ADVENTURE TIME™

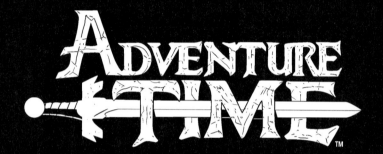

SEEING RED

PUBLISHED BY KaBOOM!

ROSS RICHIE ~ CEO & Founder

JACK CUMMINS ~ President

MARK SMYLIE ~ Founder of Archaia

MATT GAGNON ~ Editor-in-Chief

FILIP SABLIK ~ VP of Publishing & Marketing

STEPHEN CHRISTY ~ VP of Development

LANCE KREITER ~ VP of Licensing & Merchandising

PHIL BARBARO ~ VP of Finance

BRYCE CARLSON ~ Managing Editor

MEL CAYLO ~ Marketing Manager

SCOTT NEWMAN ~ Production Design Manager

IRENE BRADISH ~ Operations Manager

DAFNA PLEBAN ~ Editor

SHANNON WATTERS ~ Editor

ERIC HARBURN ~ Editor

REBECCA TAYLOR ~ Editor

IAN BRILL ~ Editor

CHRIS ROSA ~ Assistant Editor

ALEX GALER ~ Assistant Editor

WHITNEY LEOPARD ~ Assistant Editor

JASMINE AMIRI ~ Assistant Editor

CAMERON CHITTOCK ~ Assistant Editor

HANNAH NANCE PARTLOW ~ Production Designer

KELSEY DIETERICH ~ Production Designer

EMI YONEMURA BROWN ~ Production Designer

DEVIN FUNCHES ~ E-Commerce & Inventory Coordinator

ANDY LIEGL ~ Event Coordinator

BRIANNA HART ~ Executive Assistant

AARON FERRARA ~ Operations Assistant

JOSÉ MEZA ~ Sales Assistant

ELIZABETH LOUGHRIDGE ~ Accounting Assistant

ADVENTURE TIME: SEEING RED, March 2014. Published by KaBOOM!, a division of Boom Entertainment, Inc. ADVENTURE TIME, CARTOON NETWORK, the logos, and all related characters and elements are trademarks of and © Cartoon Network. (S14) All rights reserved. KaBOOM!™ and the KaBOOM! logo are trademarks of Boom Entertainment, Inc., registered in various countries and categories. All characters, events, and institutions depicted herein are fictional. Any similarity between any of the names, characters, persons, events, and/or institutions in this publication to actual names, characters, and persons, whether living or dead, events, and/or institutions is unintended and purely coincidental. KaBOOM! does not read or accept unsolicited submissions of ideas, stories, or artwork.

A catalog record of this book is available from OCLC and from the KaBOOM! website, www.kaboom-studios.com, on the Librarians Page.

BOOM! Studios, 5670 Wilshire Boulevard, Suite 450, Los Angeles, CA 90036-5679. Printed in USA. First Printing.
ISBN: 978-1-60886-356-3, eISBN: 978-1-61398-210-5

Created by **PENDLETON WARD**
Written by **KATE LETH**
Illustrated by **ZACHARY STERLING**

Inks by **RU XU**
with **TESSA STONE**
Tones by **AMANDA LAFRENAIS**
Letters by **AUBREY AIESE**

"LSP's Purse" by **MEREDITH McCLAREN**
Tones by **AMANDA LAFRENAIS**

Cover by **STEPHANIE GONZAGA**

Assistant Editor **WHITNEY LEOPARD**
Editor **SHANNON WATTERS**
Designer **HANNAH NANCE PARTLOW**

With Special Thanks to Marisa Marionakis, Rick Blanco, Curtis Lelash, Laurie Halal-Ono,
Keith Mack, Kelly Crews and the wonderful folks at Cartoon Network.

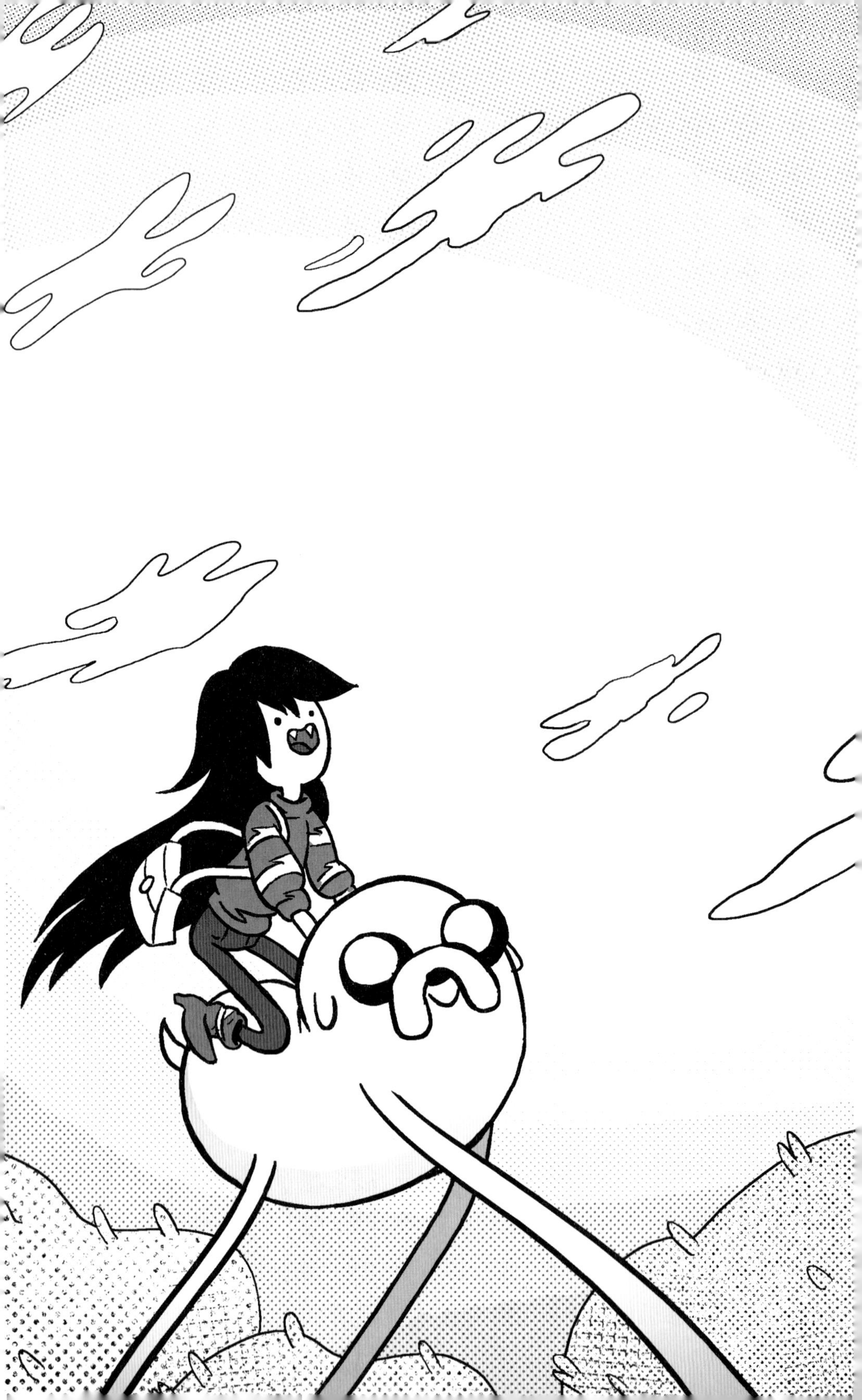

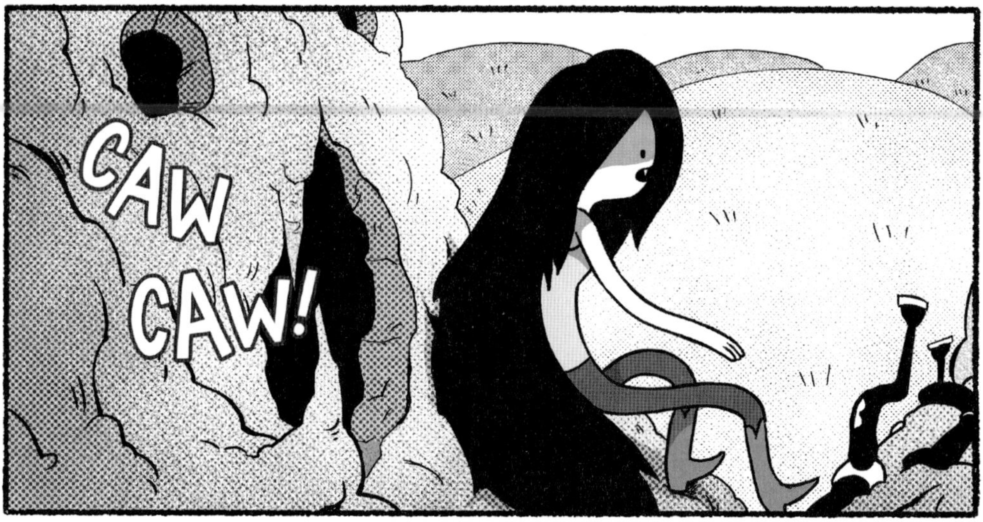
CAW CAW!

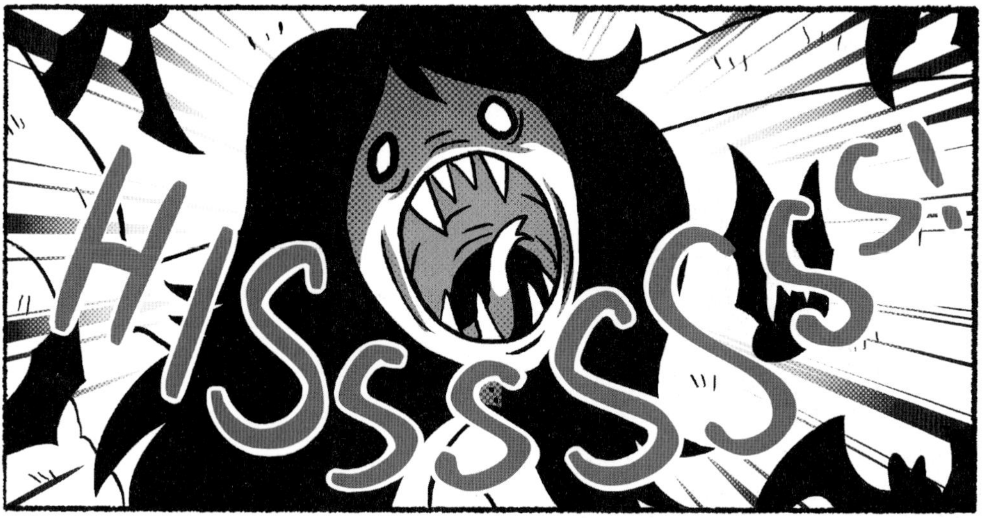
HISSSSSS!

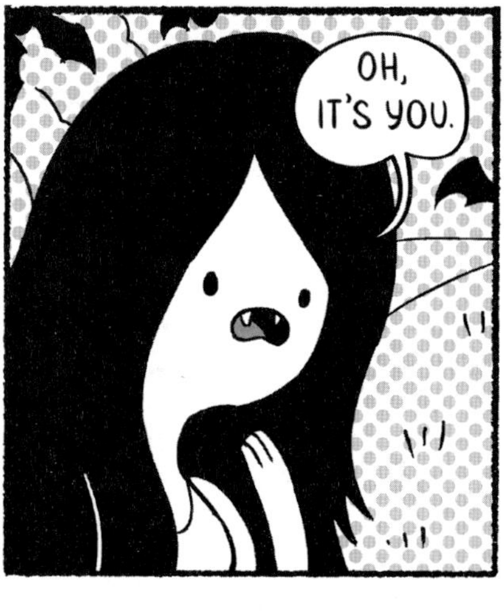
OH, IT'S YOU.

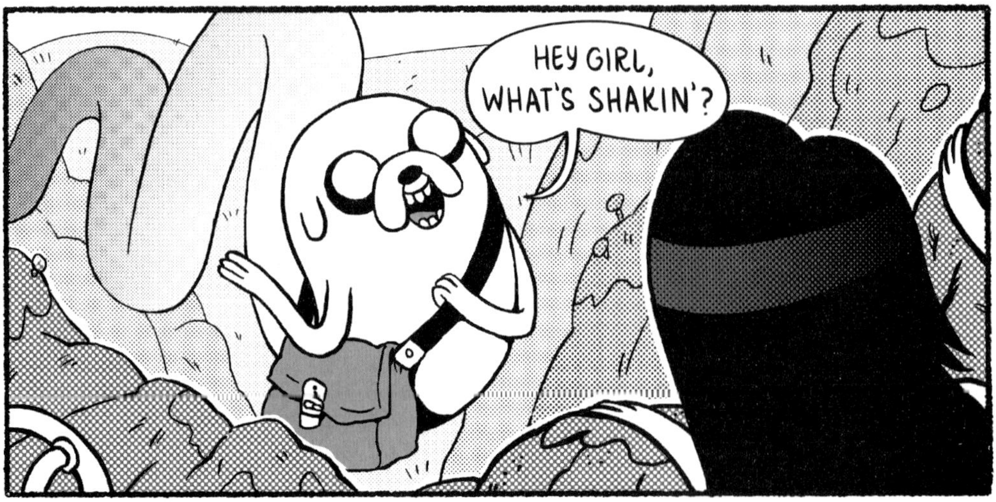
HEY GIRL, WHAT'S SHAKIN'?

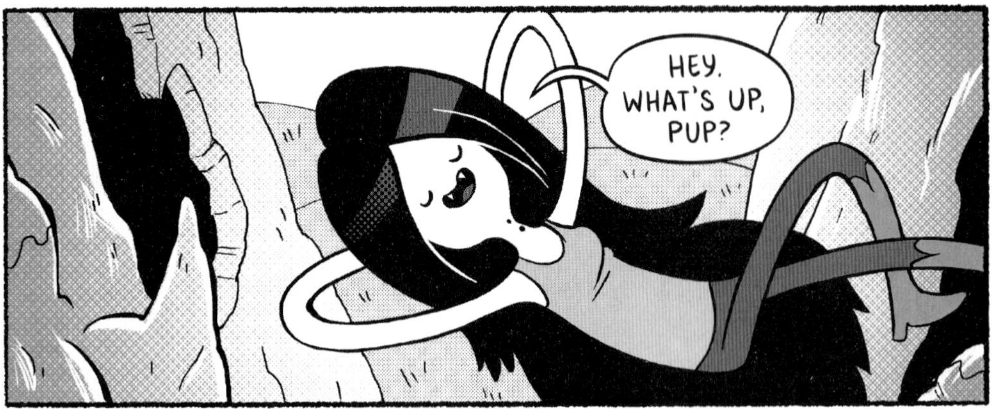
HEY. WHAT'S UP, PUP?

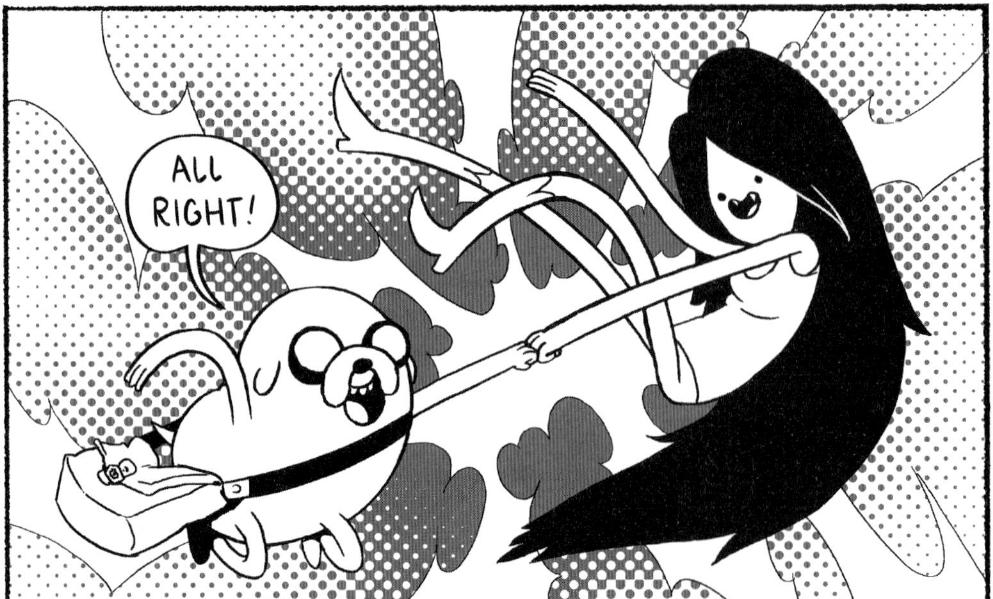
ALL RIGHT!

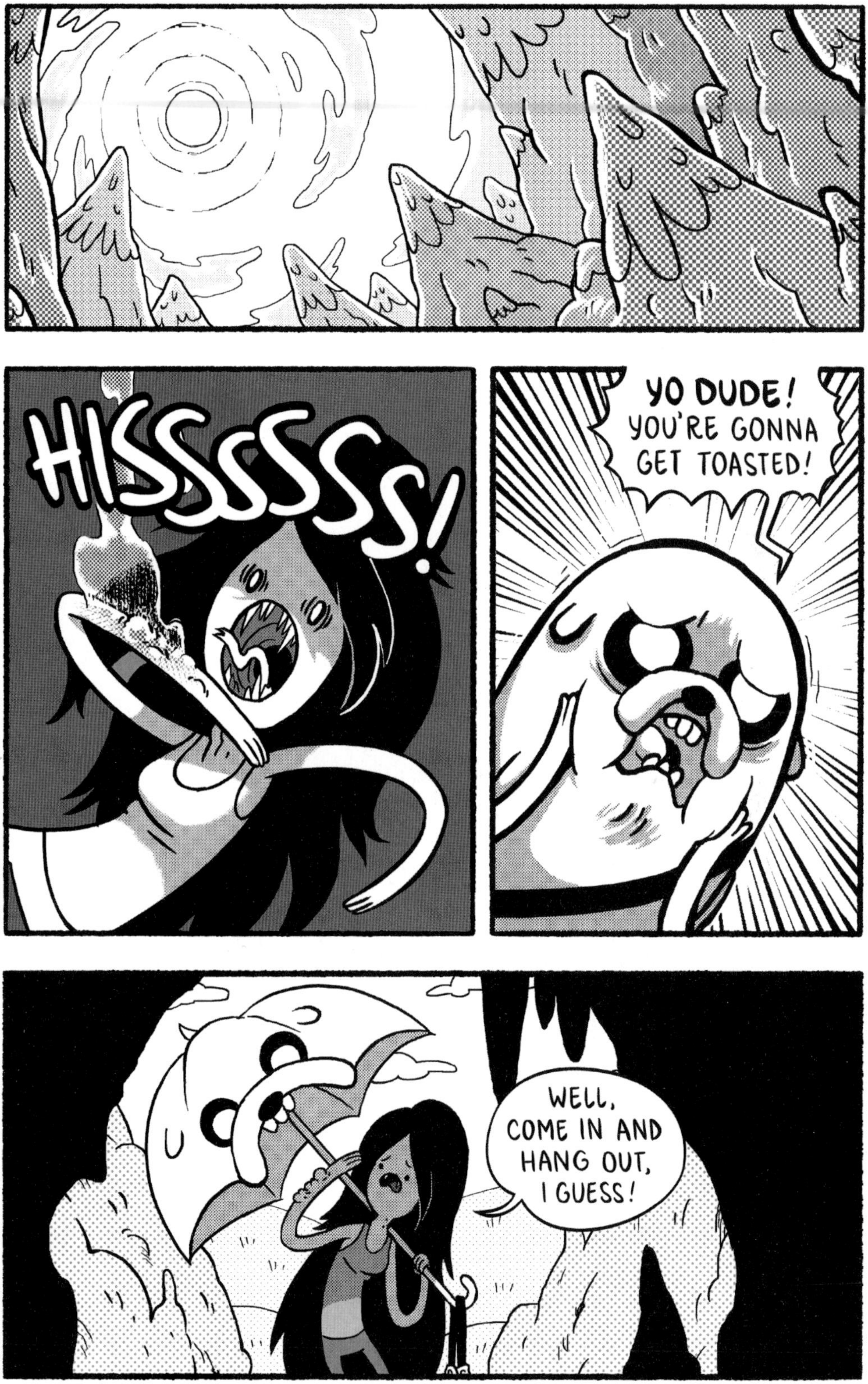
HISSSSSS!
YO DUDE! YOU'RE GONNA GET TOASTED!
WELL, COME IN AND HANG OUT, I GUESS!

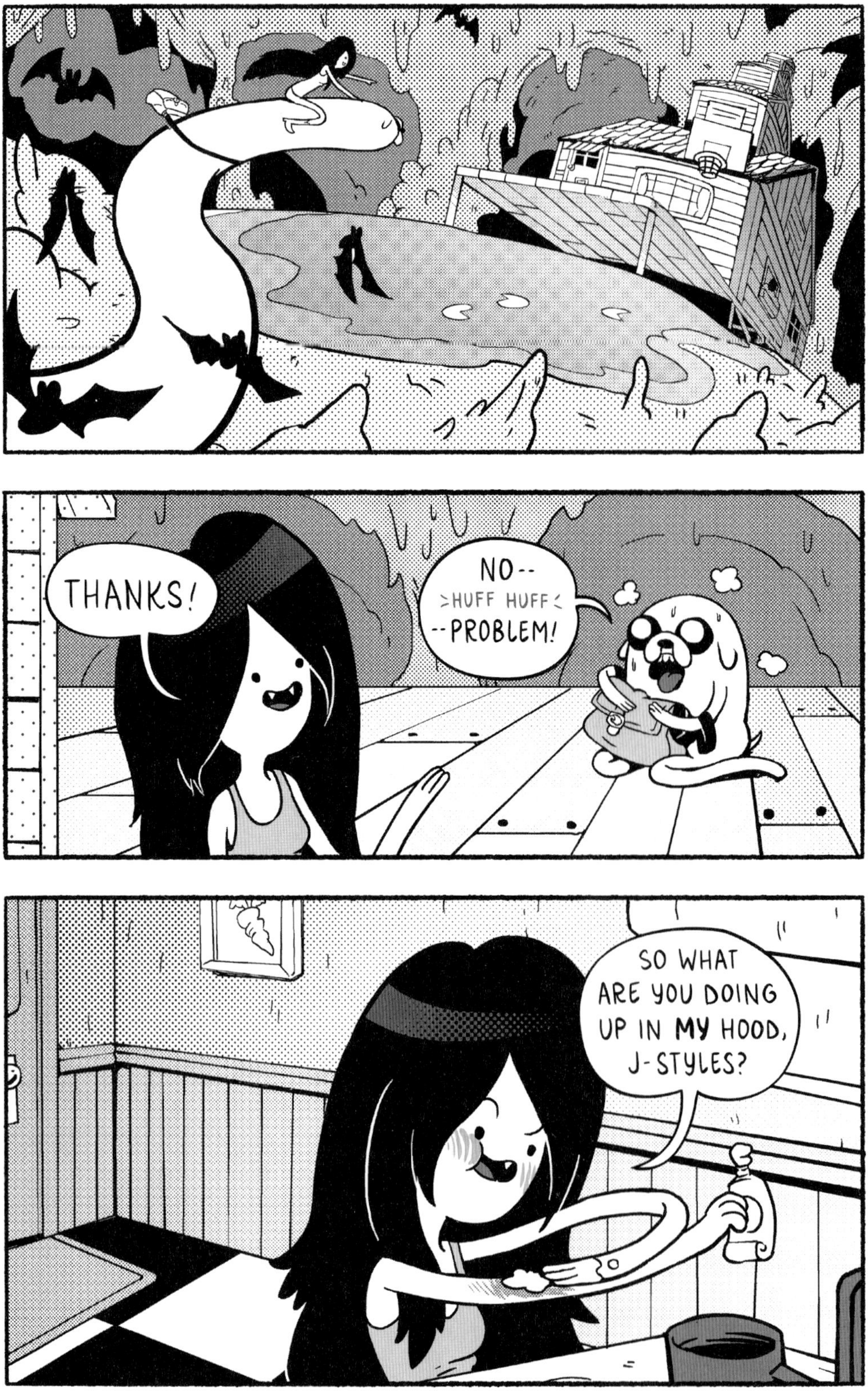
THANKS!
NO-- >HUFF HUFF< --PROBLEM!
SO WHAT ARE YOU DOING UP IN **MY** HOOD, J-STYLES?

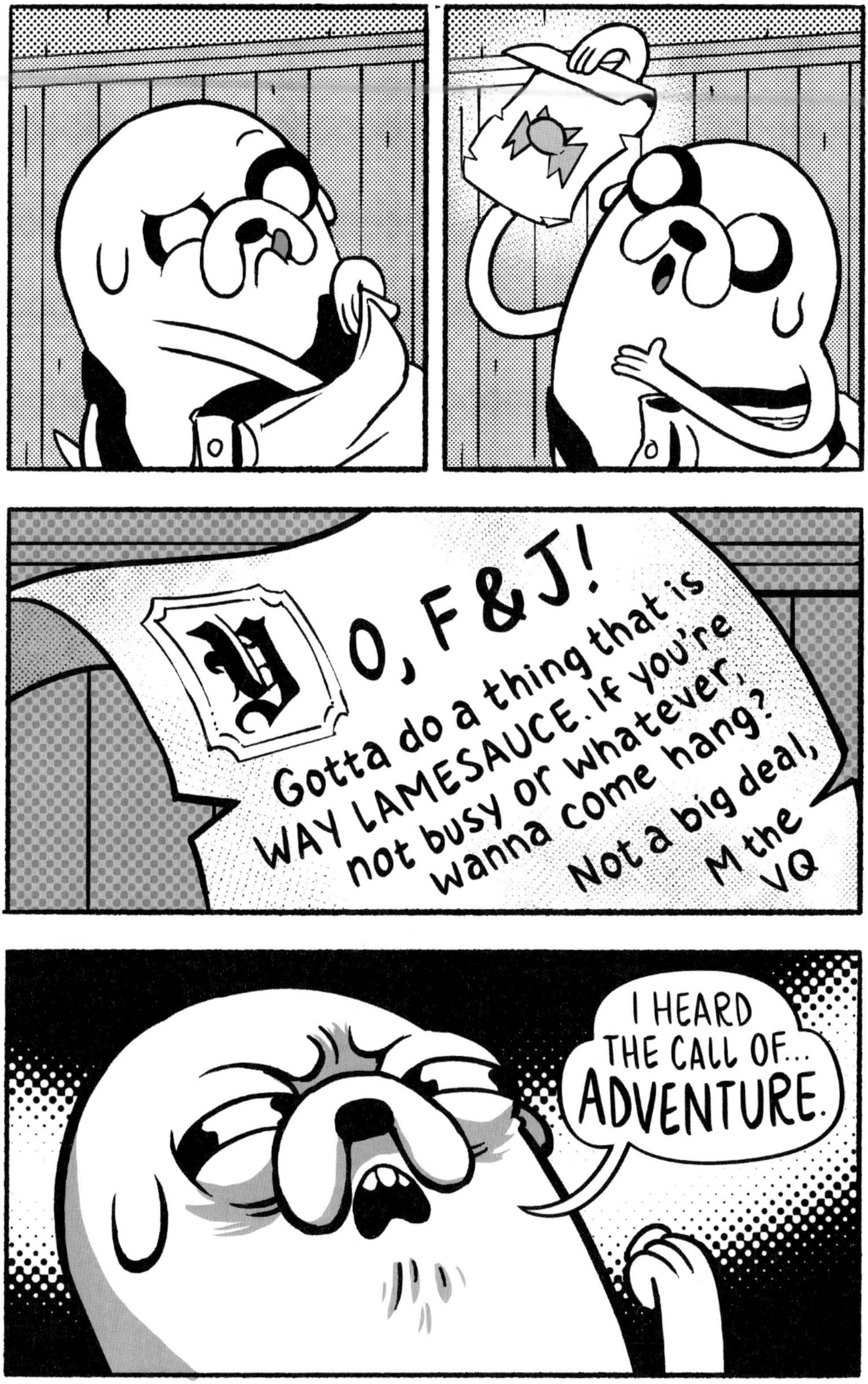
YO, F&J!
Gotta do a thing that is WAY LAMESAUCE. If you're not busy or whatever, wanna come hang?
Not a big deal,
M the VQ
I HEARD THE CALL OF... ADVENTURE.

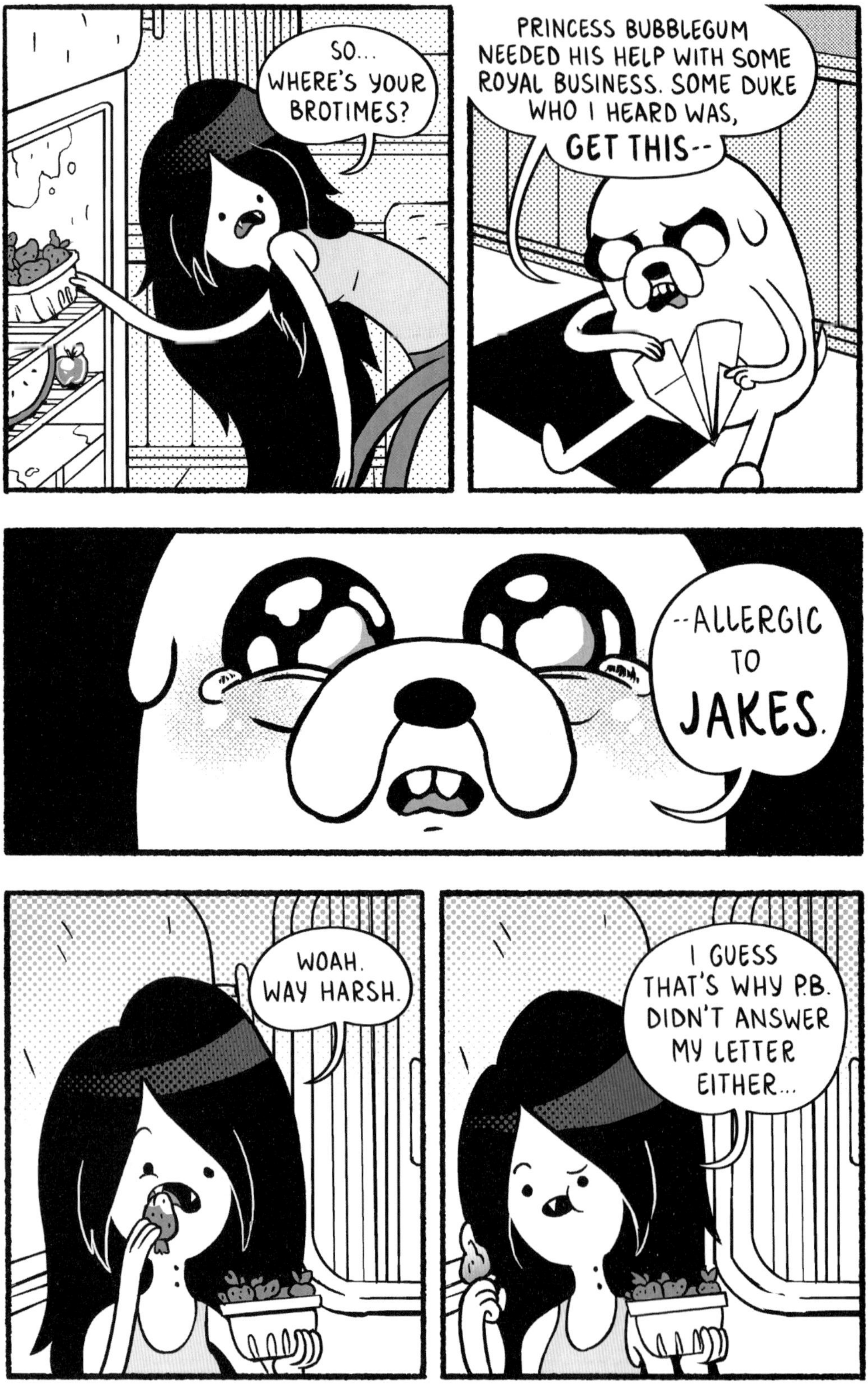
SO... WHERE'S YOUR BROTIMES?
PRINCESS BUBBLEGUM NEEDED HIS HELP WITH SOME ROYAL BUSINESS. SOME DUKE WHO I HEARD WAS, GET THIS--
--ALLERGIC TO JAKES.
WOAH. WAY HARSH.
I GUESS THAT'S WHY P.B. DIDN'T ANSWER MY LETTER EITHER...

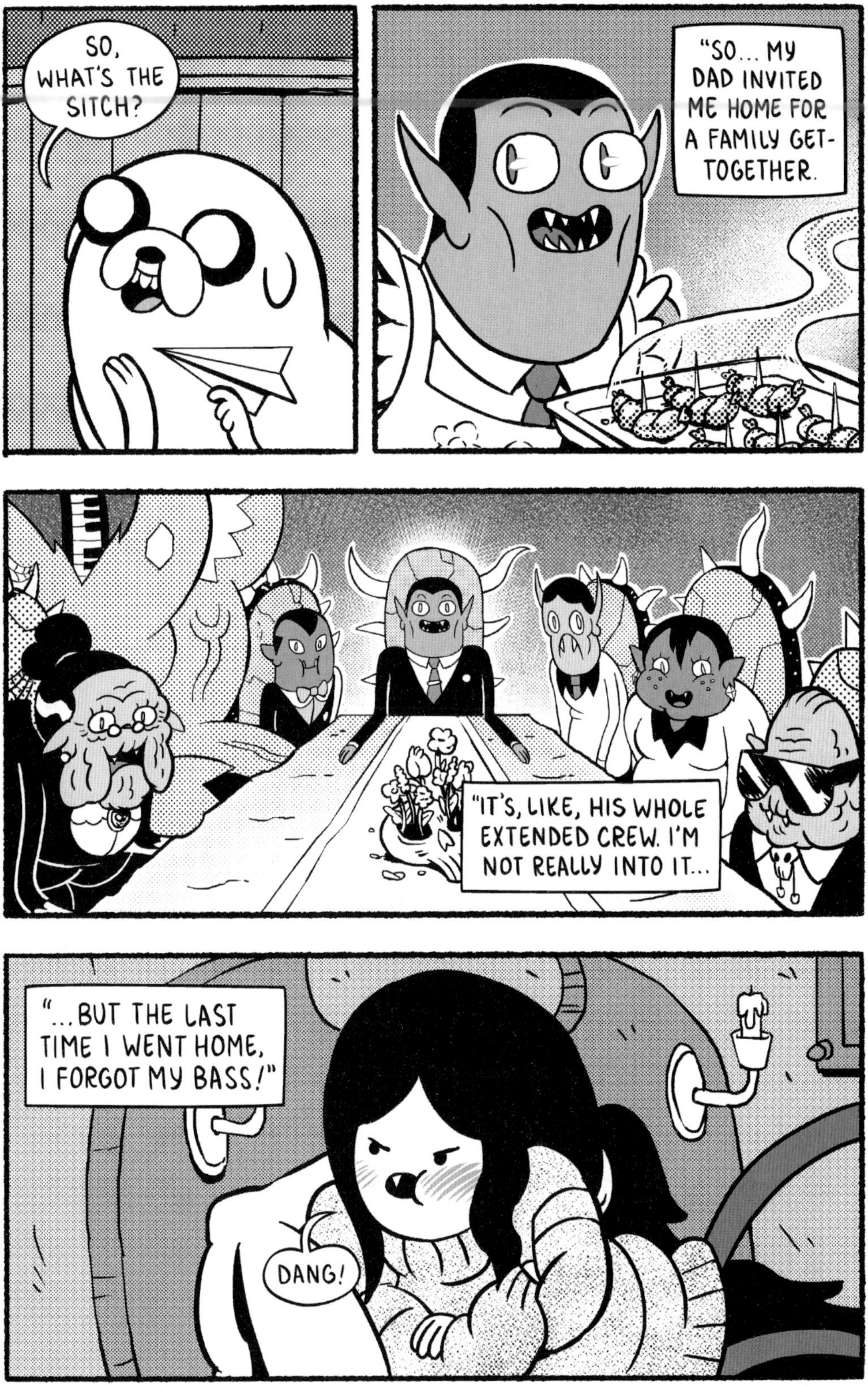

SO, WHAT'S THE SITCH?
"SO... MY DAD INVITED ME HOME FOR A FAMILY GET-TOGETHER.
"IT'S, LIKE, HIS WHOLE EXTENDED CREW. I'M NOT REALLY INTO IT...
"...BUT THE LAST TIME I WENT HOME, I FORGOT MY BASS!"
DANG!

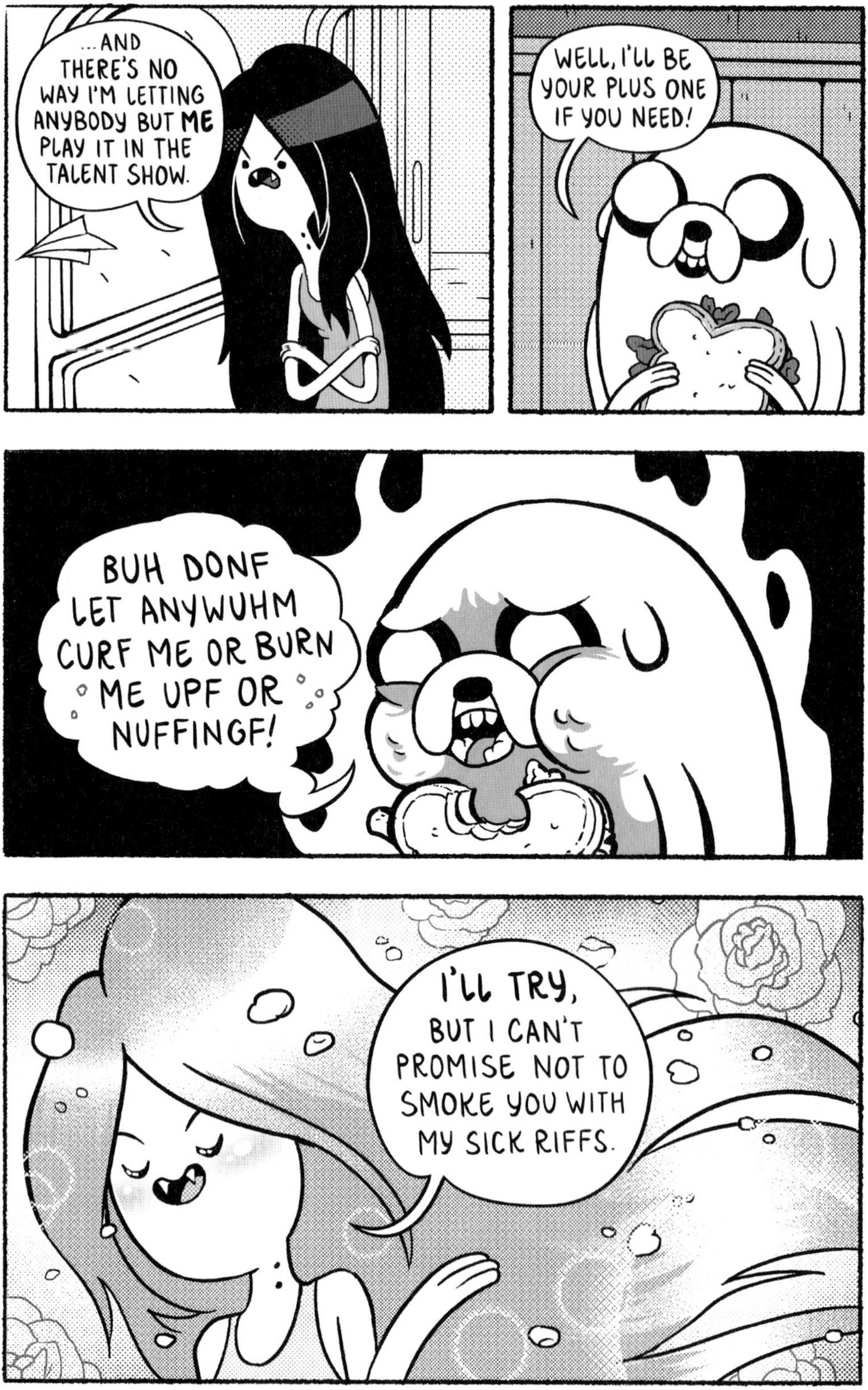
...AND THERE'S NO WAY I'M LETTING ANYBODY BUT **ME** PLAY IT IN THE TALENT SHOW.
WELL, I'LL BE YOUR PLUS ONE IF YOU NEED!
BUH DONF LET ANYWUHM CURF ME OR BURN ME UPF OR NUFFINGF!
I'LL TRY, BUT I CAN'T PROMISE NOT TO SMOKE YOU WITH MY SICK RIFFS.

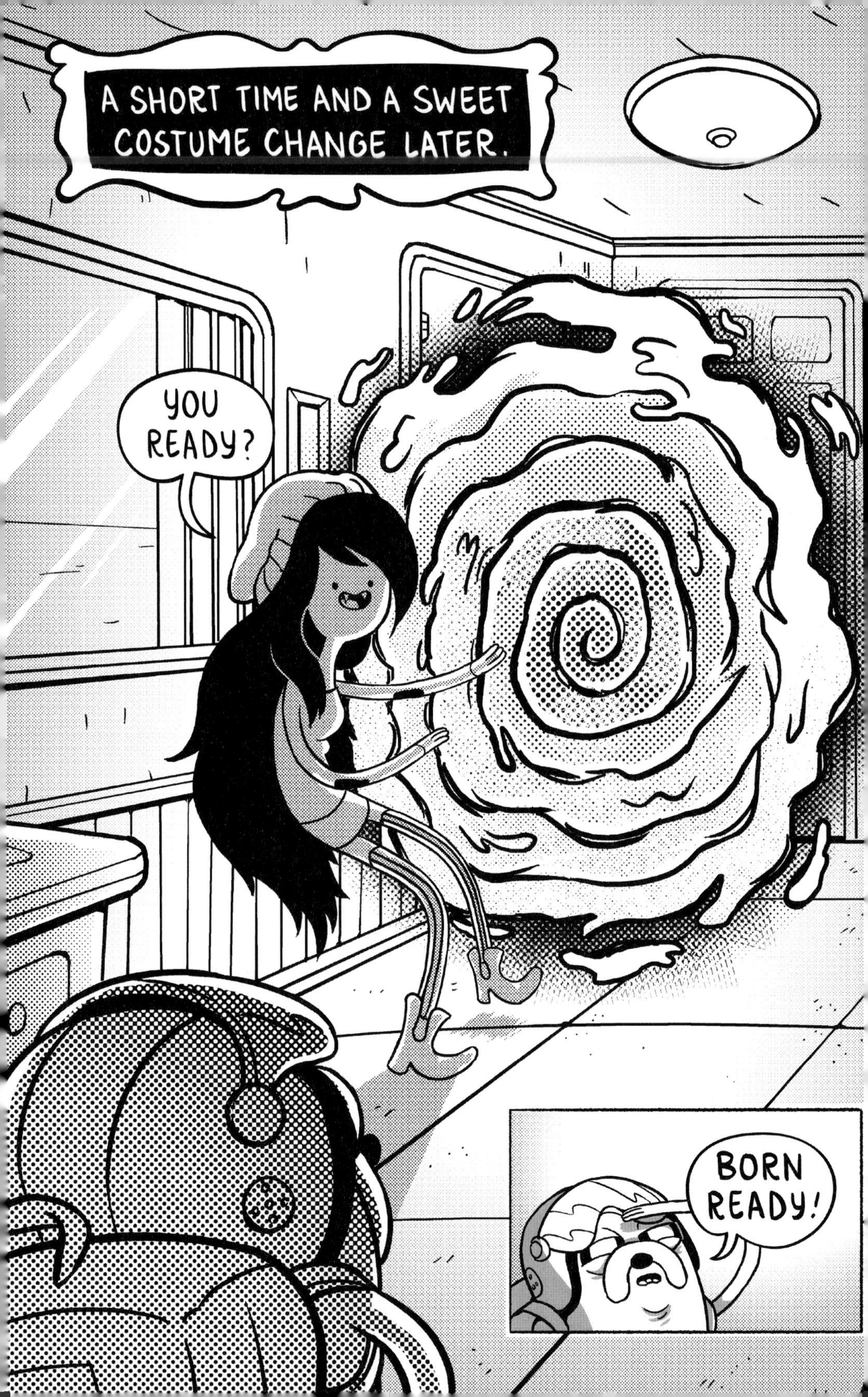
A SHORT TIME AND A SWEET COSTUME CHANGE LATER.
YOU READY?
BORN READY!

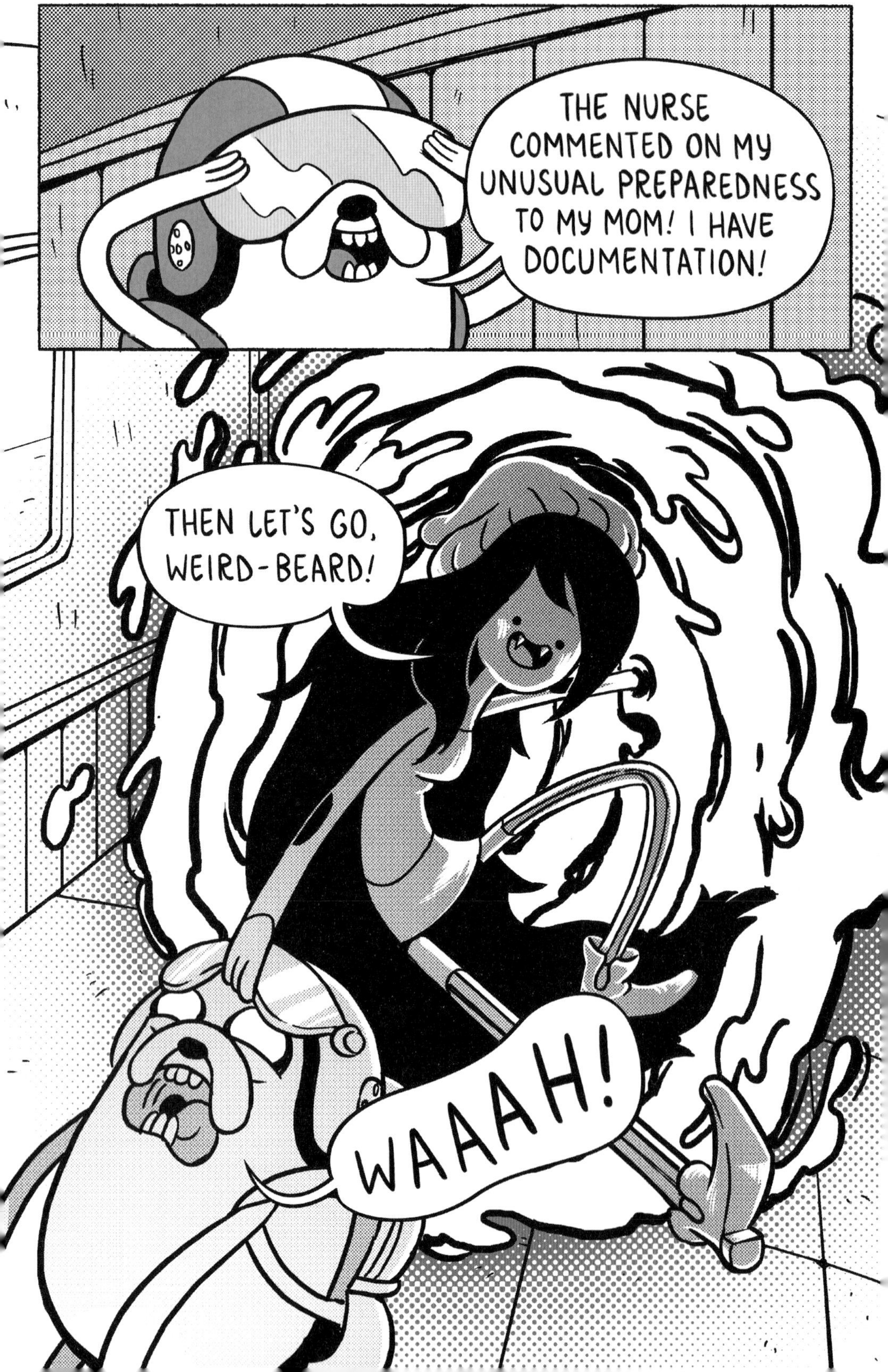
THE NURSE COMMENTED ON MY UNUSUAL PREPAREDNESS TO MY MOM! I HAVE DOCUMENTATION!
THEN LET'S GO, WEIRD-BEARD!
WAAAH!

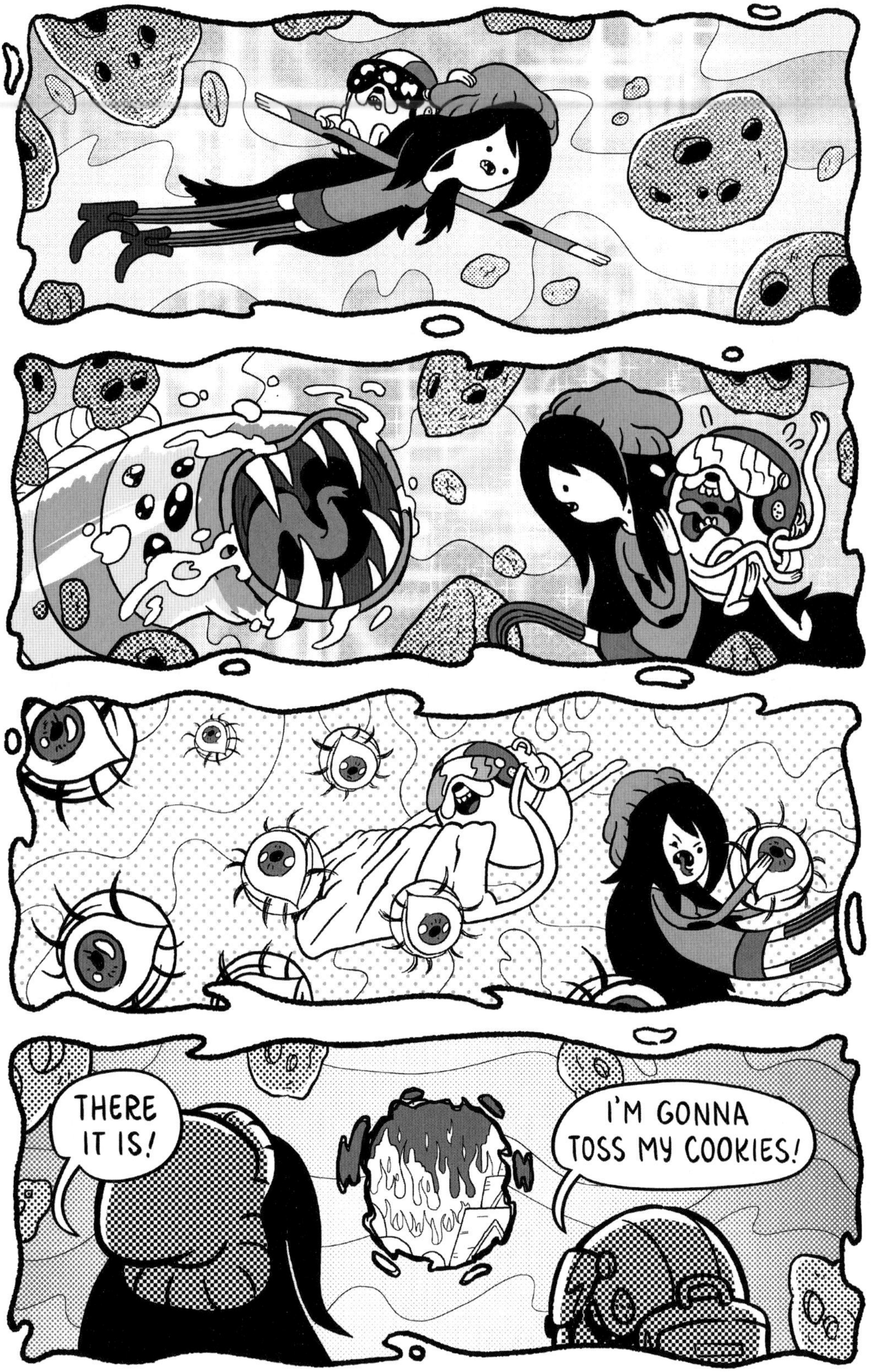
THERE IT IS!
I'M GONNA TOSS MY COOKIES!

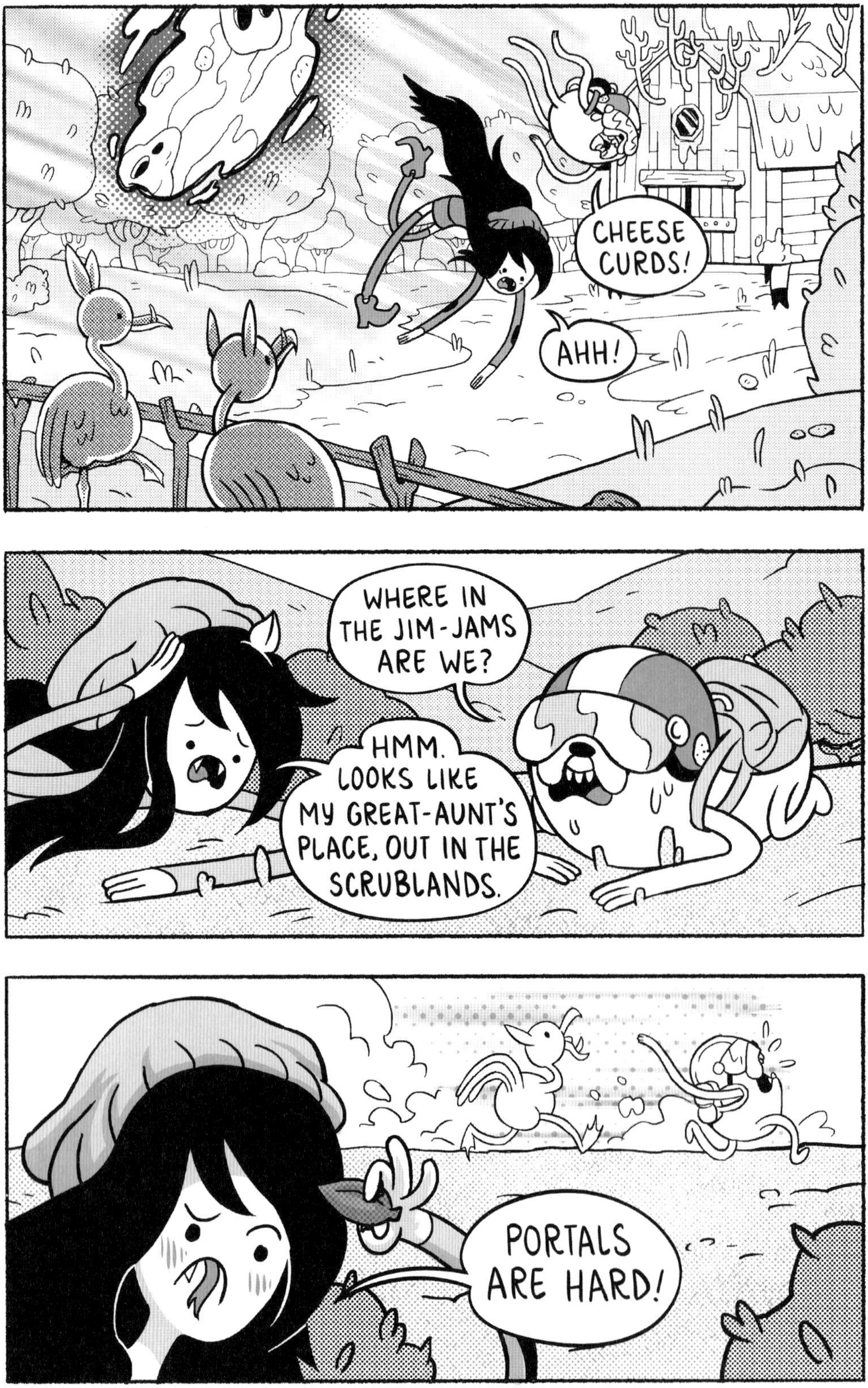
CHEESE CURDS!
AHH!
WHERE IN THE JIM-JAMS ARE WE?
HMM. LOOKS LIKE MY GREAT-AUNT'S PLACE, OUT IN THE SCRUBLANDS.
PORTALS ARE HARD!

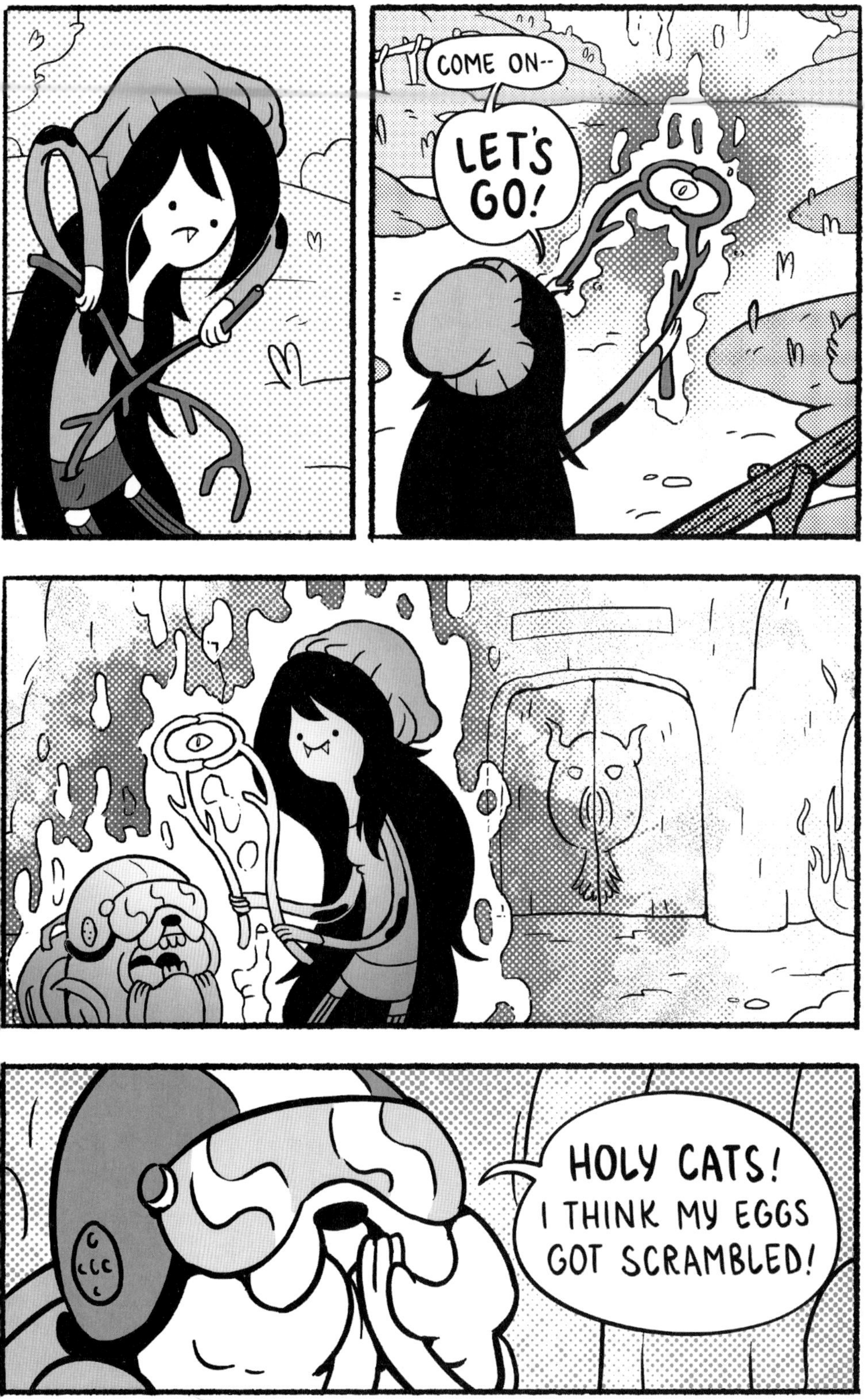
COME ON--
LET'S GO!
HOLY CATS! I THINK MY EGGS GOT SCRAMBLED!

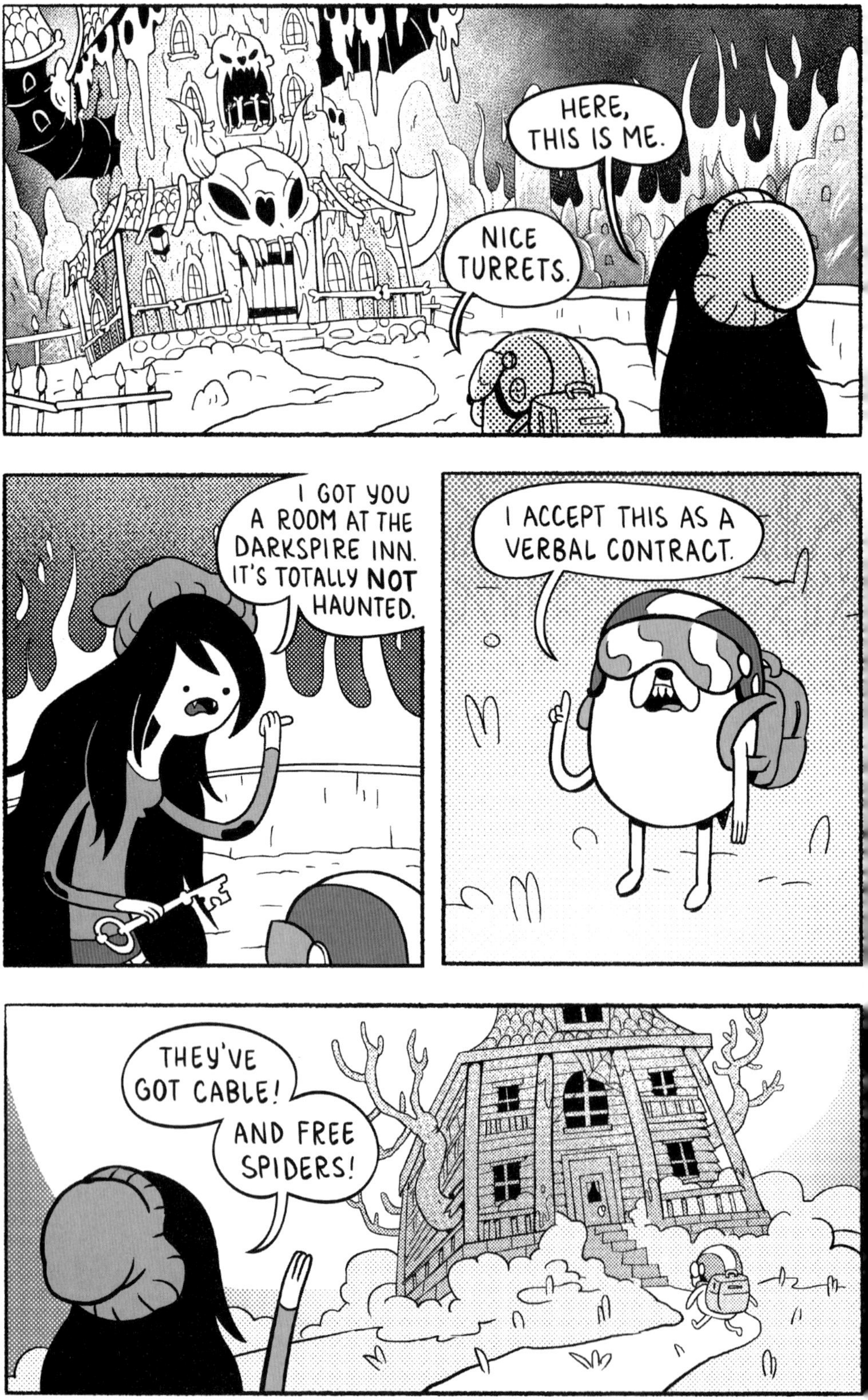
HERE, THIS IS ME.
NICE TURRETS.
I GOT YOU A ROOM AT THE DARKSPIRE INN. IT'S TOTALLY **NOT** HAUNTED.
I ACCEPT THIS AS A VERBAL CONTRACT.
THEY'VE GOT CABLE!
AND FREE SPIDERS!

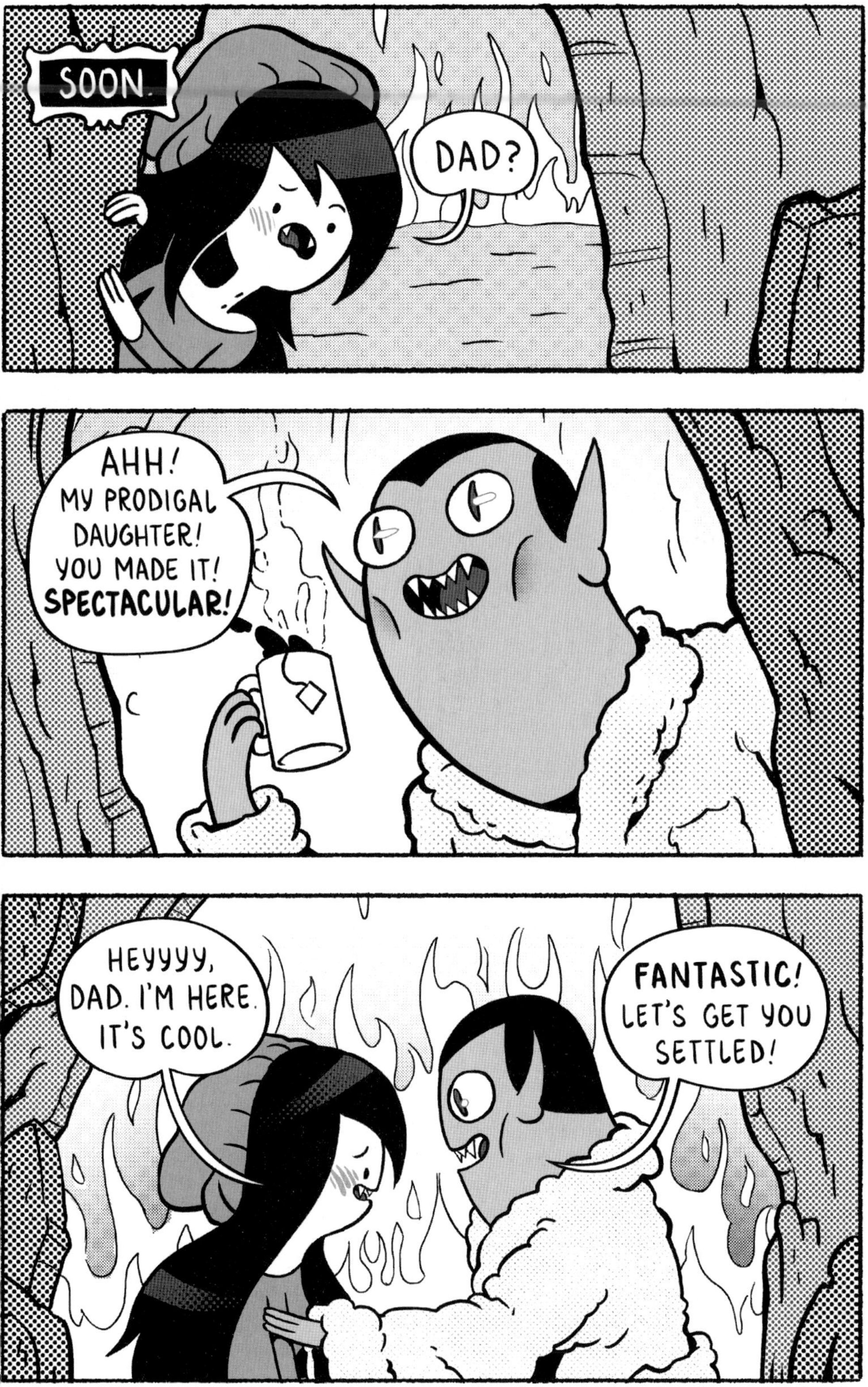
SOON.
DAD?
AHH! MY PRODIGAL DAUGHTER! YOU MADE IT! SPECTACULAR!
HEYYYY, DAD. I'M HERE. IT'S COOL.
FANTASTIC! LET'S GET YOU SETTLED!

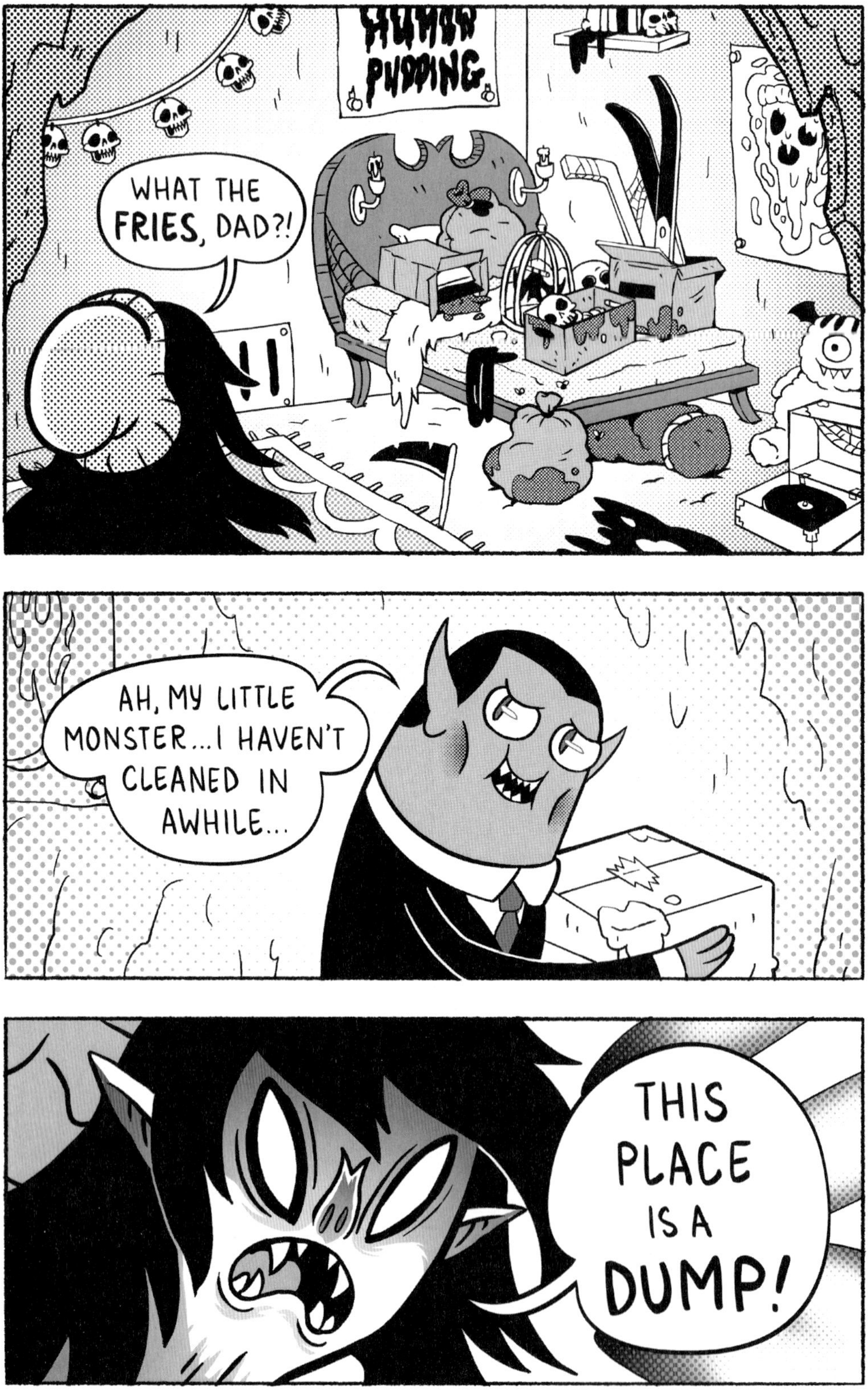
PUDDING
WHAT THE FRIES, DAD?!
AH, MY LITTLE MONSTER...I HAVEN'T CLEANED IN AWHILE...
THIS PLACE IS A DUMP!

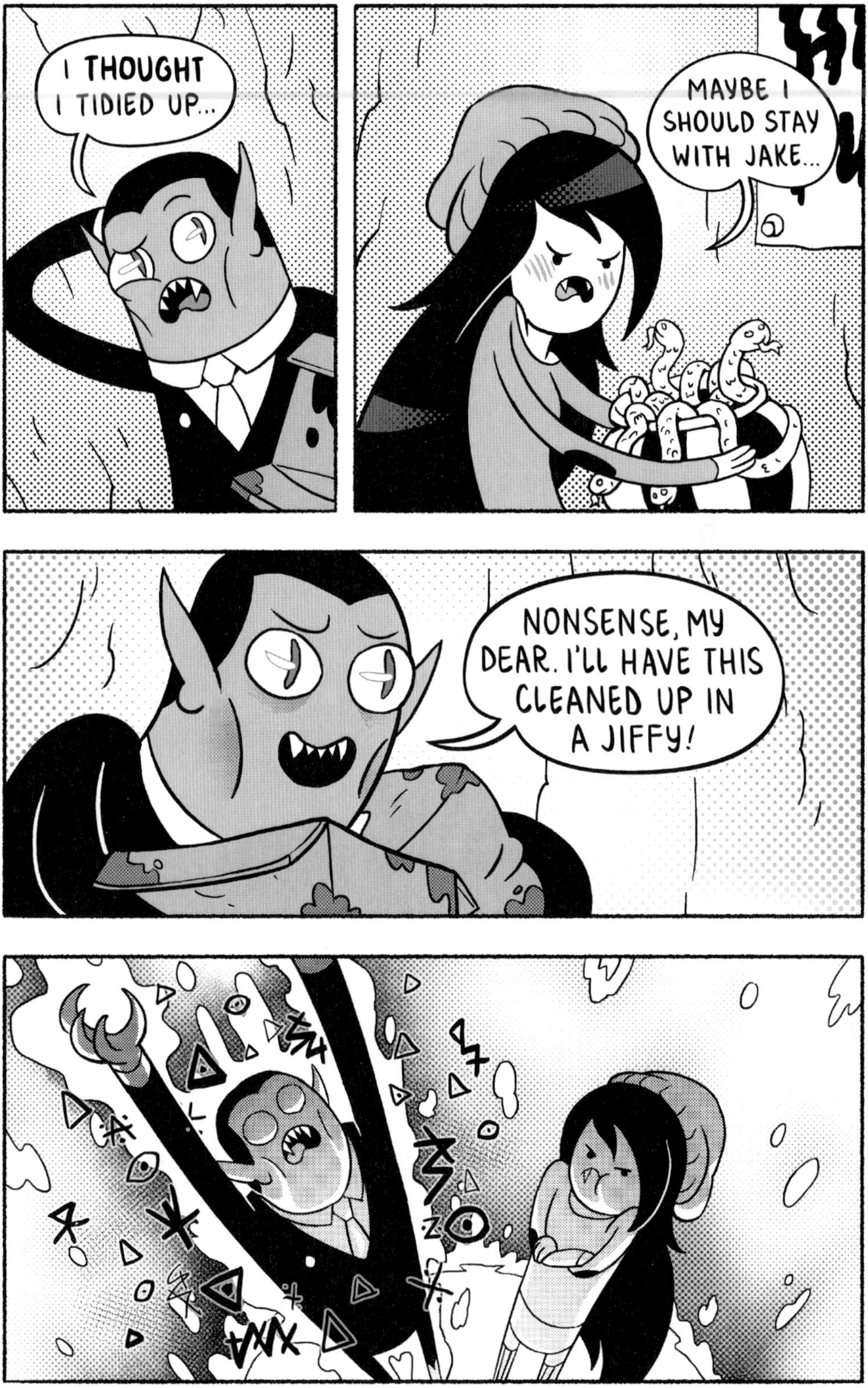
I THOUGHT I TIDIED UP...
MAYBE I SHOULD STAY WITH JAKE...
NONSENSE, MY DEAR. I'LL HAVE THIS CLEANED UP IN A JIFFY!

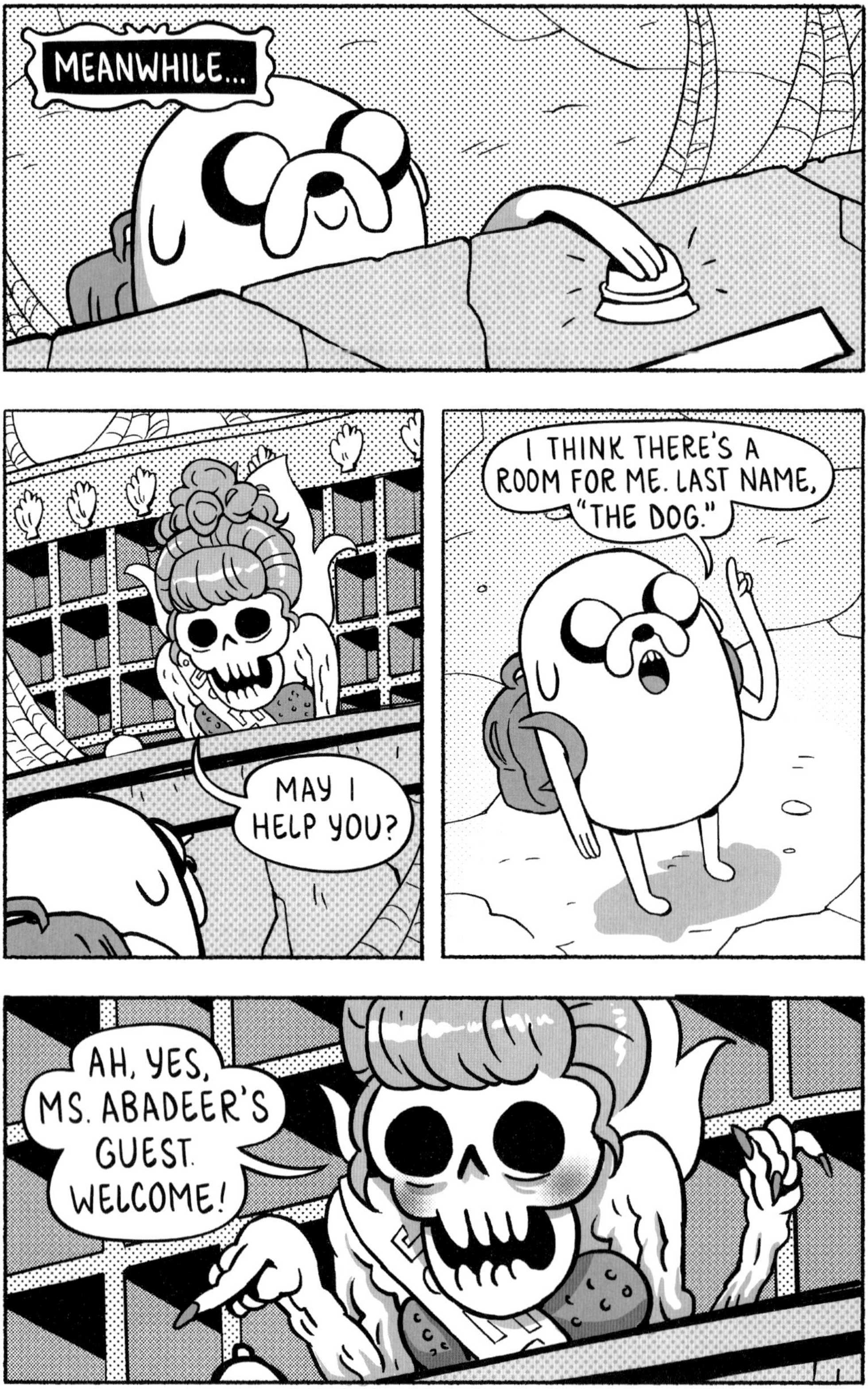
MEANWHILE...
MAY I HELP YOU?
I THINK THERE'S A ROOM FOR ME. LAST NAME, "THE DOG."
AH, YES, MS. ABADEER'S GUEST. WELCOME!

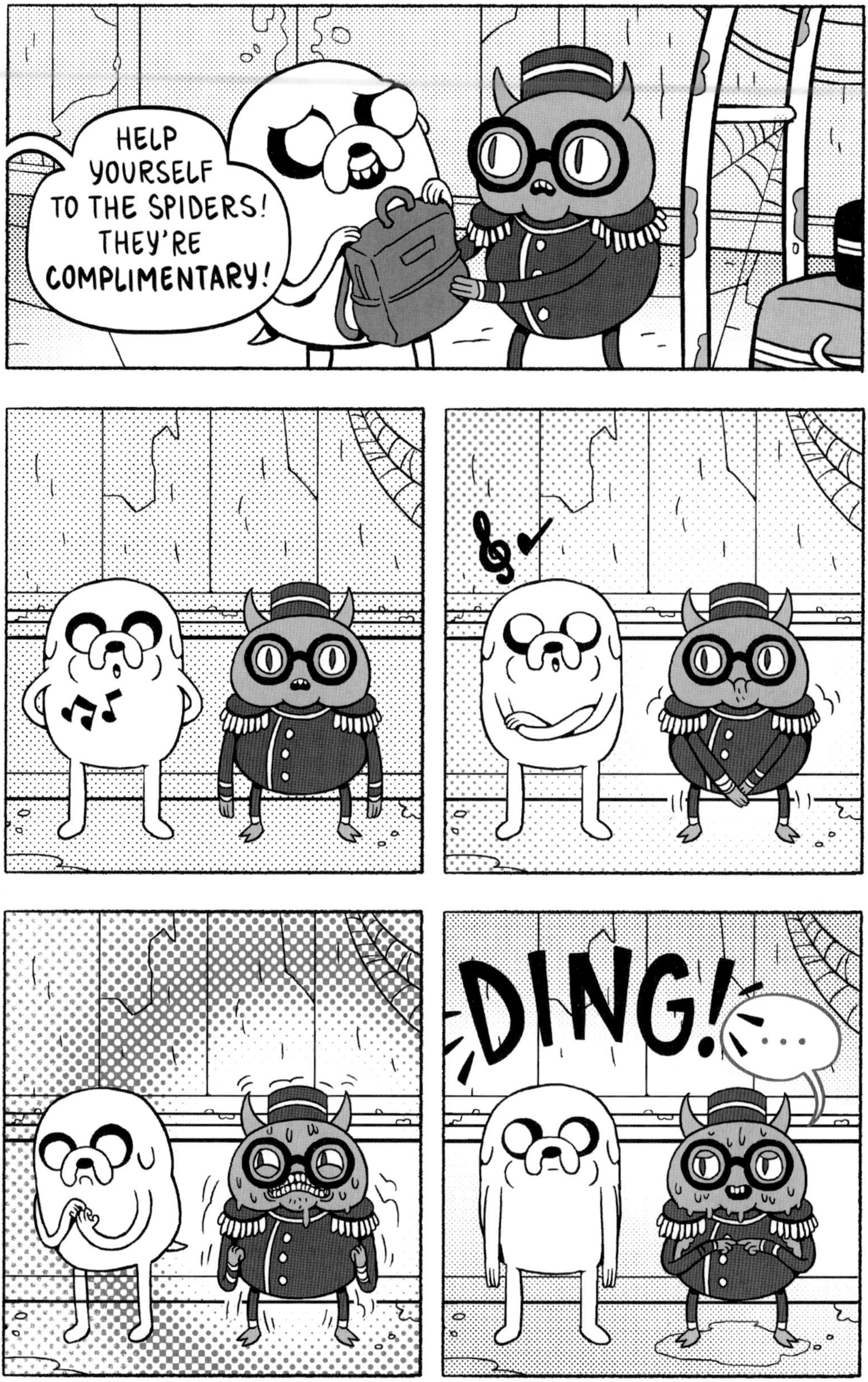
HELP YOURSELF TO THE SPIDERS! THEY'RE COMPLIMENTARY!
DING!
...

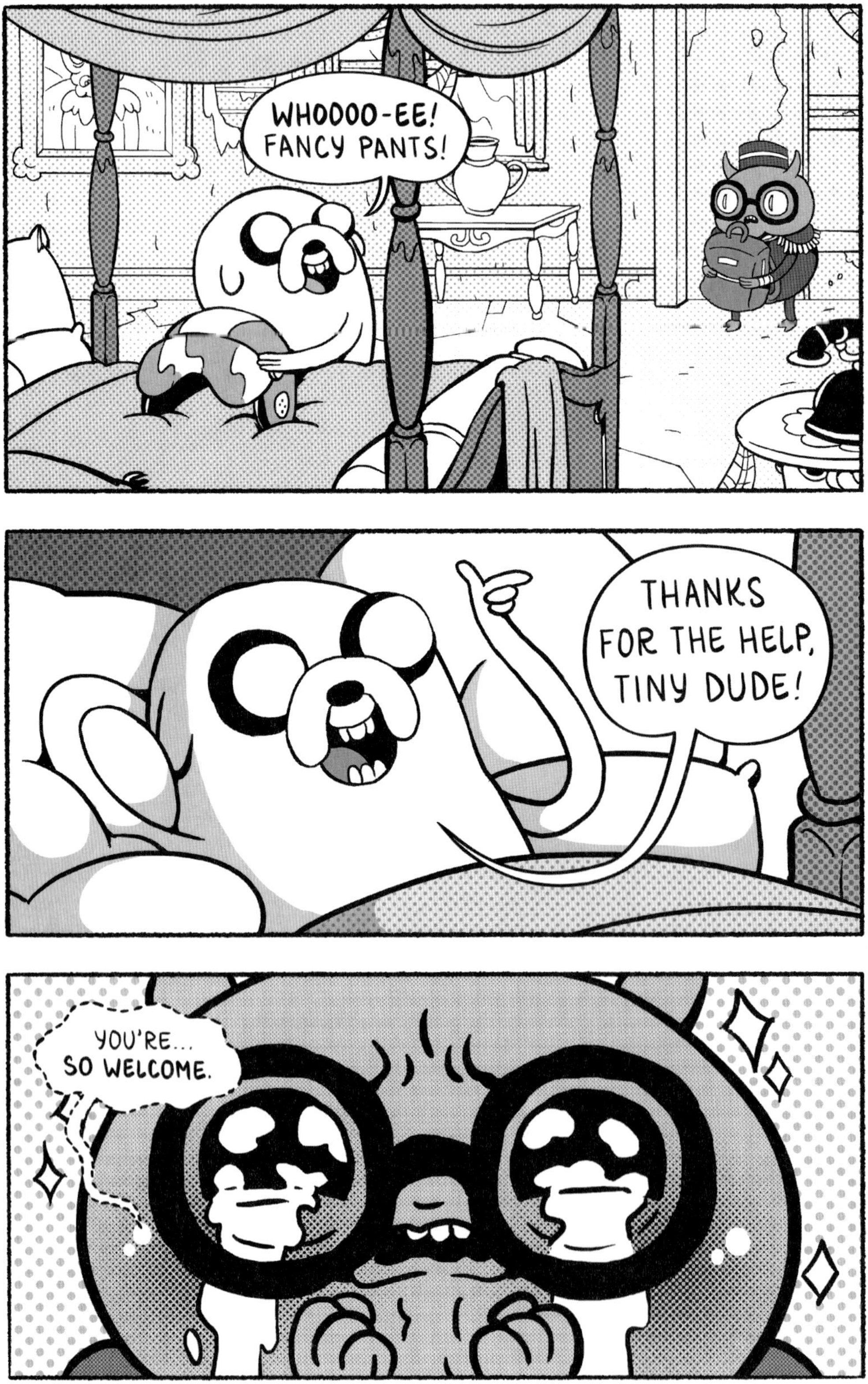
WHOOOO-EE! FANCY PANTS!
THANKS FOR THE HELP, TINY DUDE!
YOU'RE... SO WELCOME.

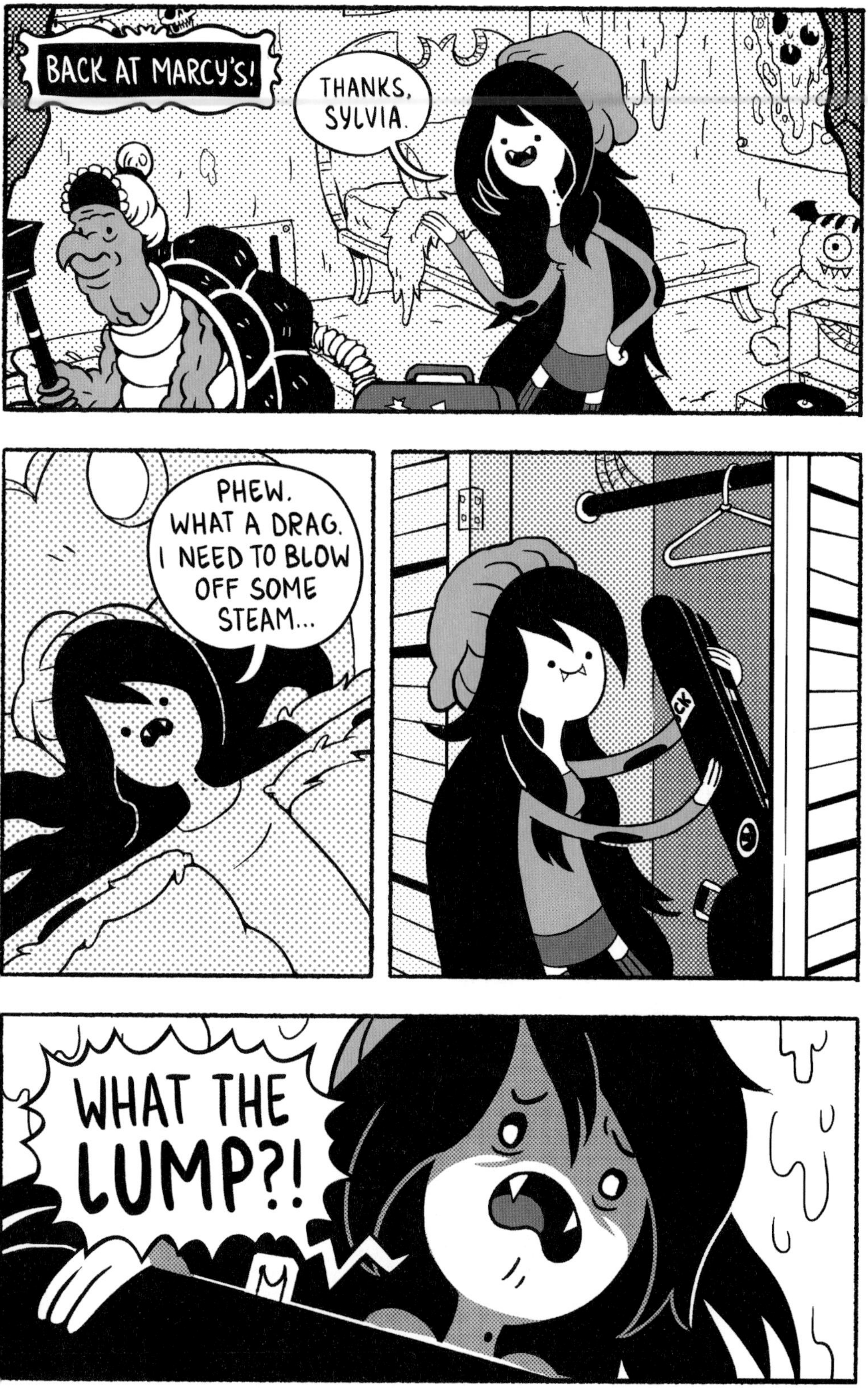
BACK AT MARCY'S!
THANKS, SYLVIA.
PHEW. WHAT A DRAG. I NEED TO BLOW OFF SOME STEAM...
WHAT THE LUMP?!

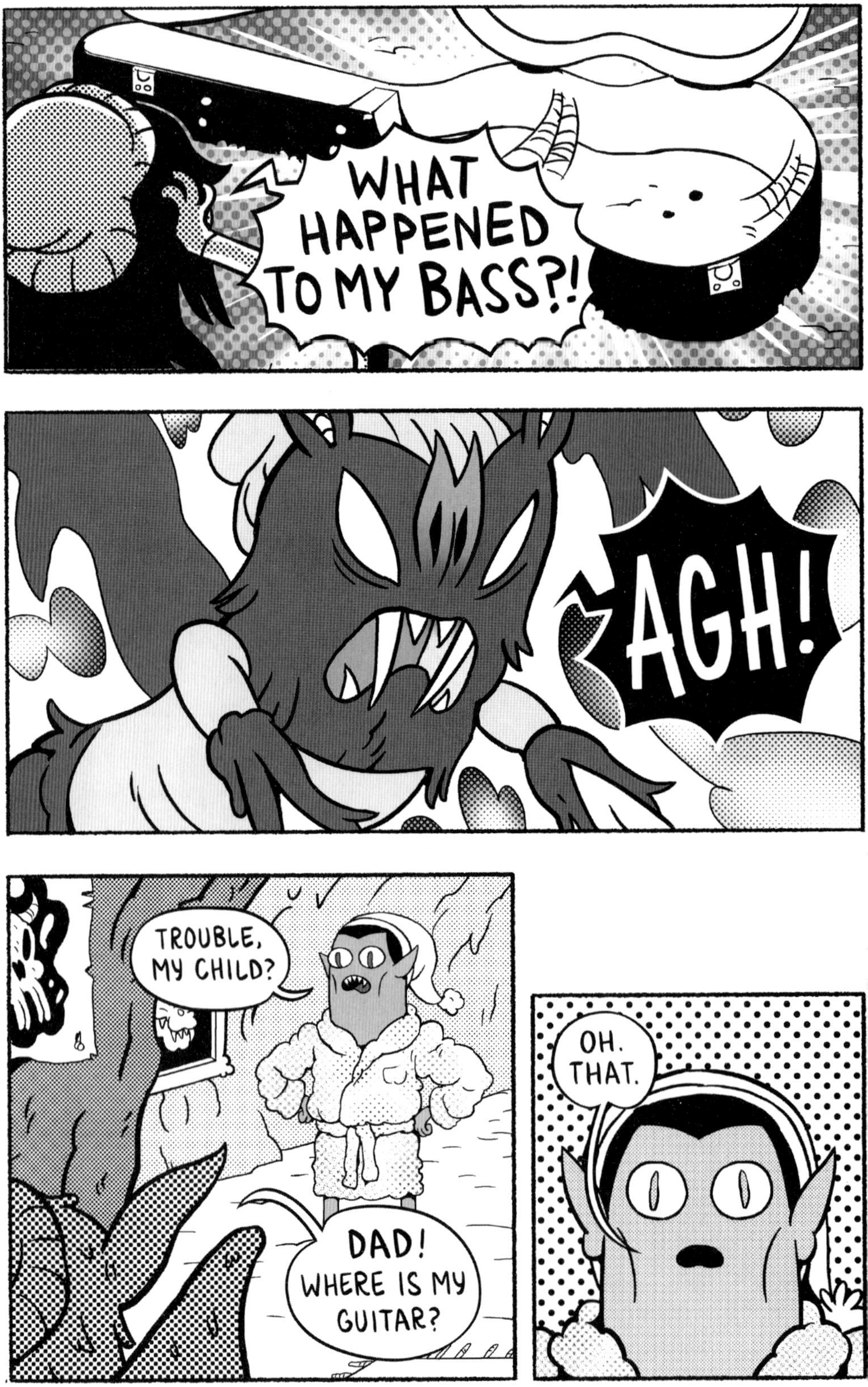
WHAT HAPPENED TO MY BASS?!
AGH!
TROUBLE, MY CHILD?
DAD! WHERE IS MY GUITAR?
OH. THAT.

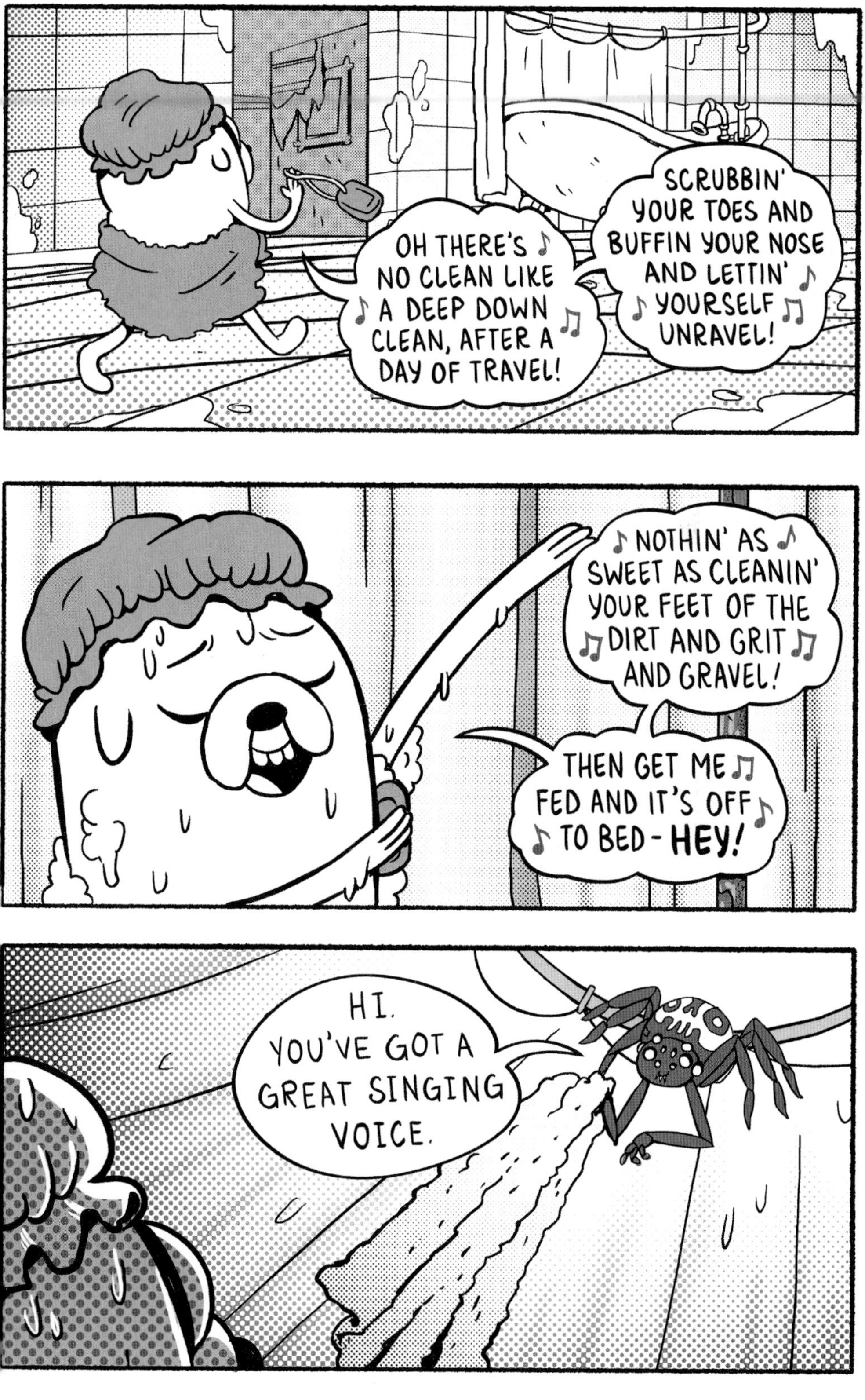
OH THERE'S NO CLEAN LIKE A DEEP DOWN CLEAN, AFTER A DAY OF TRAVEL!
SCRUBBIN' YOUR TOES AND BUFFIN YOUR NOSE AND LETTIN' YOURSELF UNRAVEL!
NOTHIN' AS SWEET AS CLEANIN' YOUR FEET OF THE DIRT AND GRIT AND GRAVEL!
THEN GET ME FED AND IT'S OFF TO BED - **HEY!**
HI. YOU'VE GOT A GREAT SINGING VOICE.

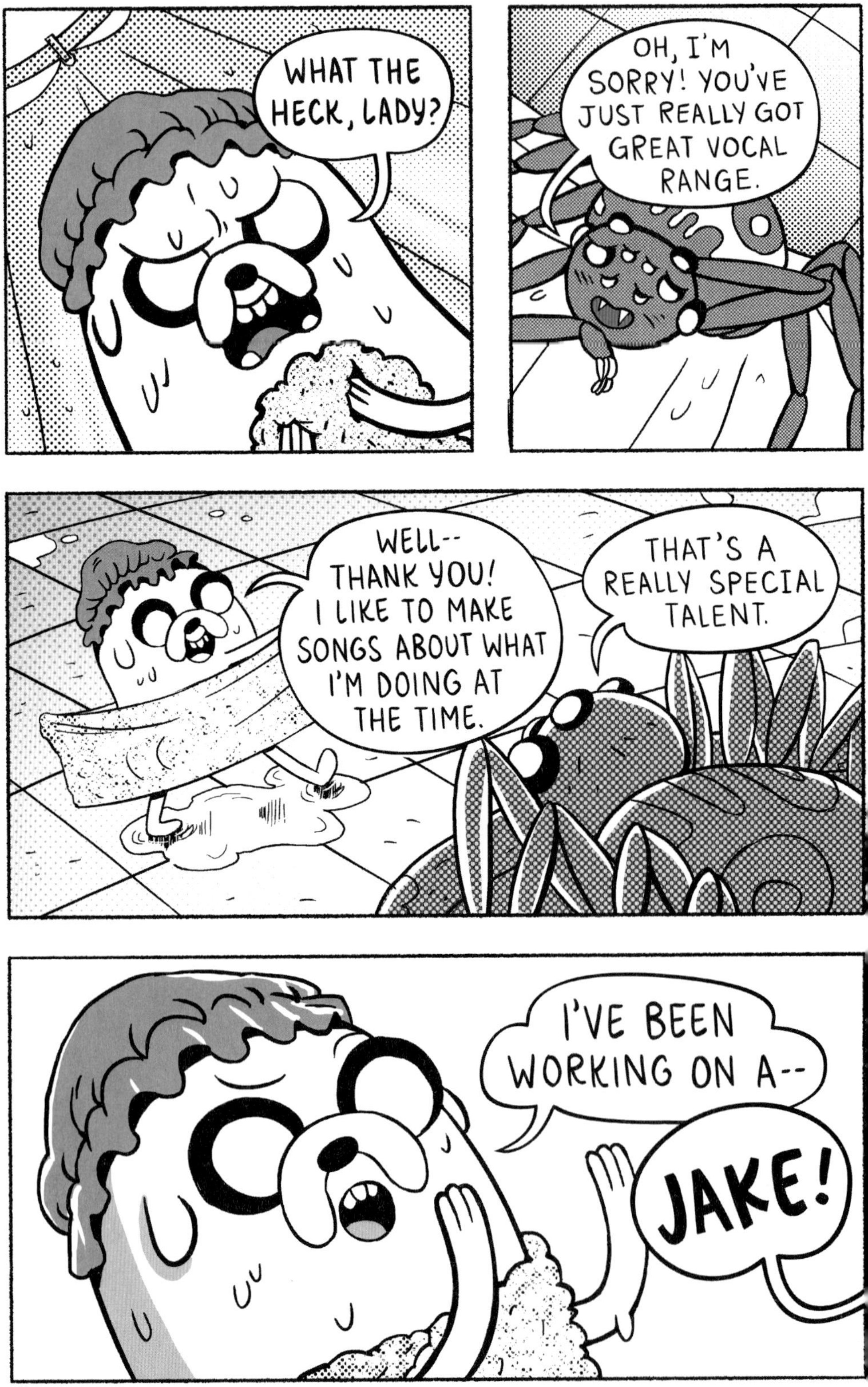
WHAT THE HECK, LADY?
OH, I'M SORRY! YOU'VE JUST REALLY GOT GREAT VOCAL RANGE.
WELL-- THANK YOU! I LIKE TO MAKE SONGS ABOUT WHAT I'M DOING AT THE TIME.
THAT'S A REALLY SPECIAL TALENT.
I'VE BEEN WORKING ON A--
JAKE!

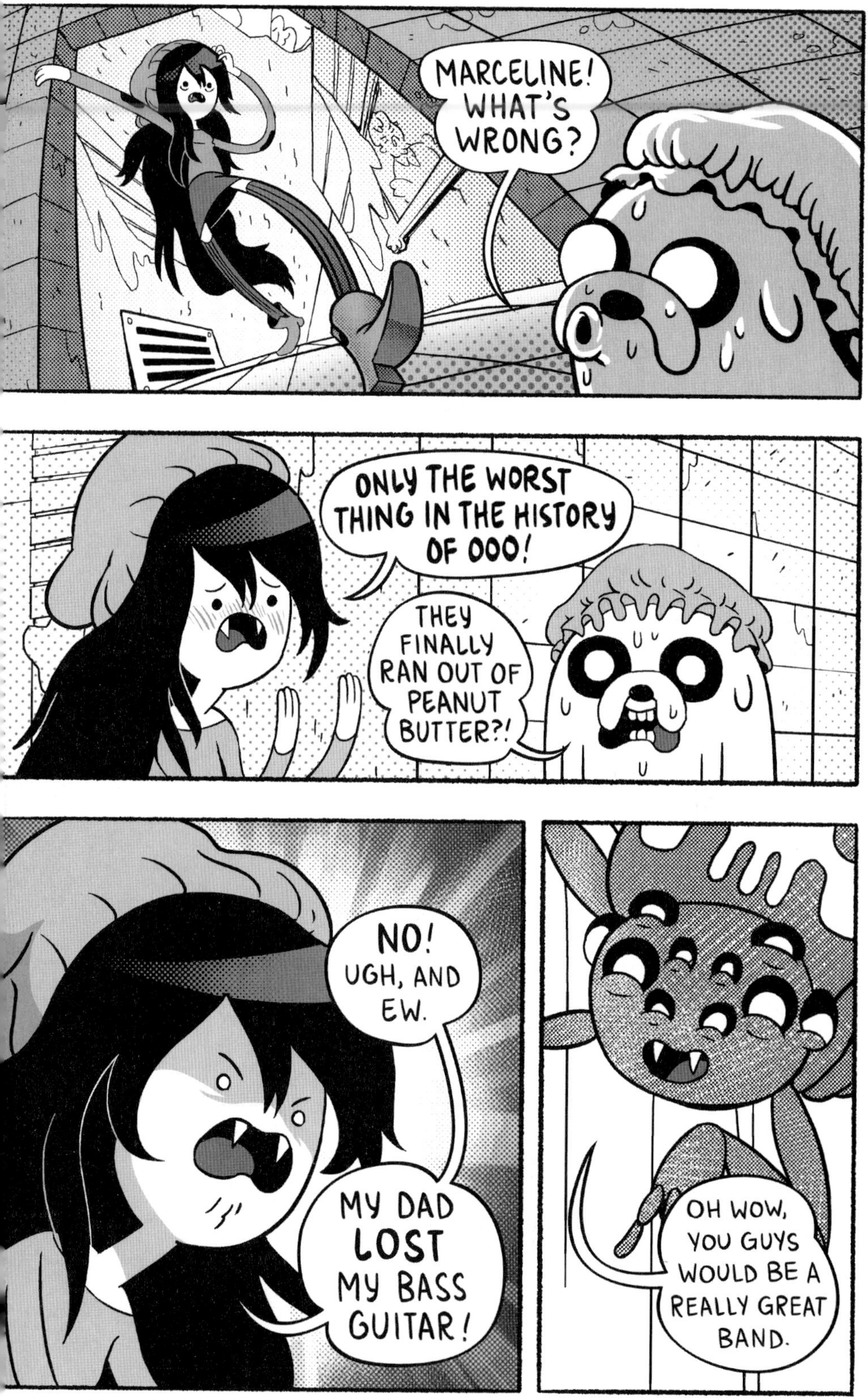
MARCELINE! WHAT'S WRONG?
ONLY THE WORST THING IN THE HISTORY OF OOO!
THEY FINALLY RAN OUT OF PEANUT BUTTER?!
NO! UGH, AND EW.
MY DAD **LOST** MY BASS GUITAR!
OH WOW, YOU GUYS WOULD BE A REALLY GREAT BAND.

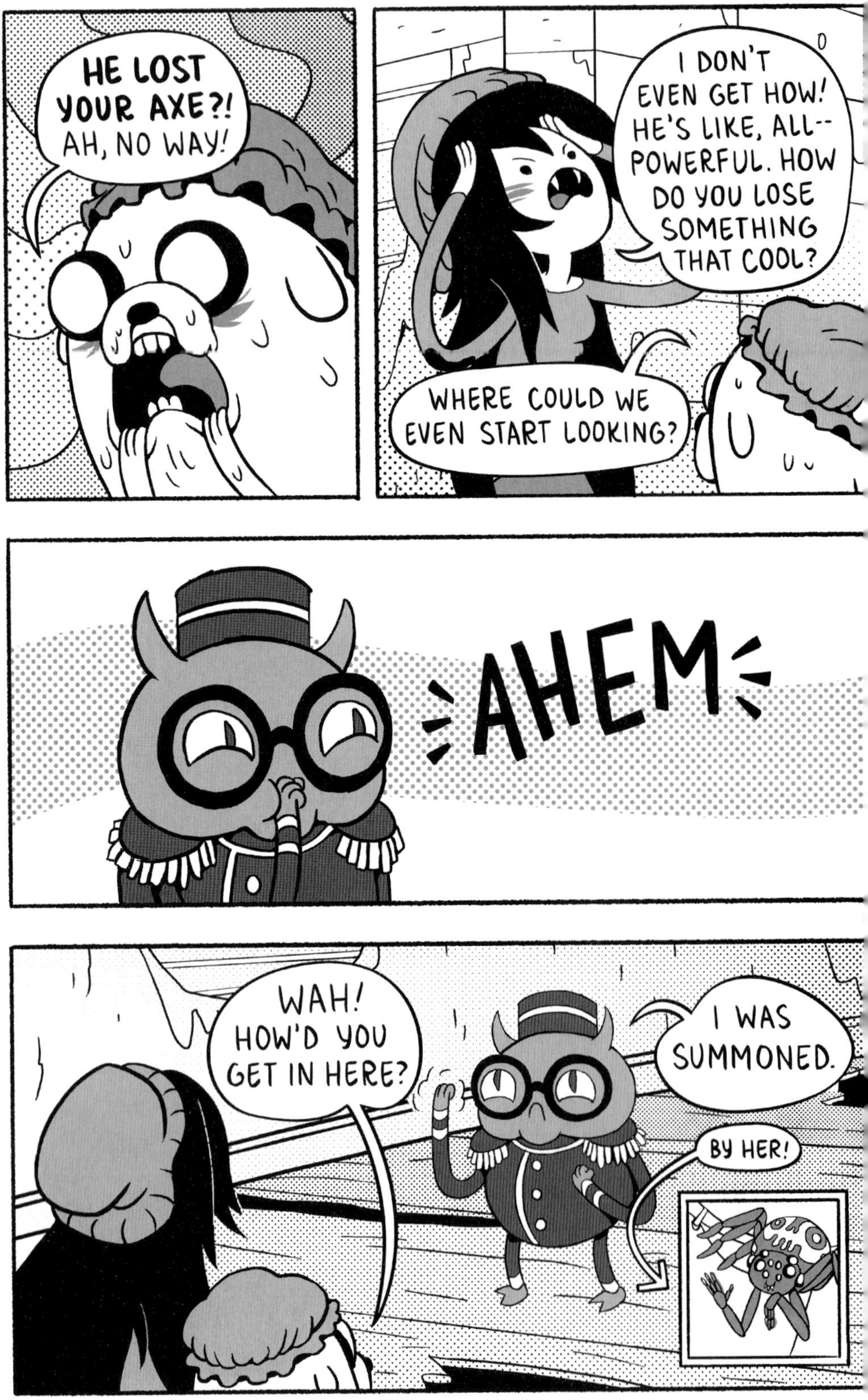
HE LOST YOUR AXE?! AH, NO WAY!
I DON'T EVEN GET HOW! HE'S LIKE, ALL-- POWERFUL. HOW DO YOU LOSE SOMETHING THAT COOL?
WHERE COULD WE EVEN START LOOKING?
AHEM
WAH! HOW'D YOU GET IN HERE?
I WAS SUMMONED.
BY HER!

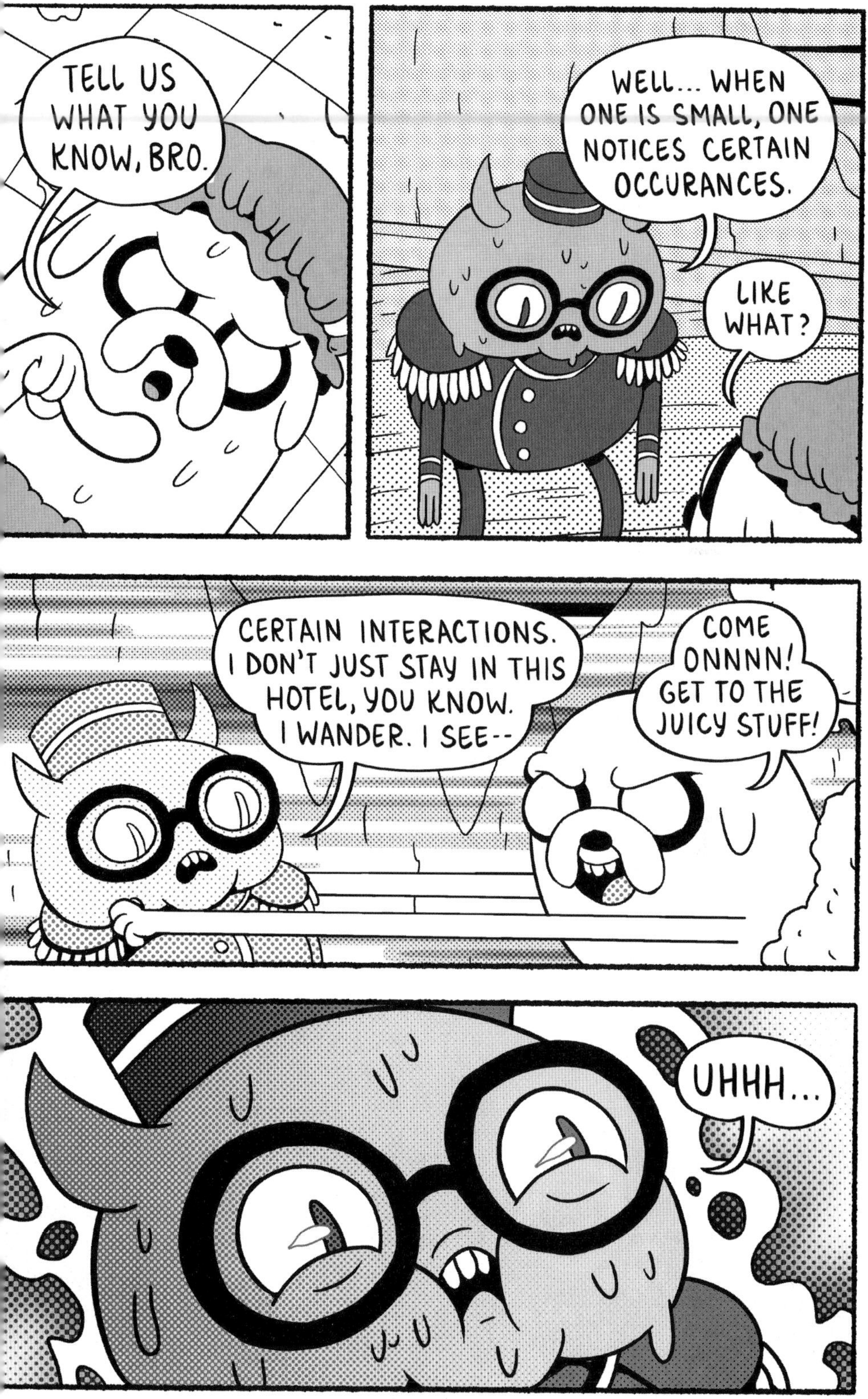
TELL US WHAT YOU KNOW, BRO.
WELL... WHEN ONE IS SMALL, ONE NOTICES CERTAIN OCCURANCES.
LIKE WHAT?
CERTAIN INTERACTIONS. I DON'T JUST STAY IN THIS HOTEL, YOU KNOW. I WANDER. I SEE--
COME ONNNN! GET TO THE JUICY STUFF!
UHHH...

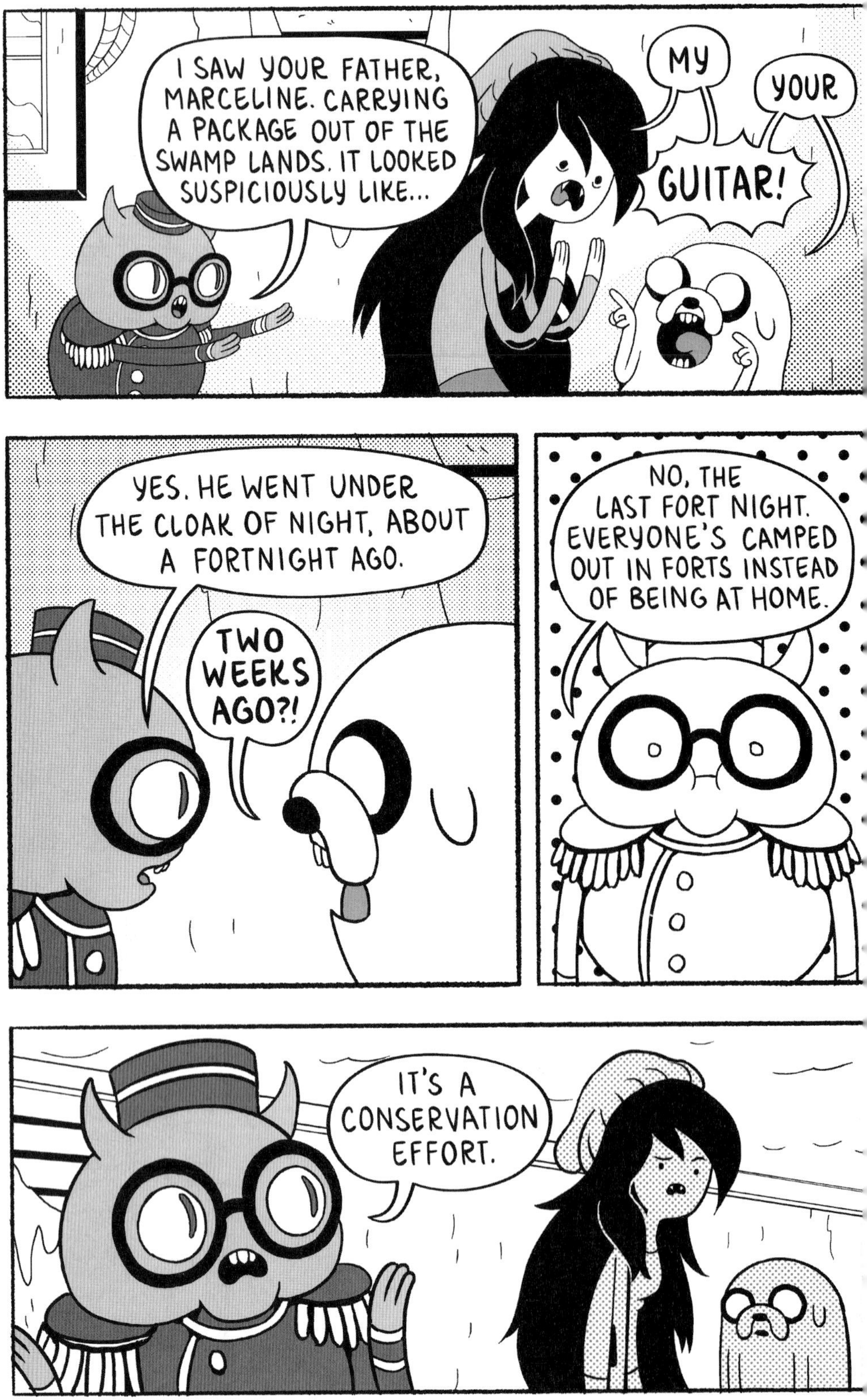
I SAW YOUR FATHER, MARCELINE. CARRYING A PACKAGE OUT OF THE SWAMP LANDS. IT LOOKED SUSPICIOUSLY LIKE...
MY
YOUR
GUITAR!
YES. HE WENT UNDER THE CLOAK OF NIGHT, ABOUT A FORTNIGHT AGO.
TWO WEEKS AGO?!
NO, THE LAST FORT NIGHT. EVERYONE'S CAMPED OUT IN FORTS INSTEAD OF BEING AT HOME.
IT'S A CONSERVATION EFFORT.

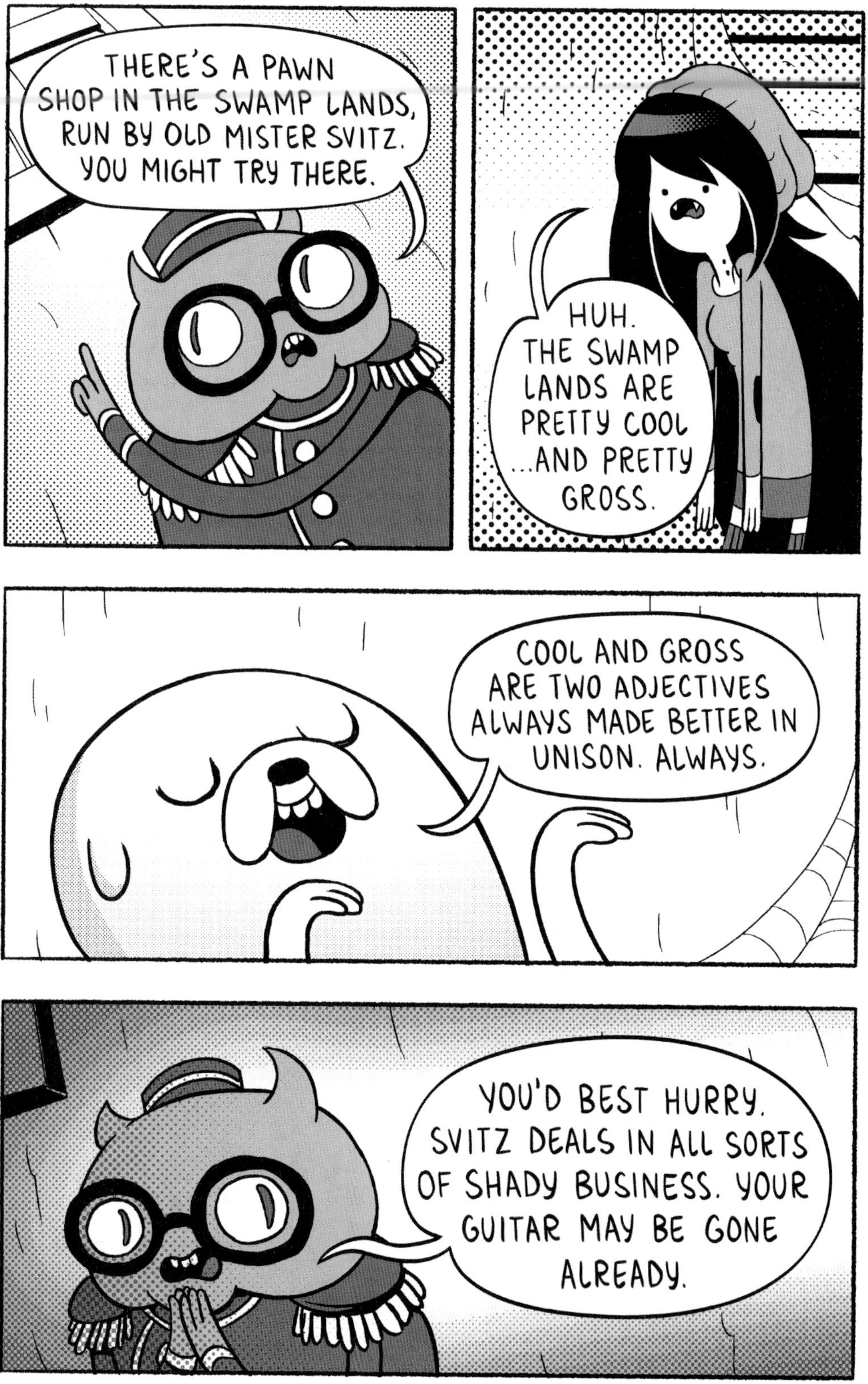
THERE'S A PAWN SHOP IN THE SWAMP LANDS, RUN BY OLD MISTER SVITZ. YOU MIGHT TRY THERE.
HUH. THE SWAMP LANDS ARE PRETTY COOL ...AND PRETTY GROSS.
COOL AND GROSS ARE TWO ADJECTIVES ALWAYS MADE BETTER IN UNISON. ALWAYS.
YOU'D BEST HURRY. SVITZ DEALS IN ALL SORTS OF SHADY BUSINESS. YOUR GUITAR MAY BE GONE ALREADY.

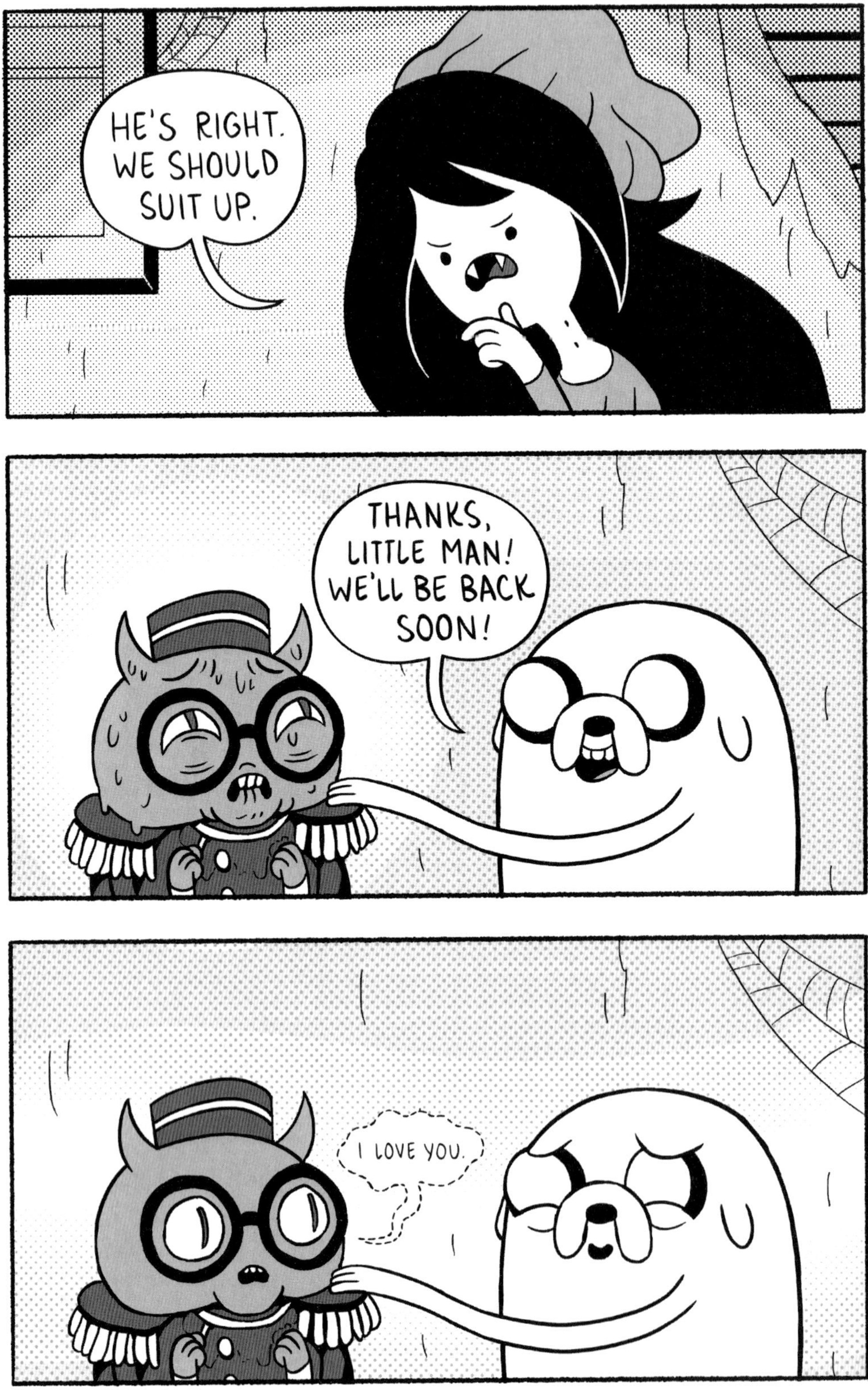
HE'S RIGHT. WE SHOULD SUIT UP.
THANKS, LITTLE MAN! WE'LL BE BACK SOON!
I LOVE YOU.

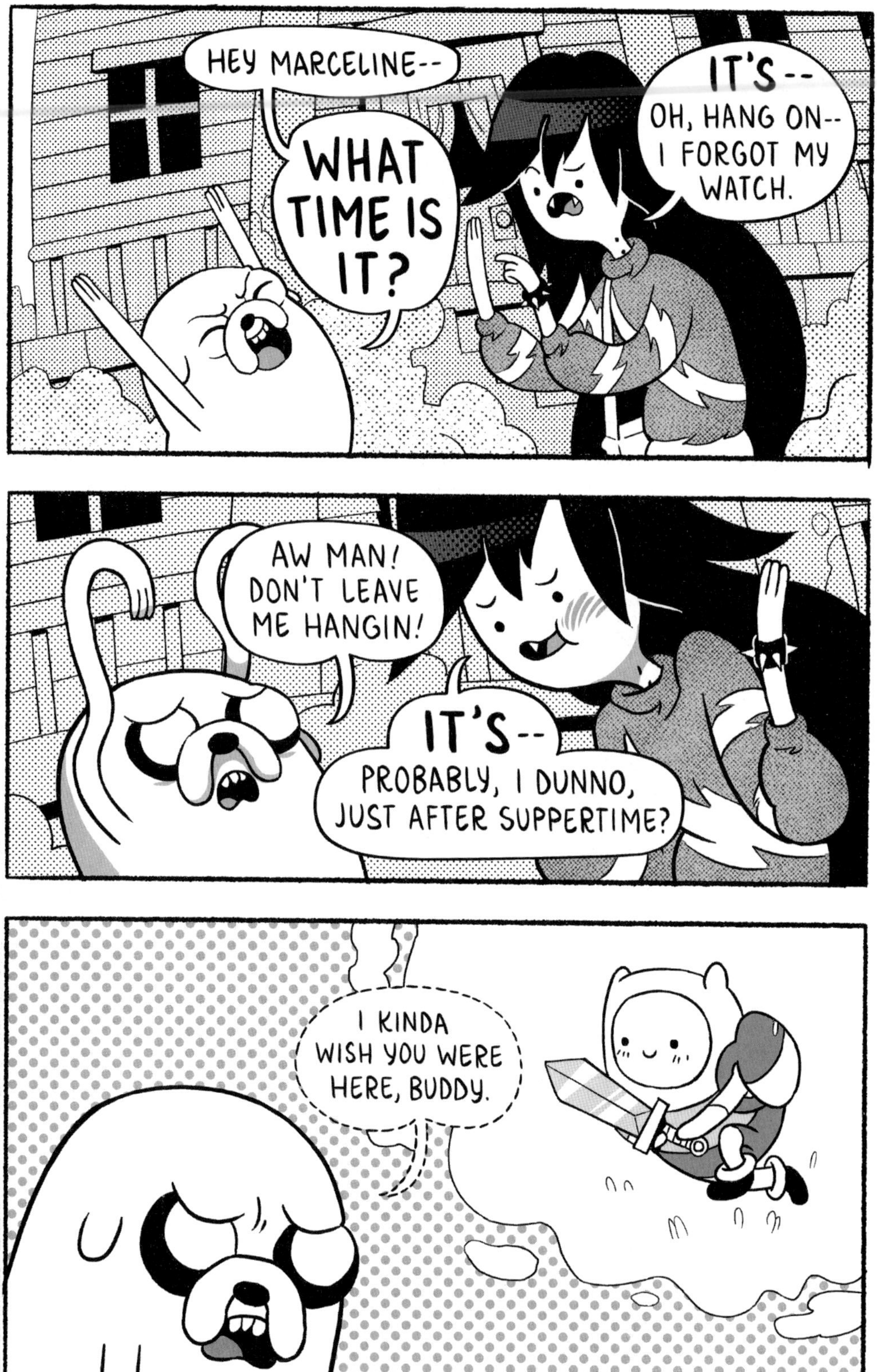
HEY MARCELINE--
WHAT TIME IS IT?
IT'S-- OH, HANG ON-- I FORGOT MY WATCH.
AW MAN! DON'T LEAVE ME HANGIN!
IT'S-- PROBABLY, I DUNNO, JUST AFTER SUPPERTIME?
I KINDA WISH YOU WERE HERE, BUDDY.

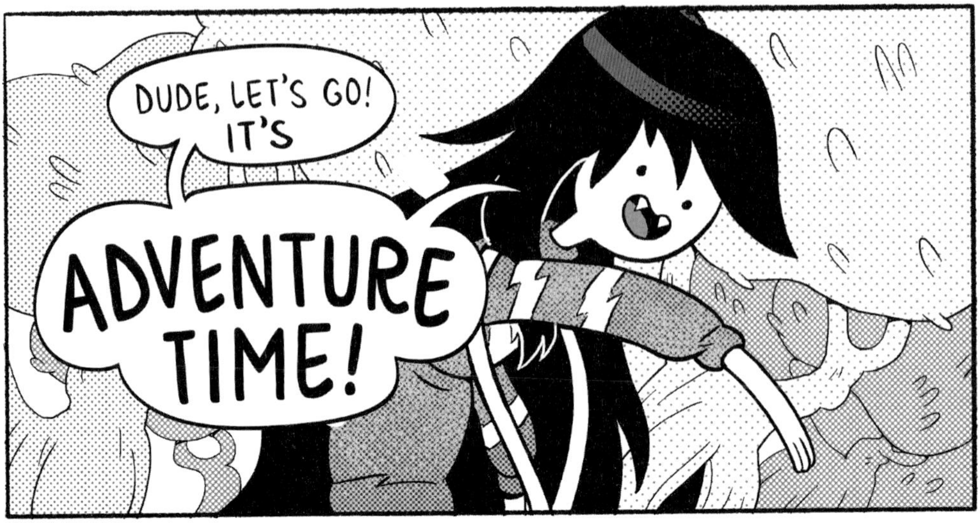
DUDE, LET'S GO! IT'S
ADVENTURE TIME!

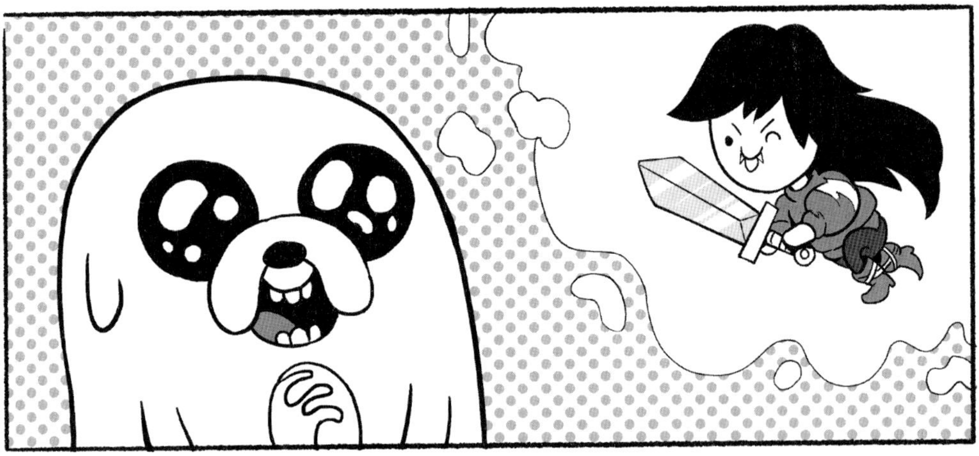

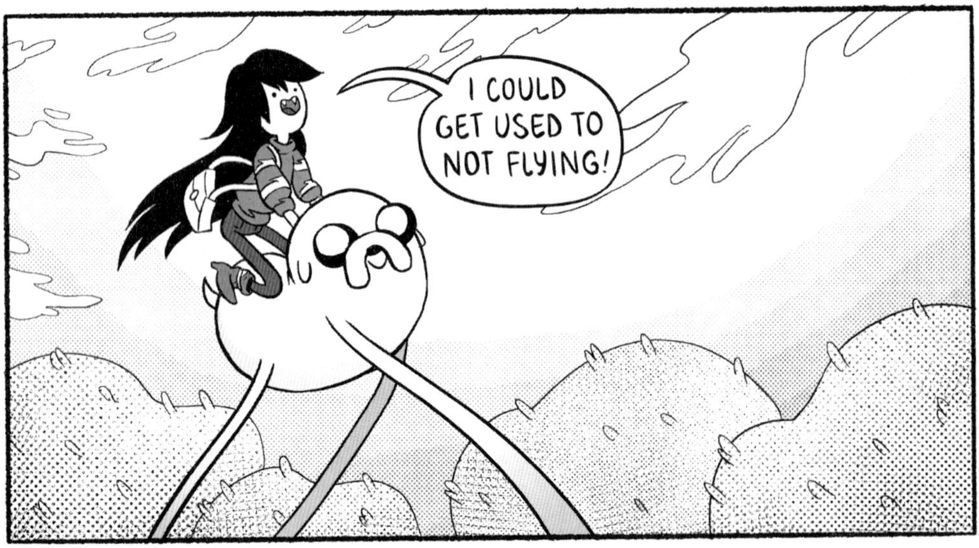
I COULD GET USED TO NOT FLYING!

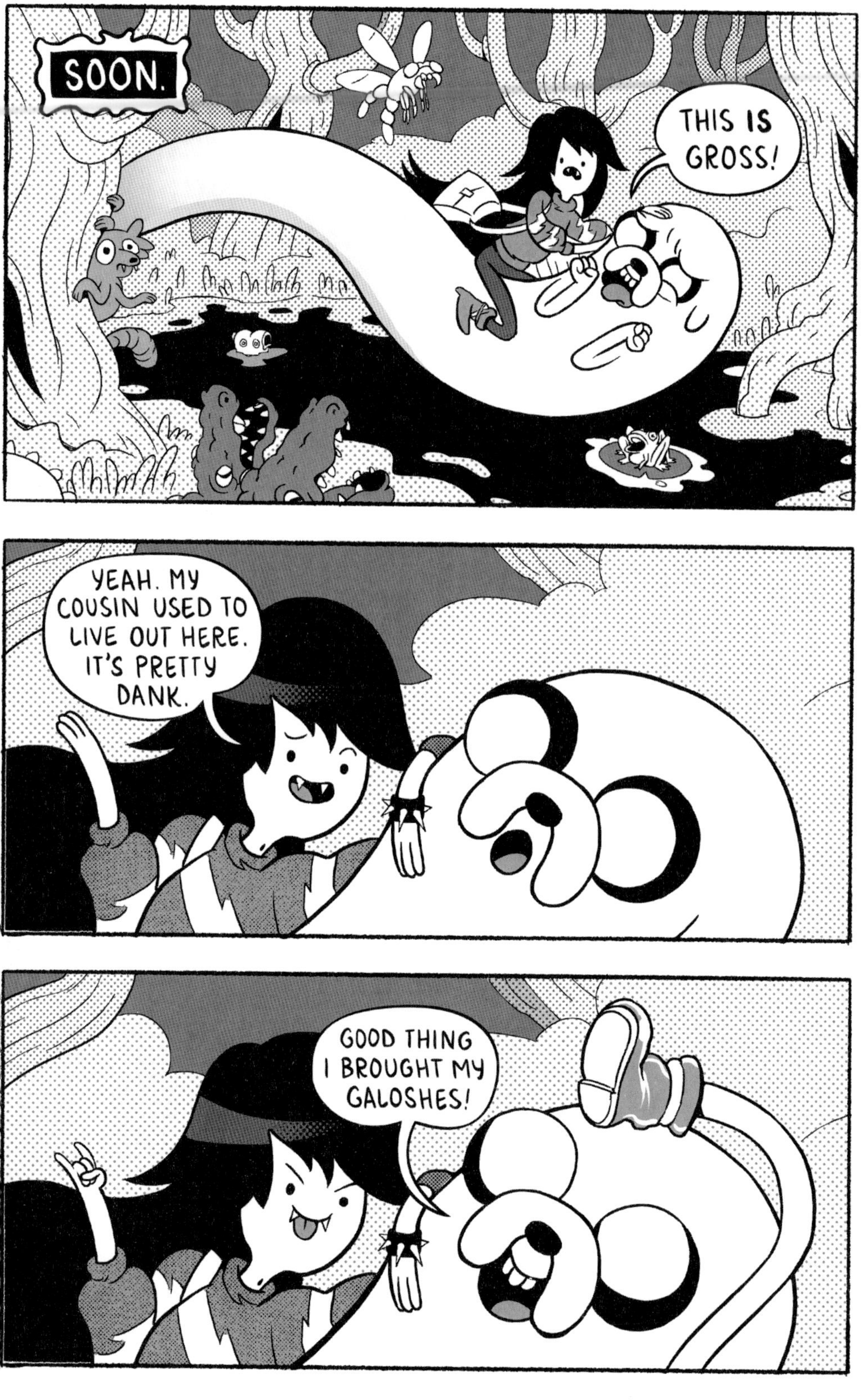
SOON.
THIS **IS** GROSS!
YEAH. MY COUSIN USED TO LIVE OUT HERE. IT'S PRETTY DANK.
GOOD THING I BROUGHT MY GALOSHES!

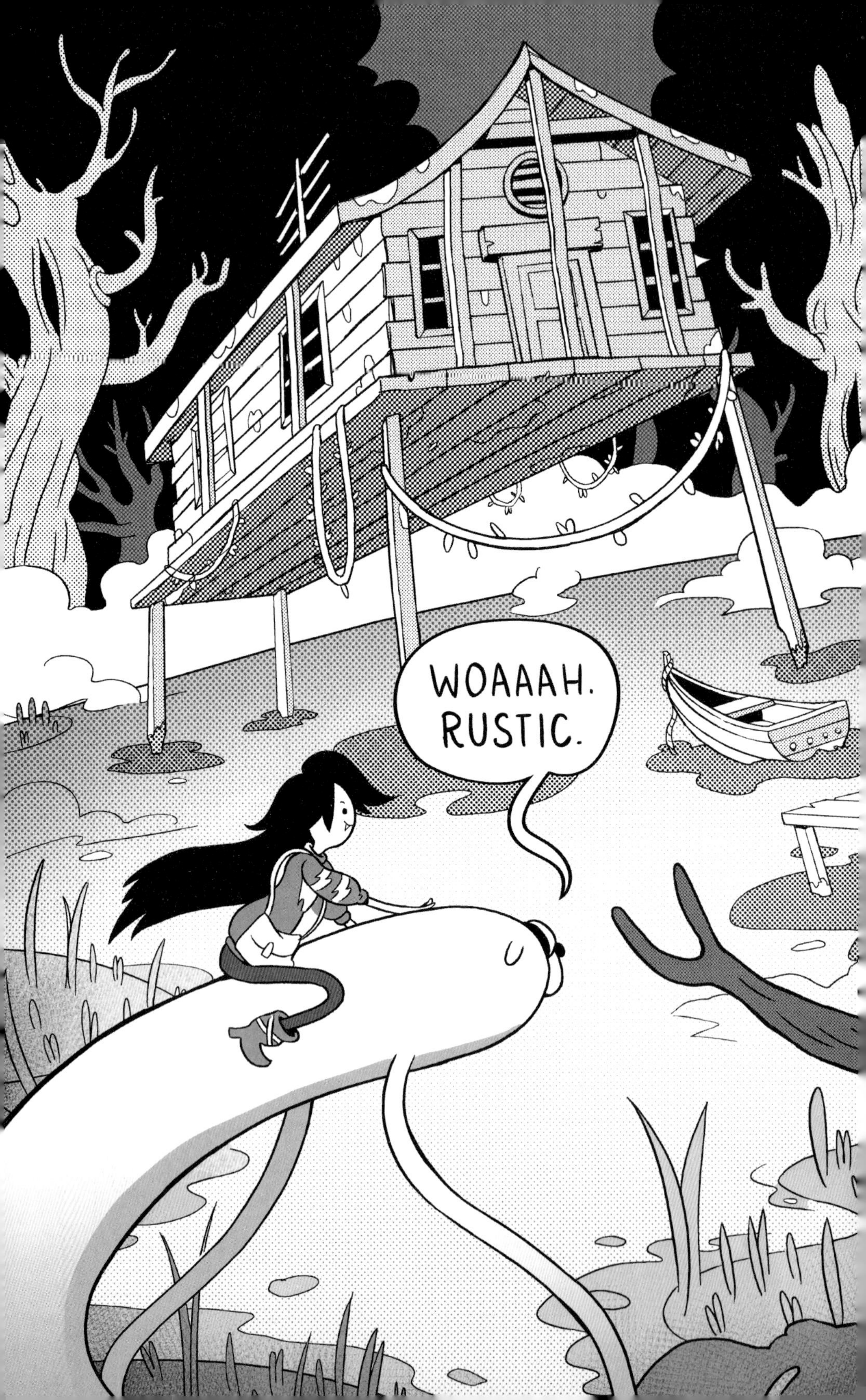
WOAAAH. RUSTIC.

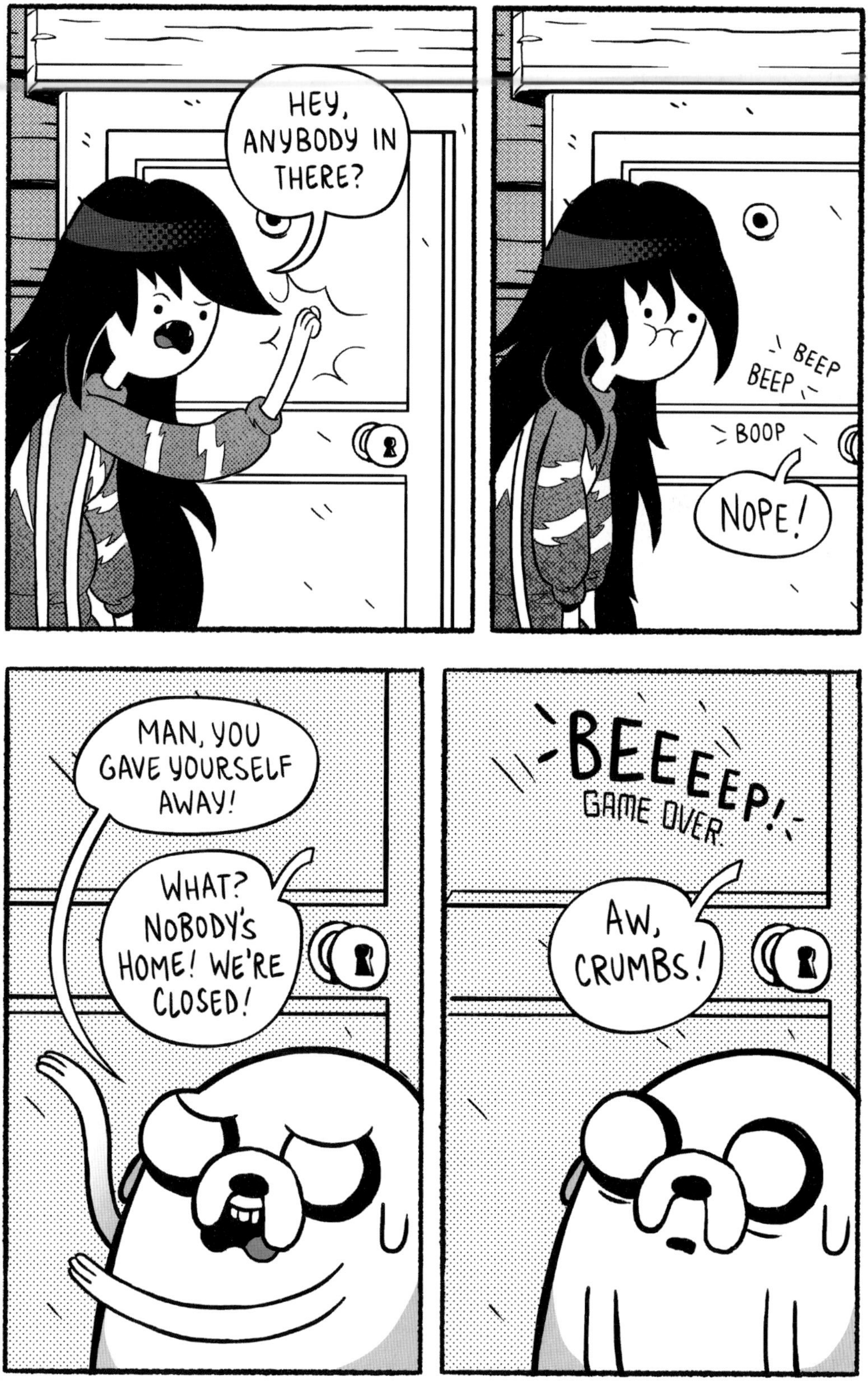
HEY, ANYBODY IN THERE?
BEEP
BEEP
BOOP
NOPE!
MAN, YOU GAVE YOURSELF AWAY!
WHAT? NOBODY'S HOME! WE'RE CLOSED!
BEEEEEP!
GAME OVER
AW, CRUMBS!

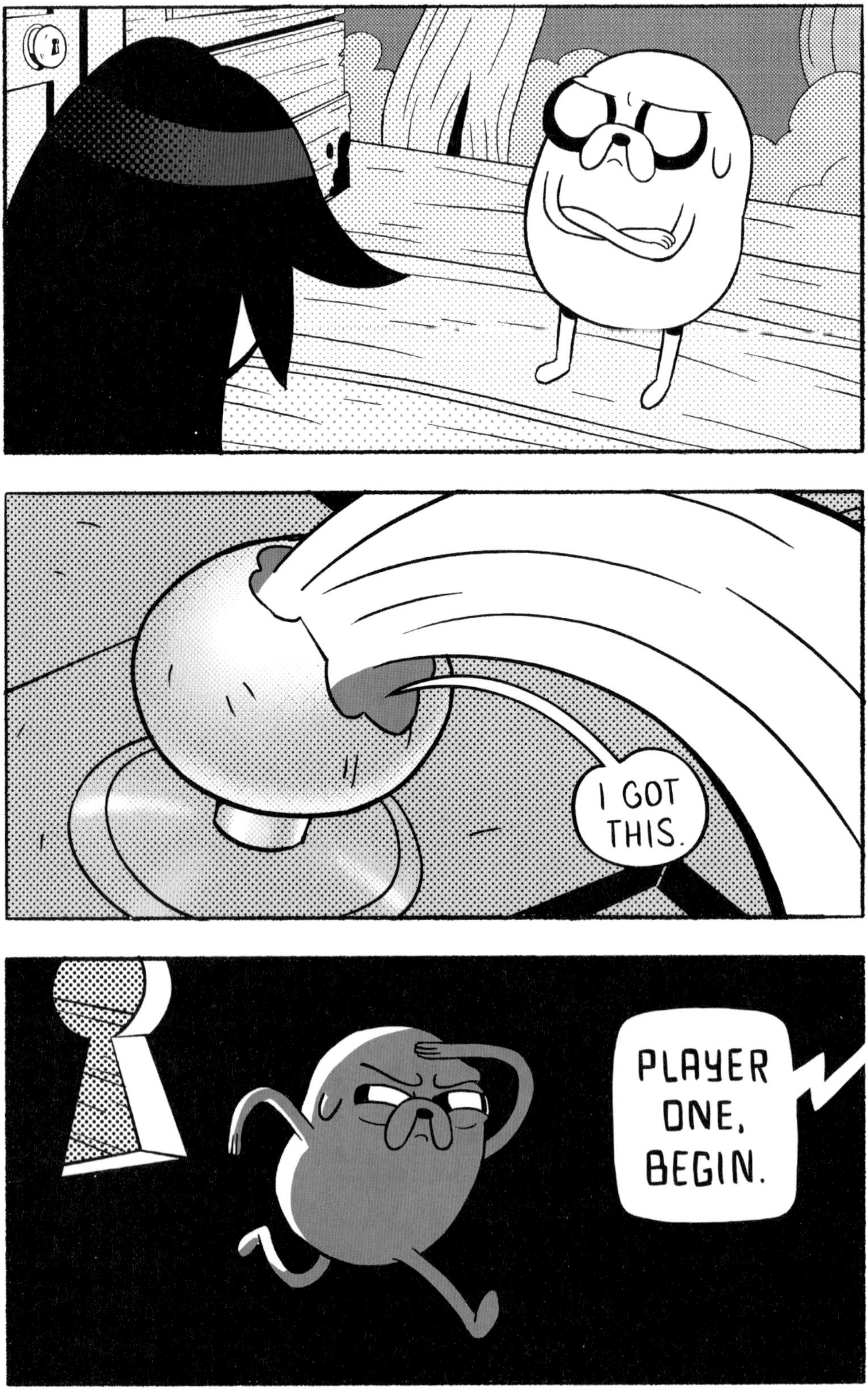
I GOT THIS.
PLAYER ONE, BEGIN.

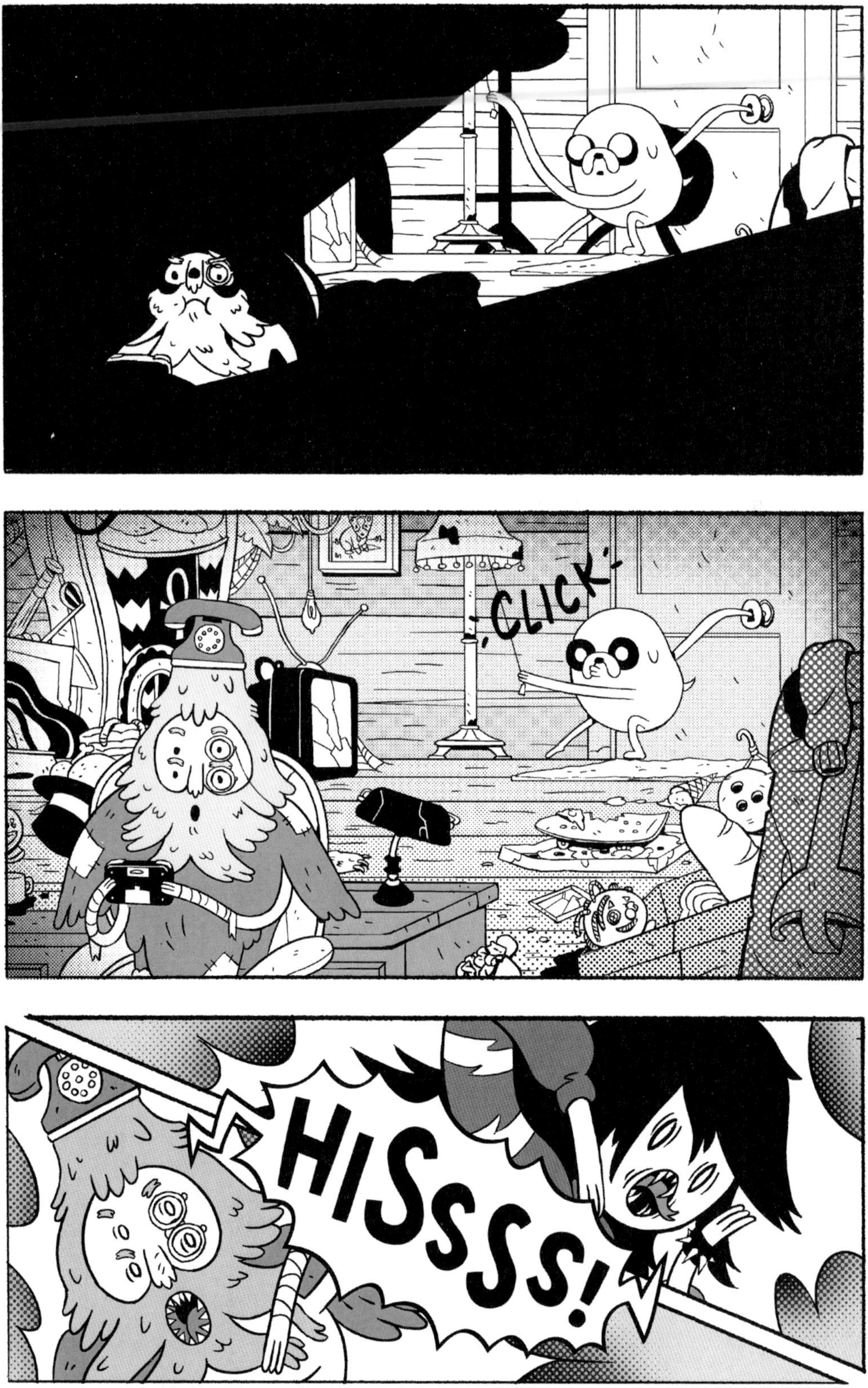
CLICK
HISSSS!

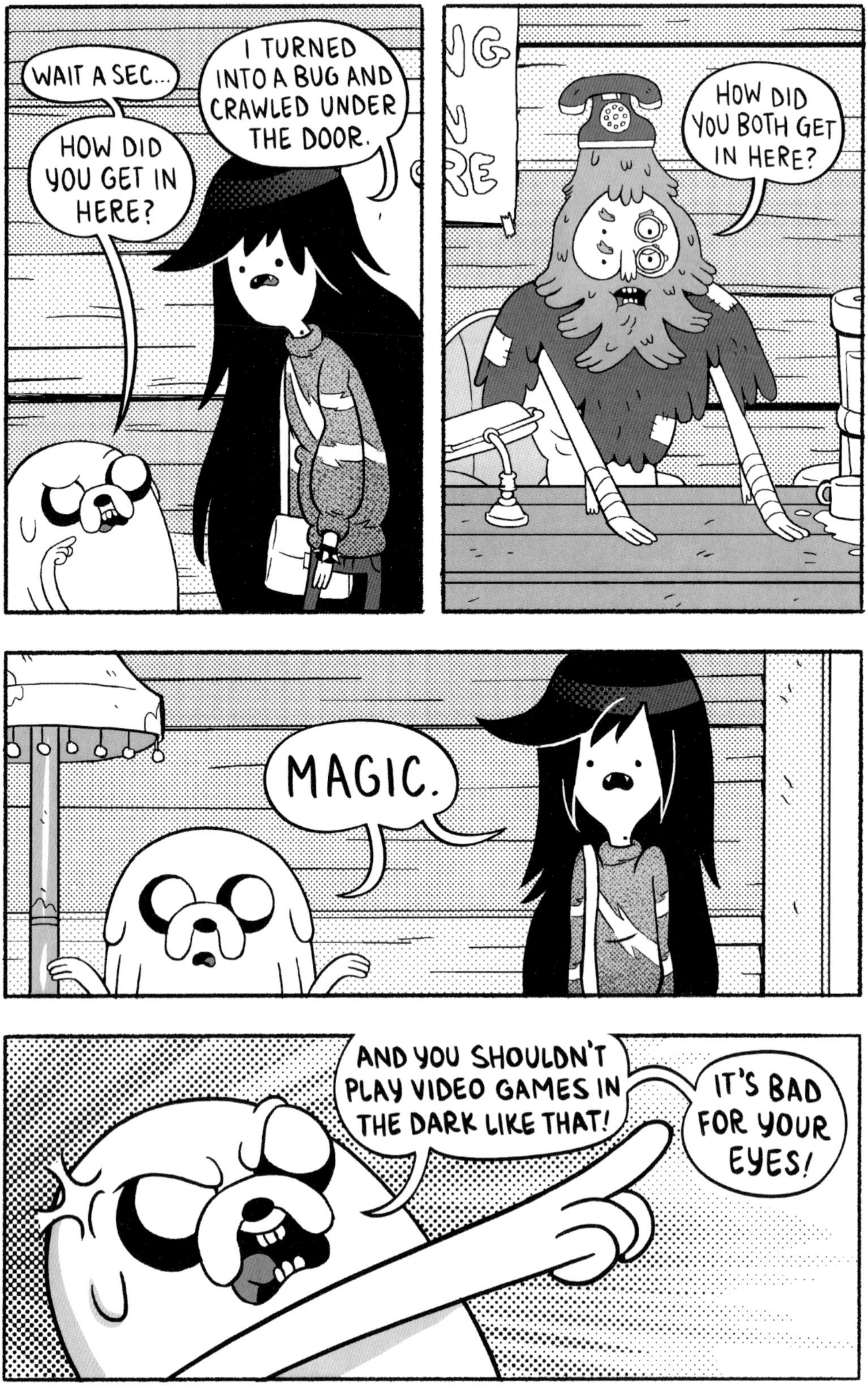
WAIT A SEC...
HOW DID YOU GET IN HERE?
I TURNED INTO A BUG AND CRAWLED UNDER THE DOOR.
HOW DID YOU BOTH GET IN HERE?
MAGIC.
AND YOU SHOULDN'T PLAY VIDEO GAMES IN THE DARK LIKE THAT!
IT'S BAD FOR YOUR EYES!

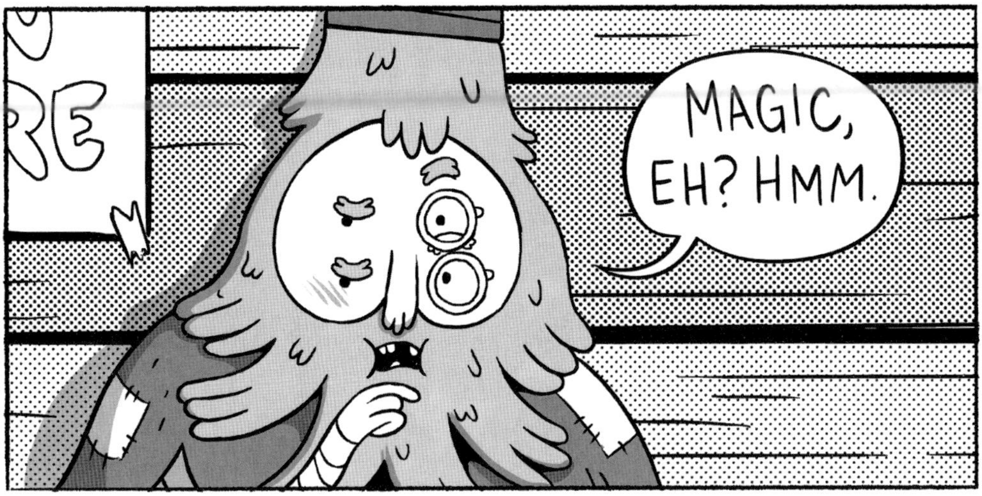
MAGIC, EH? HMM.

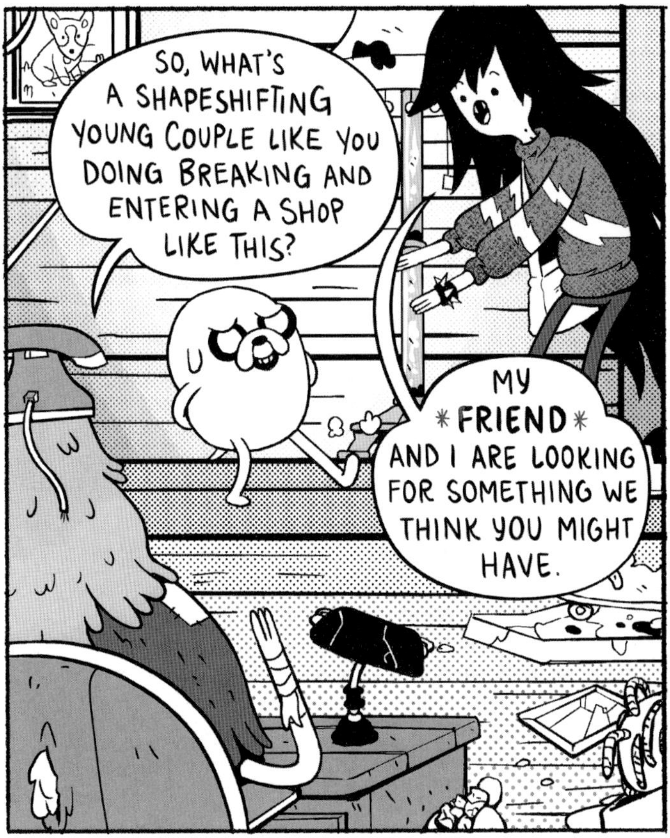
SO, WHAT'S A SHAPESHIFTING YOUNG COUPLE LIKE YOU DOING BREAKING AND ENTERING A SHOP LIKE THIS?
MY *FRIEND* AND I ARE LOOKING FOR SOMETHING WE THINK YOU MIGHT HAVE.

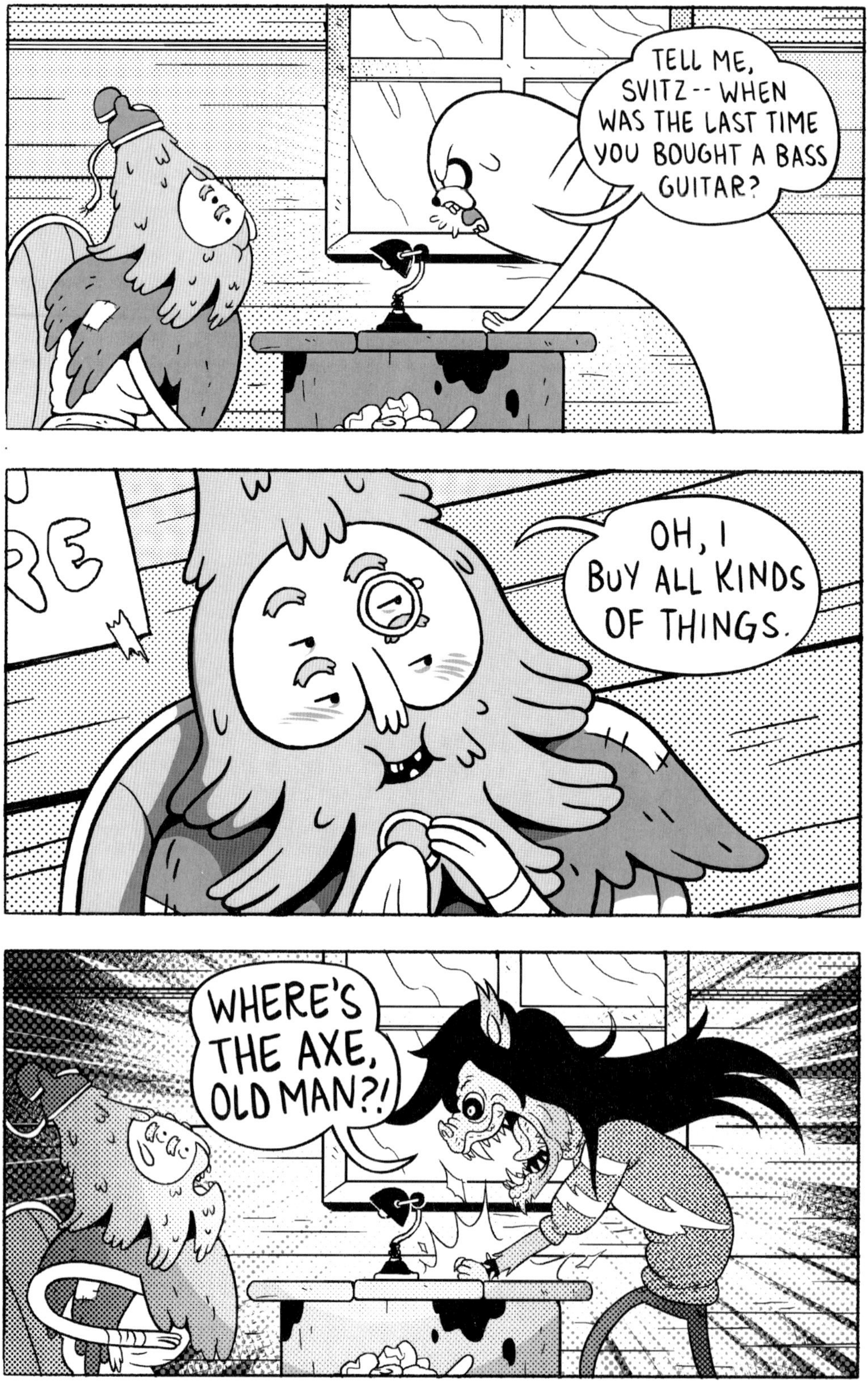
TELL ME, SVITZ -- WHEN WAS THE LAST TIME YOU BOUGHT A BASS GUITAR?
OH, I BUY ALL KINDS OF THINGS.
WHERE'S THE AXE, OLD MAN?!

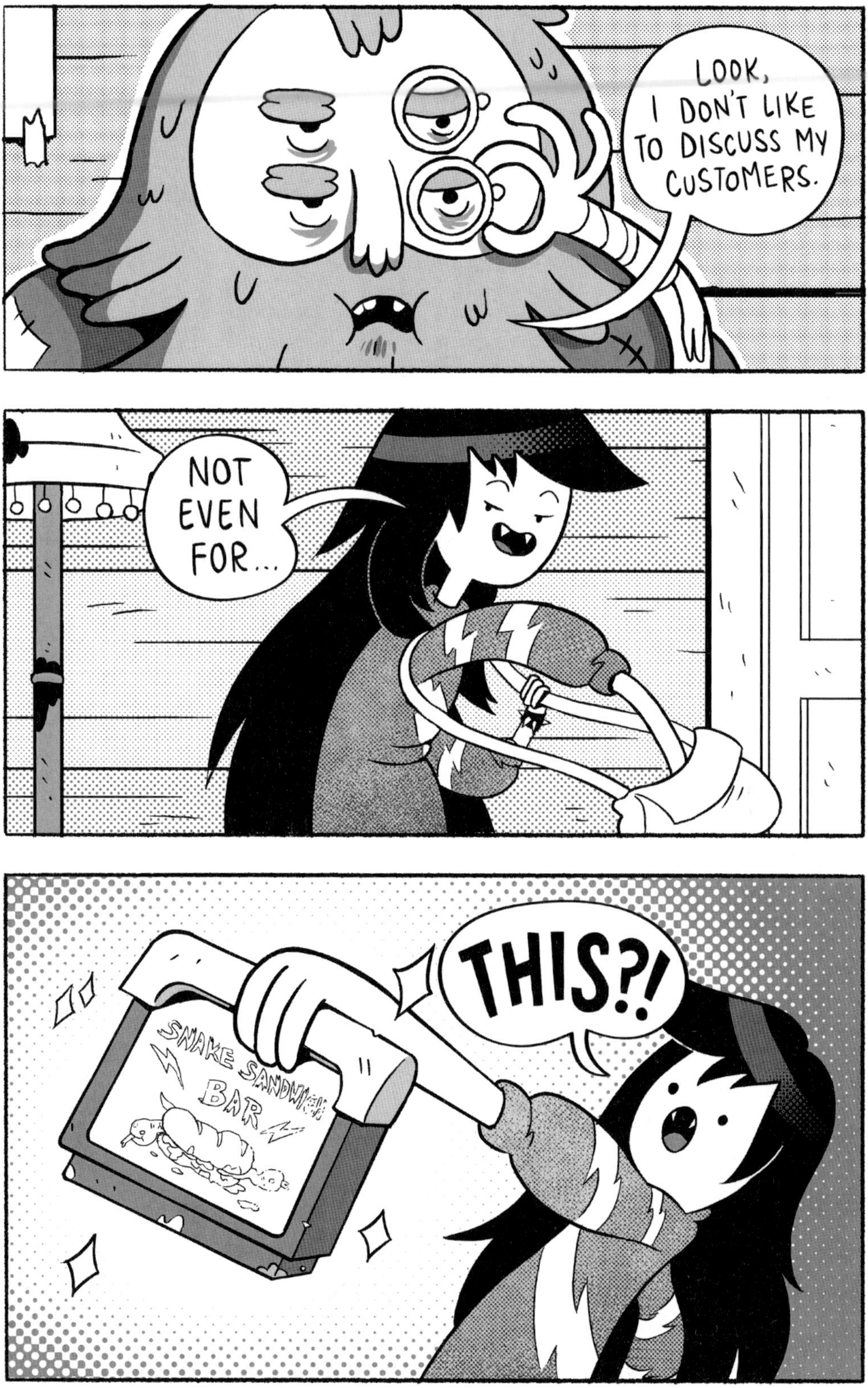
LOOK, I DON'T LIKE TO DISCUSS MY CUSTOMERS.
NOT EVEN FOR...
THIS?!
SNAKE SANDWICH BAR

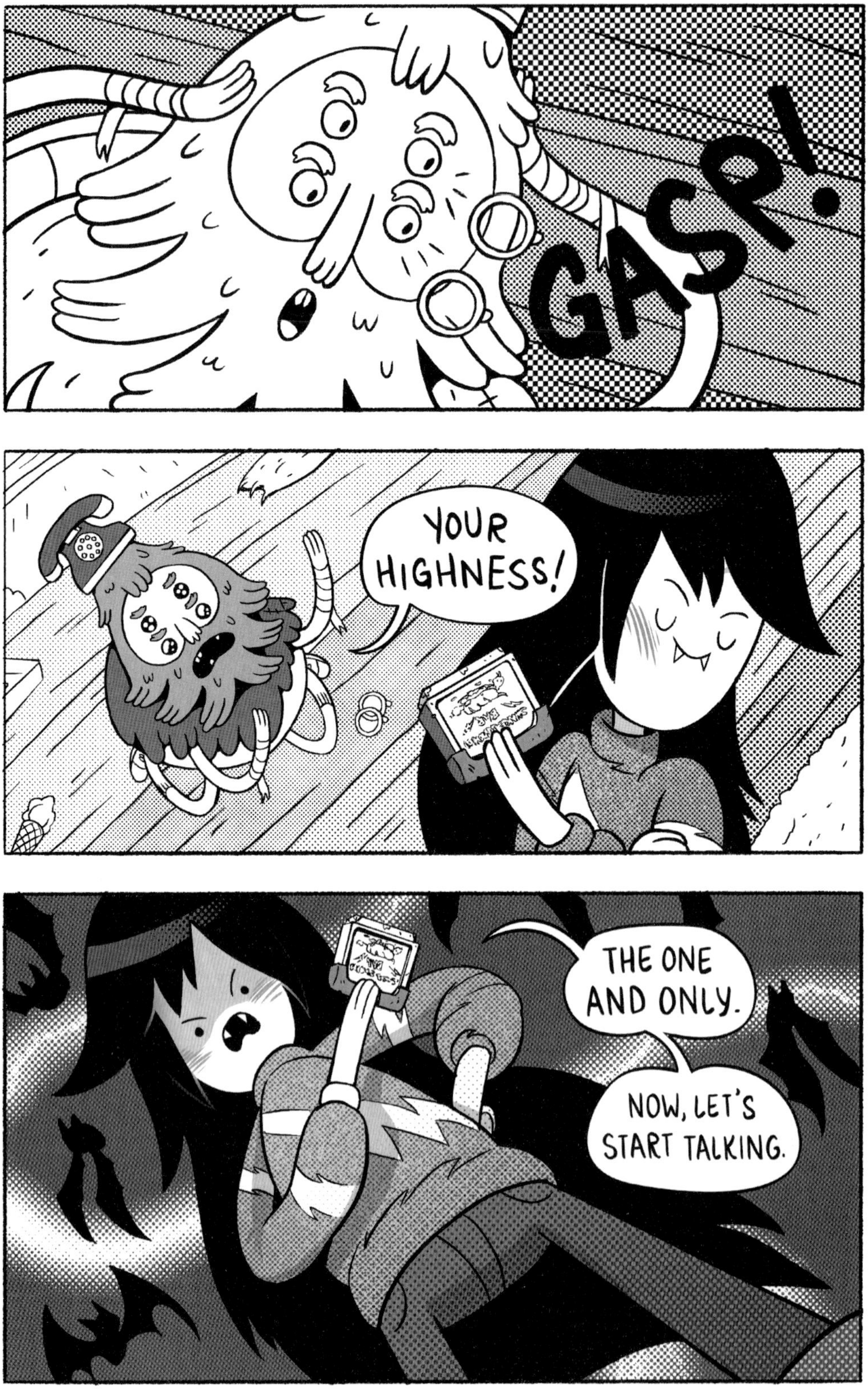
GASP!
YOUR HIGHNESS!
THE ONE AND ONLY.
NOW, LET'S START TALKING.

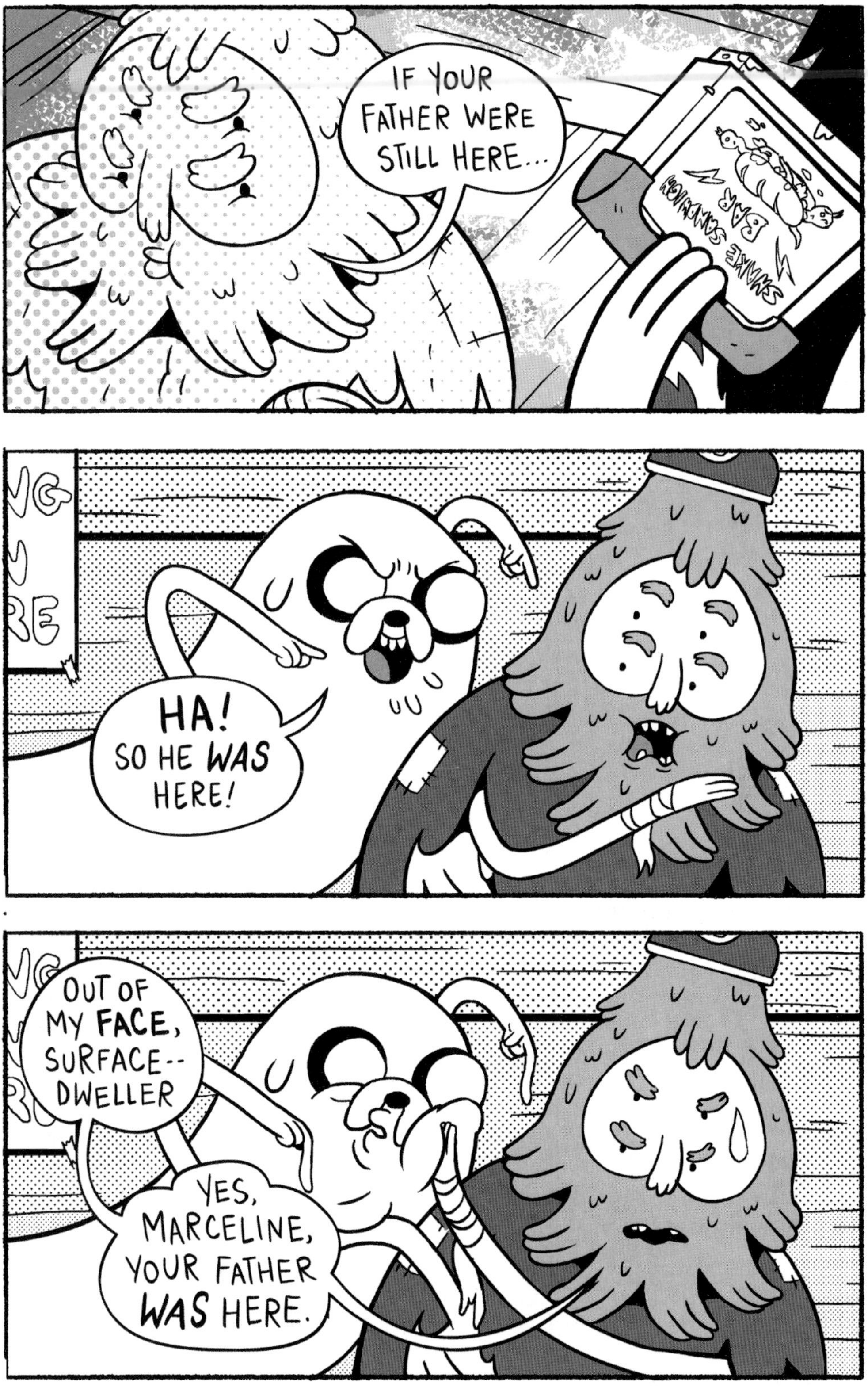

IF YOUR FATHER WERE STILL HERE...
HA! SO HE WAS HERE!
OUT OF MY FACE, SURFACE--DWELLER
YES, MARCELINE, YOUR FATHER WAS HERE.

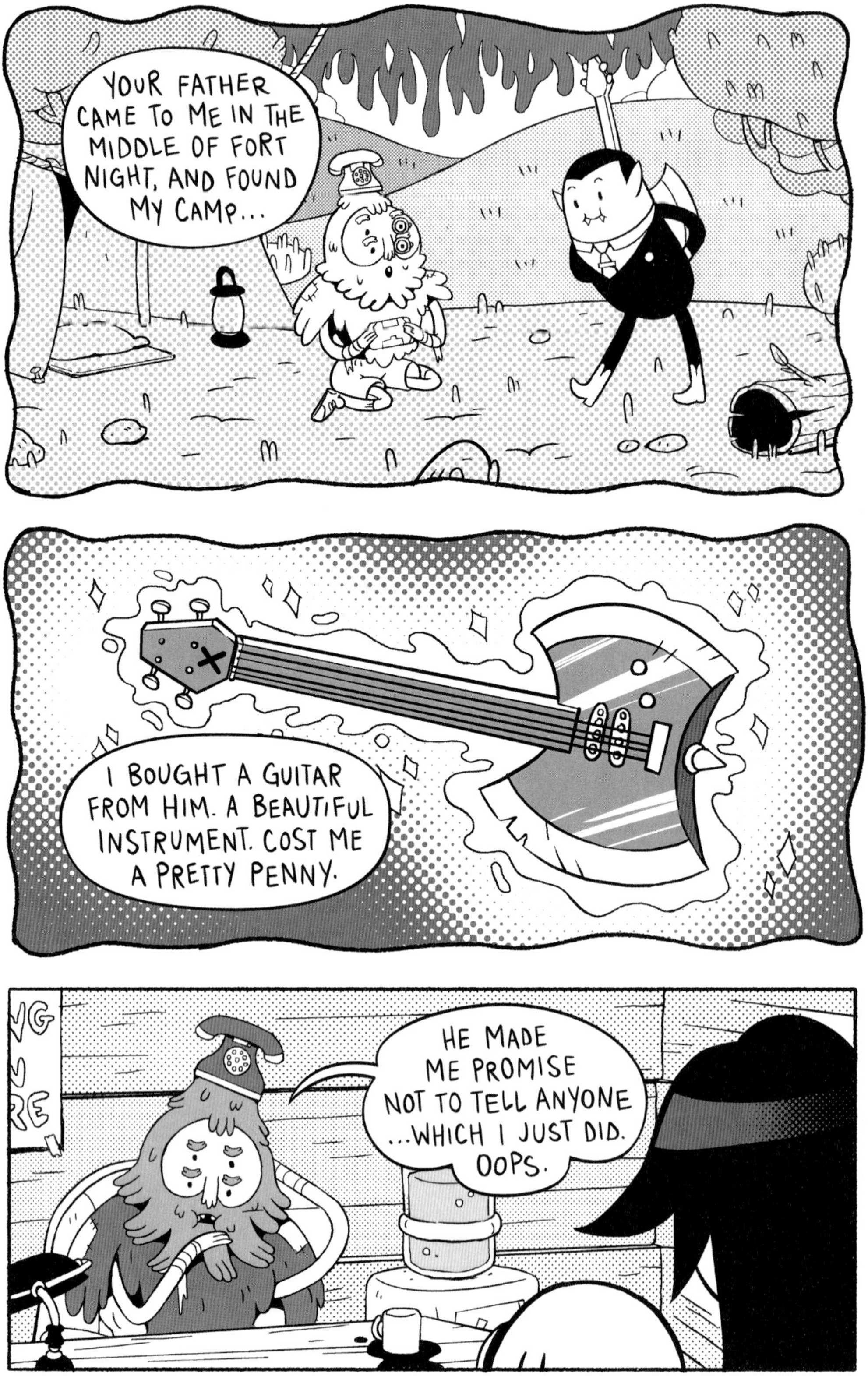
YOUR FATHER CAME TO ME IN THE MIDDLE OF FORT NIGHT, AND FOUND MY CAMP...
I BOUGHT A GUITAR FROM HIM. A BEAUTIFUL INSTRUMENT. COST ME A PRETTY PENNY.
HE MADE ME PROMISE NOT TO TELL ANYONE ...WHICH I JUST DID. OOPS.

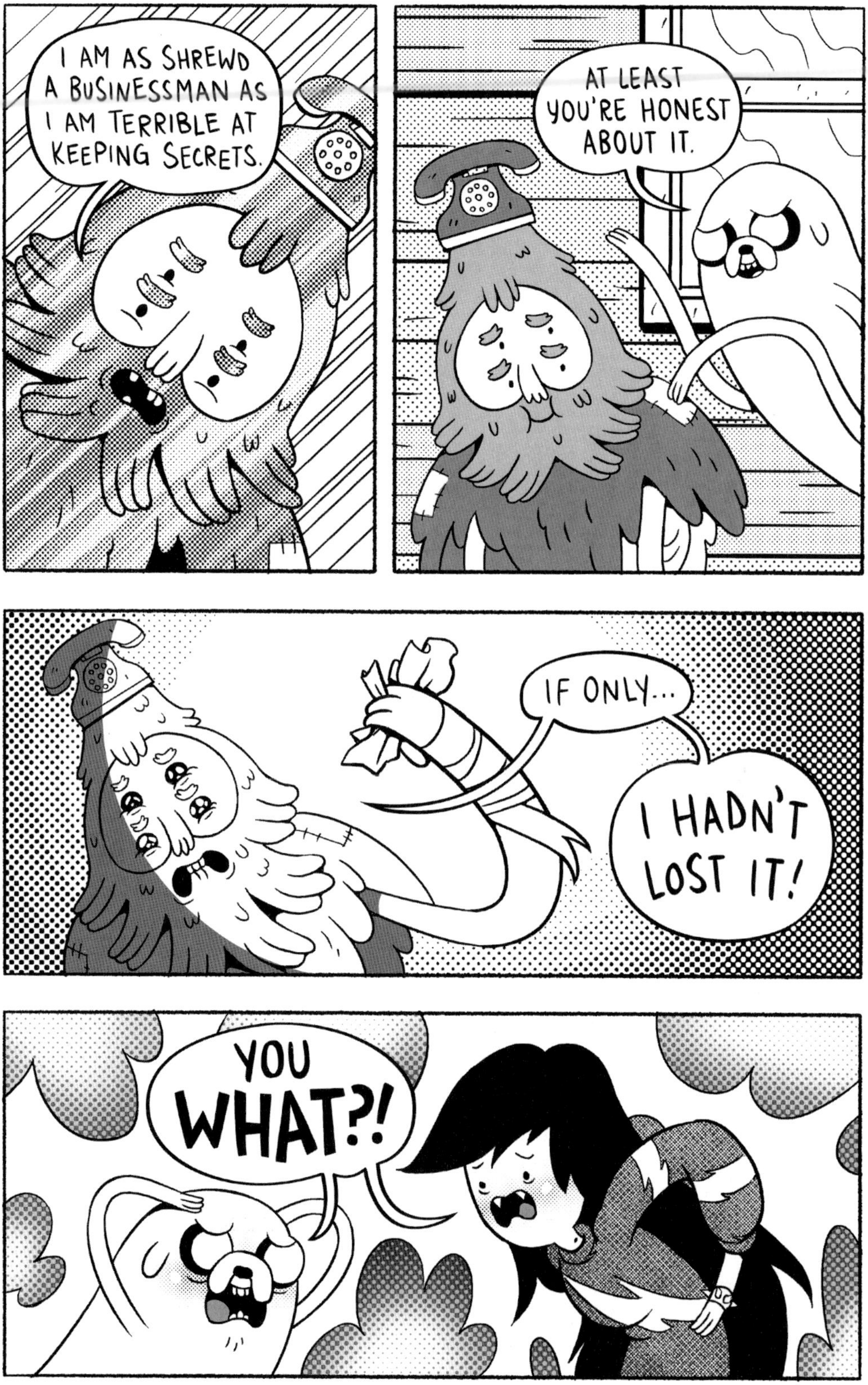
I AM AS SHREWD A BUSINESSMAN AS I AM TERRIBLE AT KEEPING SECRETS.
AT LEAST YOU'RE HONEST ABOUT IT.
IF ONLY...
I HADN'T LOST IT!
YOU WHAT?!

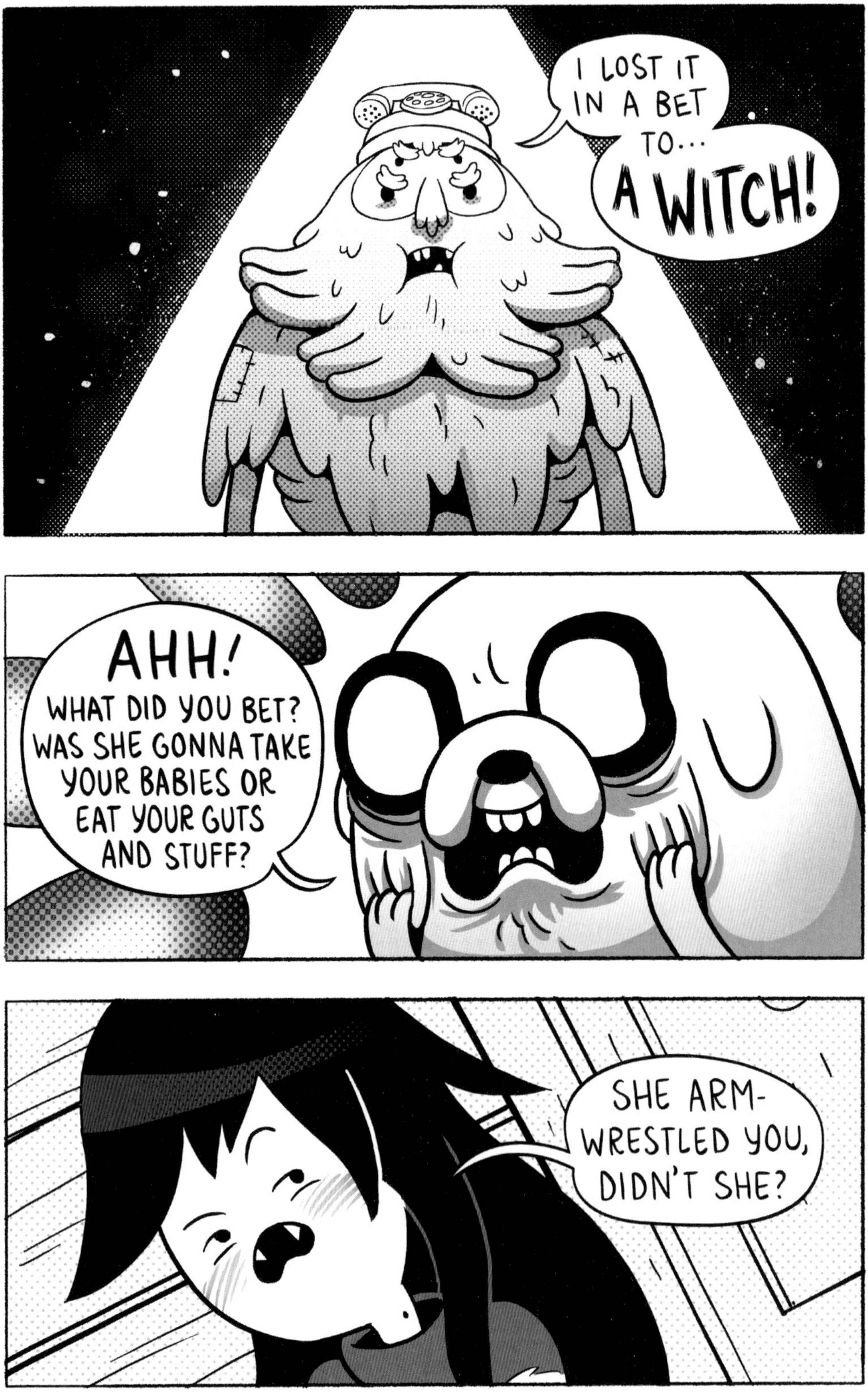
I LOST IT IN A BET TO...
A WITCH!
AHH! WHAT DID YOU BET? WAS SHE GONNA TAKE YOUR BABIES OR EAT YOUR GUTS AND STUFF?
SHE ARM-WRESTLED YOU, DIDN'T SHE?

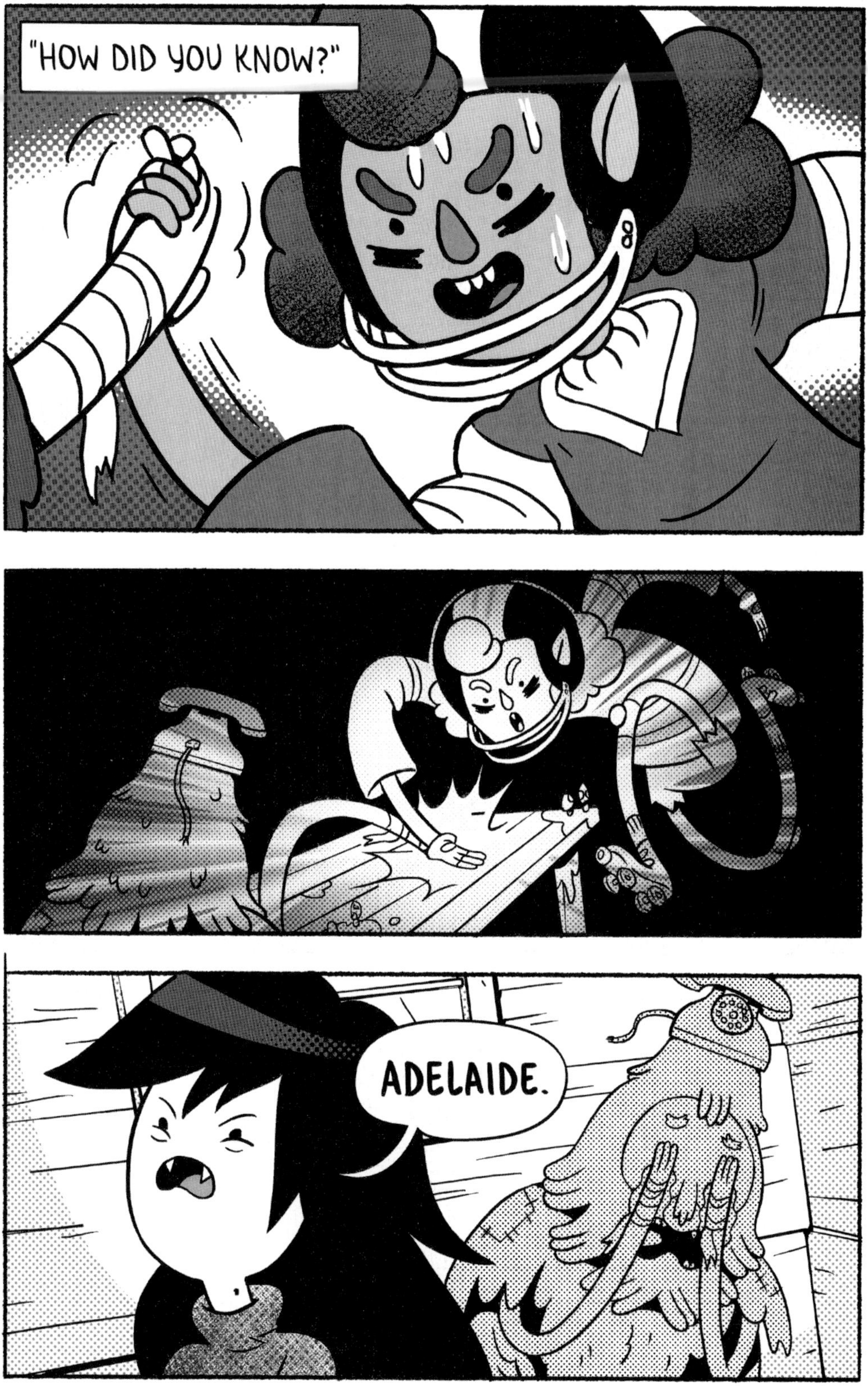
"HOW DID YOU KNOW?"
ADELAIDE.

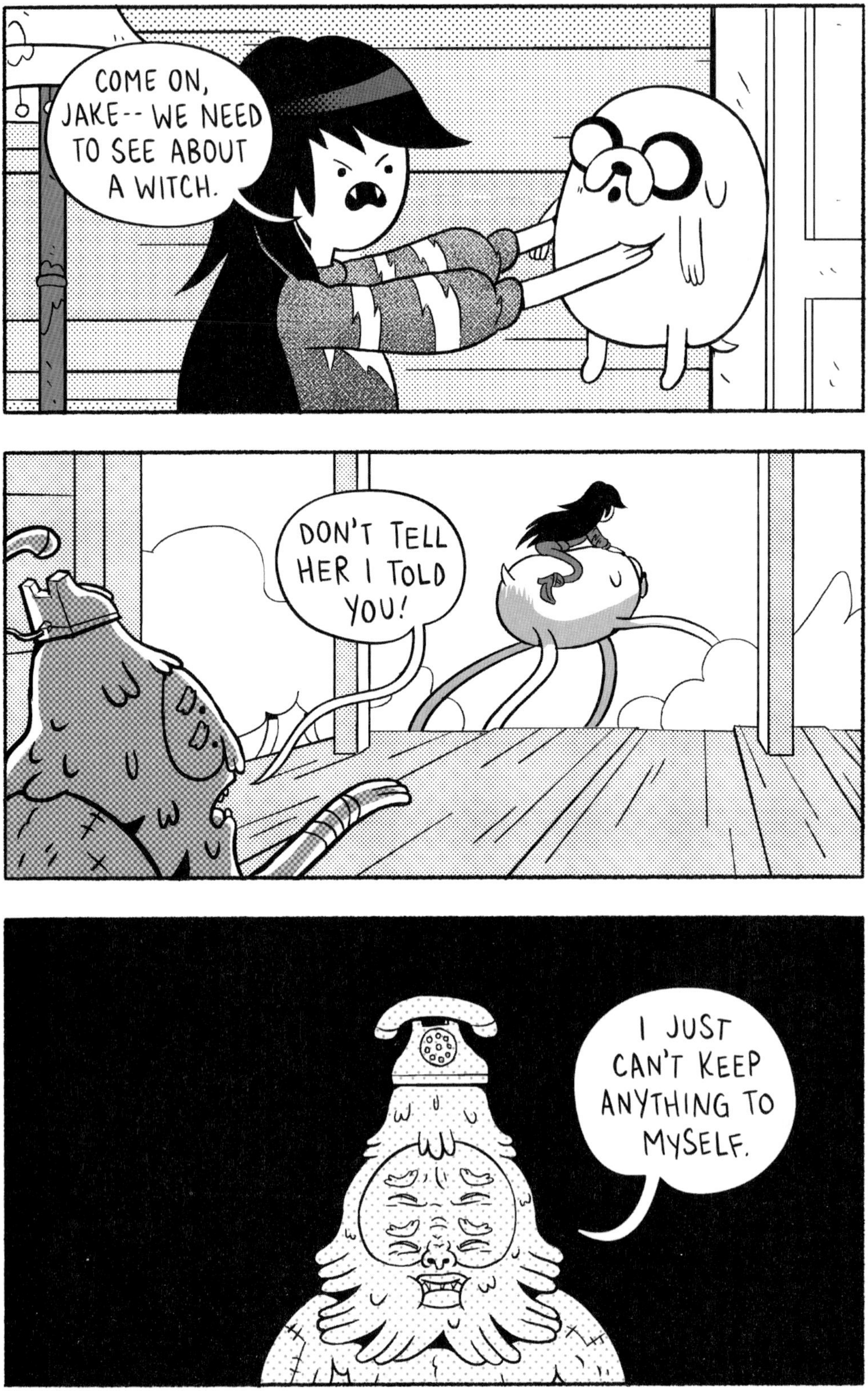
COME ON, JAKE-- WE NEED TO SEE ABOUT A WITCH.
DON'T TELL HER I TOLD YOU!
I JUST CAN'T KEEP ANYTHING TO MYSELF.

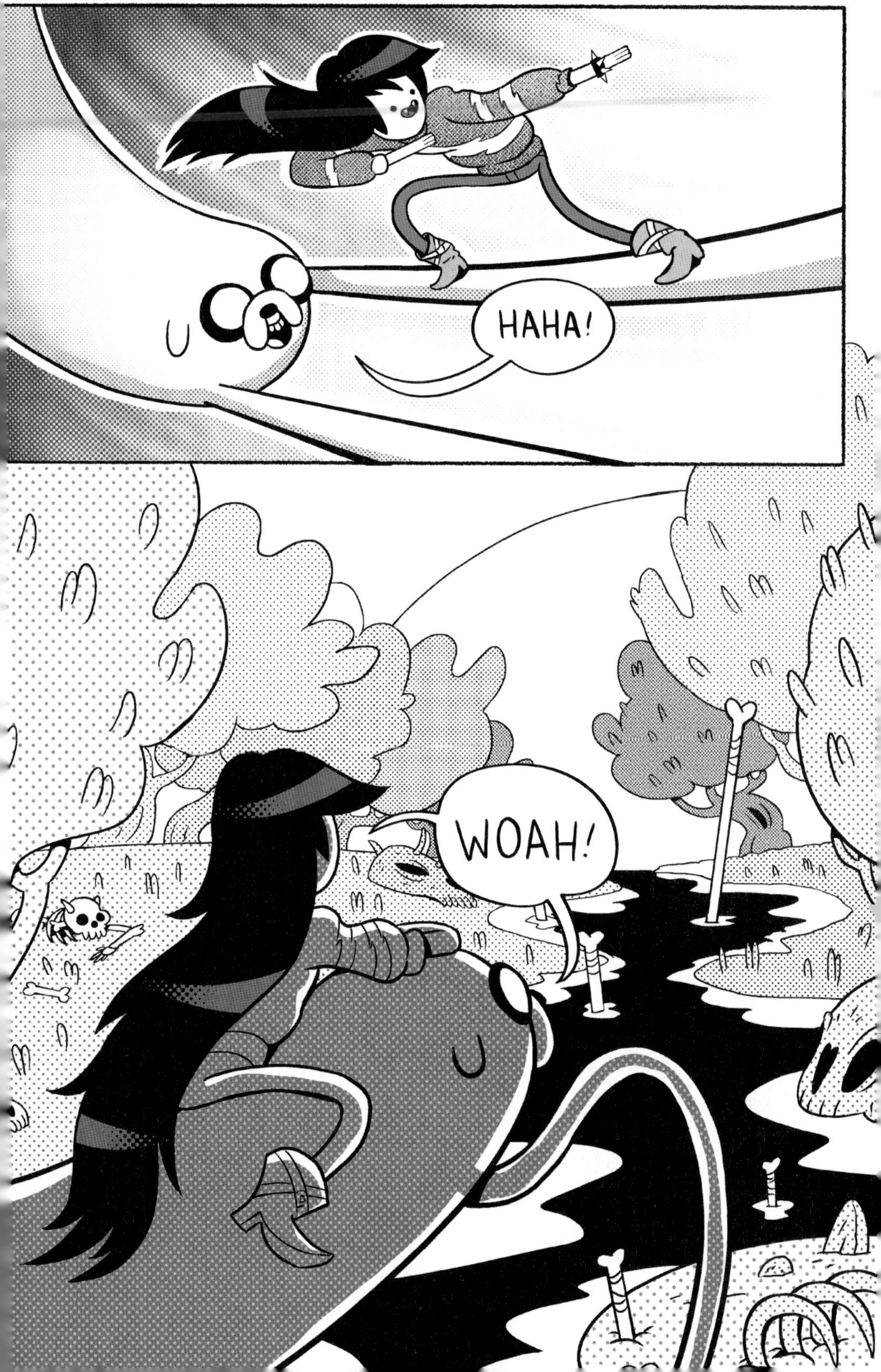
HAHA!
WOAH!

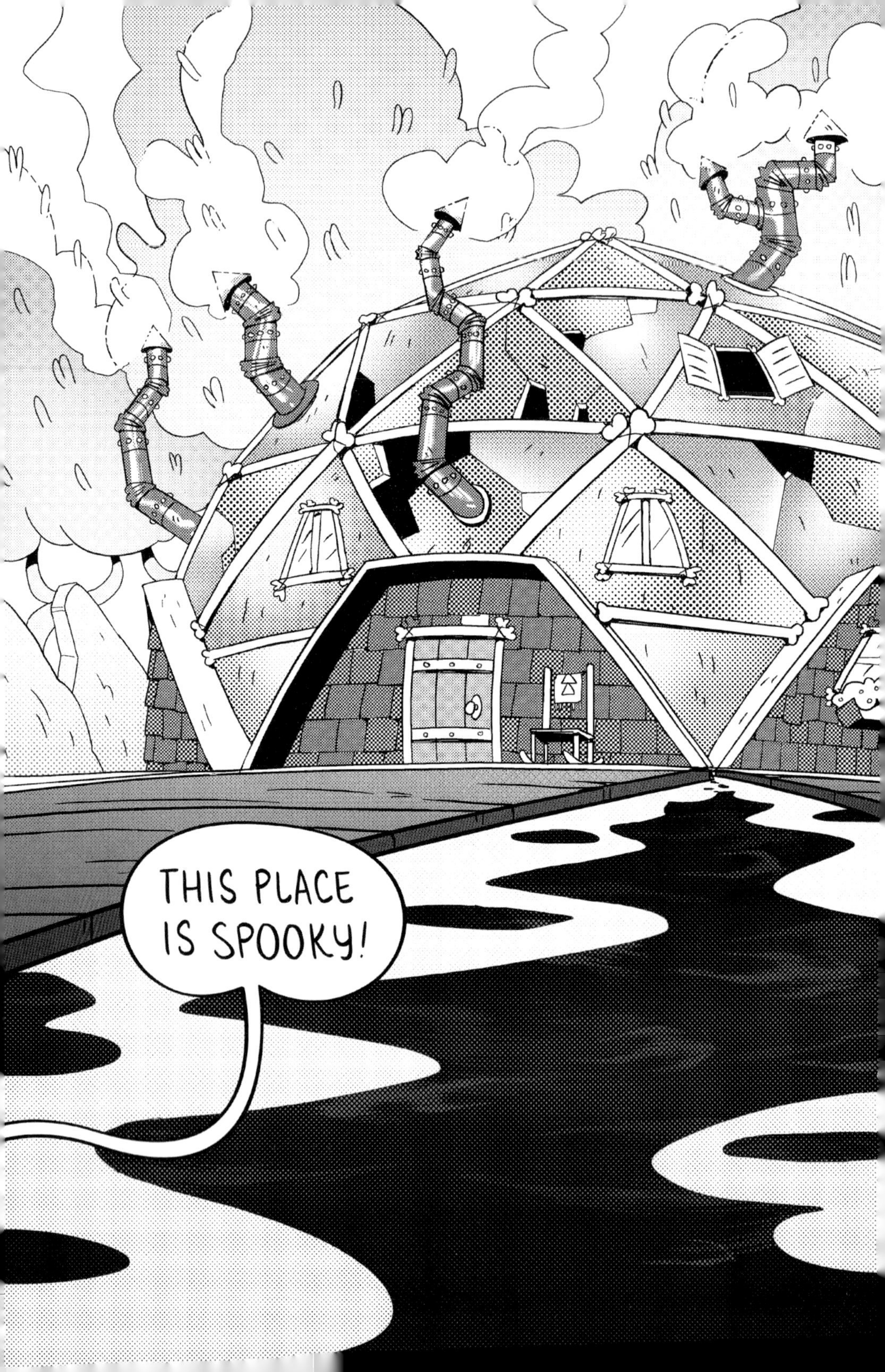
THIS PLACE IS SPOOKY!

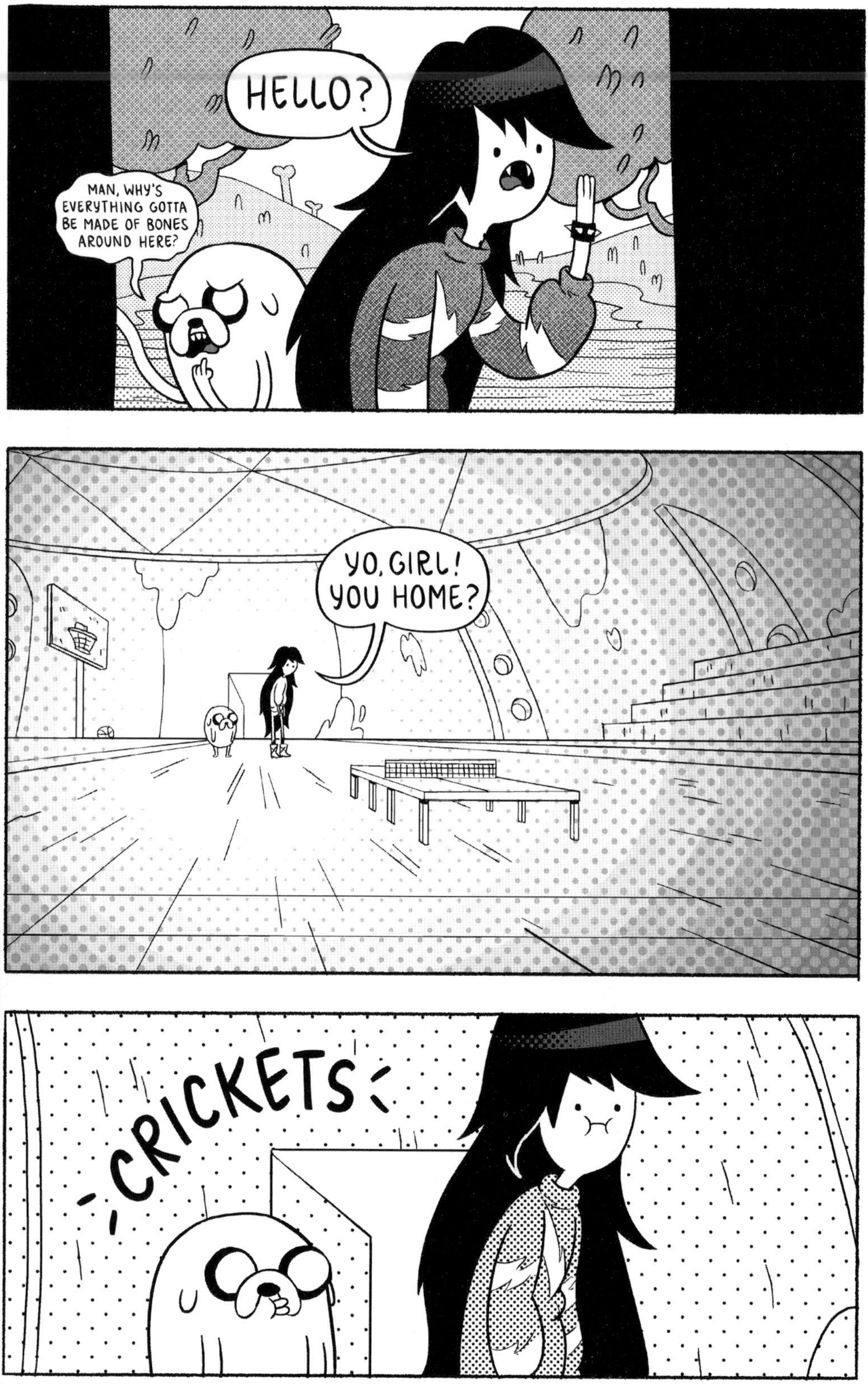
HELLO?
MAN, WHY'S EVERYTHING GOTTA BE MADE OF BONES AROUND HERE?
YO, GIRL! YOU HOME?
CRICKETS

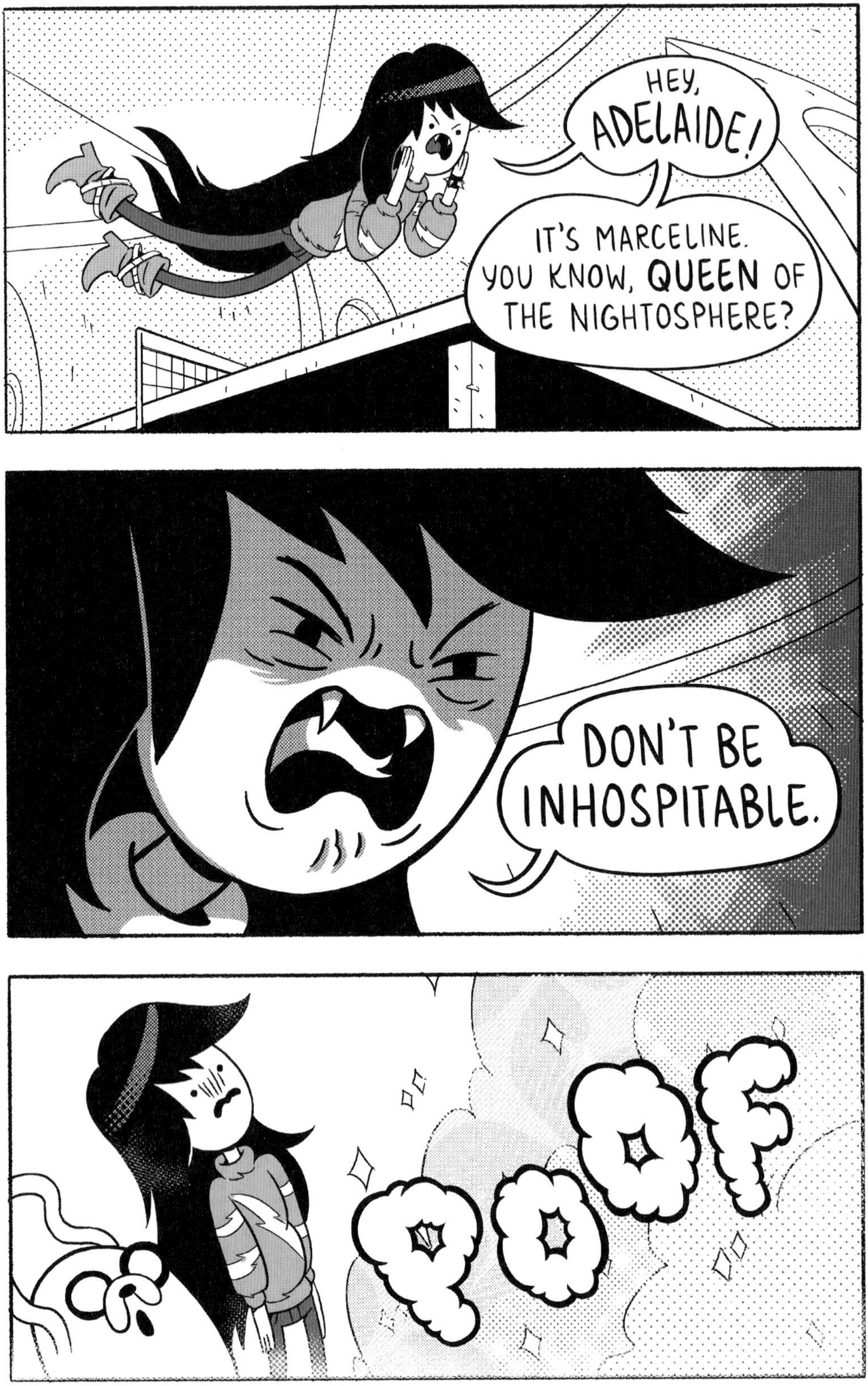
HEY, ADELAIDE!
IT'S MARCELINE. YOU KNOW, QUEEN OF THE NIGHTOSPHERE?
DON'T BE INHOSPITABLE.
POOF

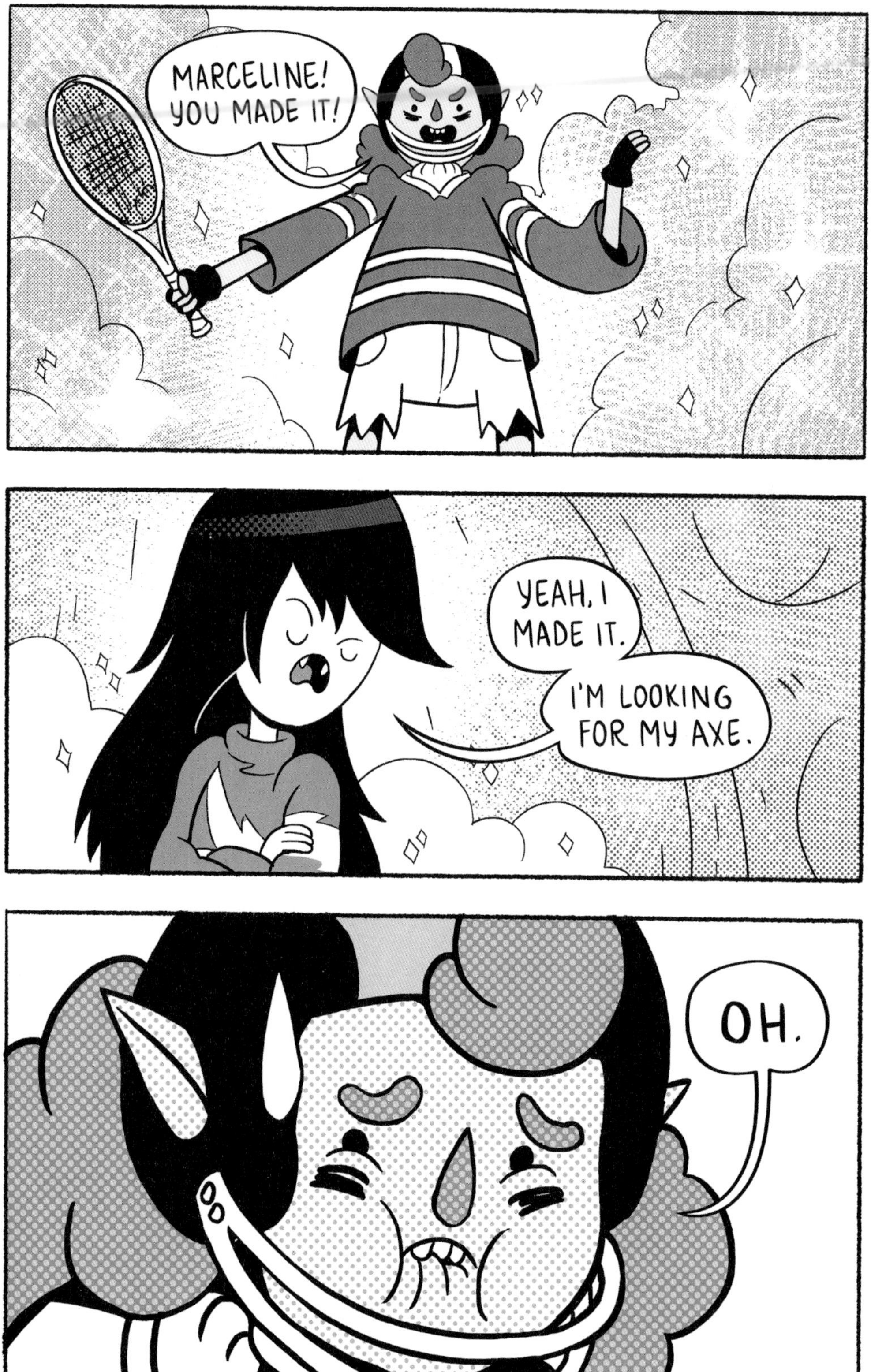
MARCELINE! YOU MADE IT!
YEAH, I MADE IT.
I'M LOOKING FOR MY AXE.
OH.

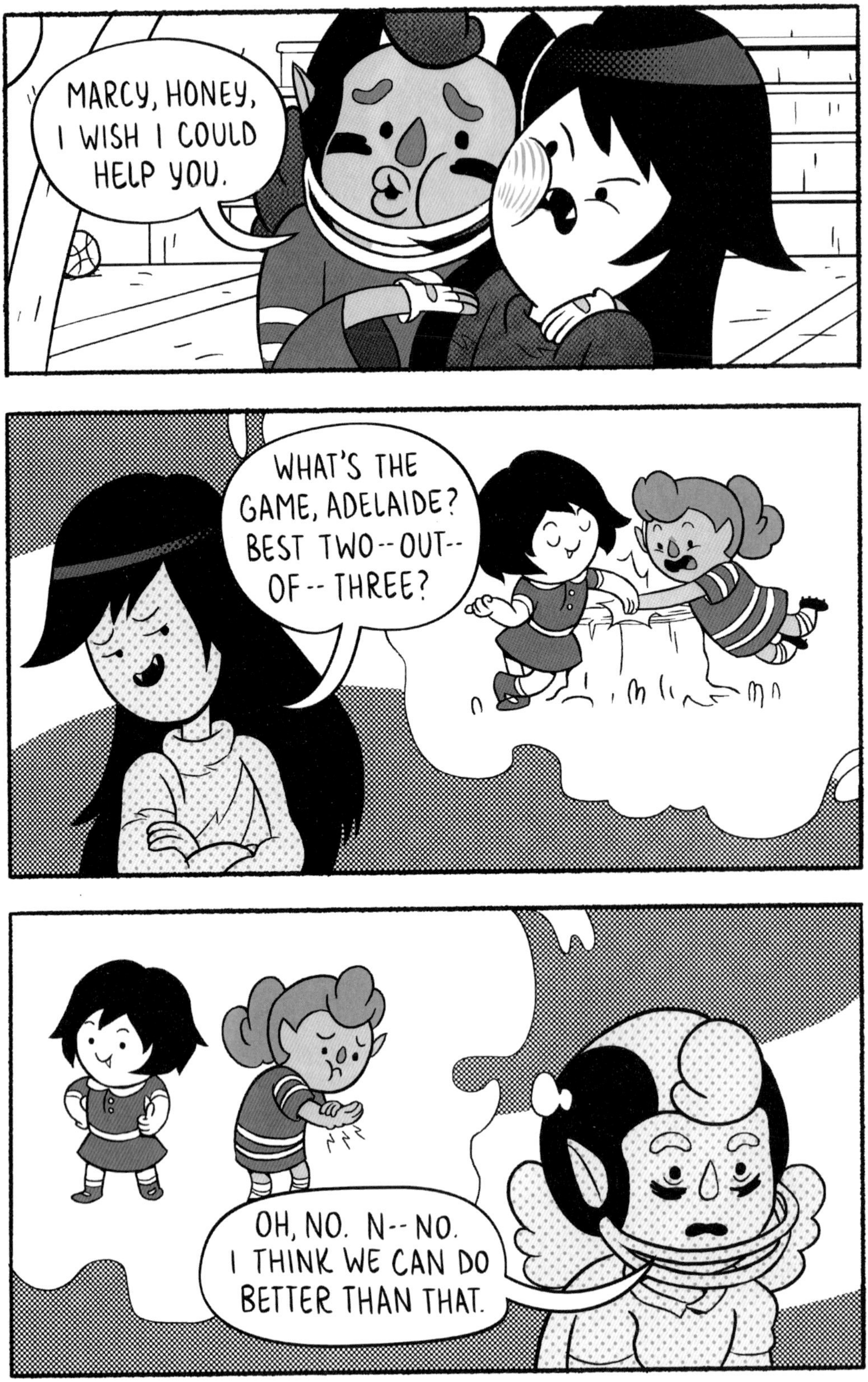
MARCY, HONEY, I WISH I COULD HELP YOU.
WHAT'S THE GAME, ADELAIDE? BEST TWO--OUT--OF--THREE?
OH, NO. N--NO. I THINK WE CAN DO BETTER THAN THAT.

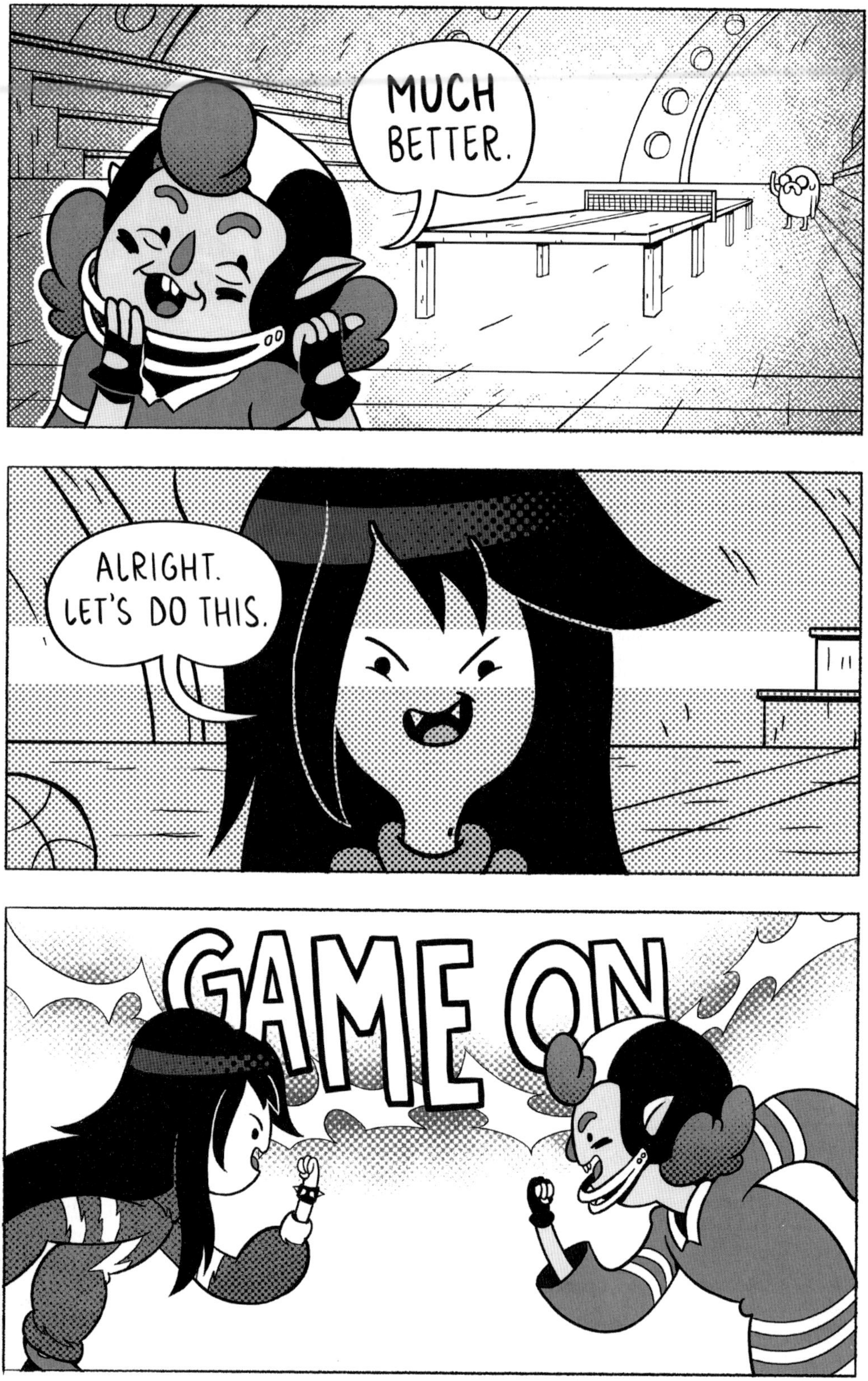
MUCH BETTER.
ALRIGHT. LET'S DO THIS.
GAME ON

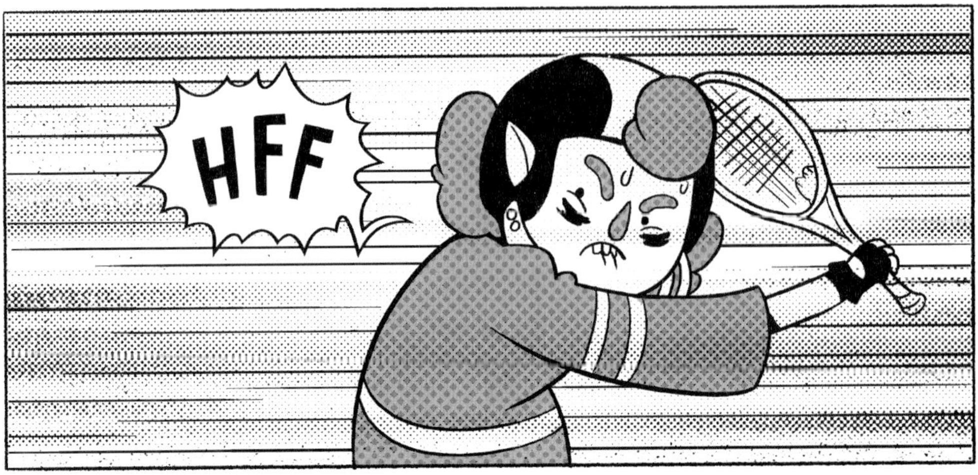
HFF

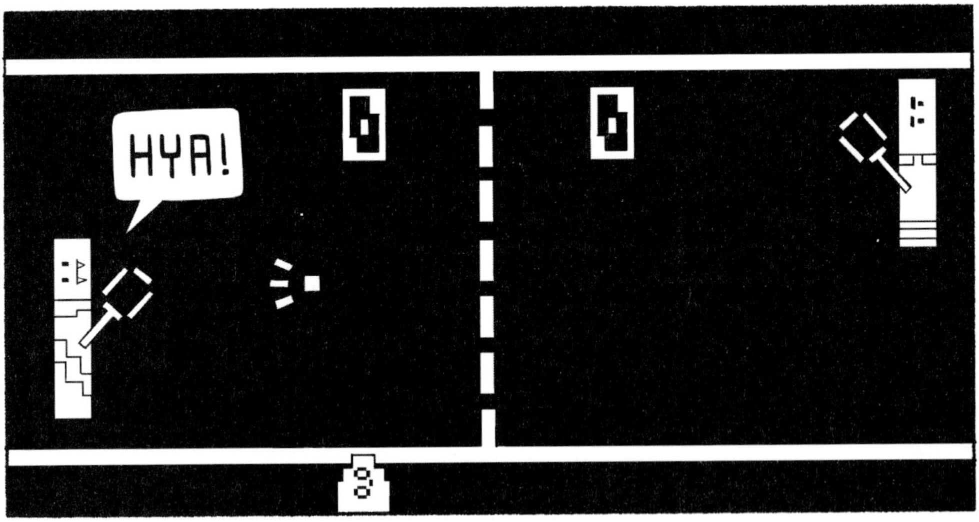
HYA!

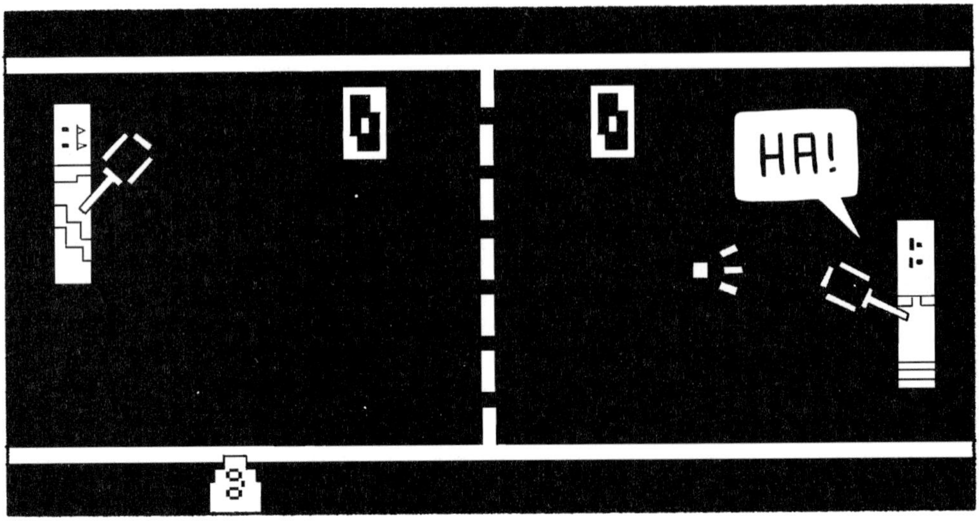
HA!

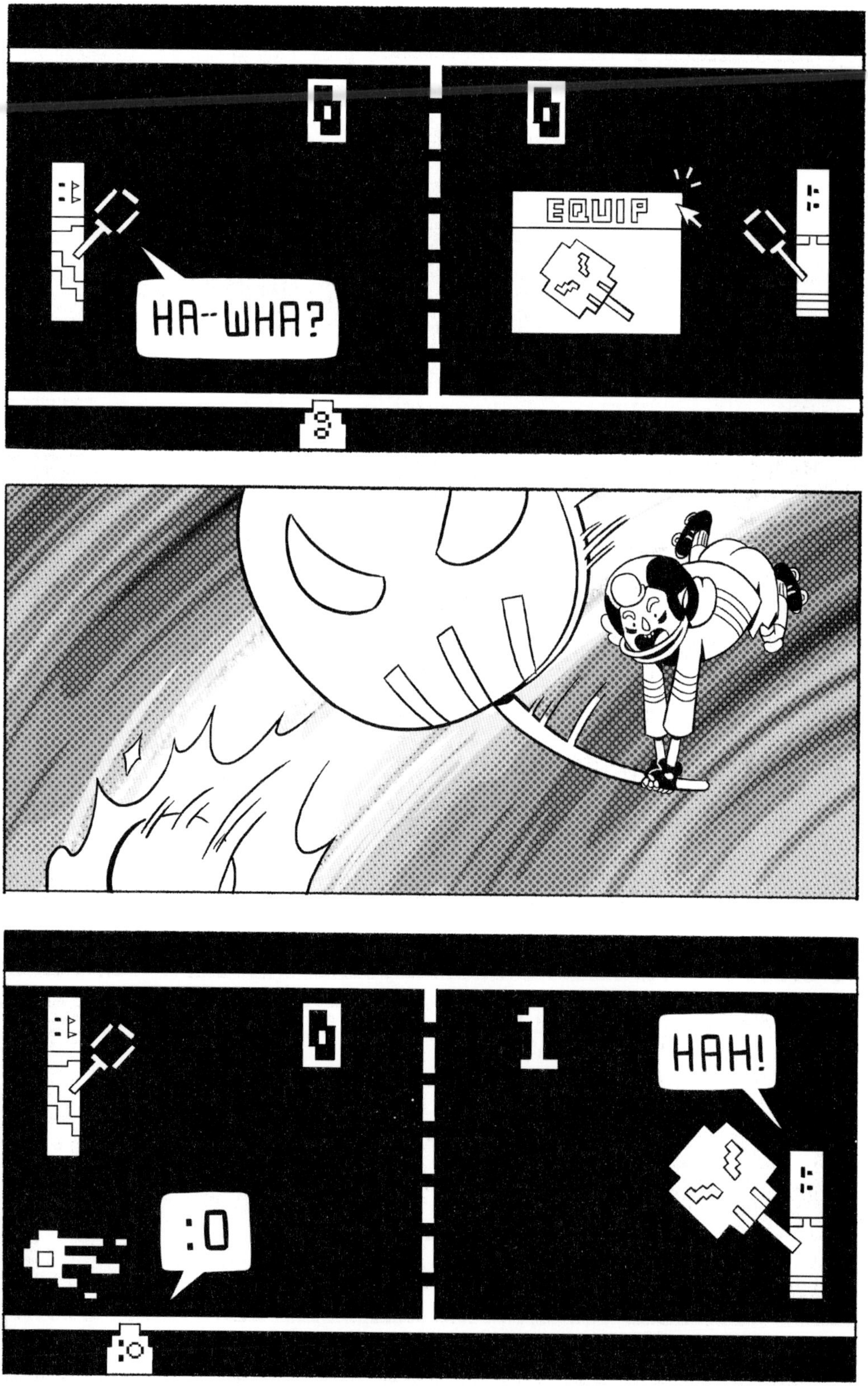
HA--WHA?
EQUIP
1
HAH!
:O

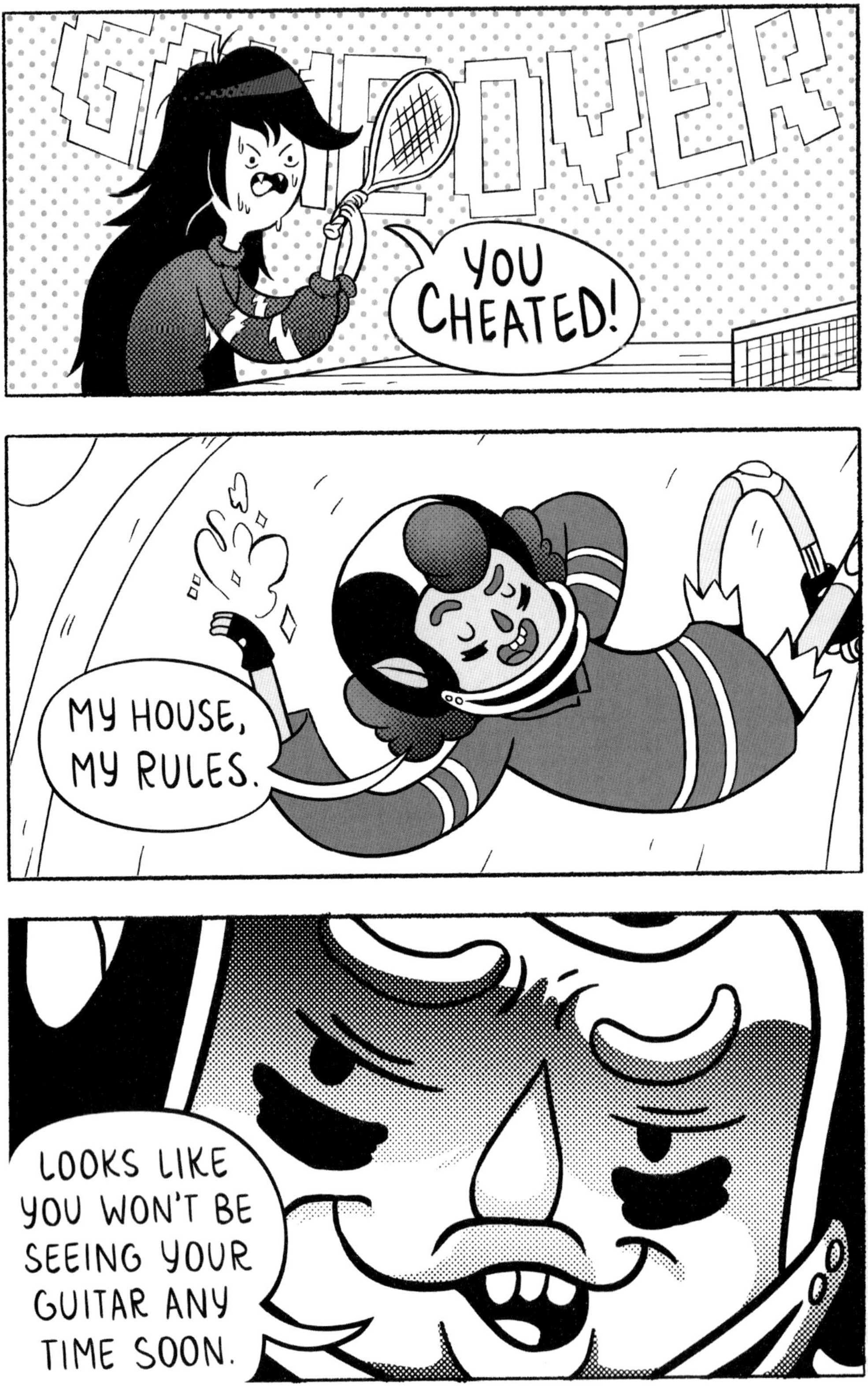
OVER
YOU CHEATED!
MY HOUSE, MY RULES.
LOOKS LIKE YOU WON'T BE SEEING YOUR GUITAR ANY TIME SOON.

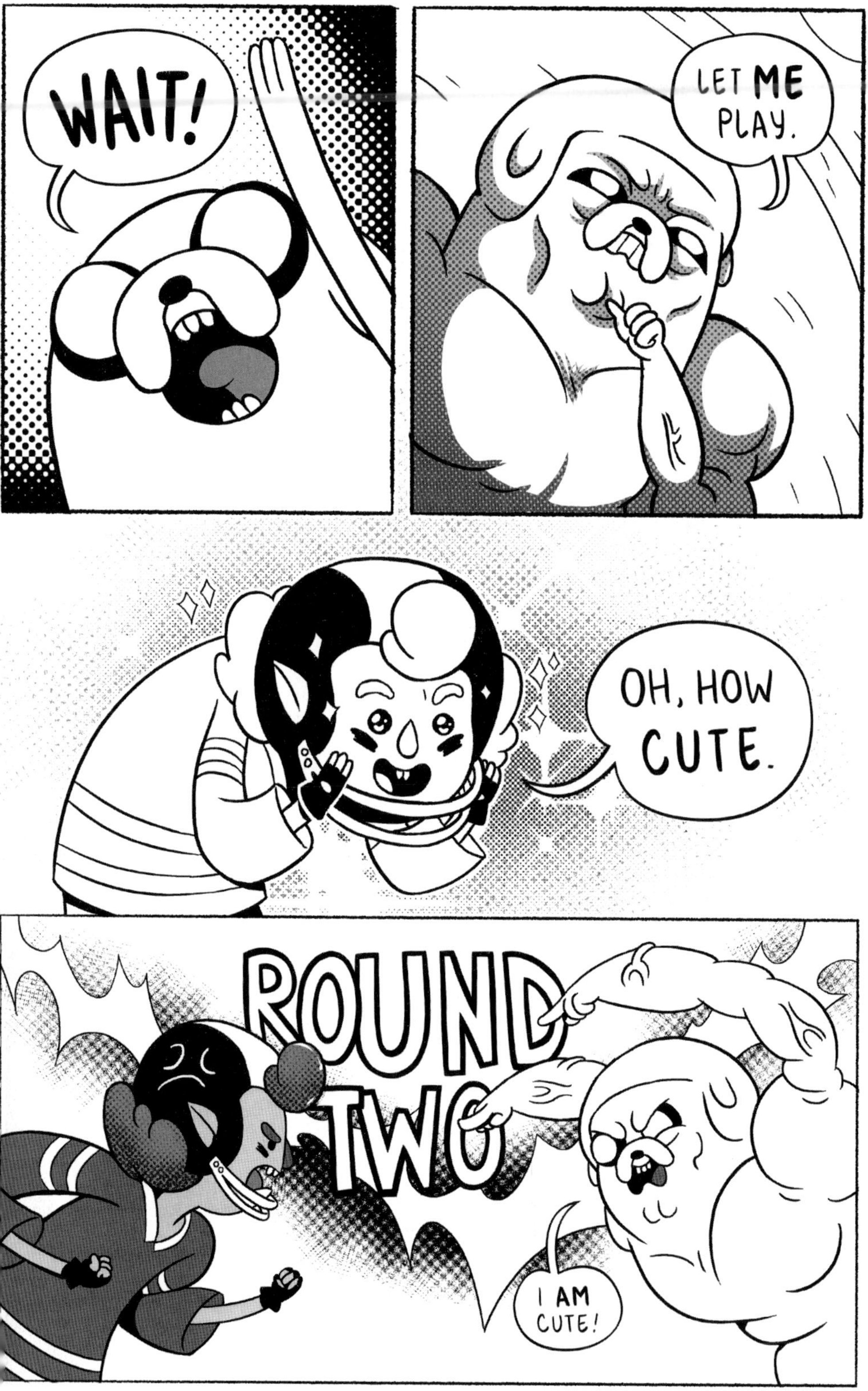
WAIT!
LET ME PLAY.
OH, HOW CUTE.
ROUND TWO
I AM CUTE!

HA!
HAHA!

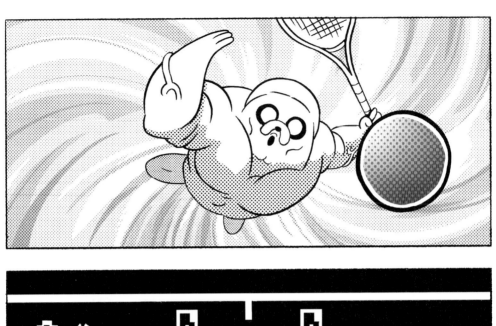

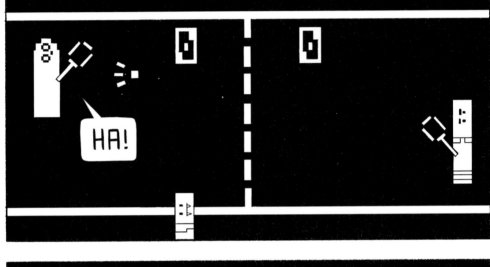

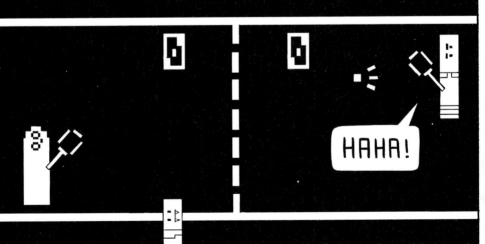

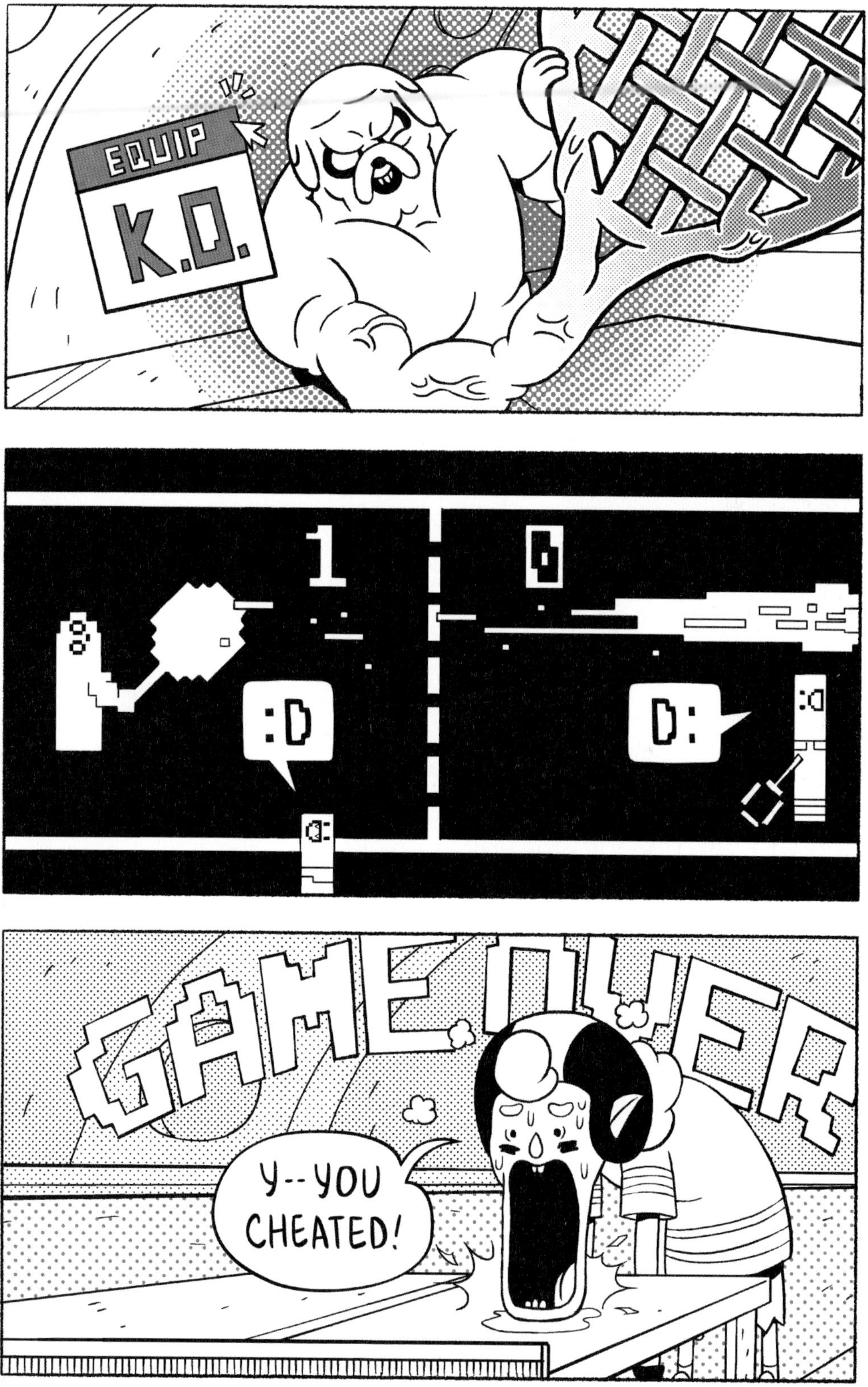
EQUIP
K.O.
1
0
:D
D:
GAME OVER
Y--YOU CHEATED!

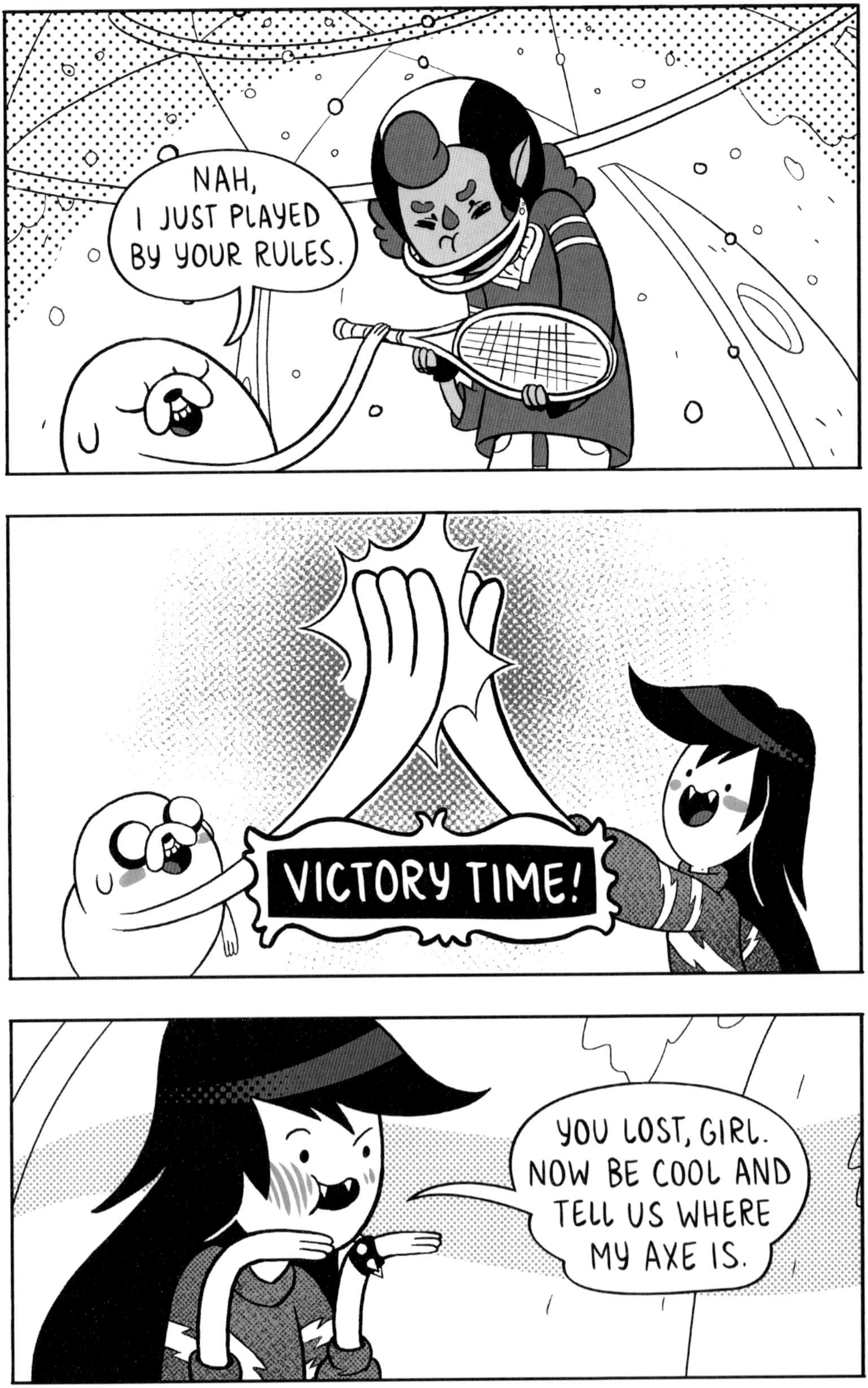
NAH, I JUST PLAYED BY YOUR RULES.
VICTORY TIME!
YOU LOST, GIRL. NOW BE COOL AND TELL US WHERE MY AXE IS.

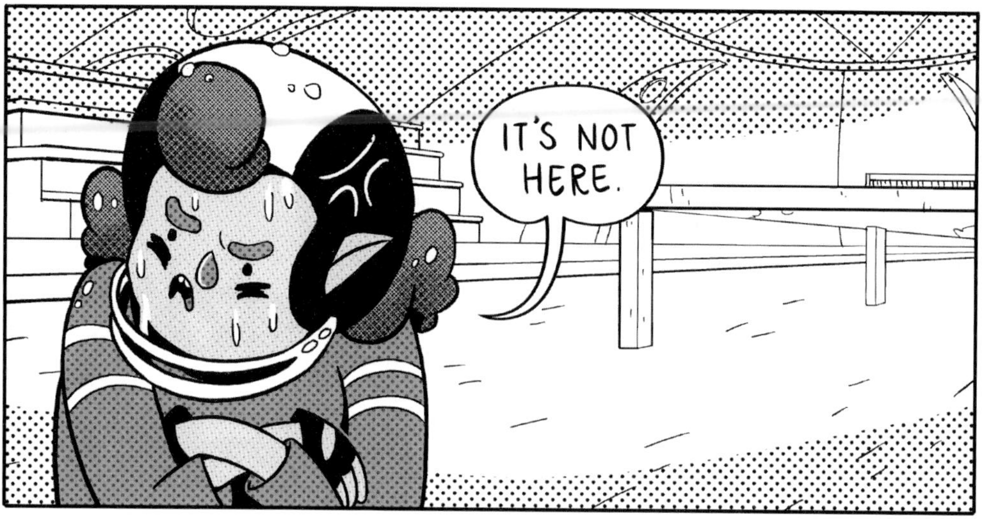
IT'S NOT HERE.

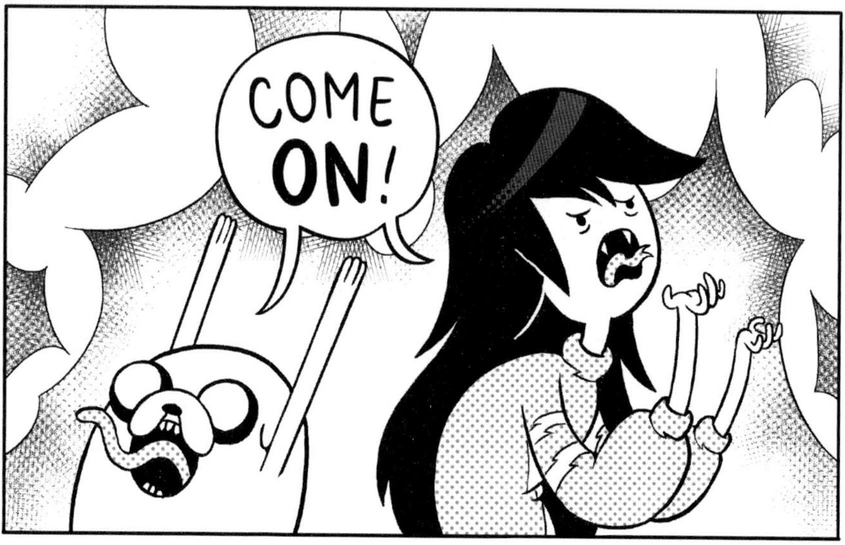
COME ON!

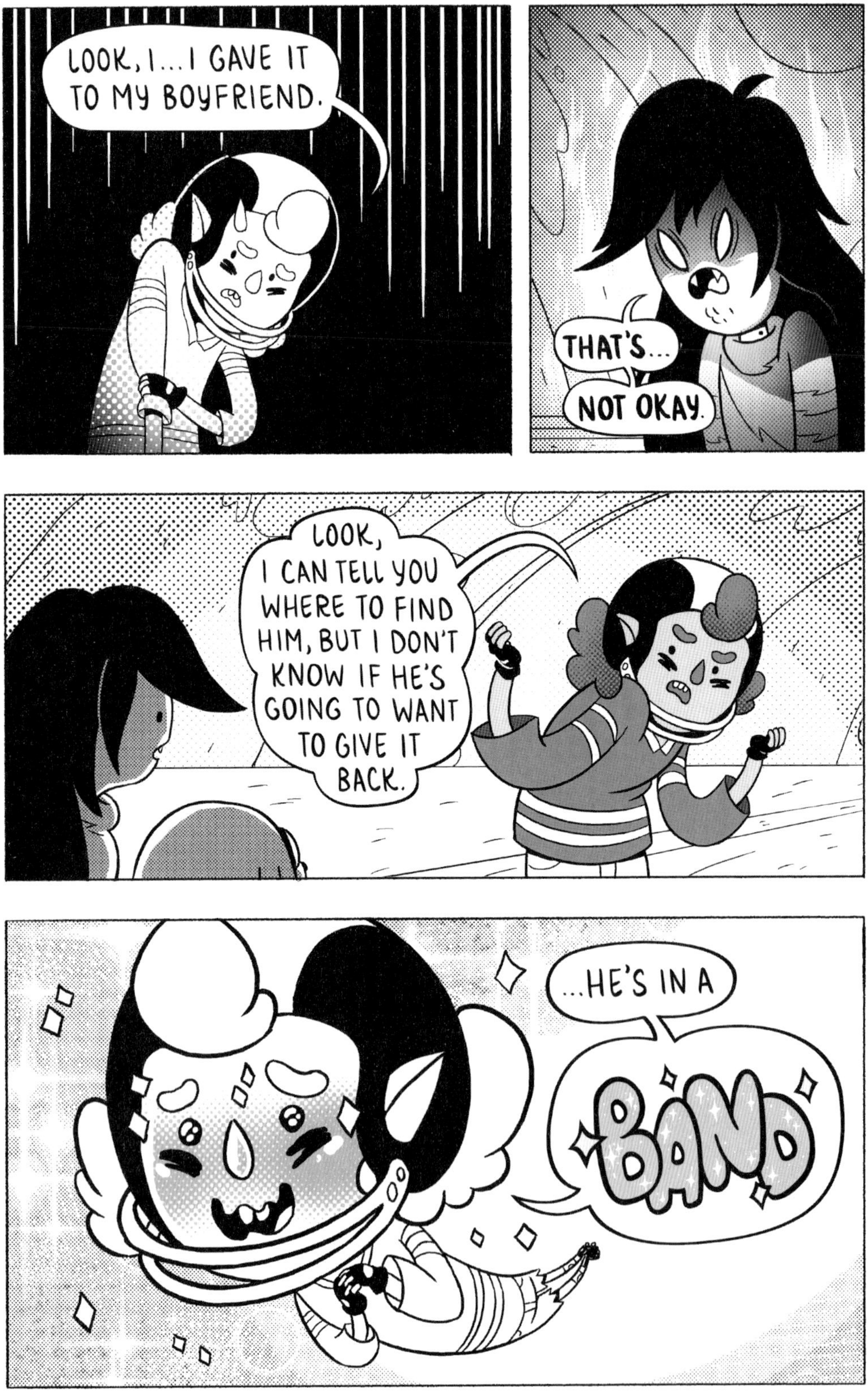
LOOK, I...I GAVE IT TO MY BOYFRIEND.
THAT'S...
NOT OKAY.
LOOK, I CAN TELL YOU WHERE TO FIND HIM, BUT I DON'T KNOW IF HE'S GOING TO WANT TO GIVE IT BACK.
...HE'S IN A
BAND

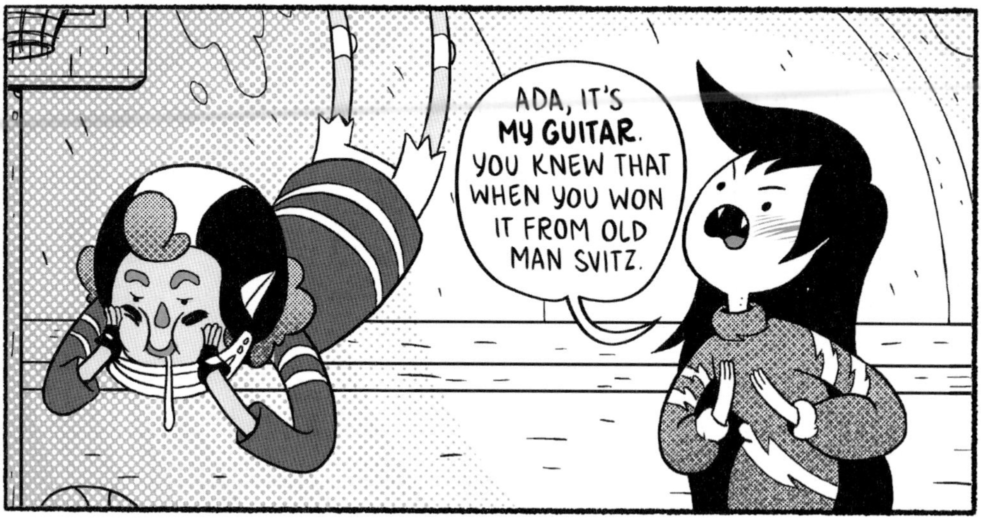
ADA, IT'S **MY GUITAR**. YOU KNEW THAT WHEN YOU WON IT FROM OLD MAN SVITZ.

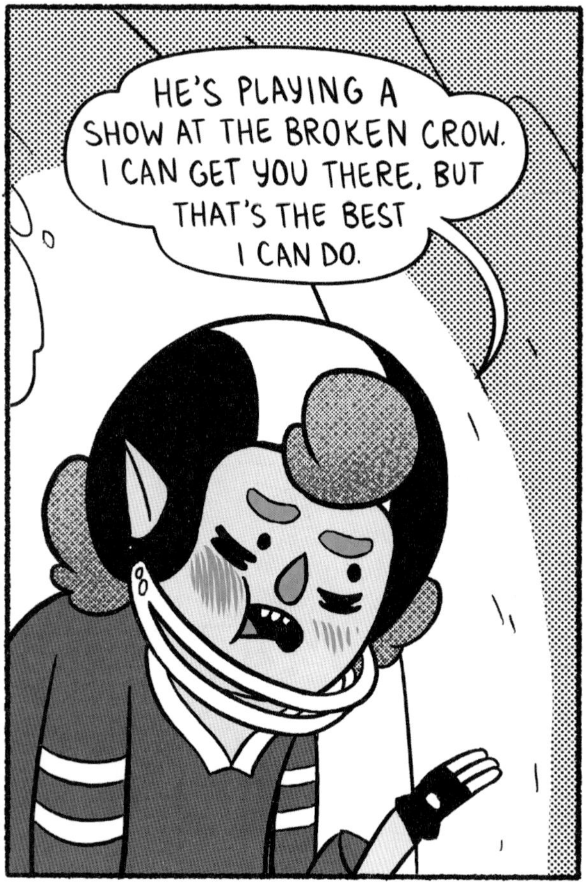
HE'S PLAYING A SHOW AT THE BROKEN CROW. I CAN GET YOU THERE, BUT THAT'S THE BEST I CAN DO.

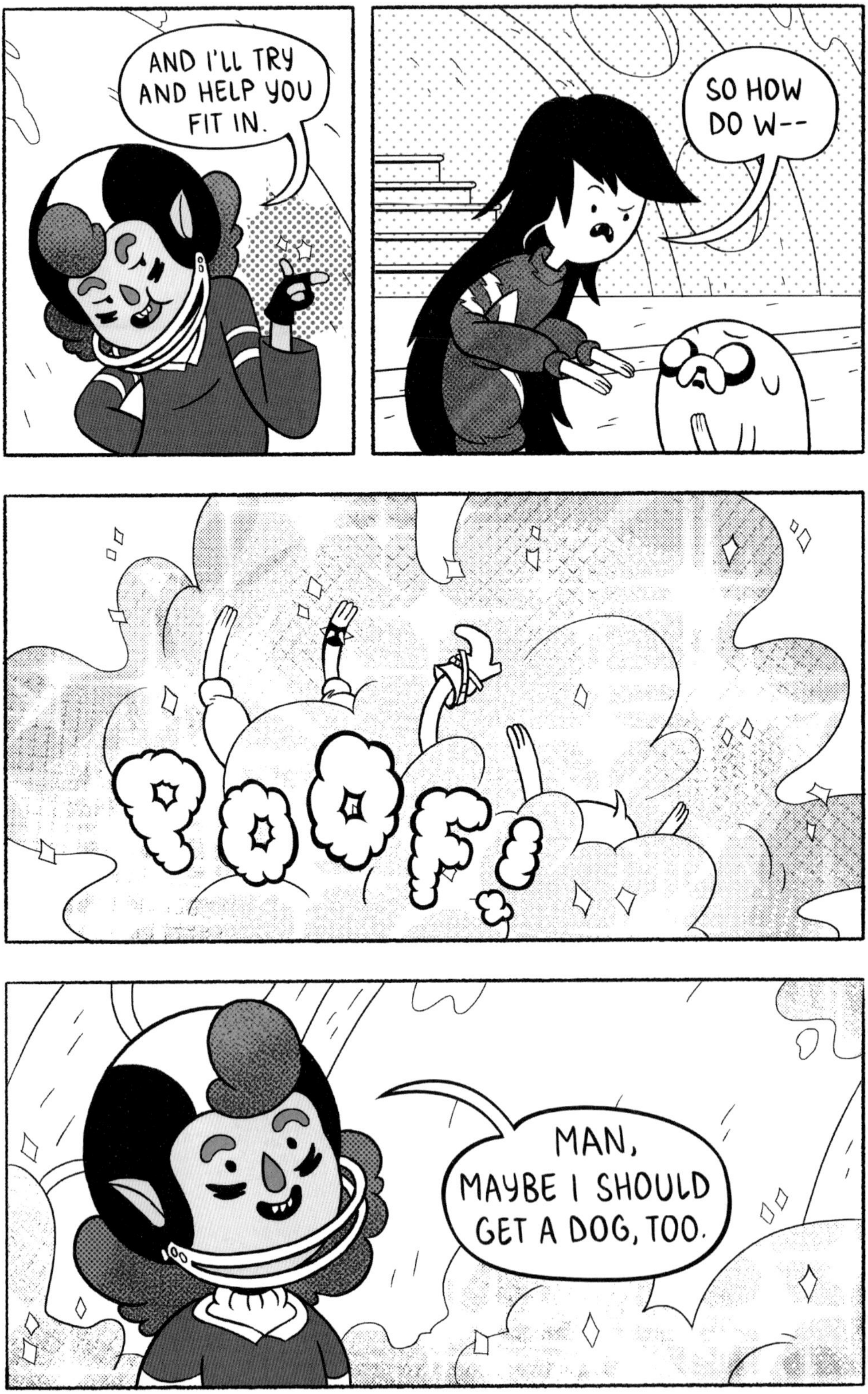
AND I'LL TRY AND HELP YOU FIT IN.
SO HOW DO W--
POOF!
MAN, MAYBE I SHOULD GET A DOG, TOO.

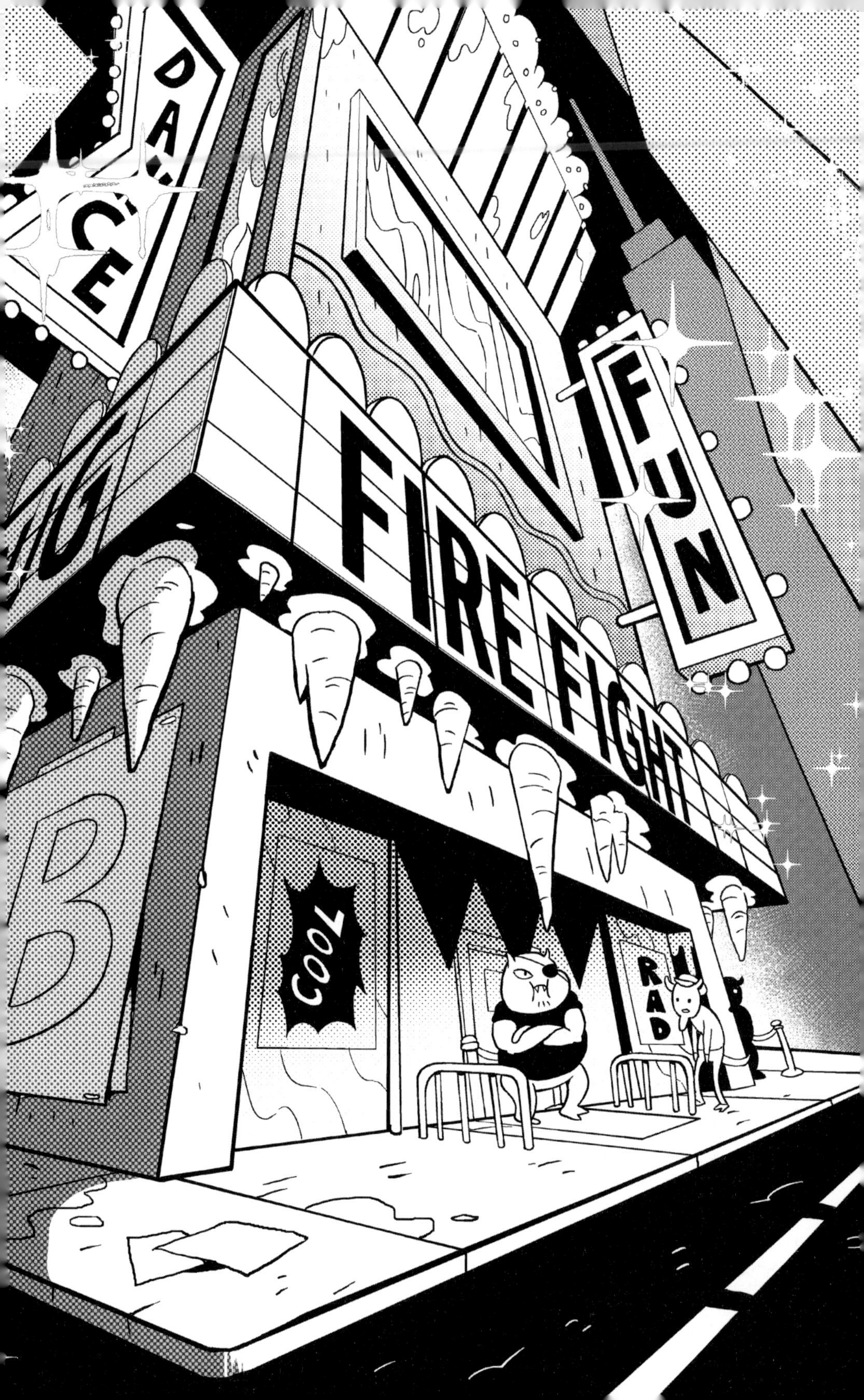
FIRE FIGHT
FUN
COOL
RAD

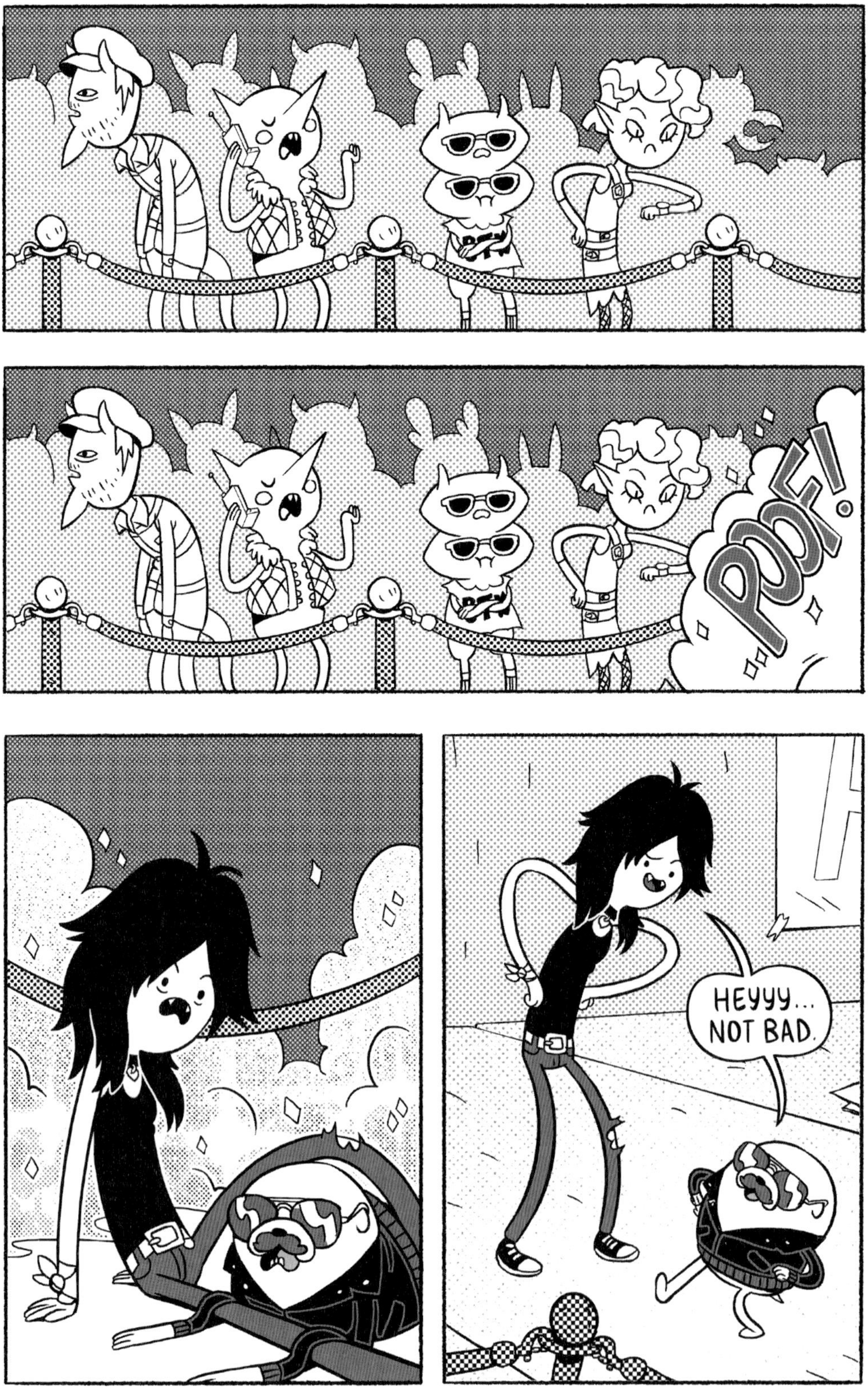
POOF!
HEYYY... NOT BAD.

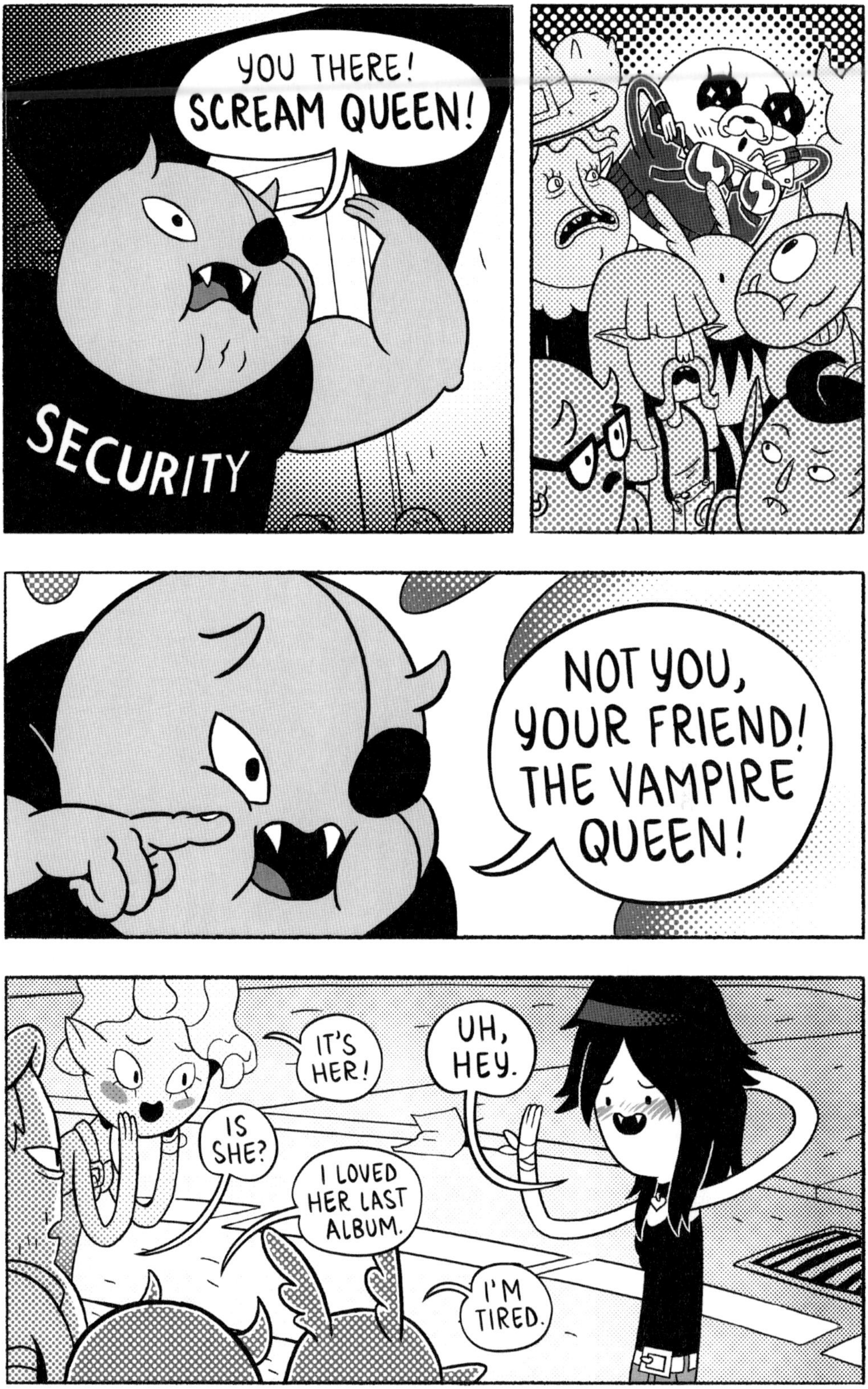
YOU THERE! SCREAM QUEEN!
SECURITY
NOT YOU, YOUR FRIEND! THE VAMPIRE QUEEN!
IT'S HER!
UH, HEY.
IS SHE?
I LOVED HER LAST ALBUM.
I'M TIRED.

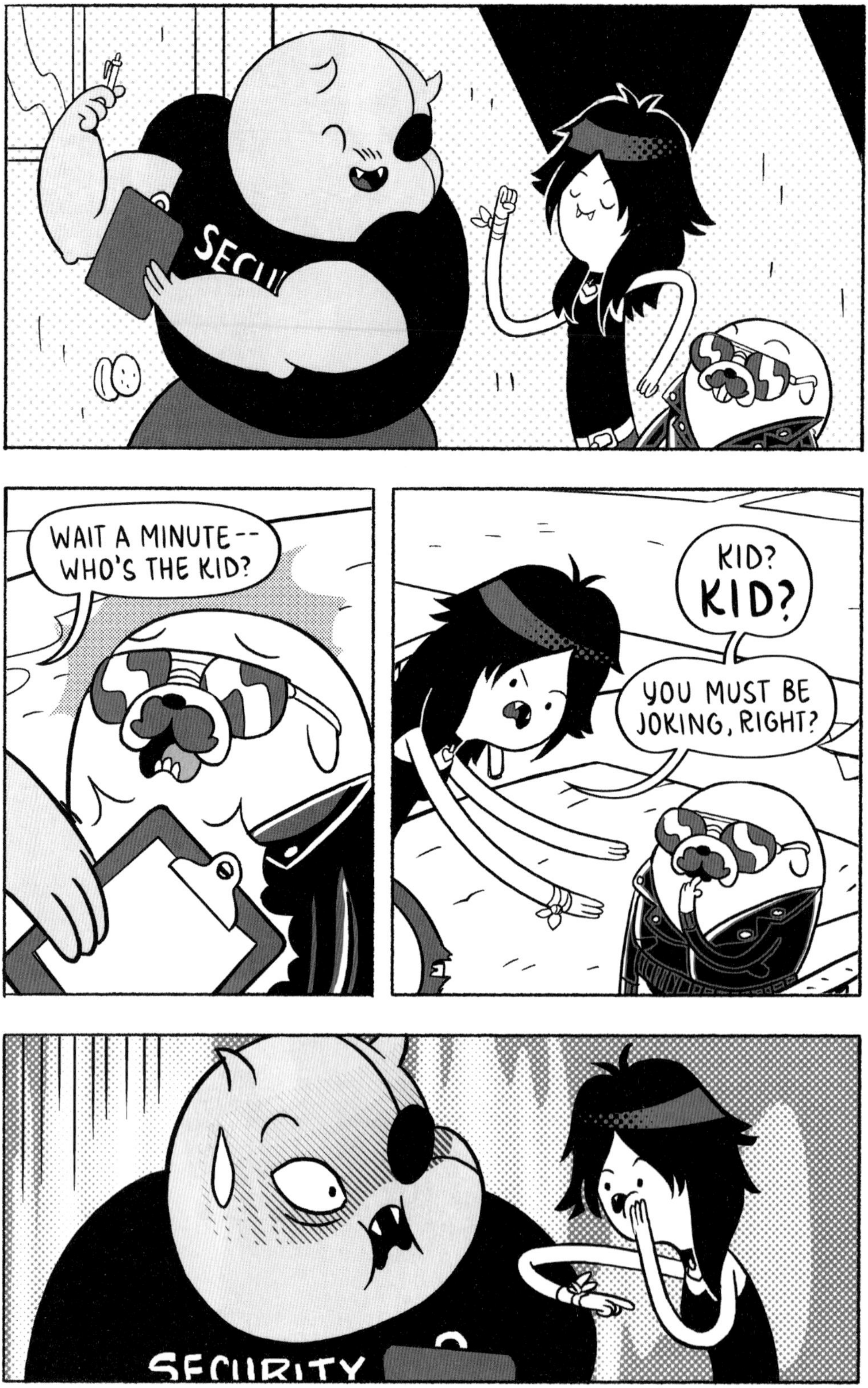

SECU
WAIT A MINUTE-- WHO'S THE KID?
KID? KID?
YOU MUST BE JOKING, RIGHT?
SECURITY

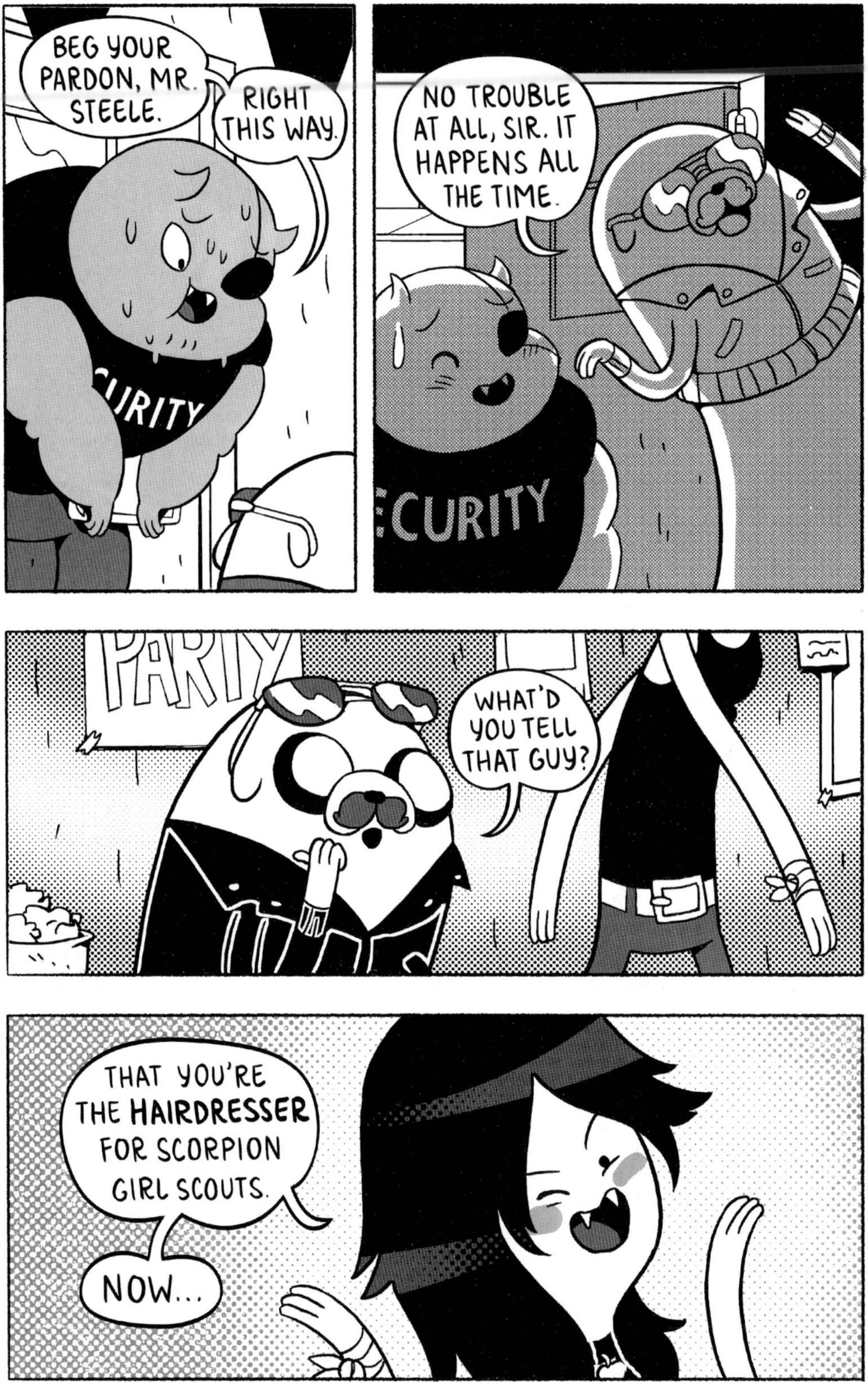
BEG YOUR PARDON, MR. STEELE.
RIGHT THIS WAY.
CURITY
NO TROUBLE AT ALL, SIR. IT HAPPENS ALL THE TIME.
ECURITY
PARTY
WHAT'D YOU TELL THAT GUY?
THAT YOU'RE THE **HAIRDRESSER** FOR SCORPION GIRL SCOUTS.
NOW...

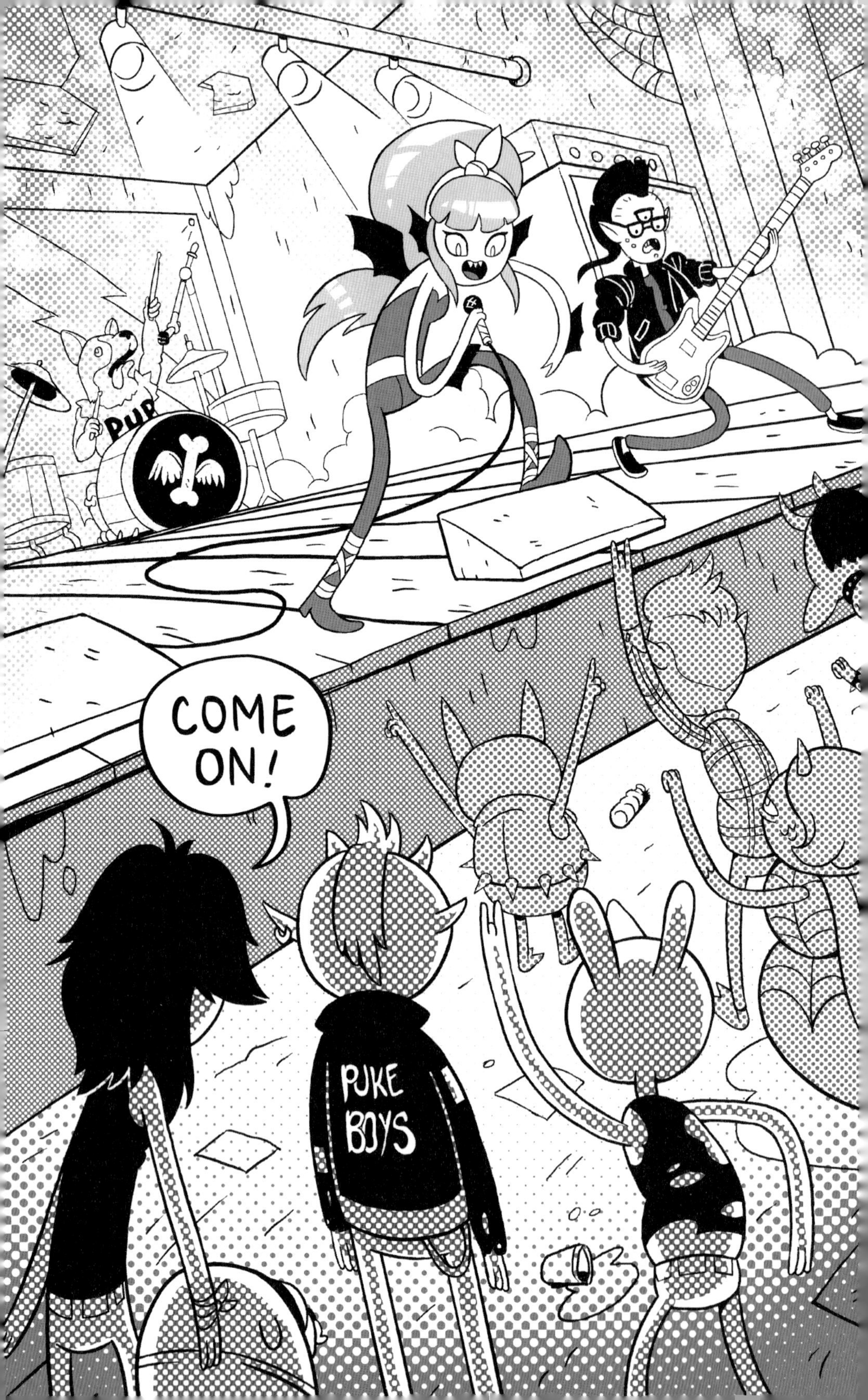
PUP
COME ON!
PUKE BOYS

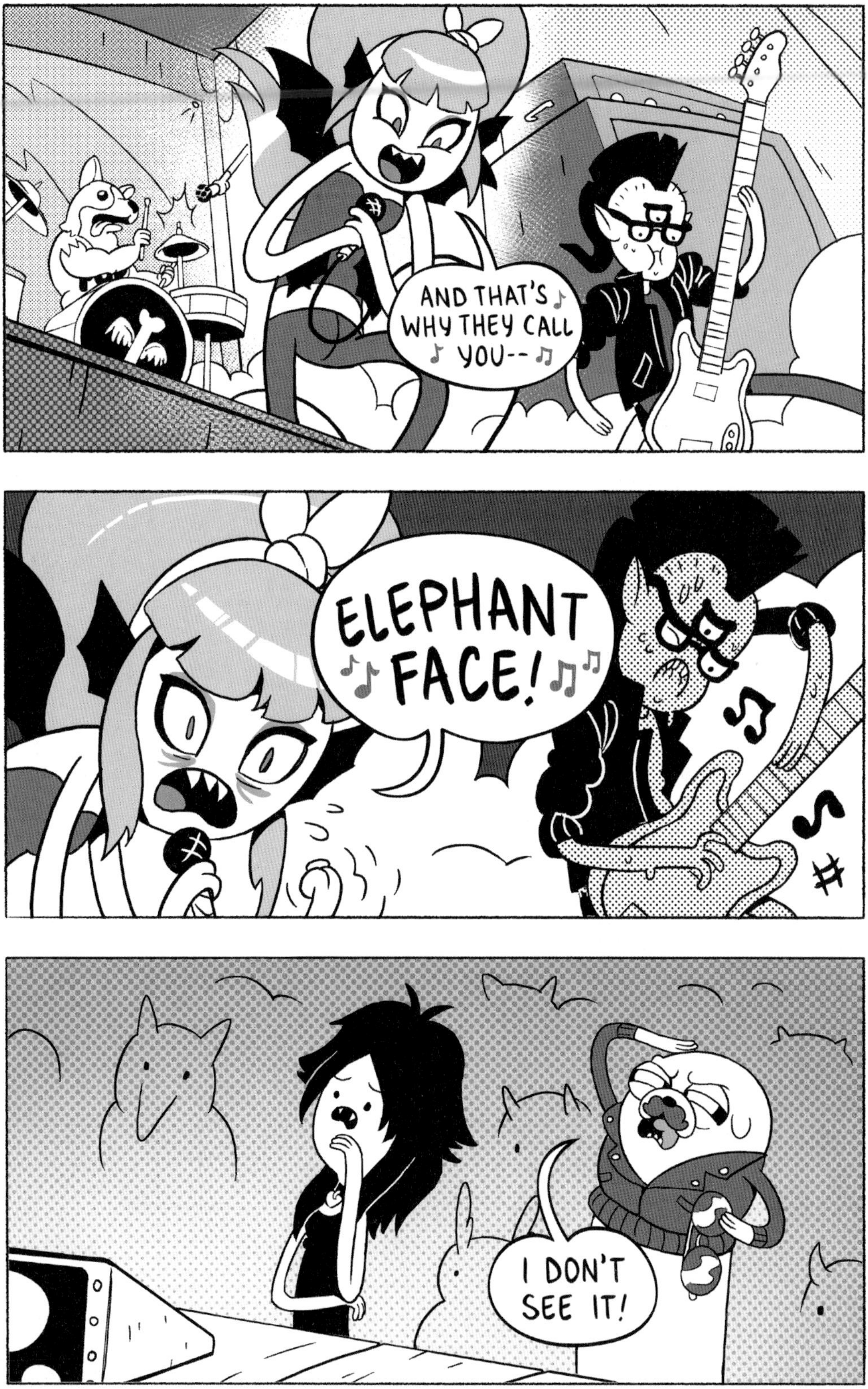
AND THAT'S WHY THEY CALL YOU--
ELEPHANT FACE!
I DON'T SEE IT!

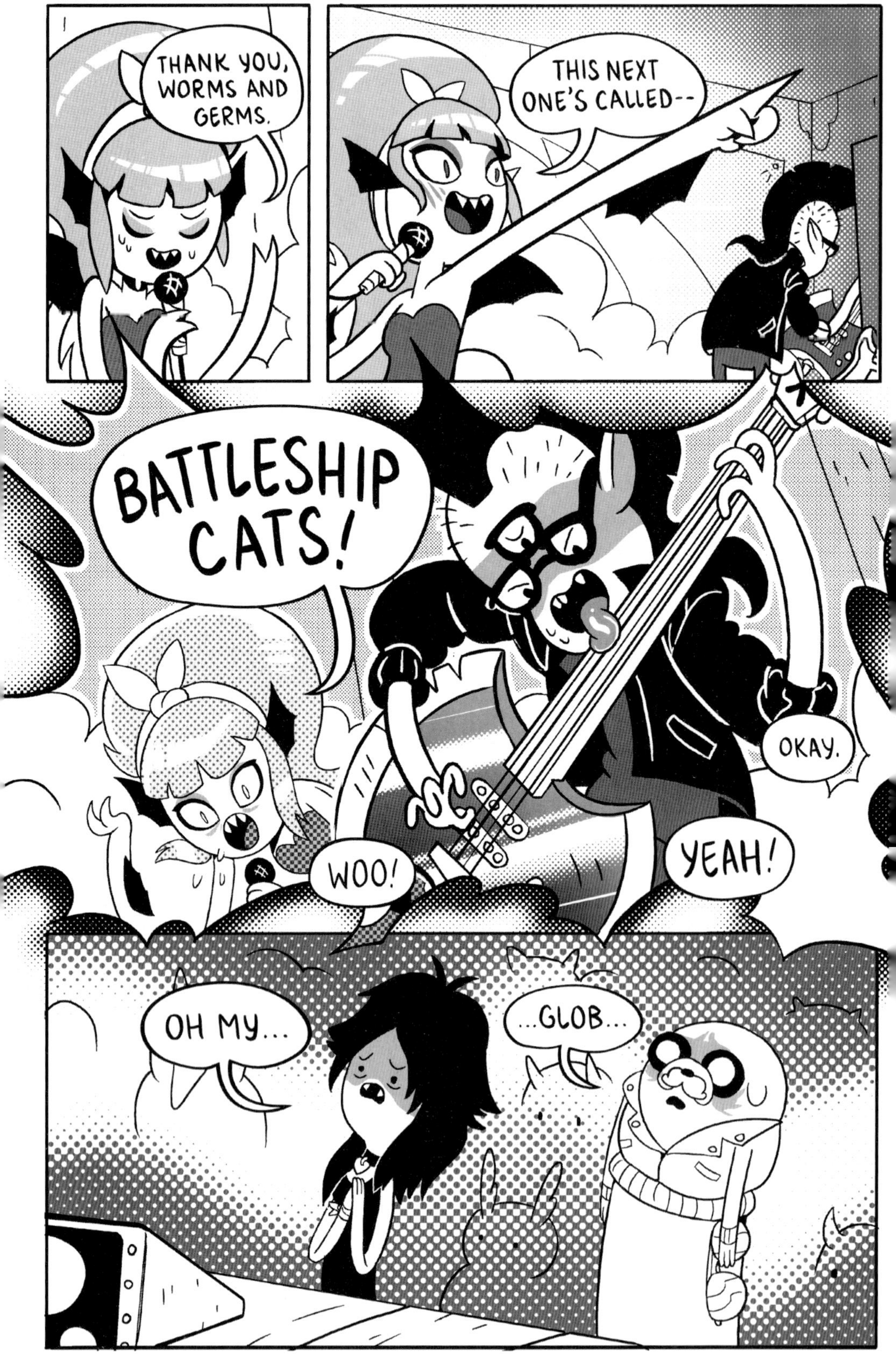
THANK YOU, WORMS AND GERMS.
THIS NEXT ONE'S CALLED--
BATTLESHIP CATS!
OKAY.
WOO!
YEAH!
OH MY...
...GLOB...

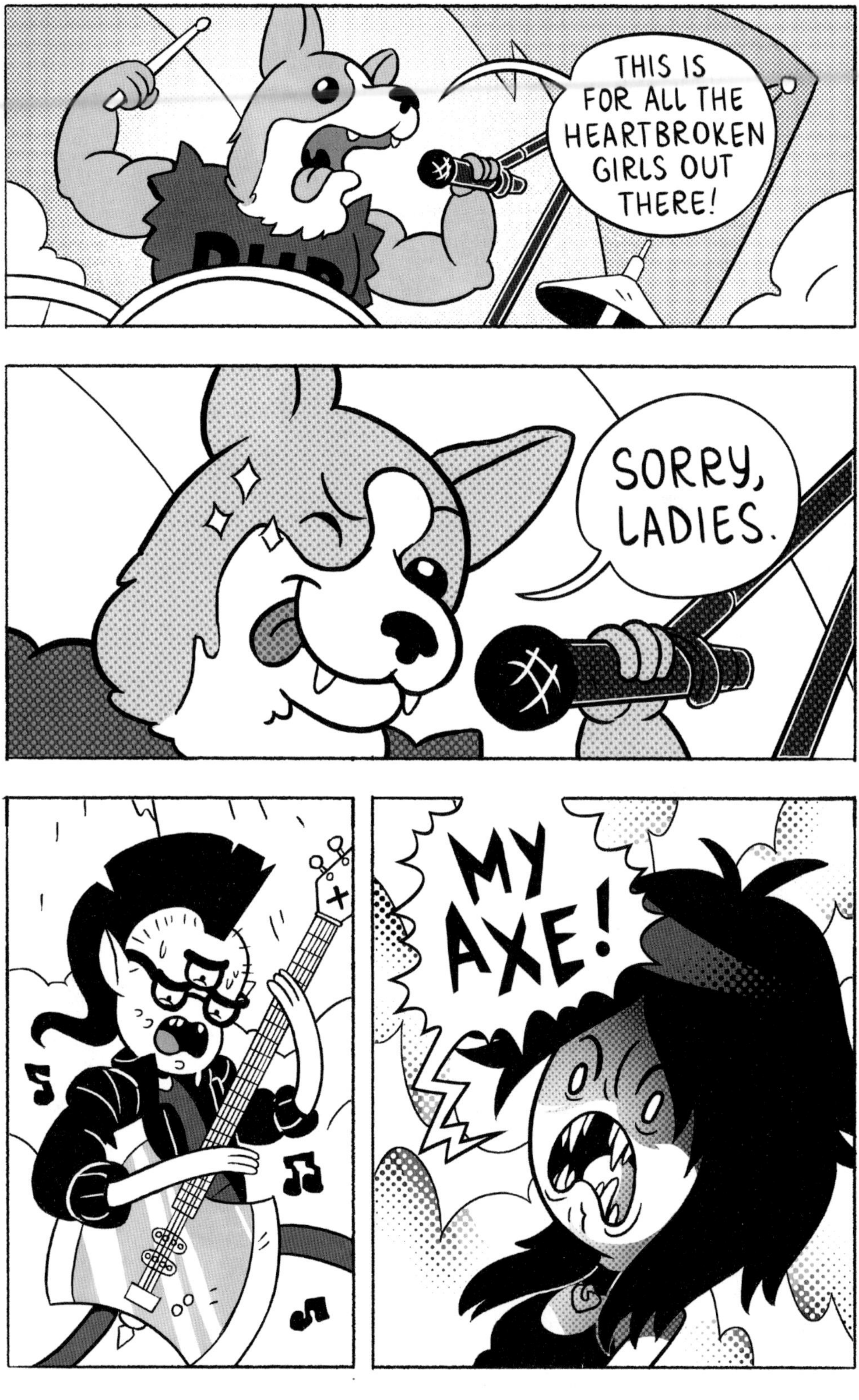
THIS IS FOR ALL THE HEARTBROKEN GIRLS OUT THERE!
SORRY, LADIES.
MY AXE!

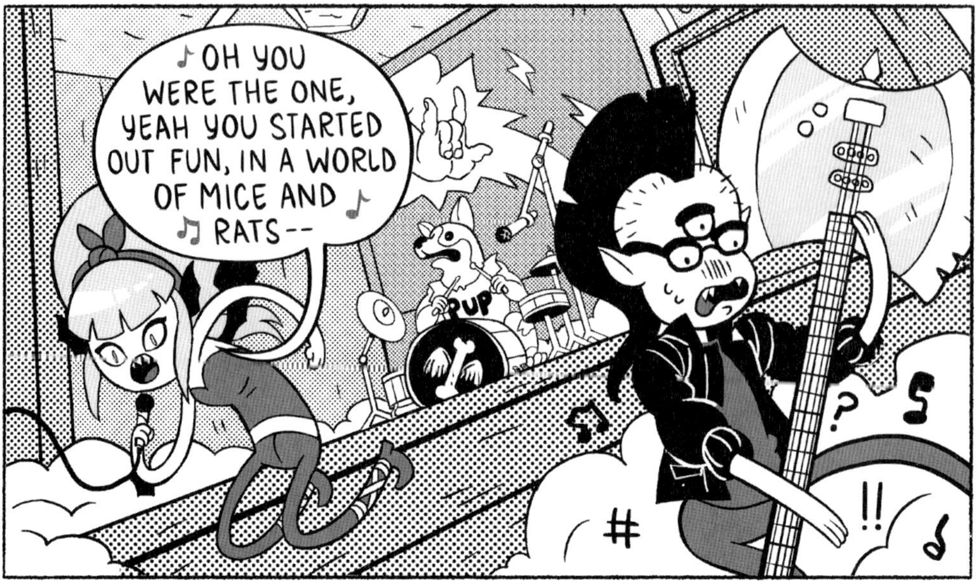
♪ OH YOU WERE THE ONE, YEAH YOU STARTED OUT FUN, IN A WORLD OF MICE AND ♪ ♫ RATS--
PUP
#
?
!!

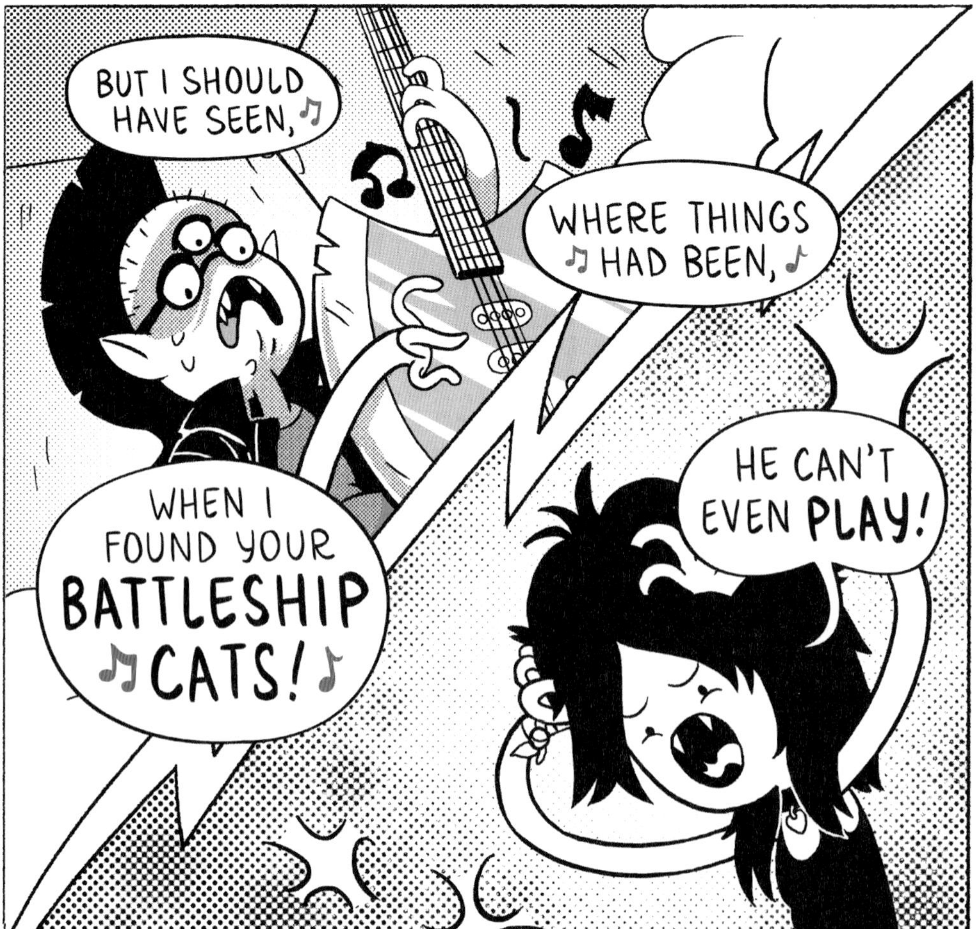
BUT I SHOULD HAVE SEEN, ♫
WHERE THINGS ♫ HAD BEEN, ♪
WHEN I FOUND YOUR BATTLESHIP ♫ CATS! ♪
HE CAN'T EVEN PLAY!

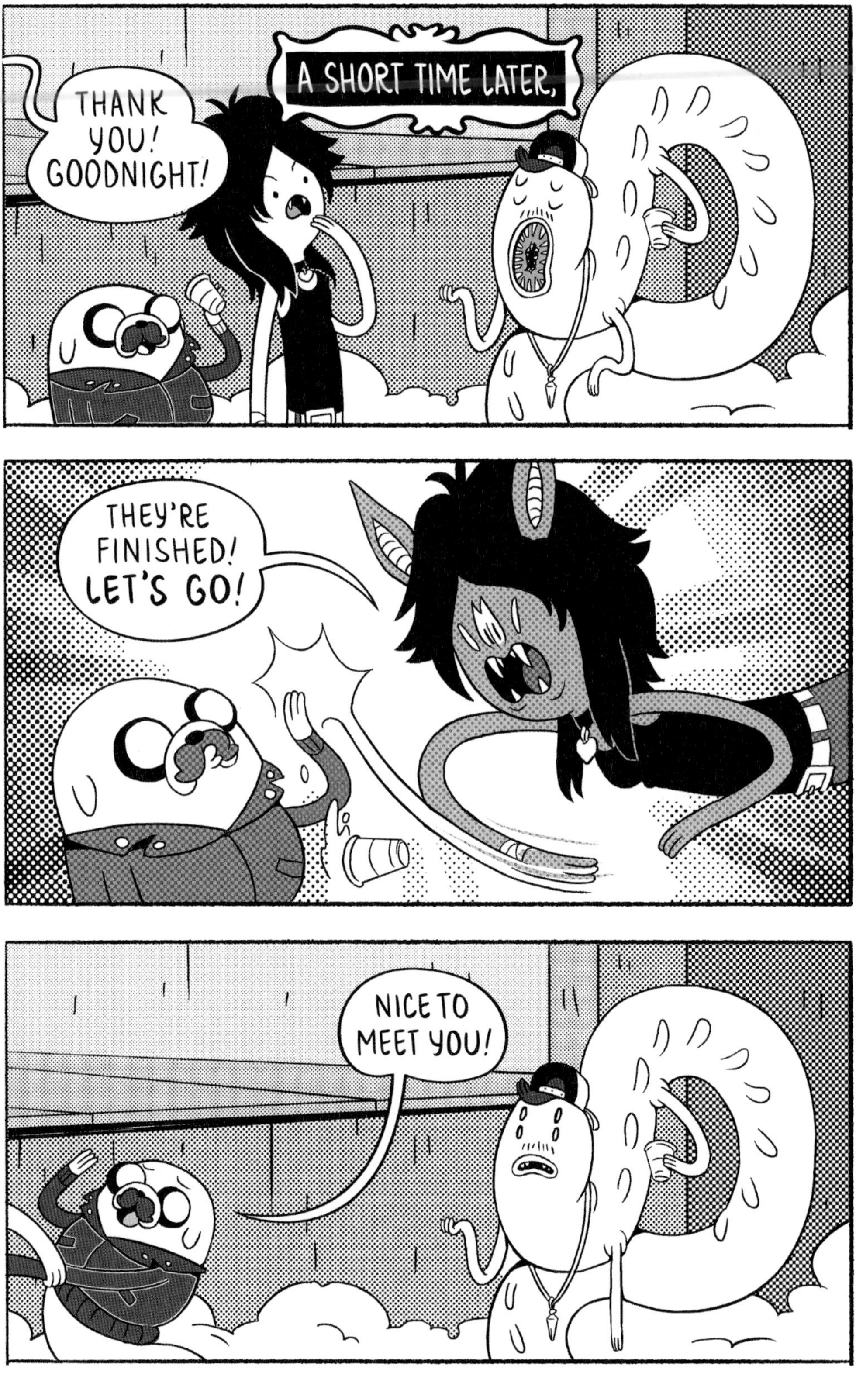
A SHORT TIME LATER,
THANK YOU! GOODNIGHT!
THEY'RE FINISHED! LET'S GO!
NICE TO MEET YOU!

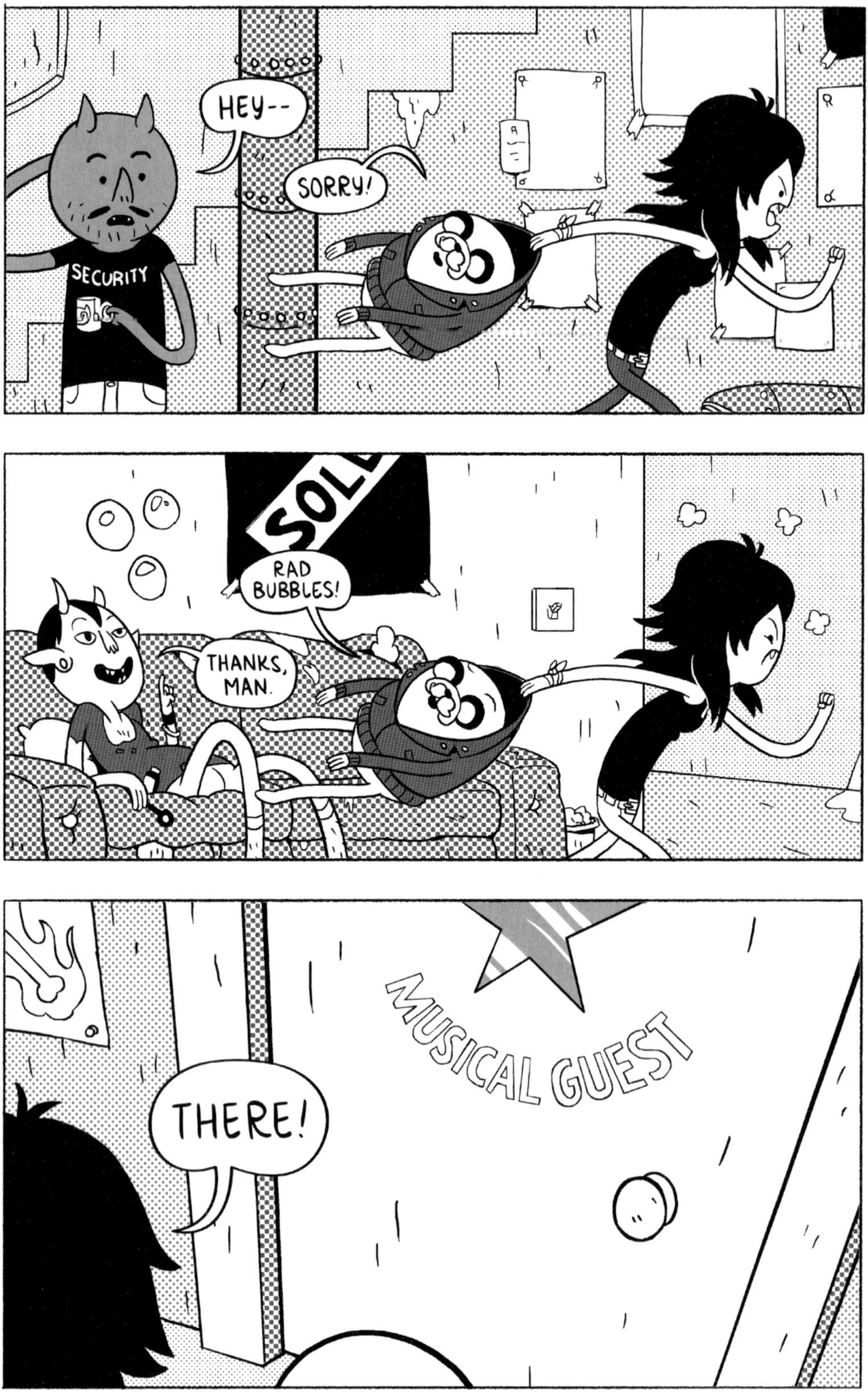
HEY--
SECURITY
SORRY!
SOLD
RAD BUBBLES!
THANKS, MAN.
MUSICAL GUEST
THERE!

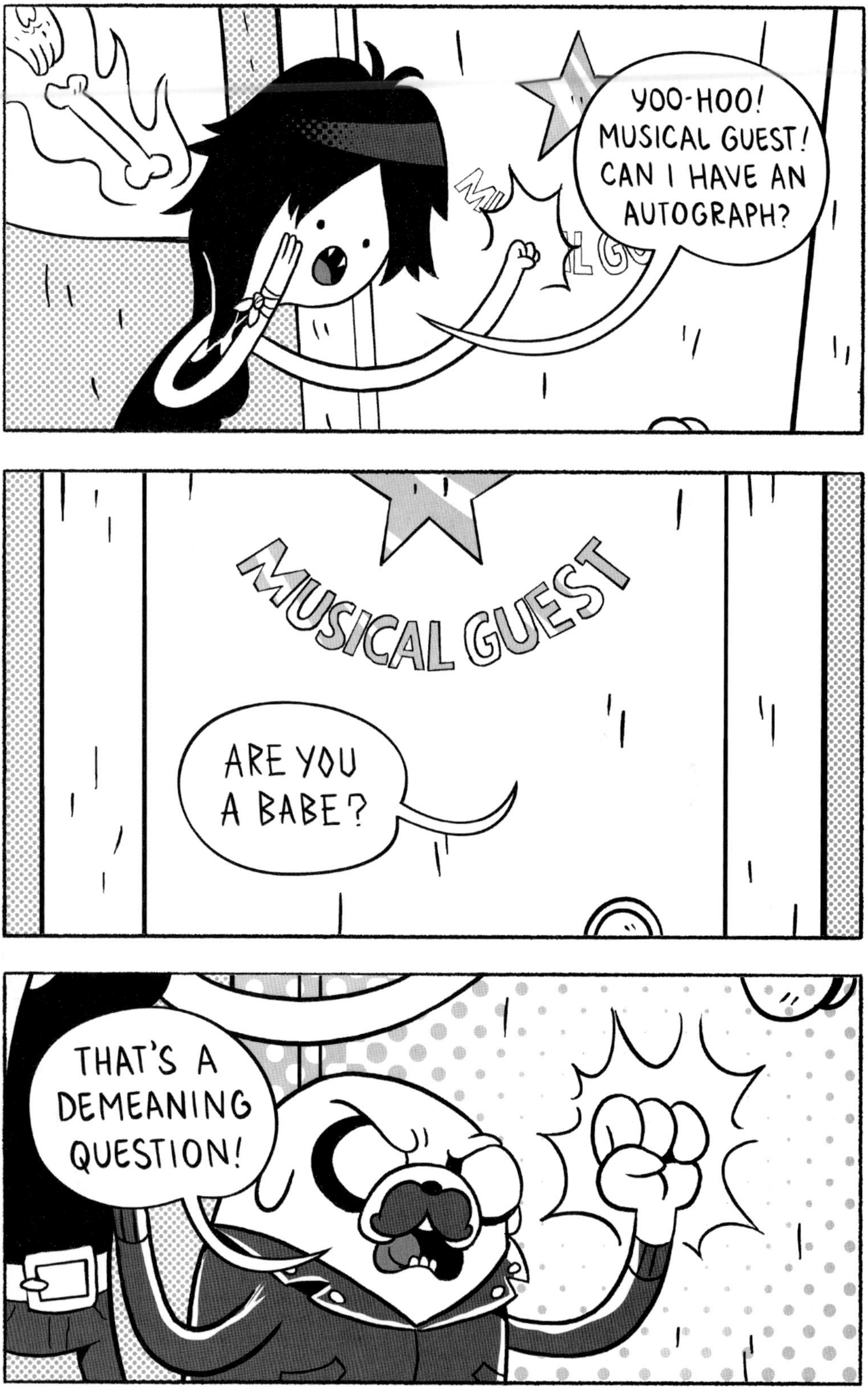
YOO-HOO! MUSICAL GUEST! CAN I HAVE AN AUTOGRAPH?
MUSICAL GUEST
ARE YOU A BABE?
THAT'S A DEMEANING QUESTION!

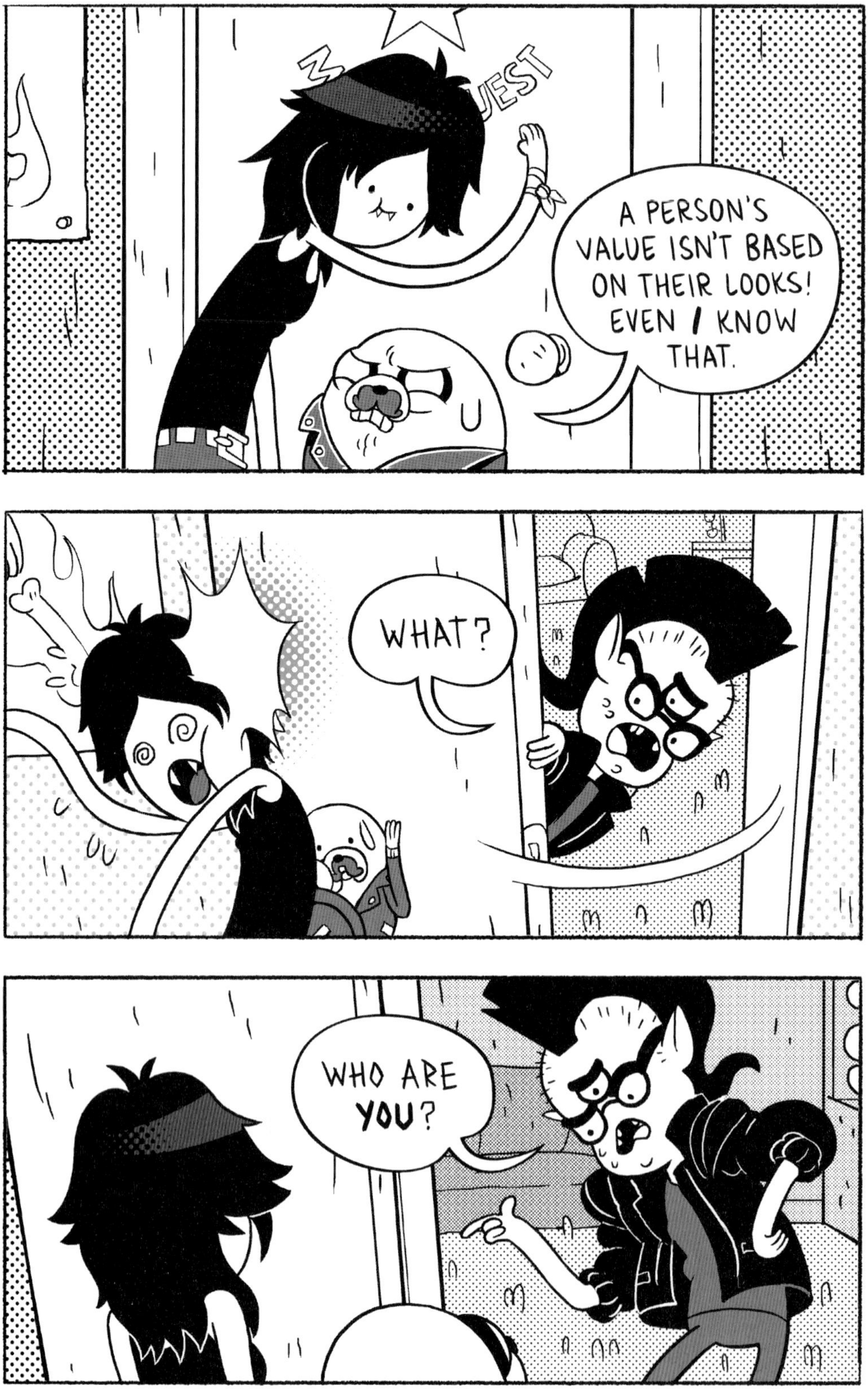
A PERSON'S VALUE ISN'T BASED ON THEIR LOOKS! EVEN I KNOW THAT.
WHAT?
WHO ARE **YOU**?

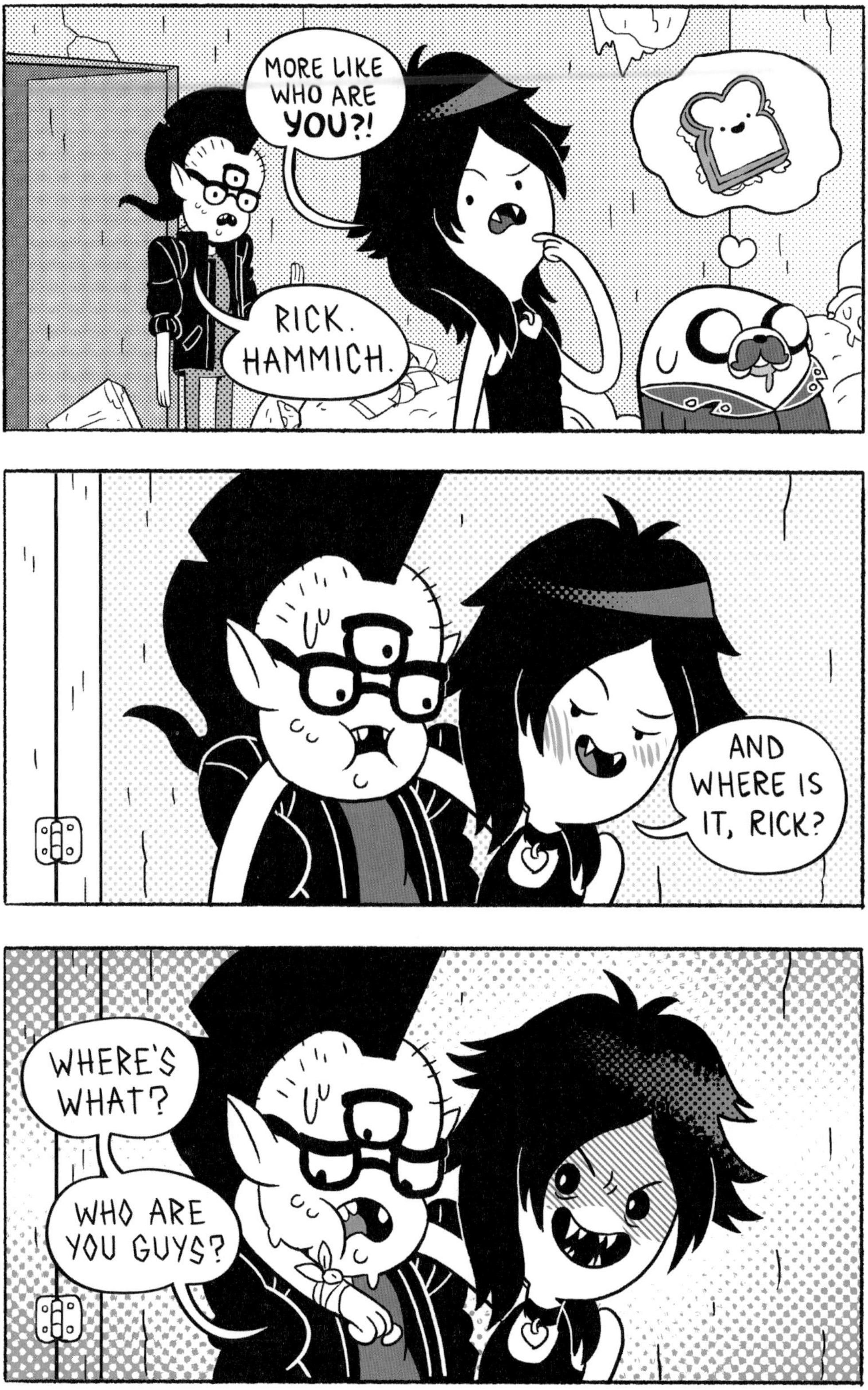
MORE LIKE WHO ARE YOU?!
RICK. HAMMICH.
AND WHERE IS IT, RICK?
WHERE'S WHAT?
WHO ARE YOU GUYS?

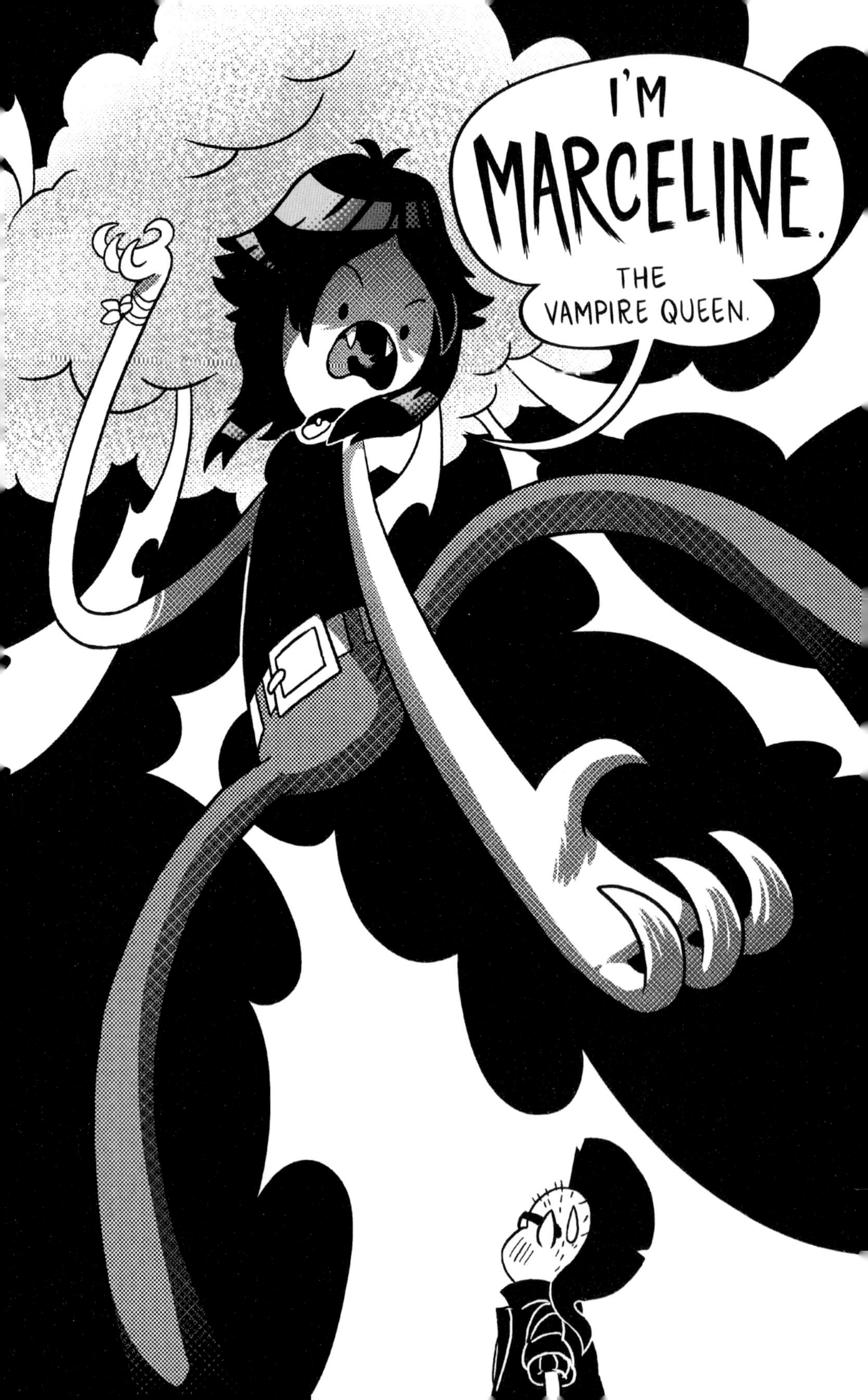
I'M
MARCELINE.
THE
VAMPIRE QUEEN.

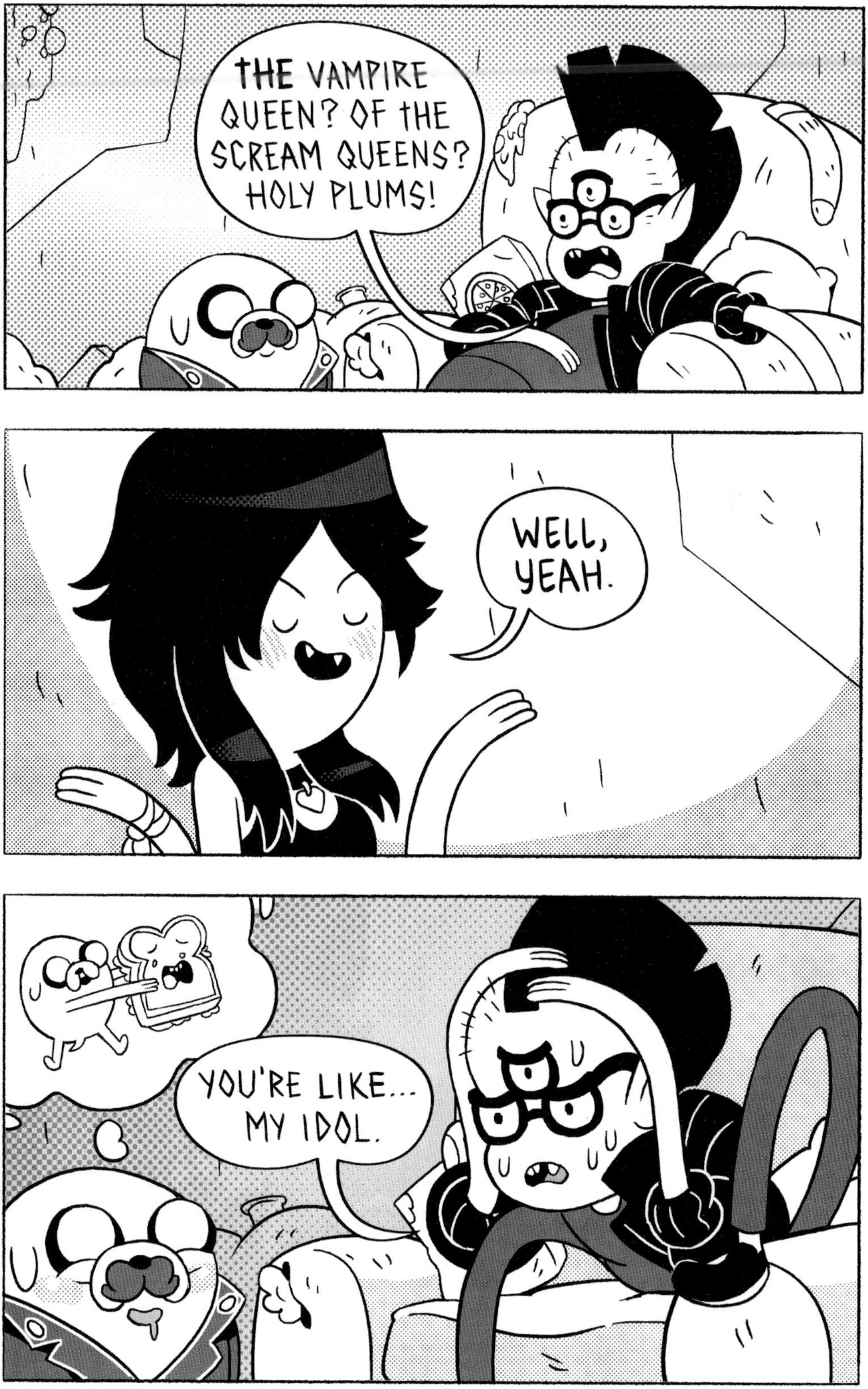
THE VAMPIRE QUEEN? OF THE SCREAM QUEENS? HOLY PLUMS!
WELL, YEAH.
YOU'RE LIKE... MY IDOL.

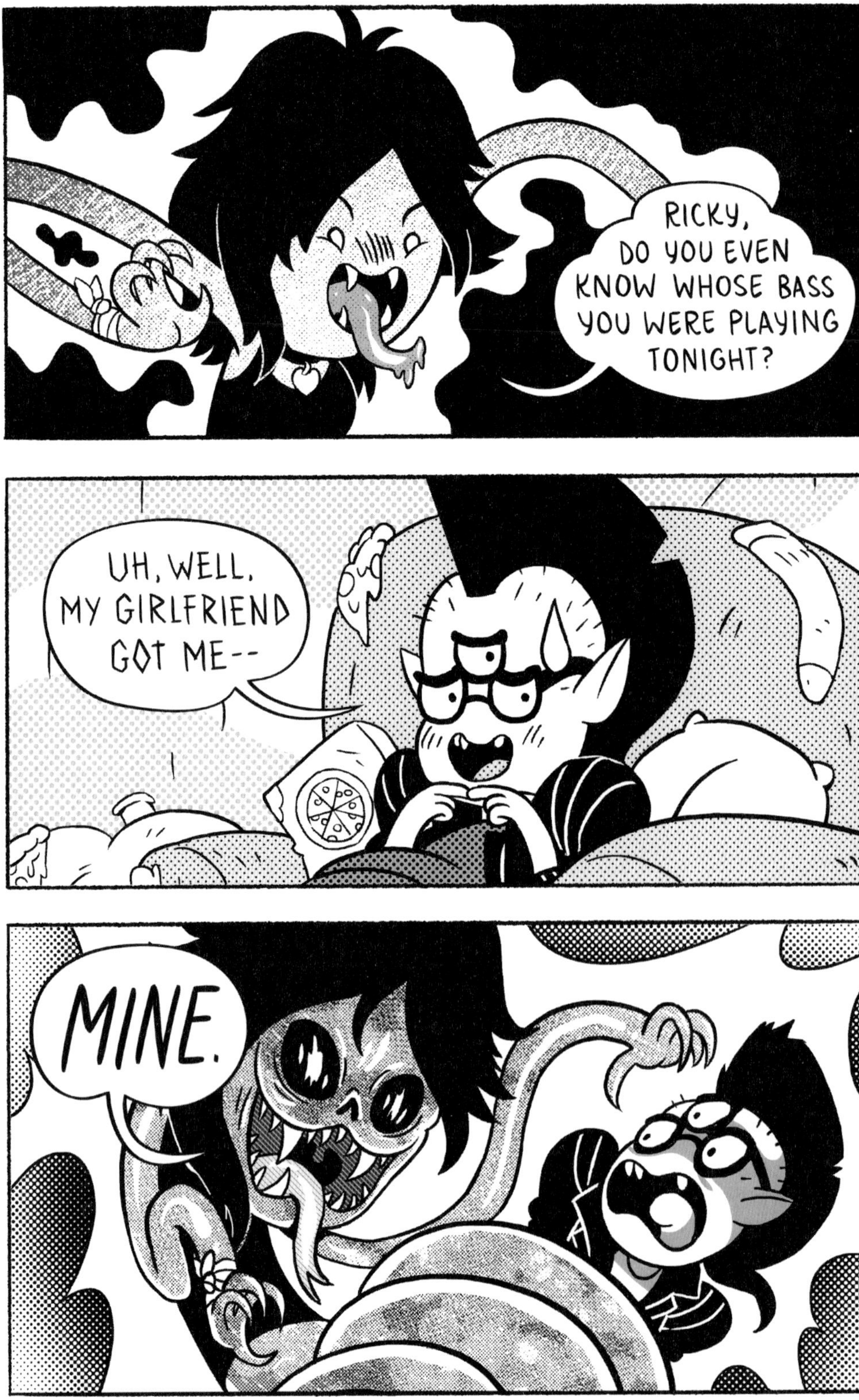
RICKY, DO YOU EVEN KNOW WHOSE BASS YOU WERE PLAYING TONIGHT?
UH, WELL. MY GIRLFRIEND GOT ME--
MINE.

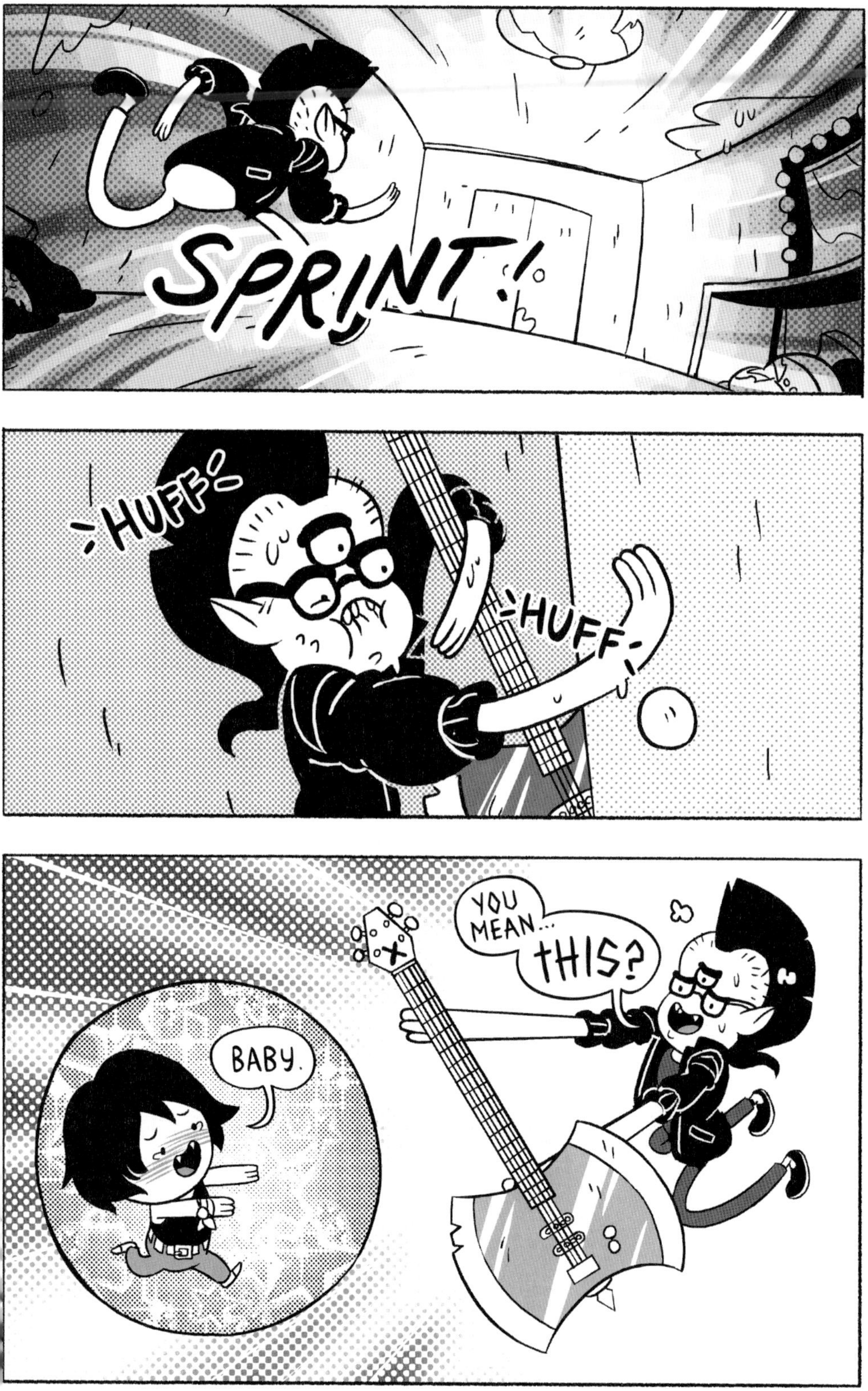
SPRINT!
HUFF
HUFF
YOU MEAN... THIS?
BABY.

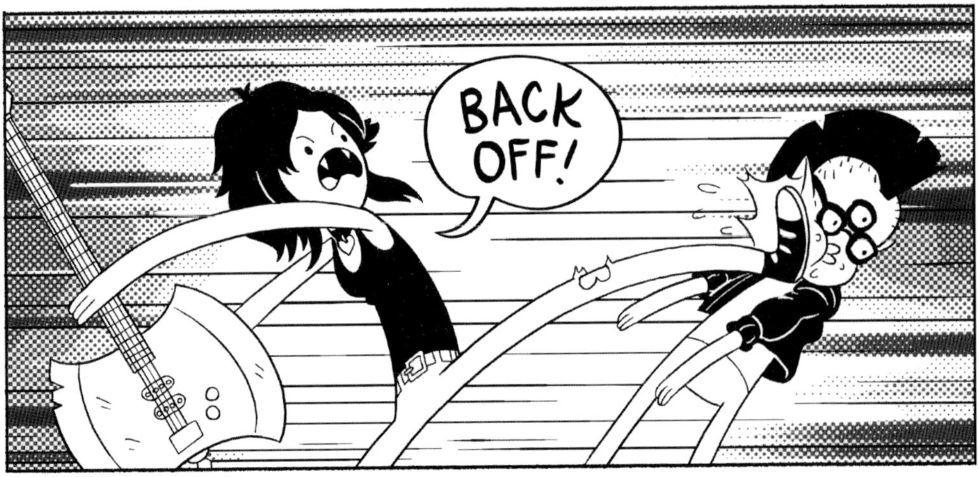
BACK OFF!

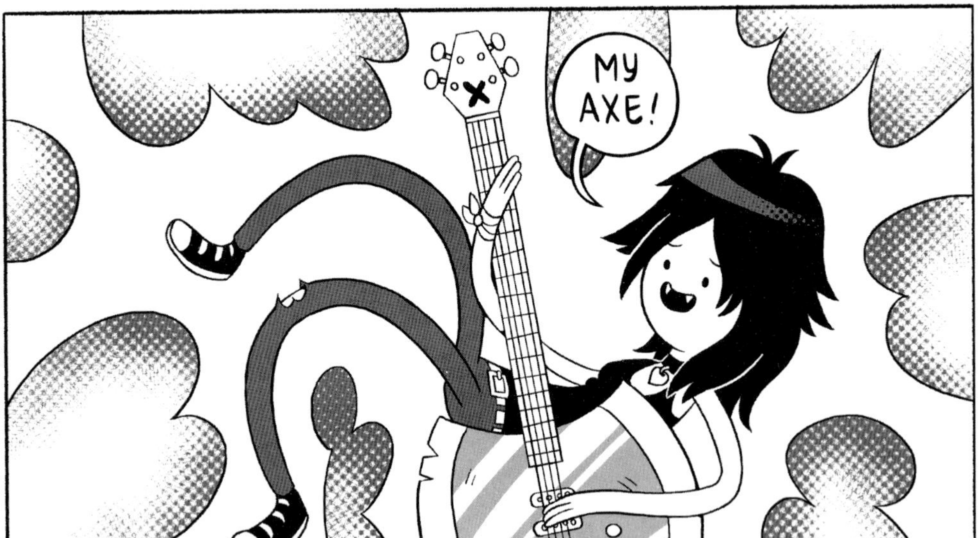
MY AXE!

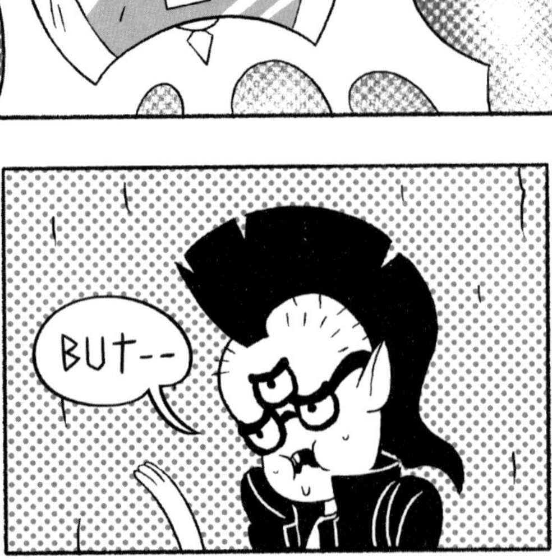
BUT--

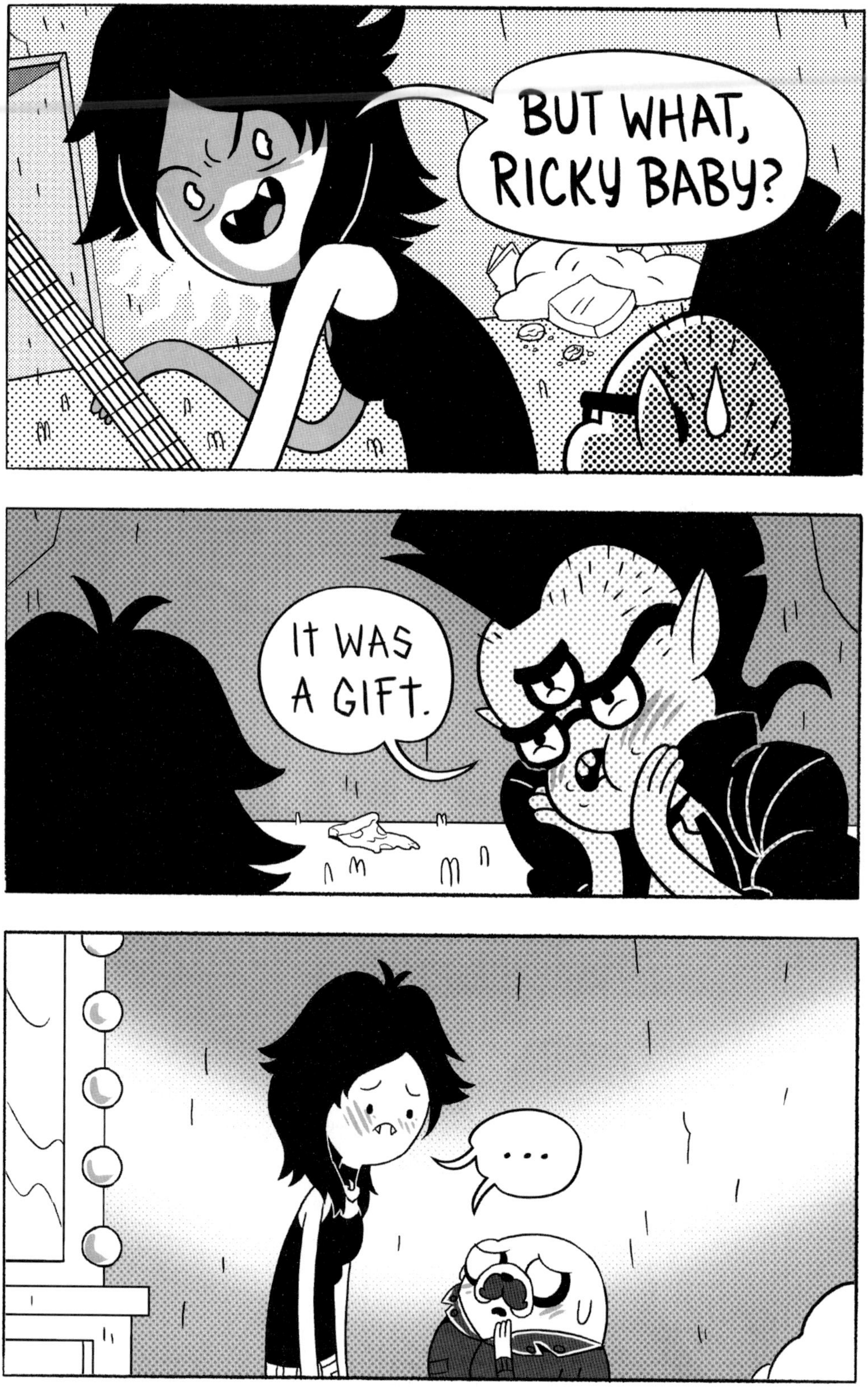
BUT WHAT, RICKY BABY?
IT WAS A GIFT.
...

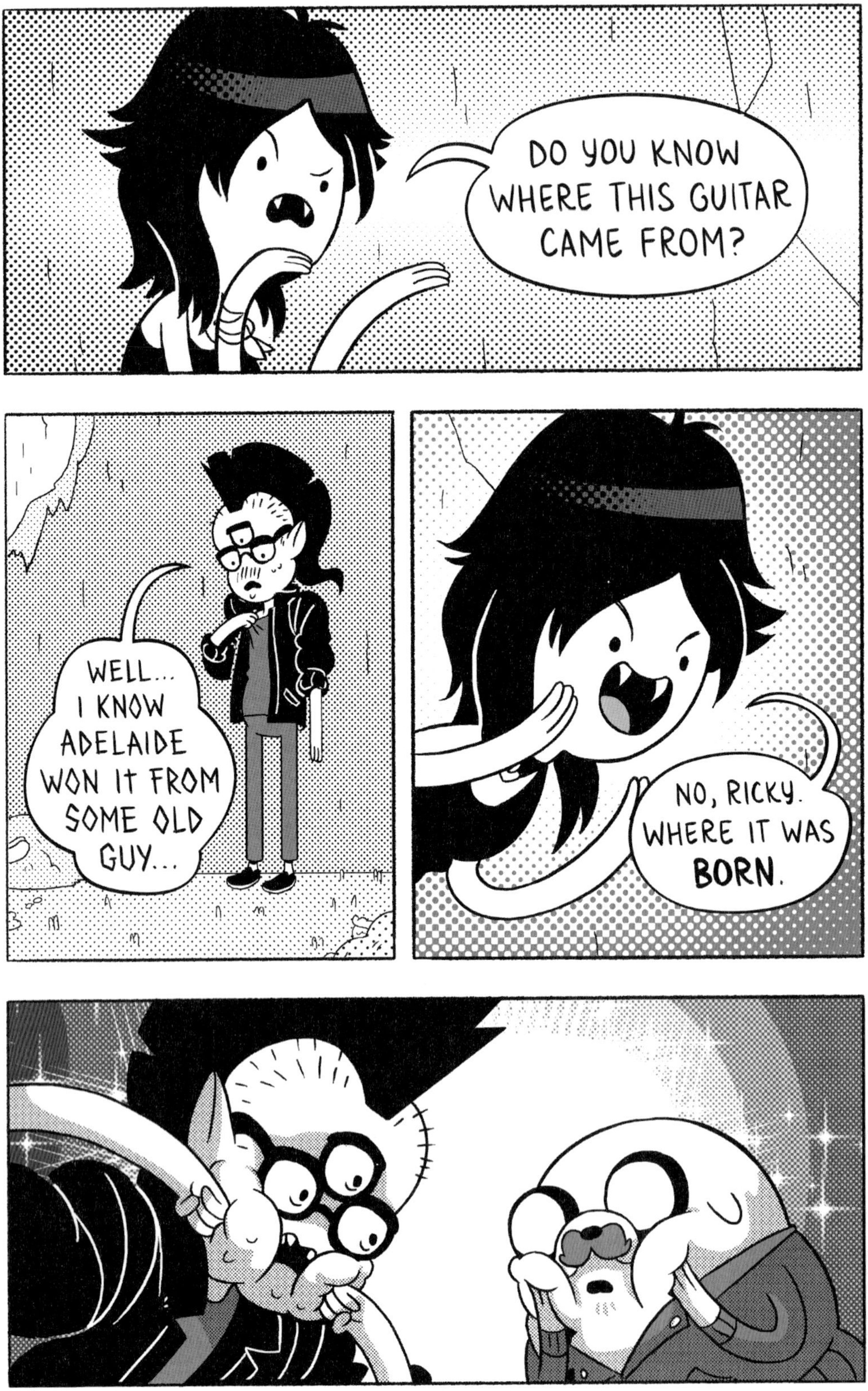
DO YOU KNOW WHERE THIS GUITAR CAME FROM?
WELL... I KNOW ADELAIDE WON IT FROM SOME OLD GUY...
NO, RICKY. WHERE IT WAS **BORN**.

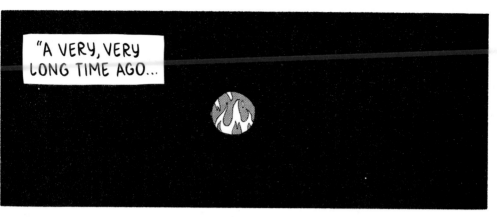

"A VERY, VERY LONG TIME AGO...

"THE NIGHTOSPHERE WAS A VERY DIFFERENT PLACE.

"IT WAS CHAOTIC. LAWLESS. A REAL NASTY PLACE."

hey.

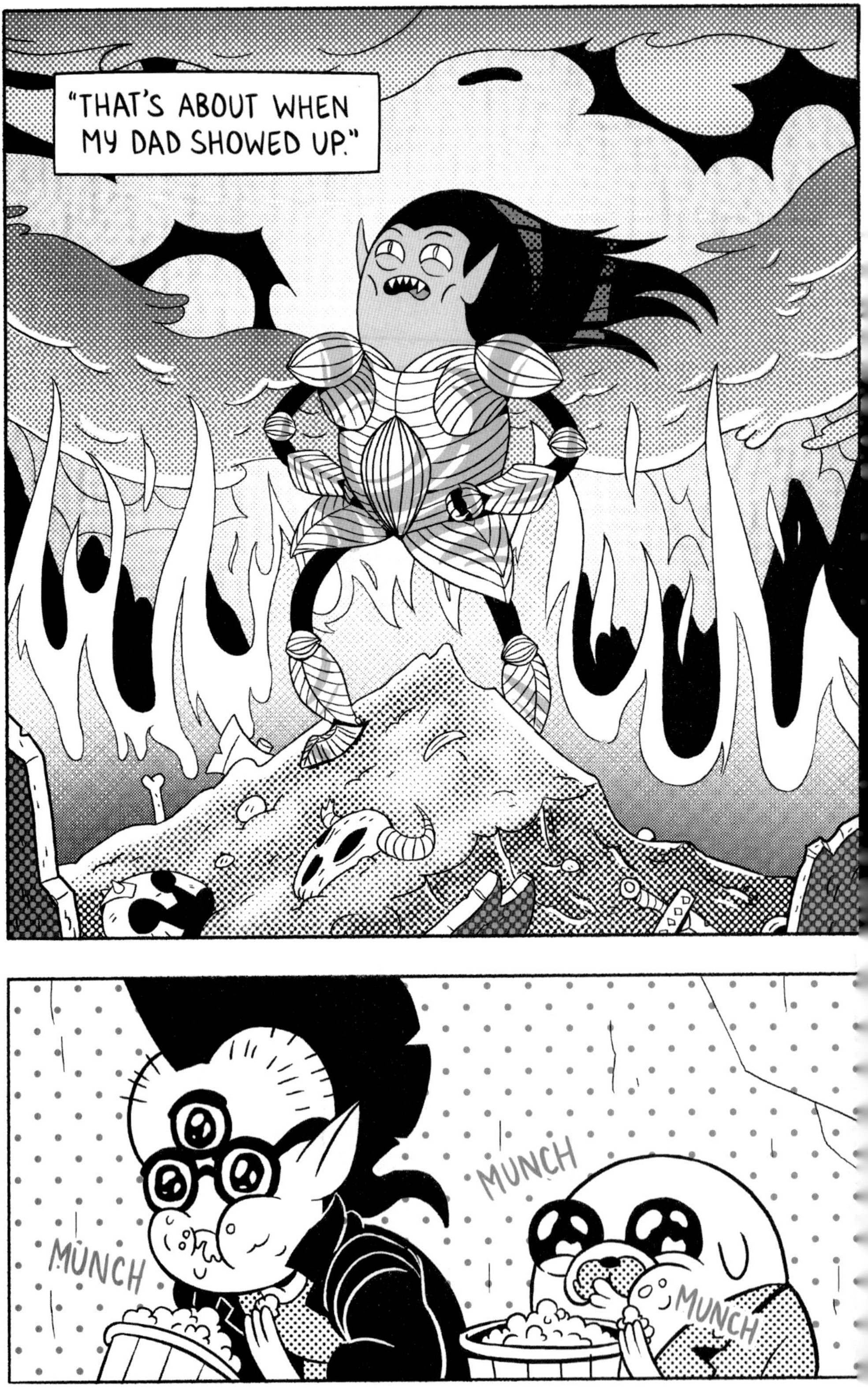
"THAT'S ABOUT WHEN MY DAD SHOWED UP."
MUNCH
MUNCH
MUNCH

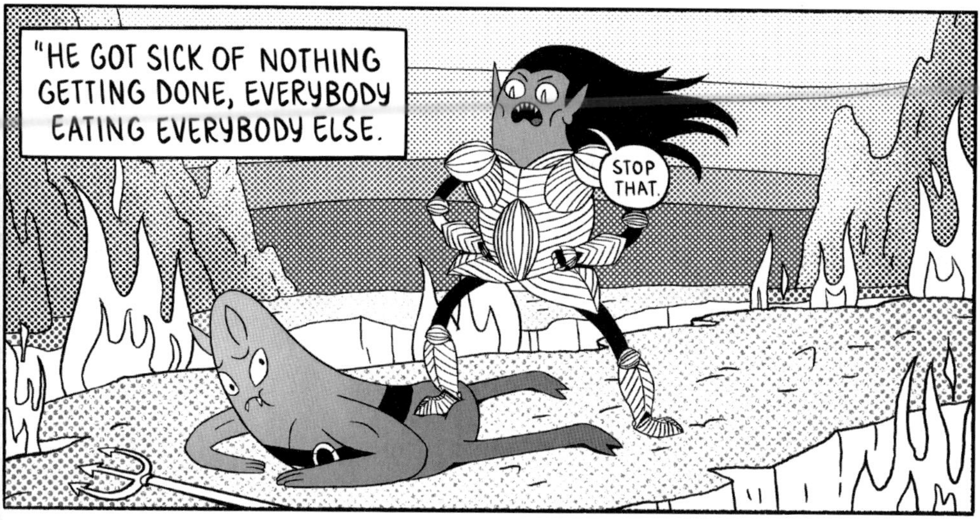
"HE GOT SICK OF NOTHING GETTING DONE, EVERYBODY EATING EVERYBODY ELSE.
STOP THAT.

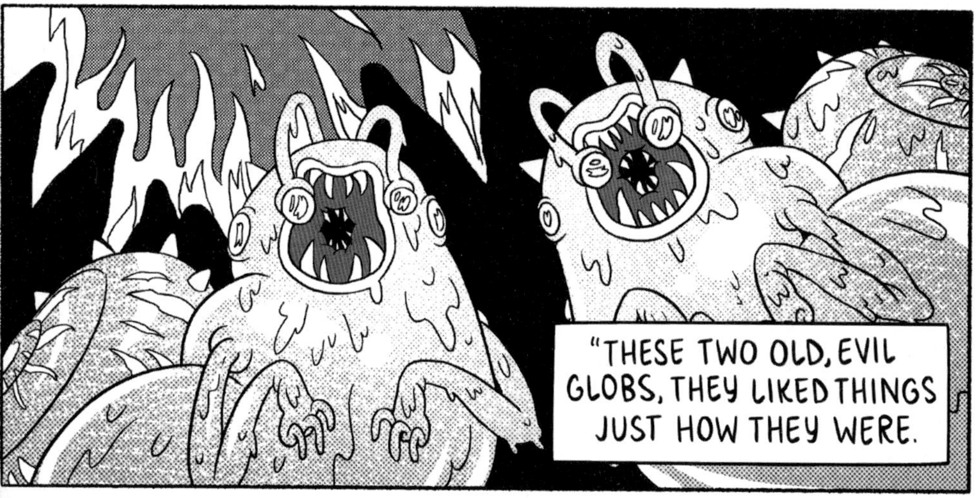
"THESE TWO OLD, EVIL GLOBS, THEY LIKED THINGS JUST HOW THEY WERE.

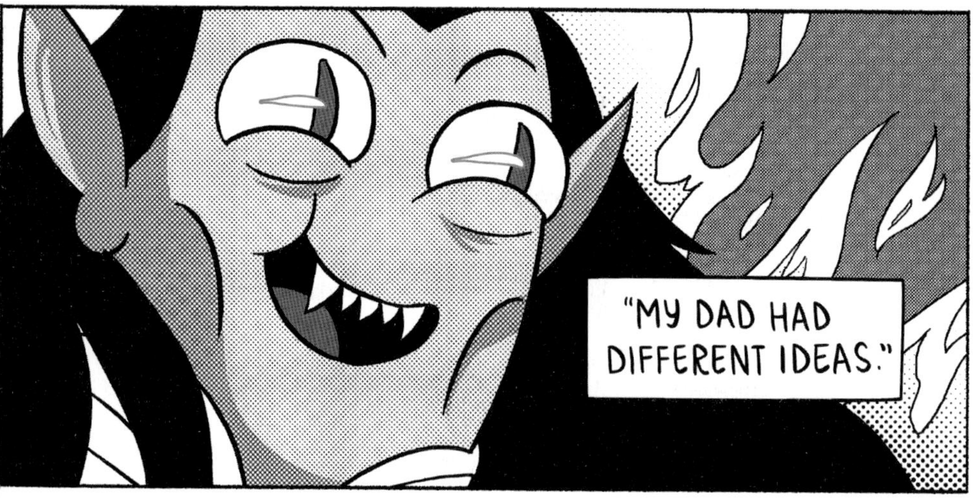
"MY DAD HAD DIFFERENT IDEAS."

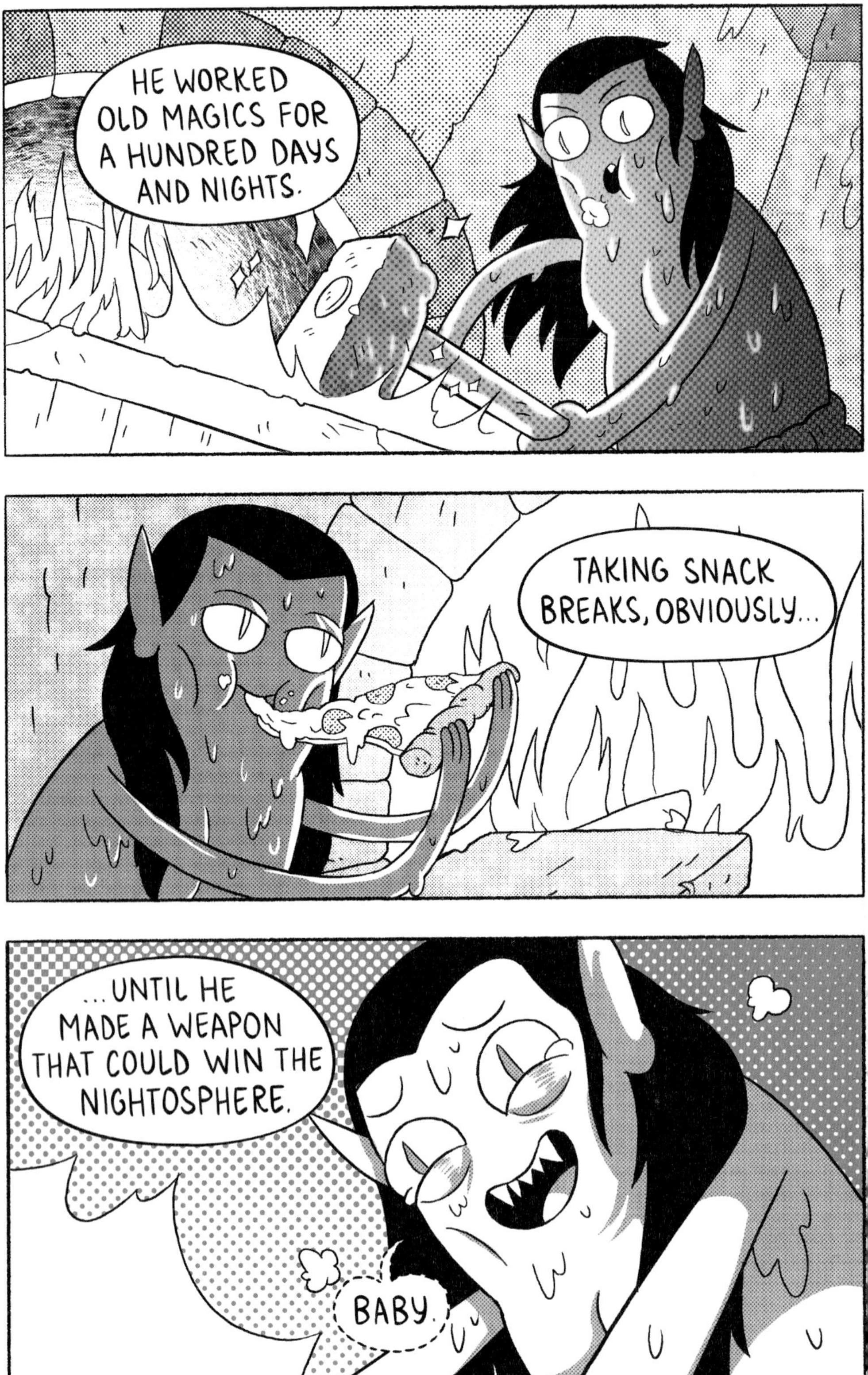
HE WORKED OLD MAGICS FOR A HUNDRED DAYS AND NIGHTS.
TAKING SNACK BREAKS, OBVIOUSLY...
...UNTIL HE MADE A WEAPON THAT COULD WIN THE NIGHTOSPHERE.
BABY.

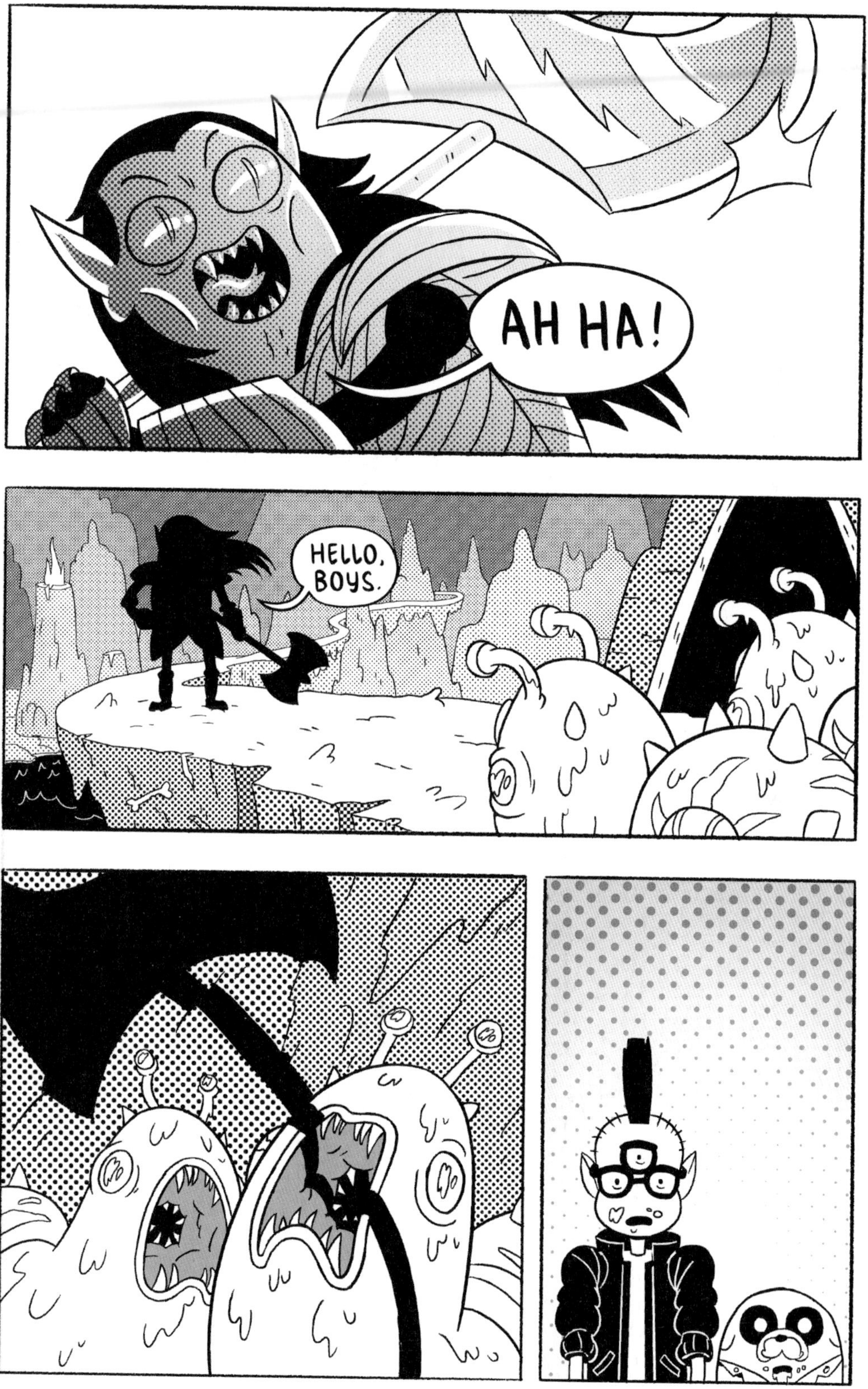
AH HA!
HELLO, BOYS.

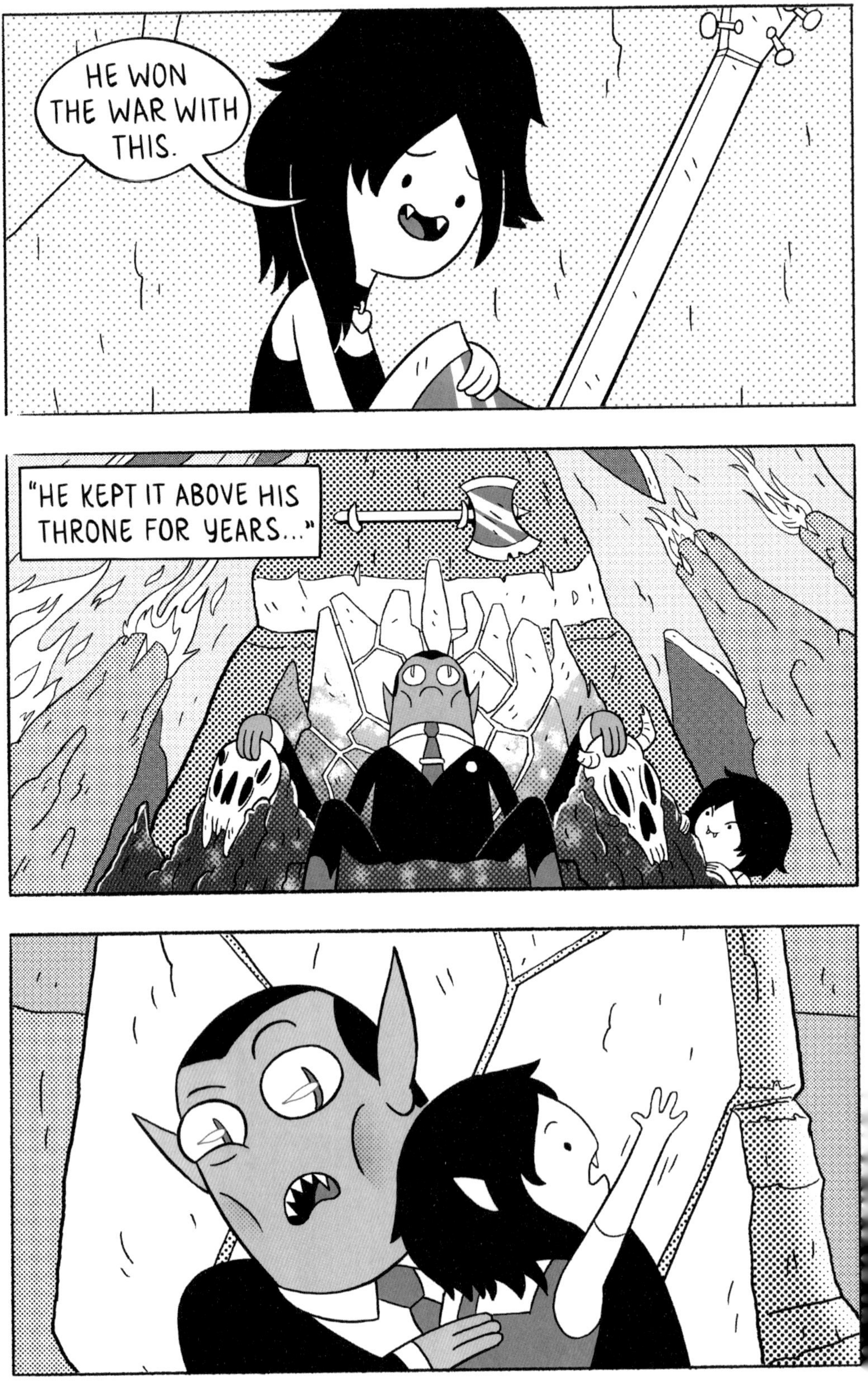
HE WON THE WAR WITH THIS.
"HE KEPT IT ABOVE HIS THRONE FOR YEARS..."

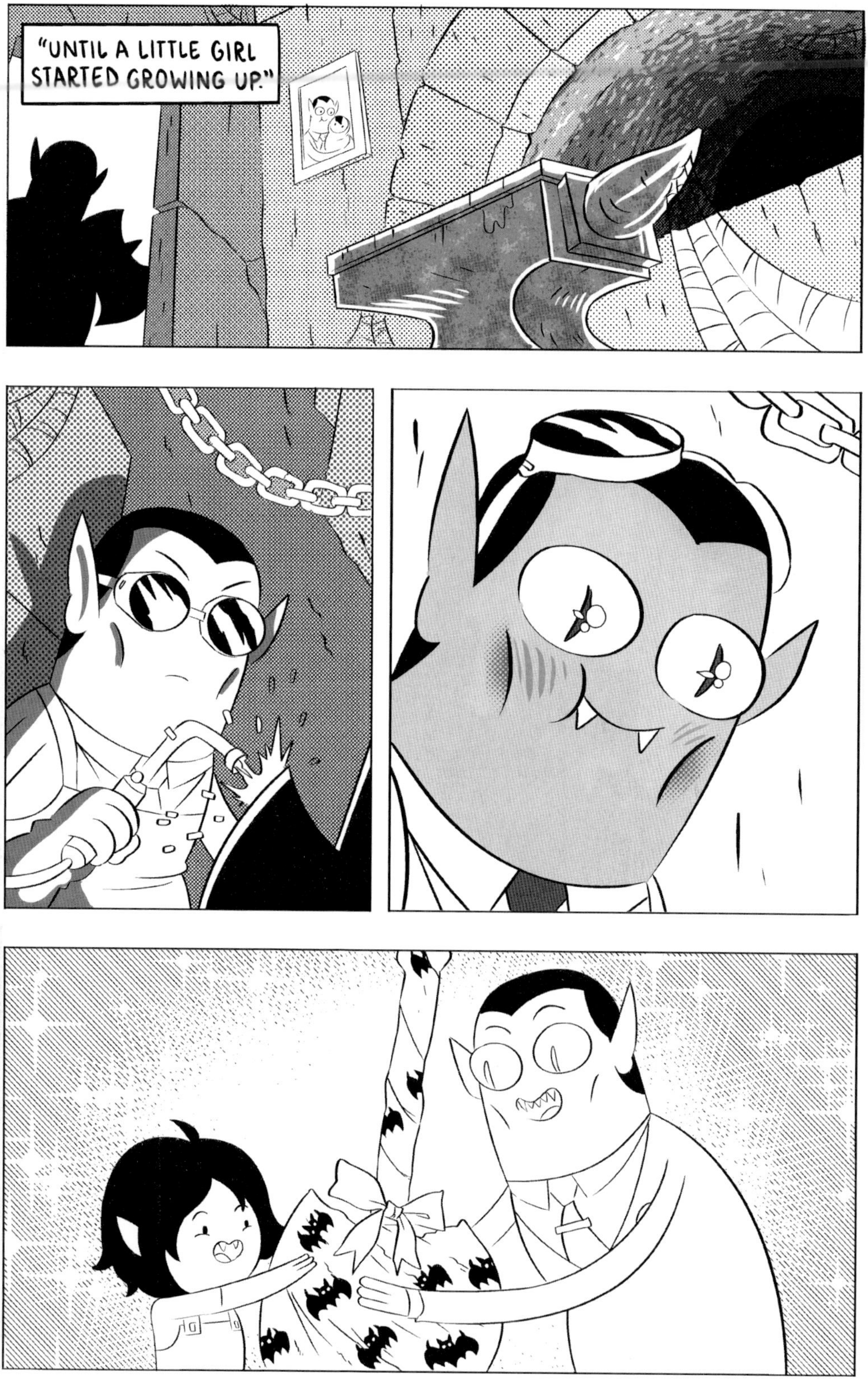
"UNTIL A LITTLE GIRL STARTED GROWING UP."

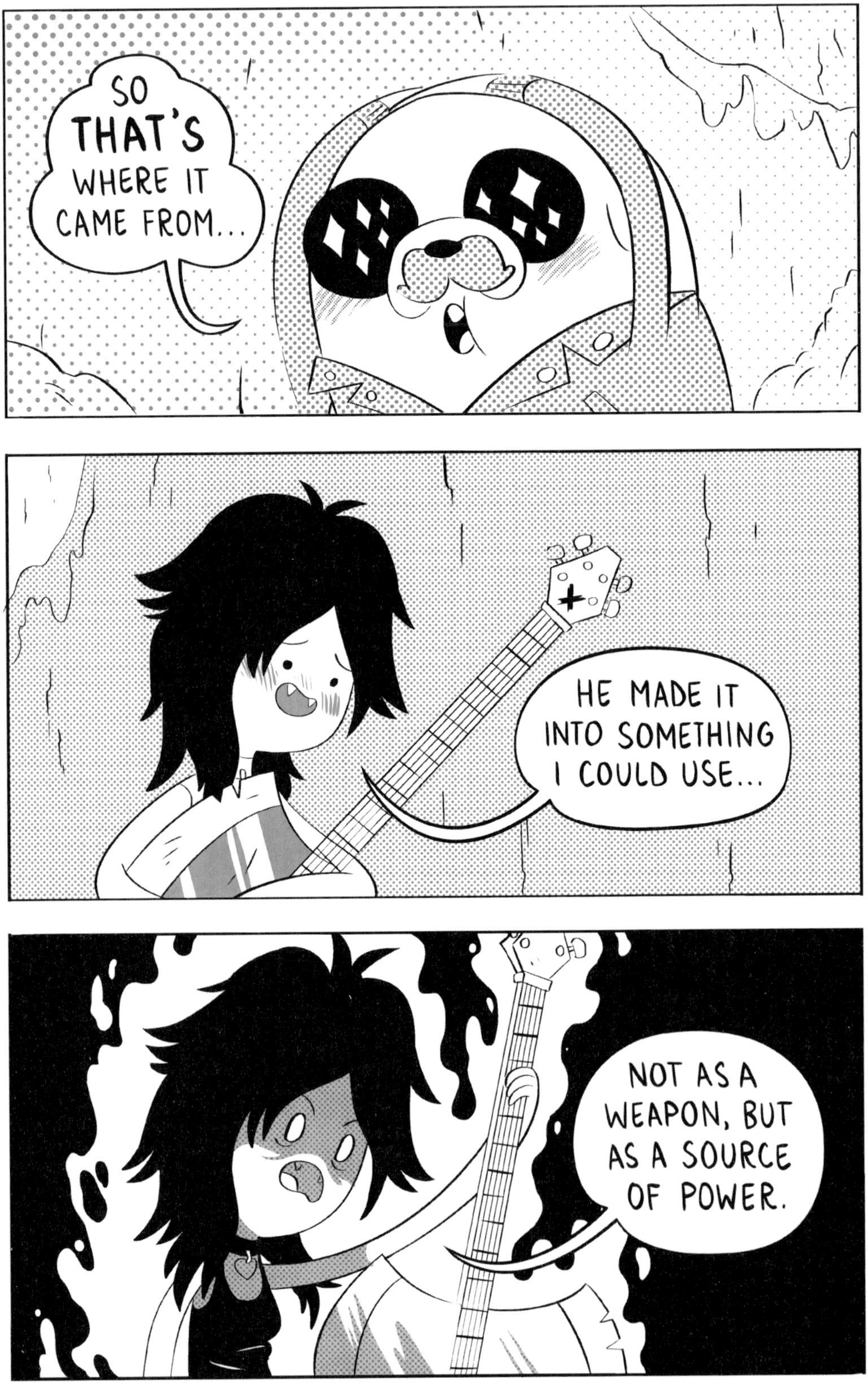
SO THAT'S WHERE IT CAME FROM...
HE MADE IT INTO SOMETHING I COULD USE...
NOT AS A WEAPON, BUT AS A SOURCE OF POWER.

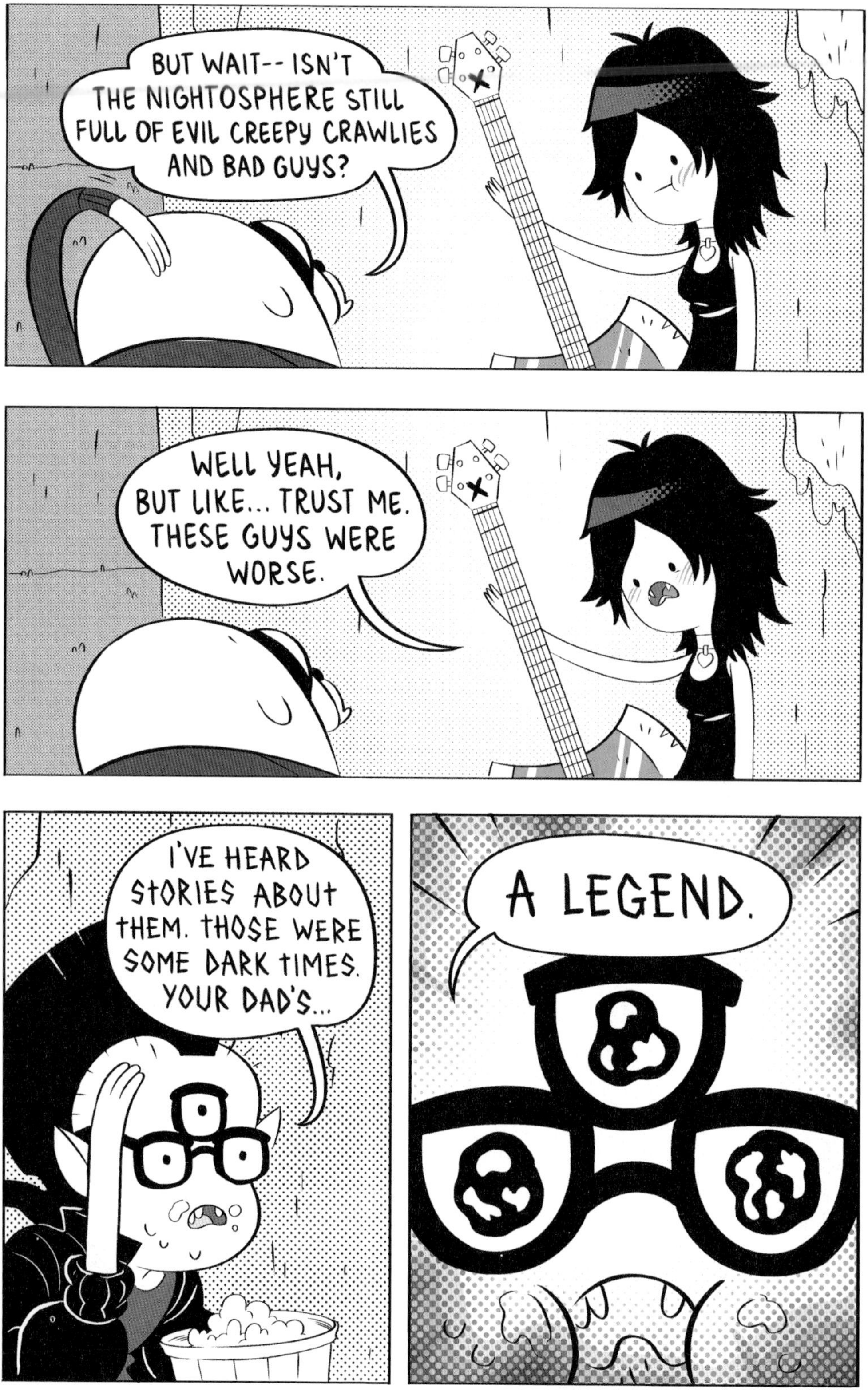
BUT WAIT-- ISN'T THE NIGHTOSPHERE STILL FULL OF EVIL CREEPY CRAWLIES AND BAD GUYS?
WELL YEAH, BUT LIKE... TRUST ME. THESE GUYS WERE WORSE.
I'VE HEARD STORIES ABOUT THEM. THOSE WERE SOME DARK TIMES. YOUR DAD'S...
A LEGEND.

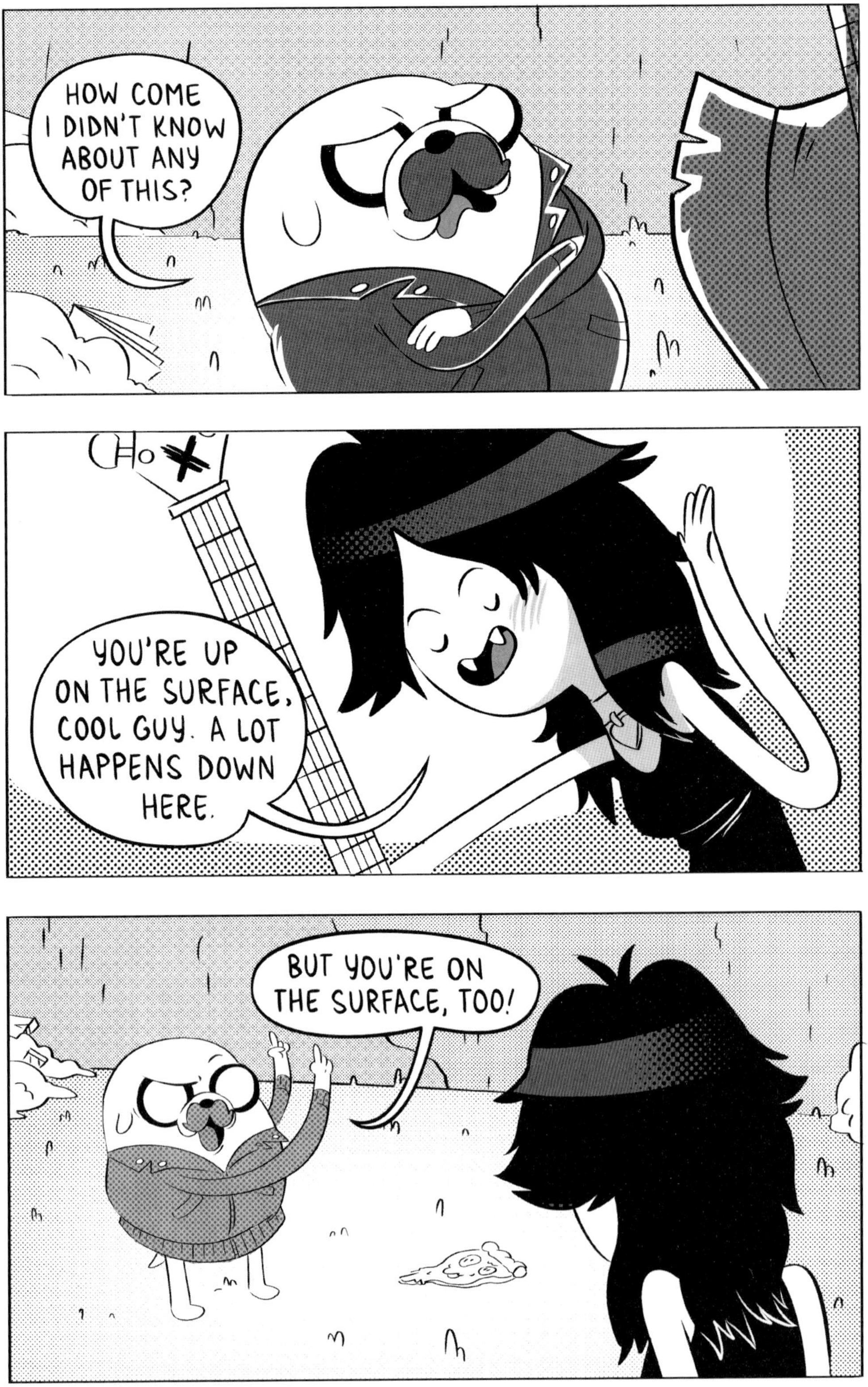
HOW COME I DIDN'T KNOW ABOUT ANY OF THIS?
YOU'RE UP ON THE SURFACE, COOL GUY. A LOT HAPPENS DOWN HERE.
BUT YOU'RE ON THE SURFACE, TOO!

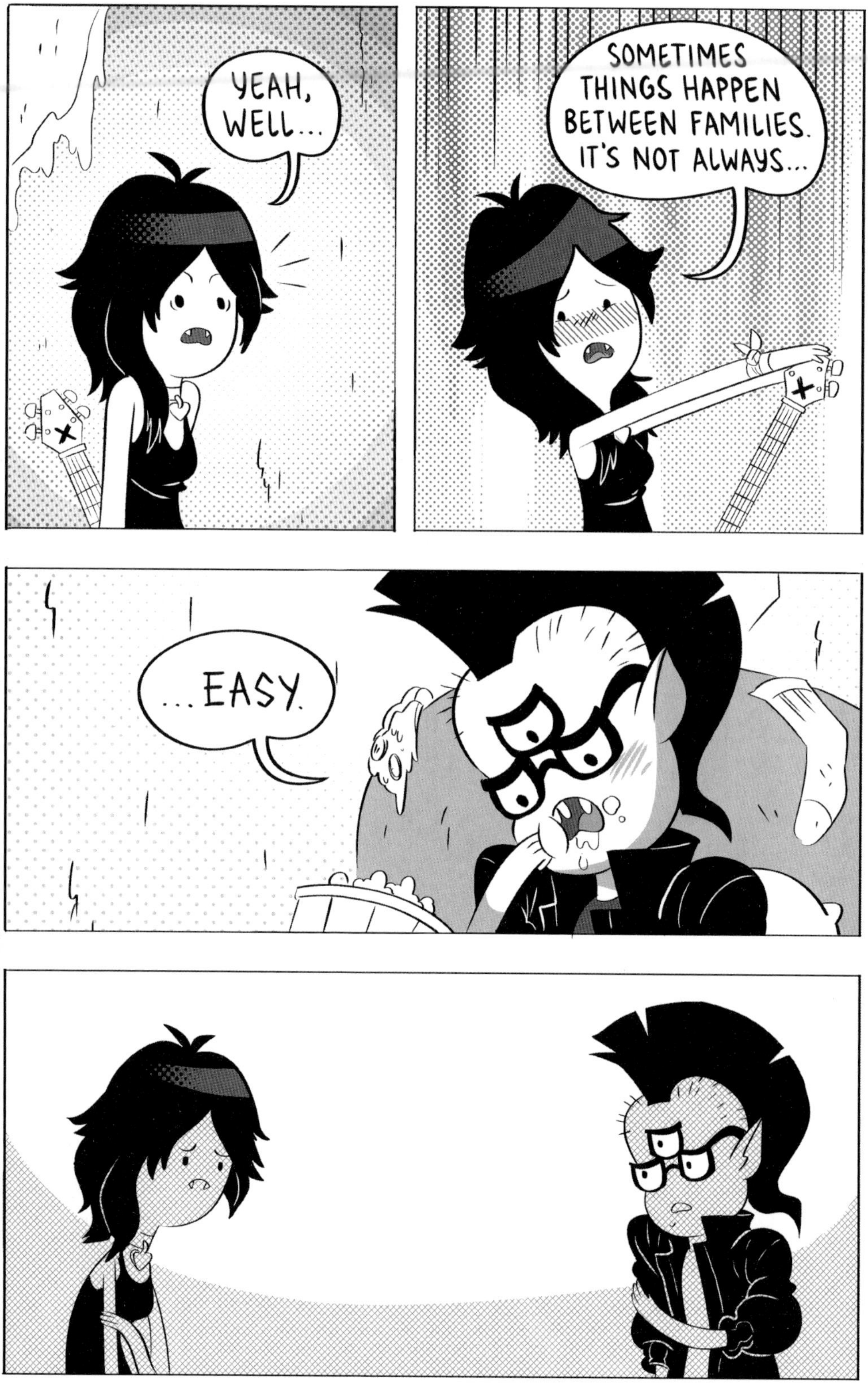
YEAH, WELL...
SOMETIMES THINGS HAPPEN BETWEEN FAMILIES. IT'S NOT ALWAYS...
...EASY.

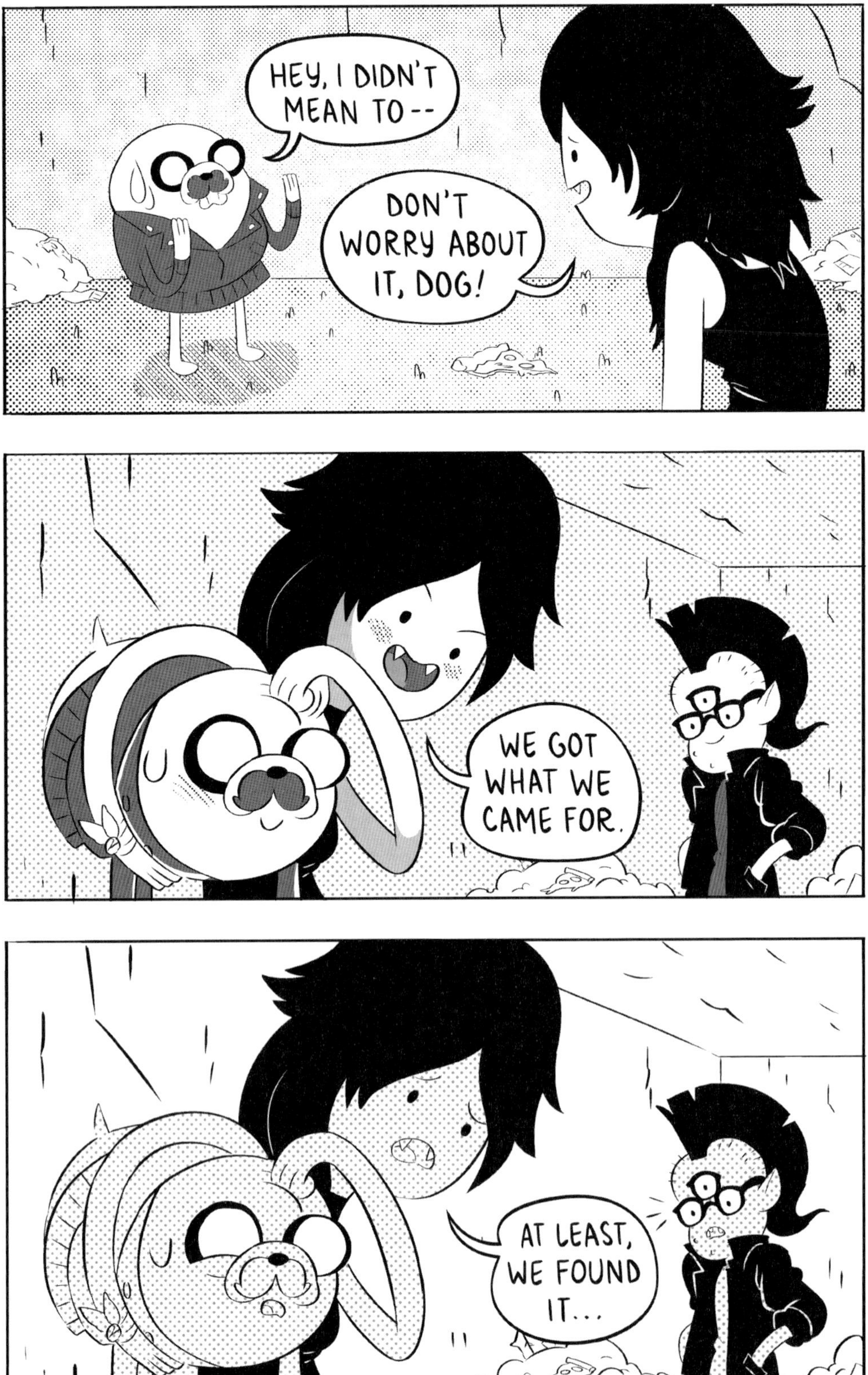
HEY, I DIDN'T MEAN TO--
DON'T WORRY ABOUT IT, DOG!
WE GOT WHAT WE CAME FOR.
AT LEAST, WE FOUND IT...

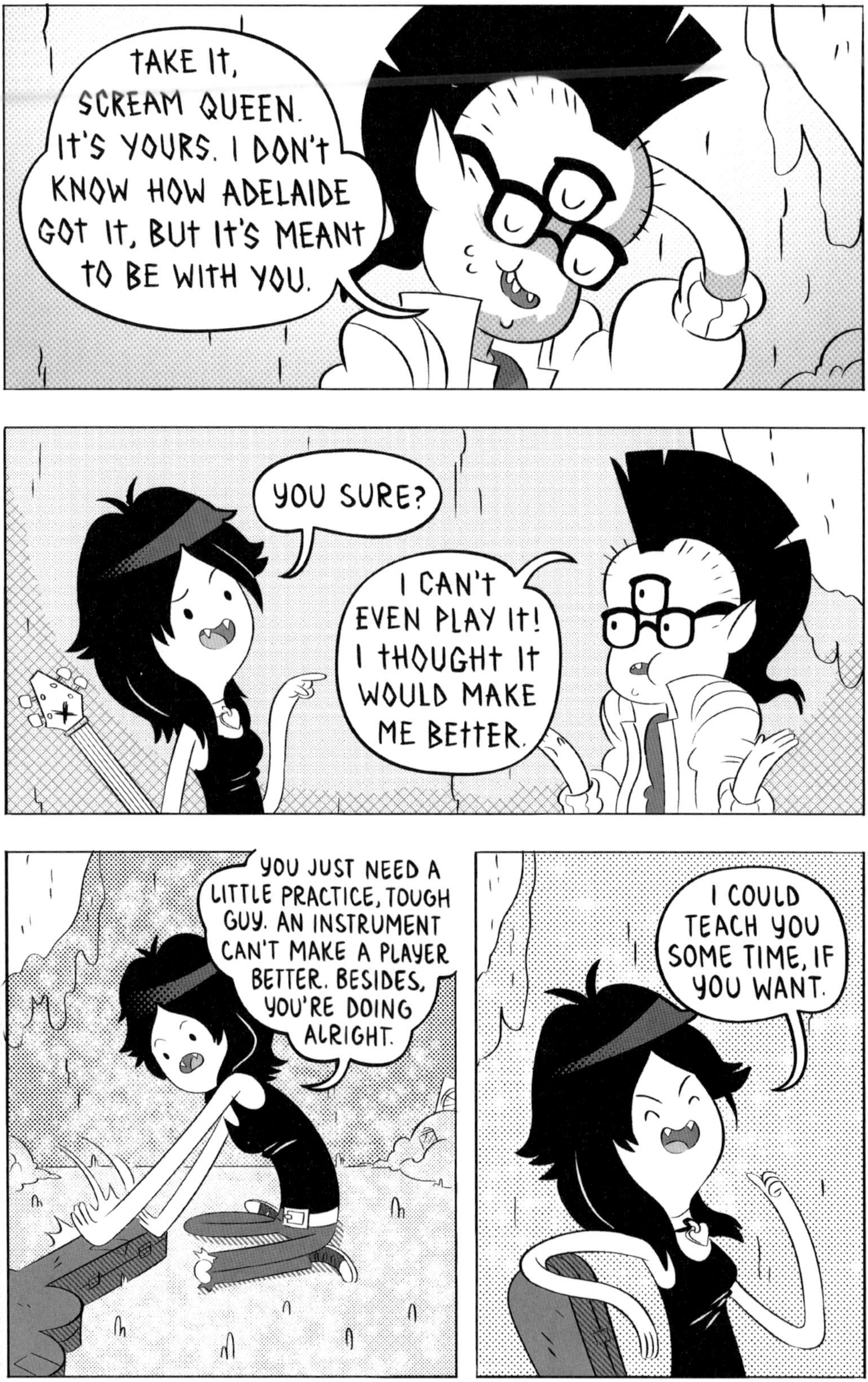
TAKE IT, SCREAM QUEEN. IT'S YOURS. I DON'T KNOW HOW ADELAIDE GOT IT, BUT IT'S MEANT TO BE WITH YOU.
YOU SURE?
I CAN'T EVEN PLAY IT! I THOUGHT IT WOULD MAKE ME BETTER.
YOU JUST NEED A LITTLE PRACTICE, TOUGH GUY. AN INSTRUMENT CAN'T MAKE A PLAYER BETTER. BESIDES, YOU'RE DOING ALRIGHT.
I COULD TEACH YOU SOME TIME, IF YOU WANT.

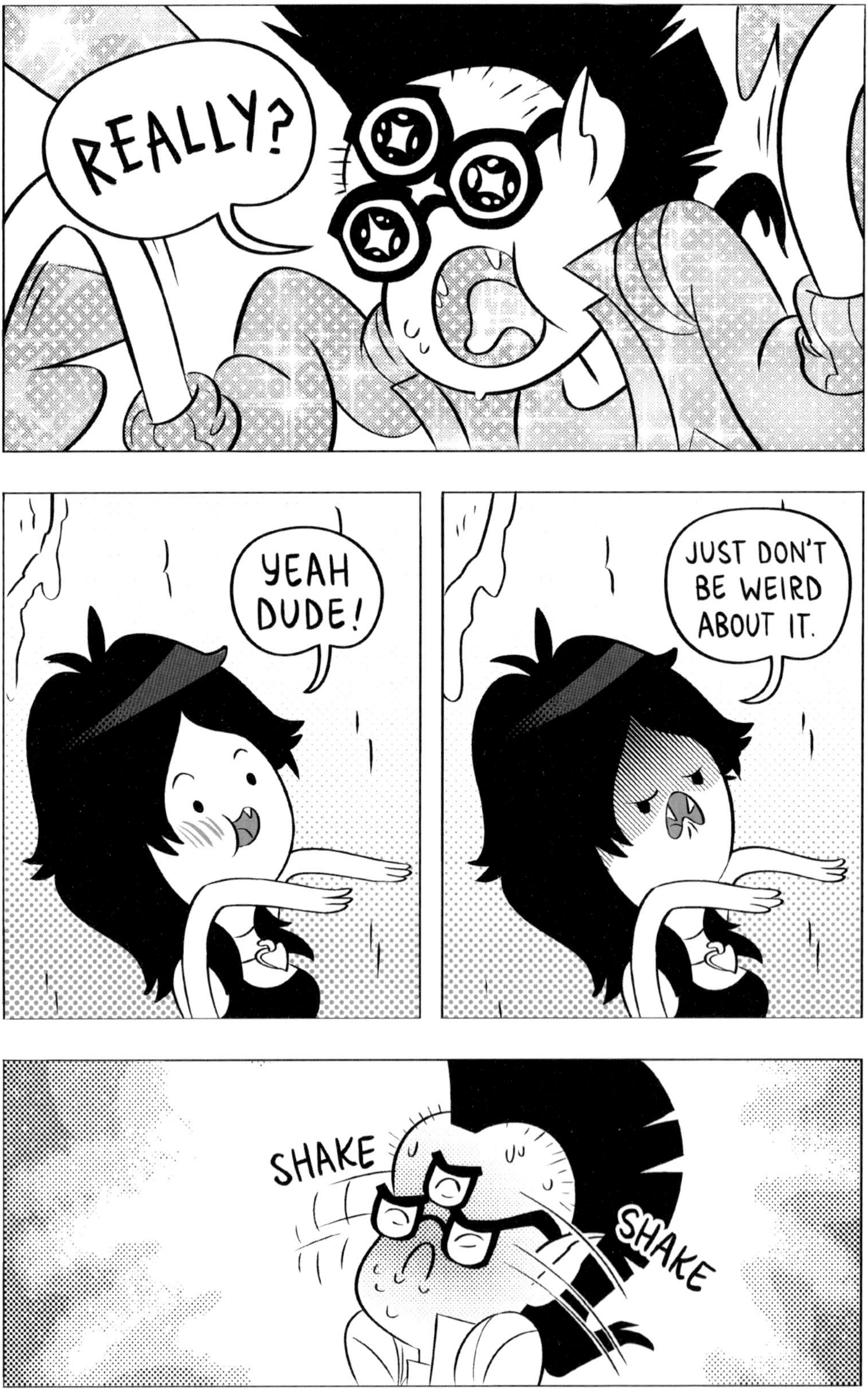
REALLY?
YEAH DUDE!
JUST DON'T BE WEIRD ABOUT IT.
SHAKE
SHAKE

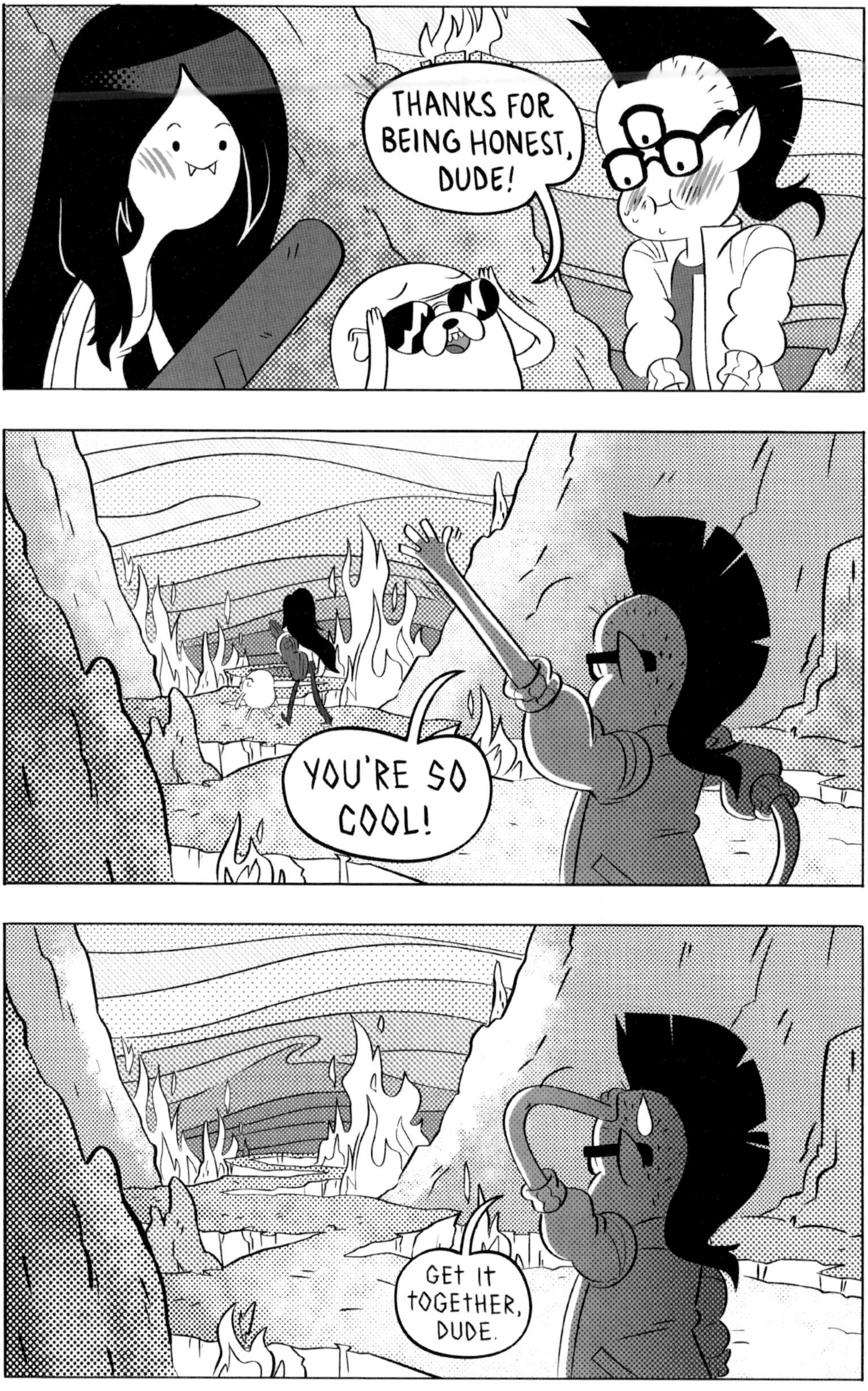
THANKS FOR BEING HONEST, DUDE!
YOU'RE SO COOL!
GET IT TOGETHER, DUDE.

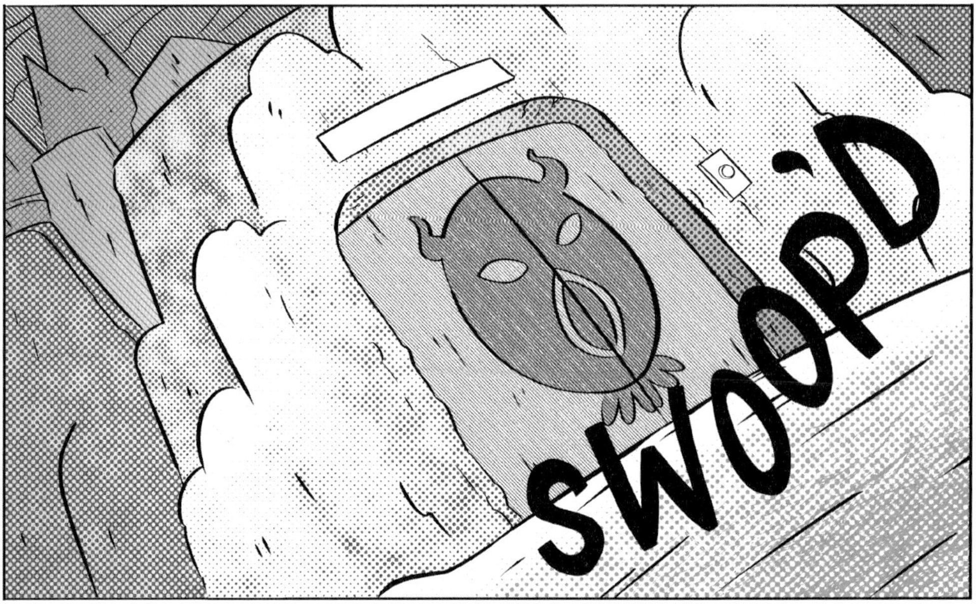
SWOOP'D

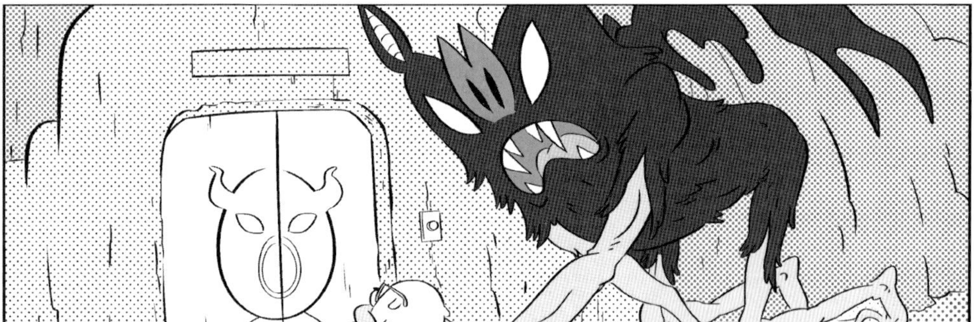

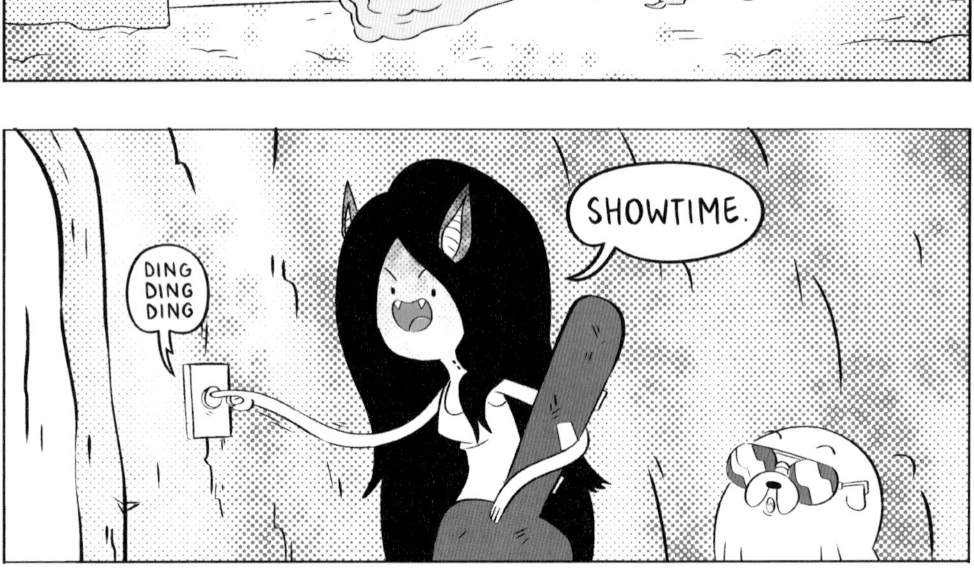
DING
DING
DING
SHOWTIME.

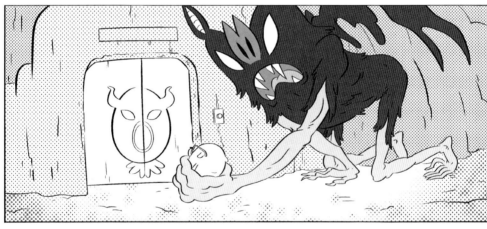

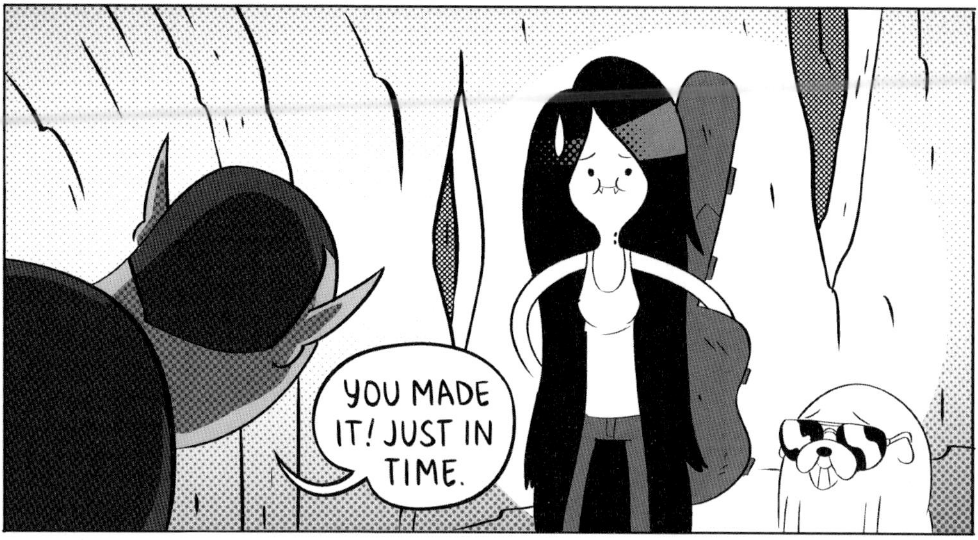
YOU MADE IT! JUST IN TIME.

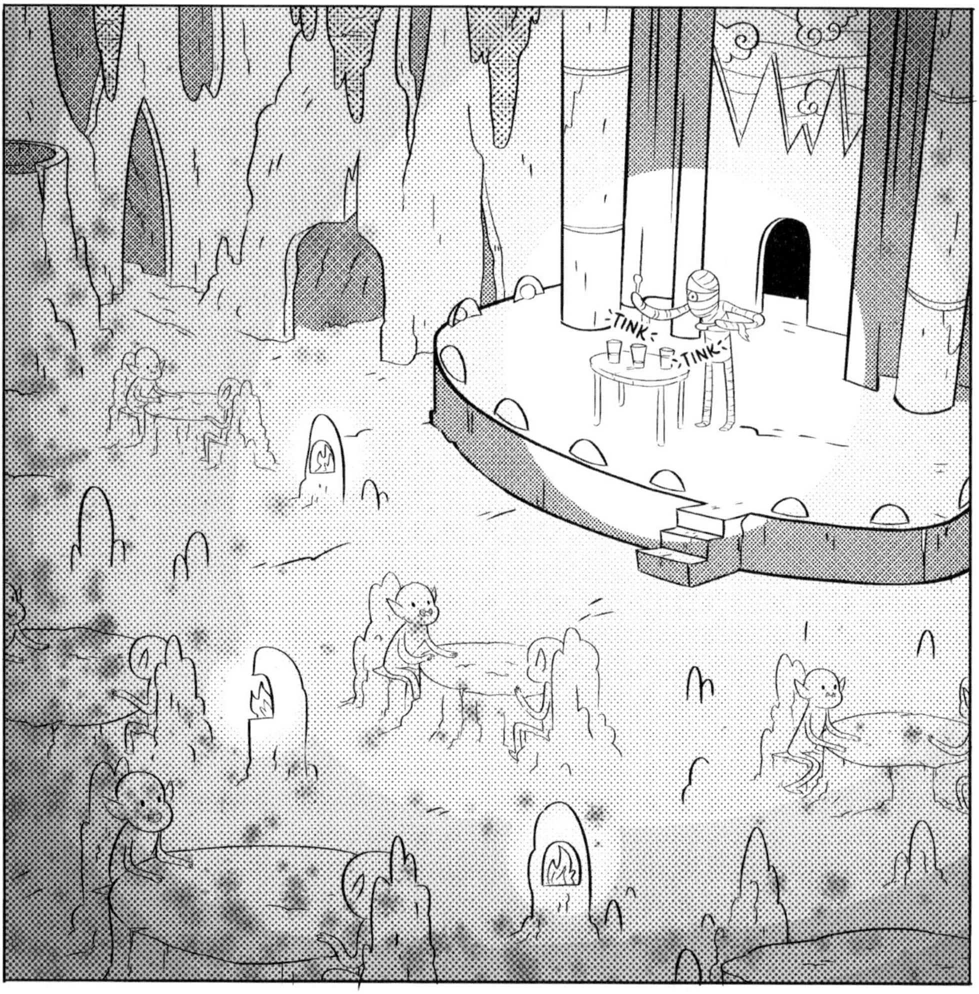
TINK
TINK

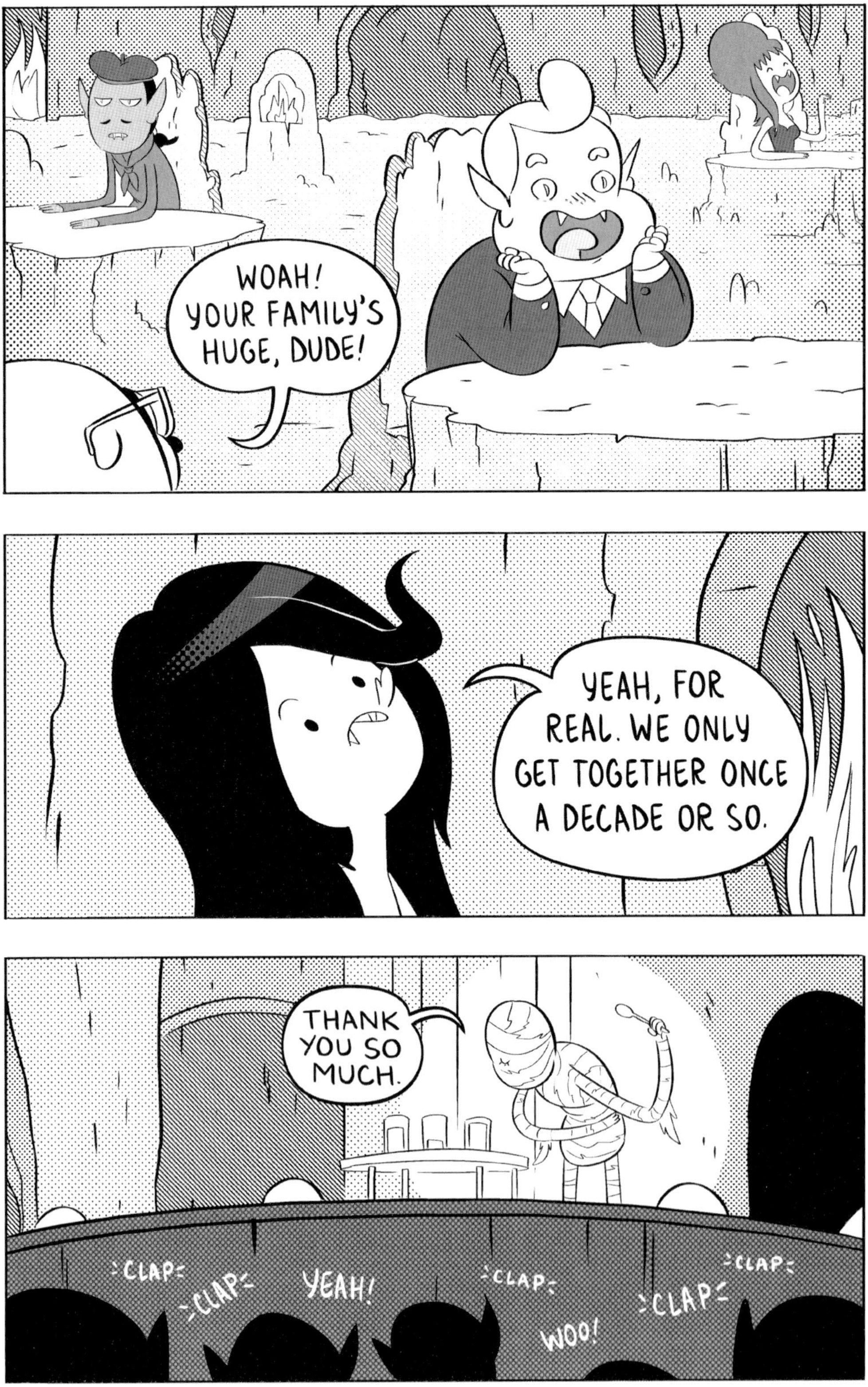
WOAH! YOUR FAMILY'S HUGE, DUDE!
YEAH, FOR REAL. WE ONLY GET TOGETHER ONCE A DECADE OR SO.
THANK YOU SO MUCH.
CLAP
CLAP
YEAH!
CLAP
CLAP
CLAP
WOO!

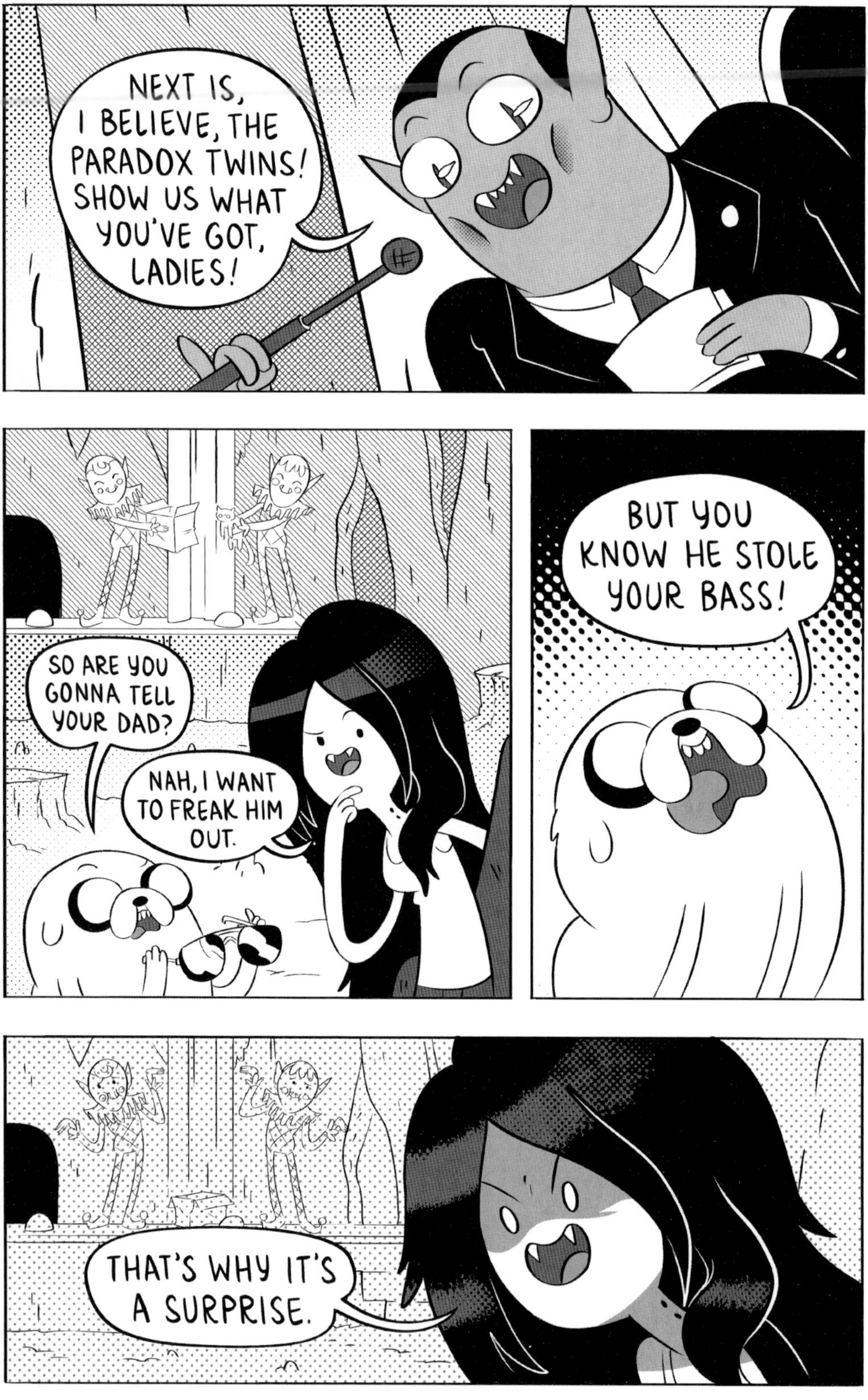
NEXT IS, I BELIEVE, THE PARADOX TWINS! SHOW US WHAT YOU'VE GOT, LADIES!
SO ARE YOU GONNA TELL YOUR DAD?
NAH, I WANT TO FREAK HIM OUT.
BUT YOU KNOW HE STOLE YOUR BASS!
THAT'S WHY IT'S A SURPRISE.

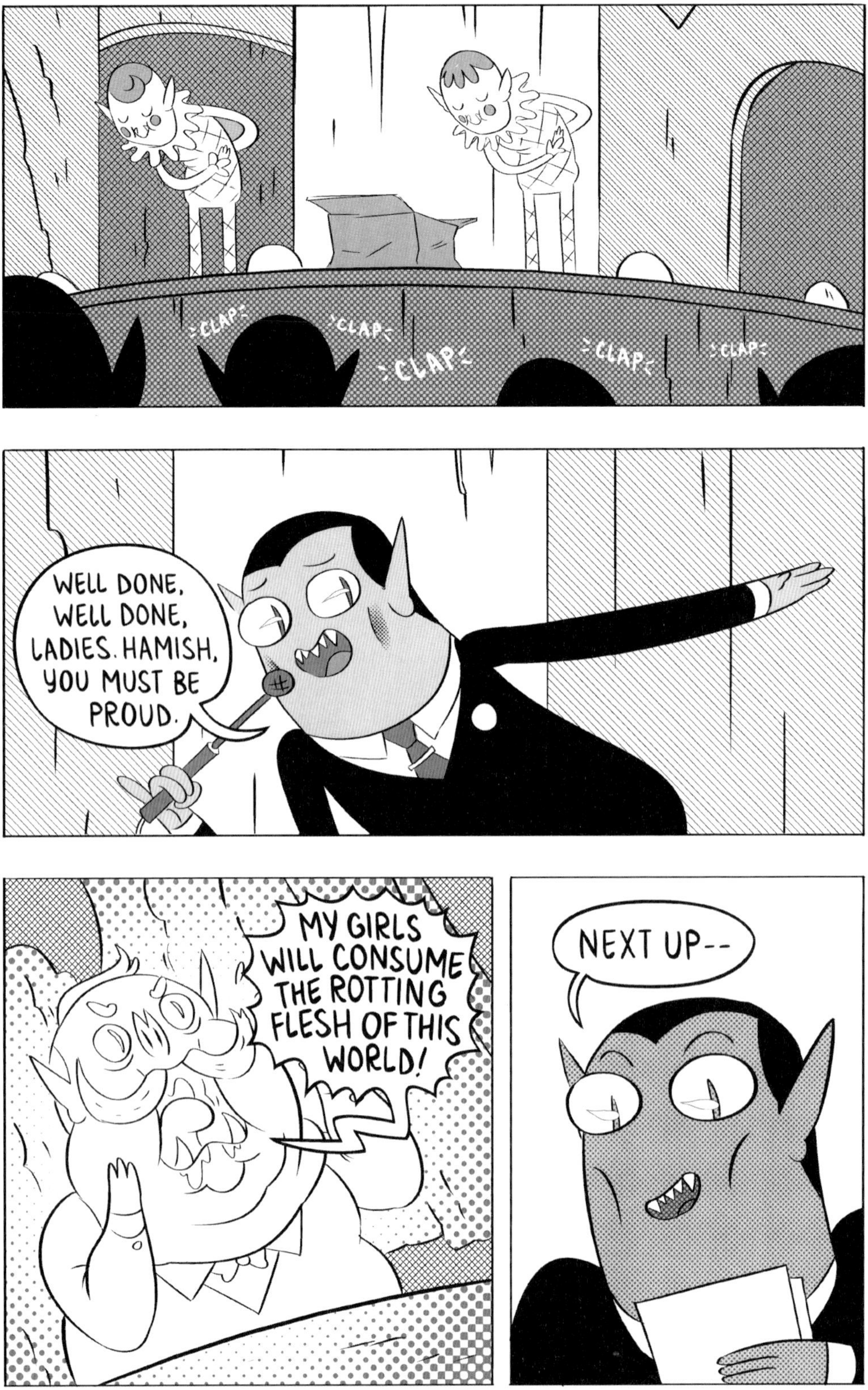
CLAP
CLAP
CLAP
CLAP
CLAP
WELL DONE, WELL DONE, LADIES. HAMISH, YOU MUST BE PROUD.
MY GIRLS WILL CONSUME THE ROTTING FLESH OF THIS WORLD!
NEXT UP--

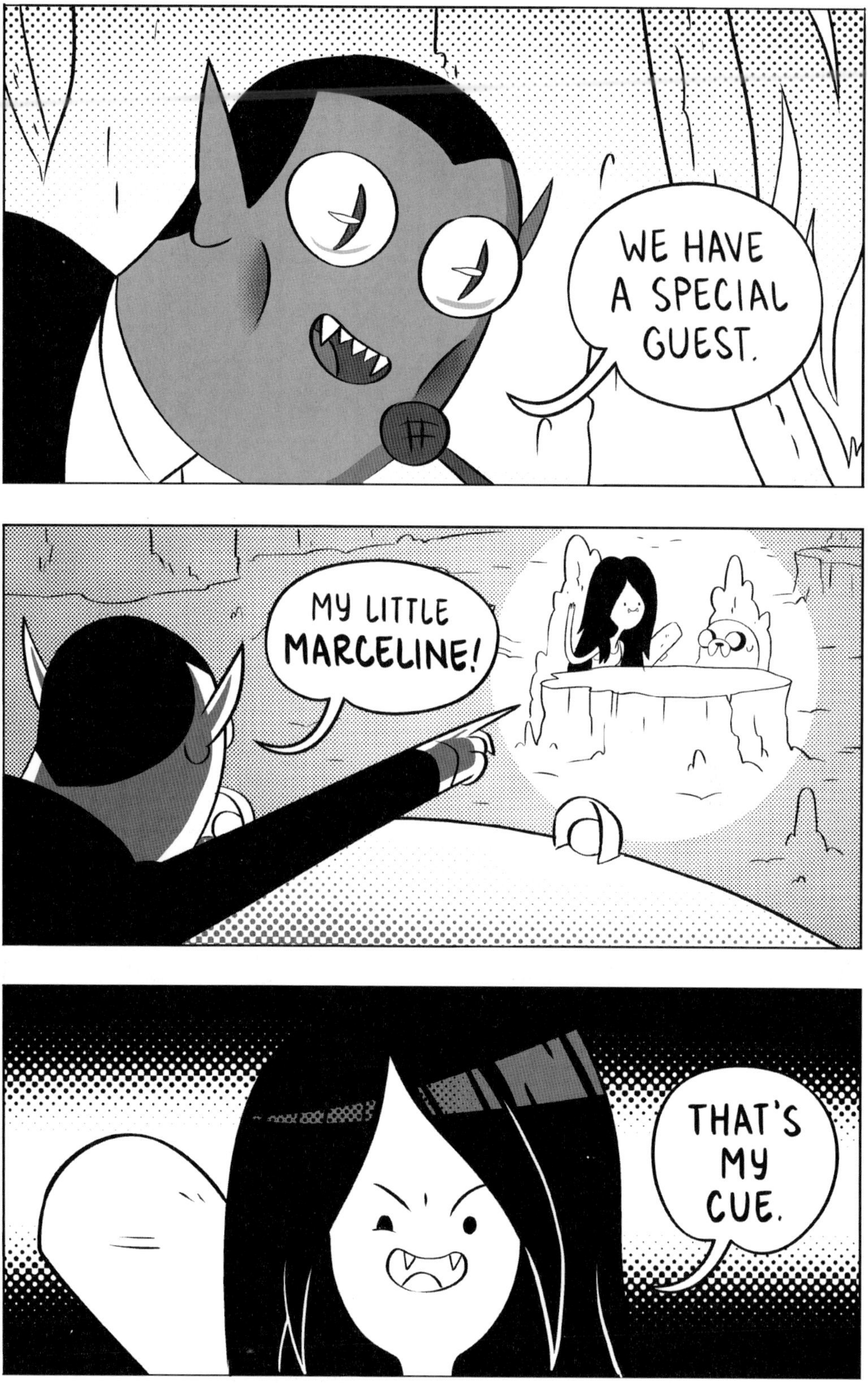
WE HAVE A SPECIAL GUEST.
MY LITTLE MARCELINE!
THAT'S MY CUE.

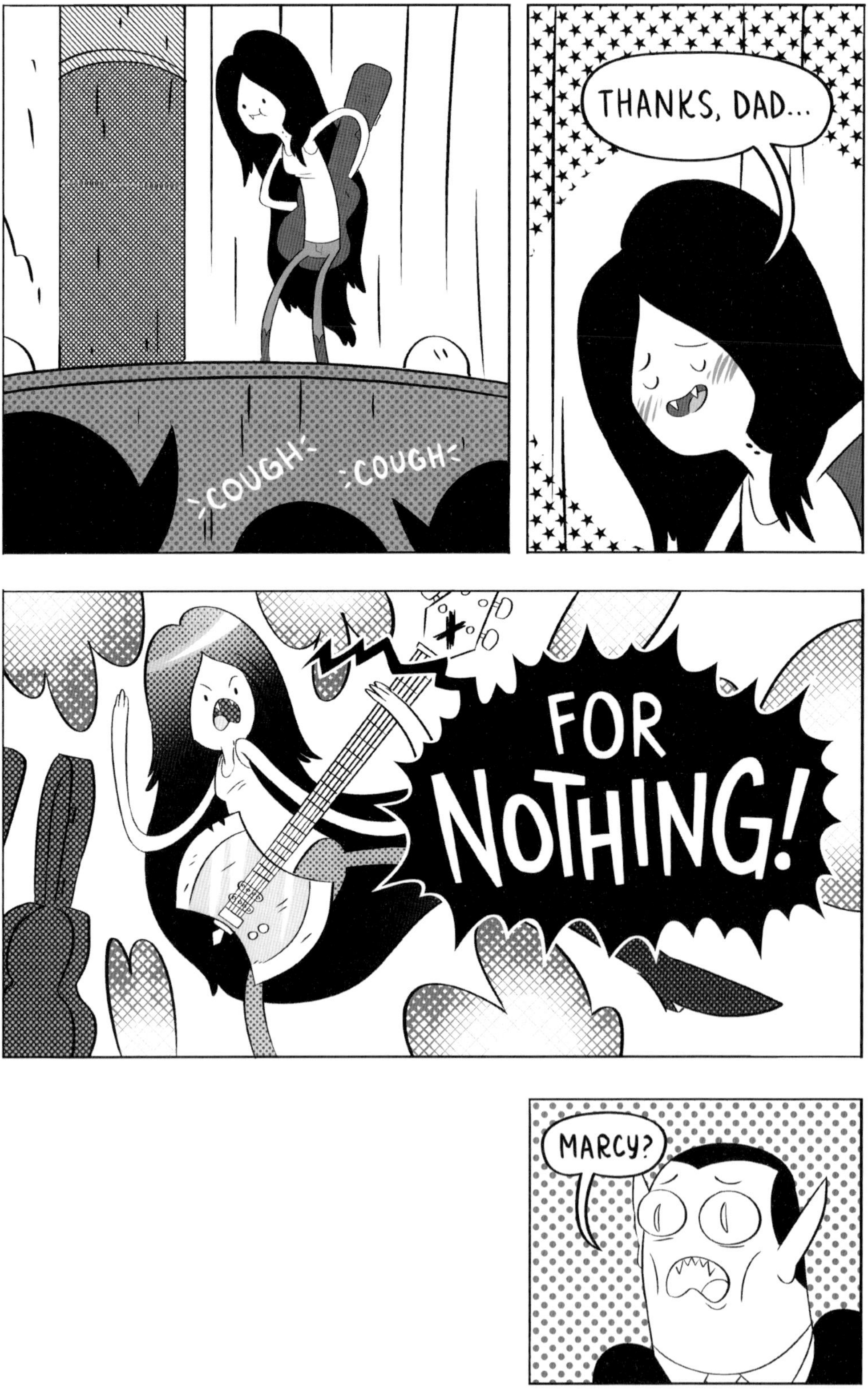
COUGH
COUGH
THANKS, DAD...
FOR NOTHING!
MARCY?

Well I took a long trip,
Through the long, dark night,
Fought my battles hard,
Ended up alright.
But I just don't
know what it means
To be back home.
Cause you didn't care
When I went away,
Took all the reasons
That I had to stay,
And I'm just not
sure you can be
A home sweet home.

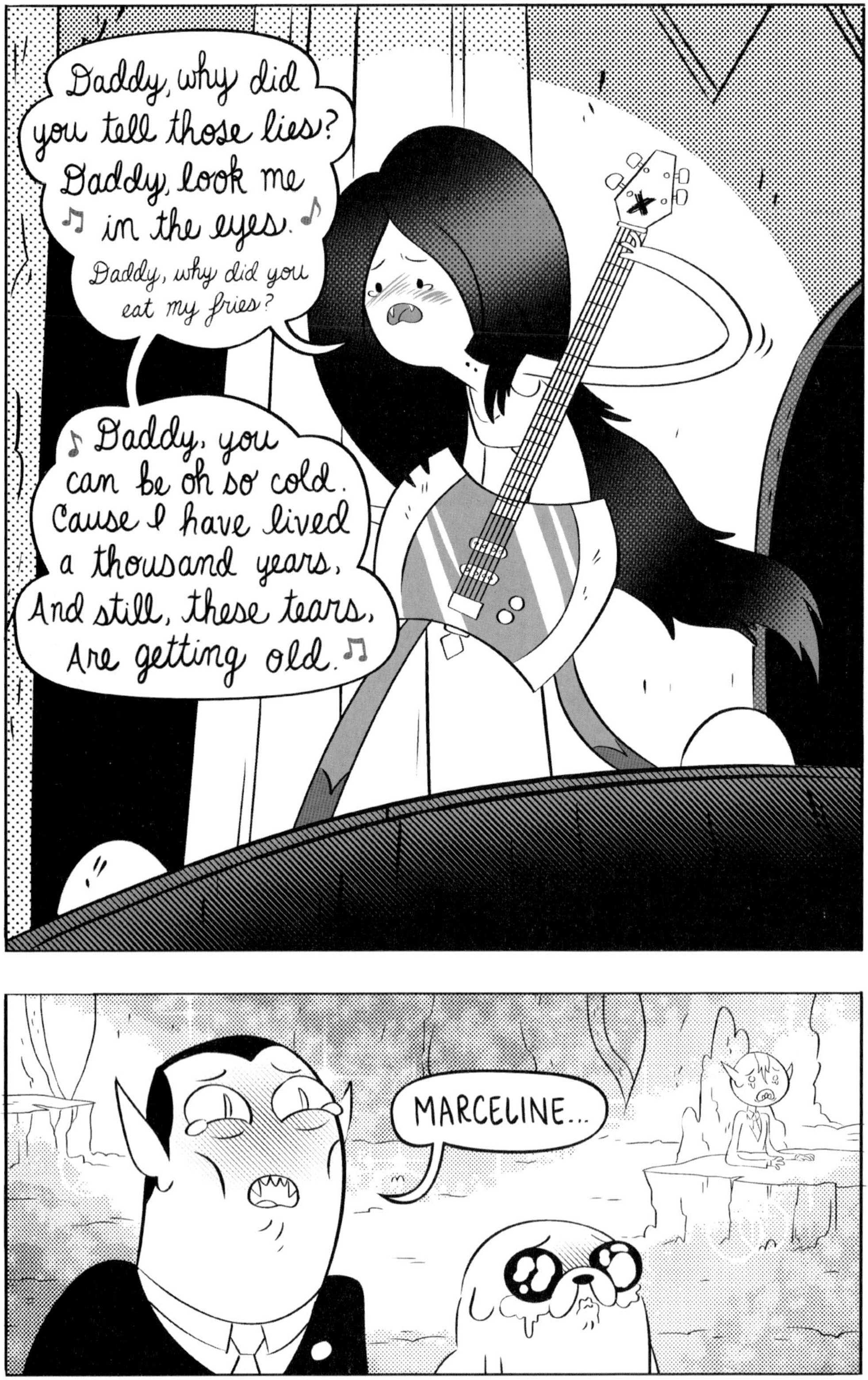
♫ Daddy, why did you tell those lies? Daddy, look me in the eyes. ♪
Daddy, why did you eat my fries?
♪ Daddy, you can be oh so cold. Cause I have lived a thousand years, And still, these tears, Are getting old. ♫
MARCELINE...

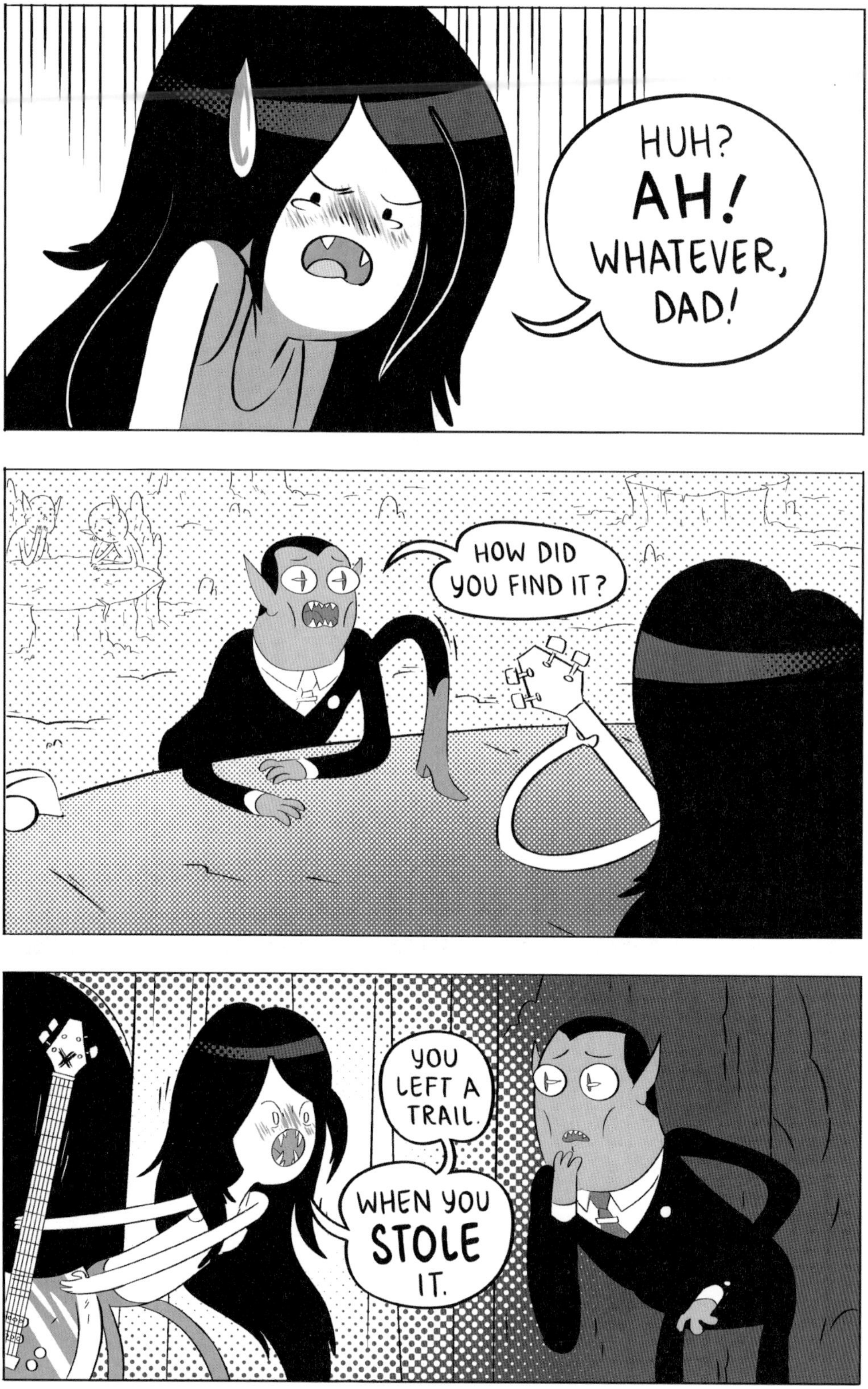
HUH? AH! WHATEVER, DAD!
HOW DID YOU FIND IT?
YOU LEFT A TRAIL.
WHEN YOU STOLE IT.

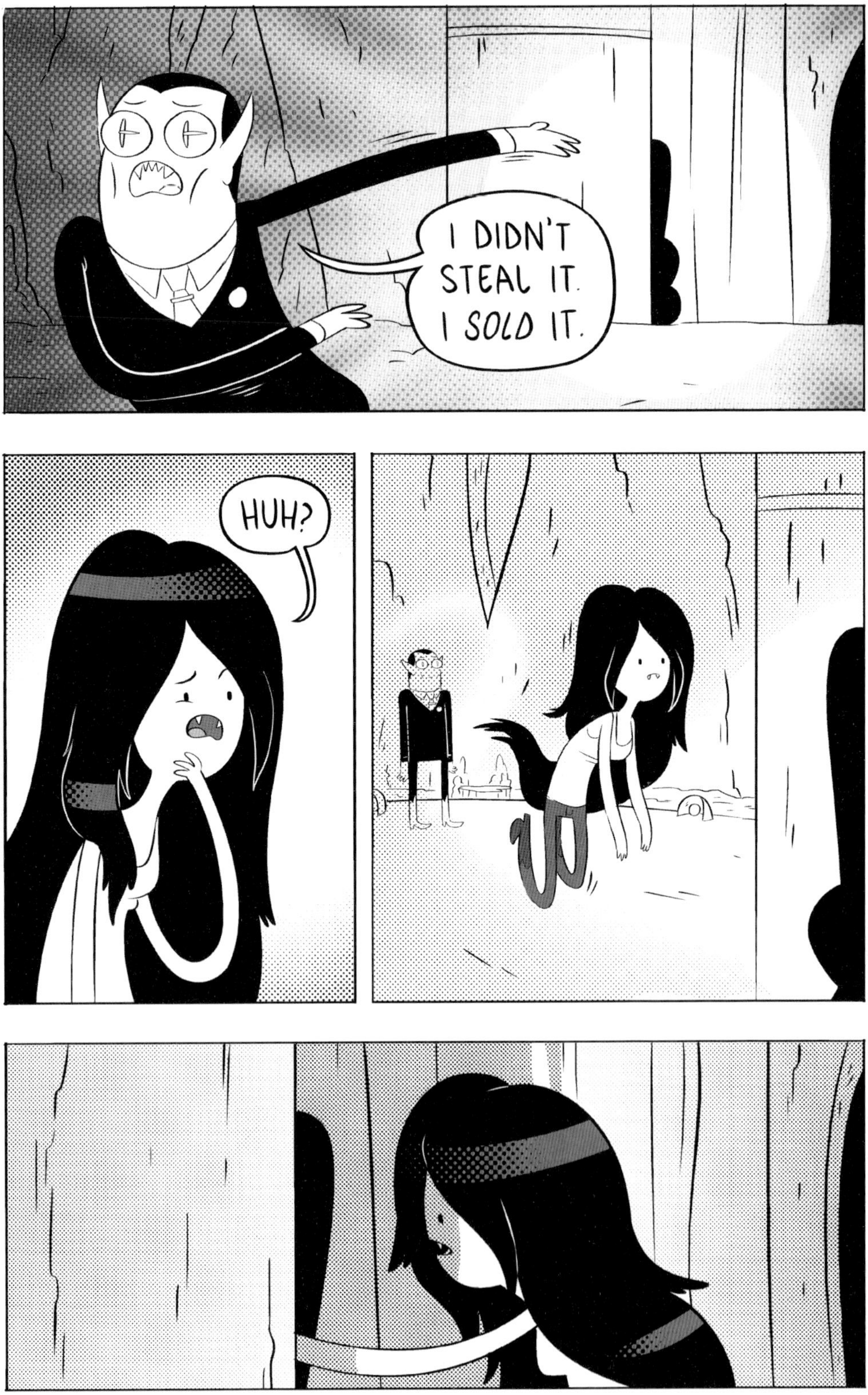
I DIDN'T STEAL IT. I SOLD IT.
HUH?

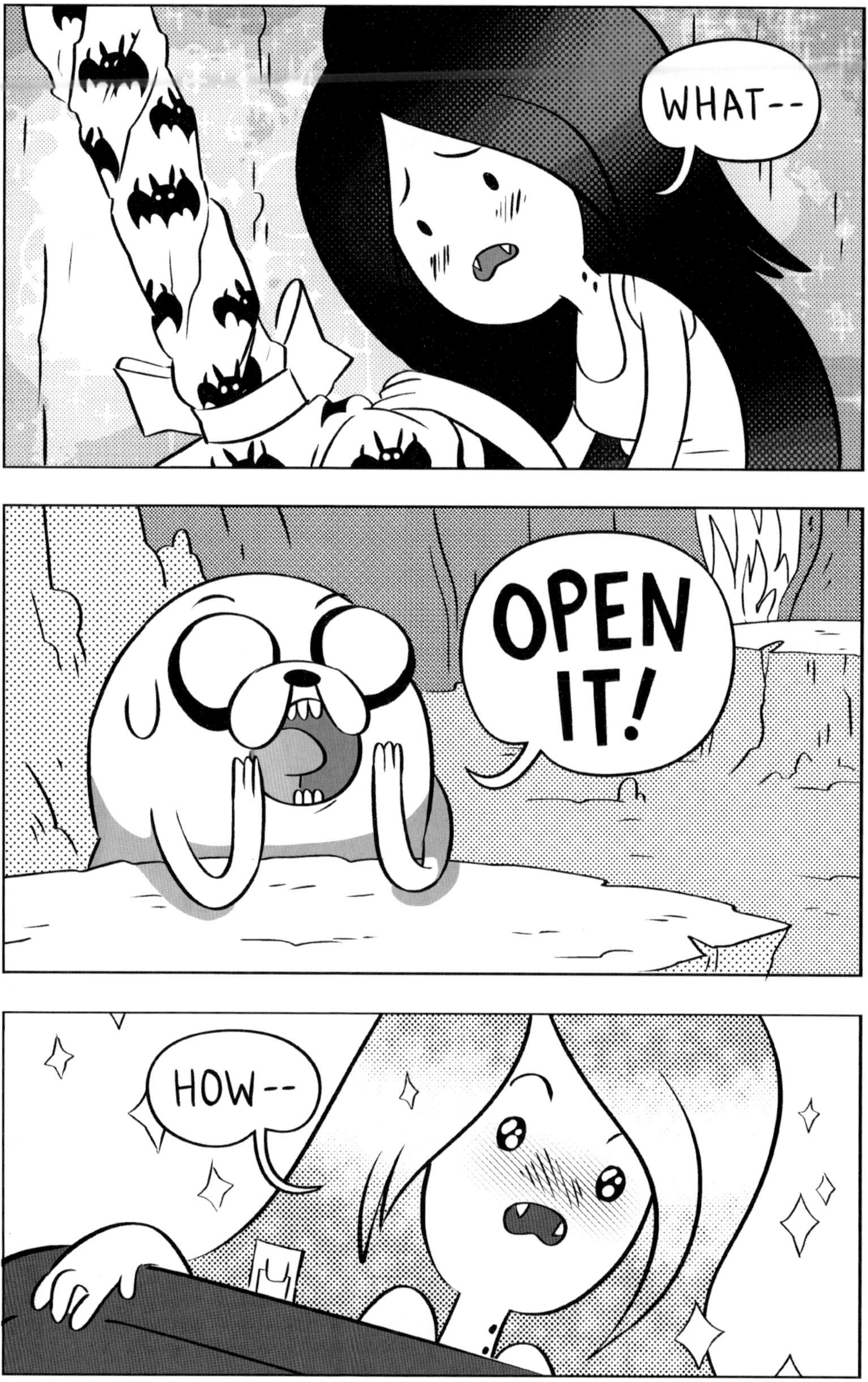
WHAT--
OPEN IT!
HOW--

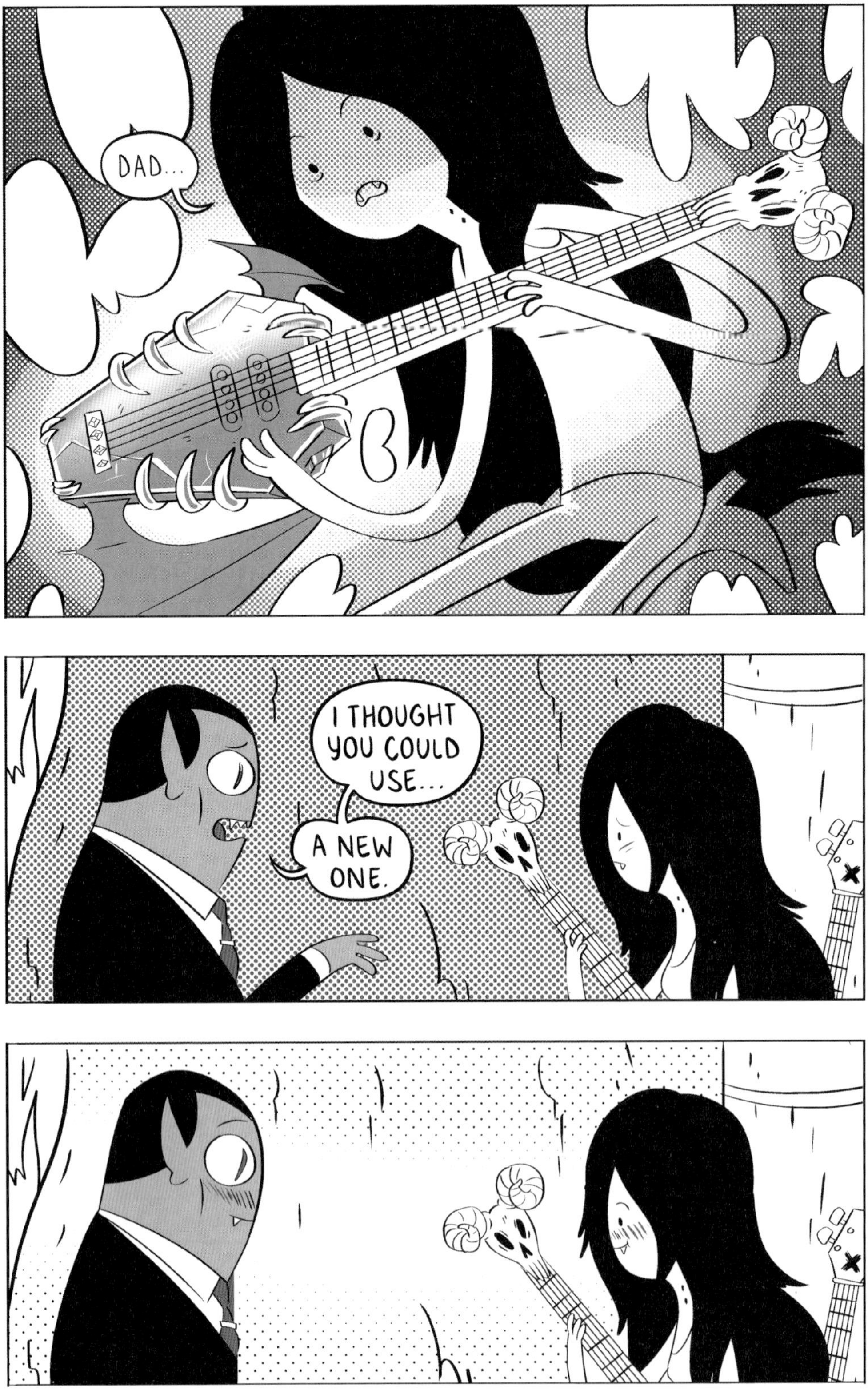
DAD...
I THOUGHT YOU COULD USE...
A NEW ONE.

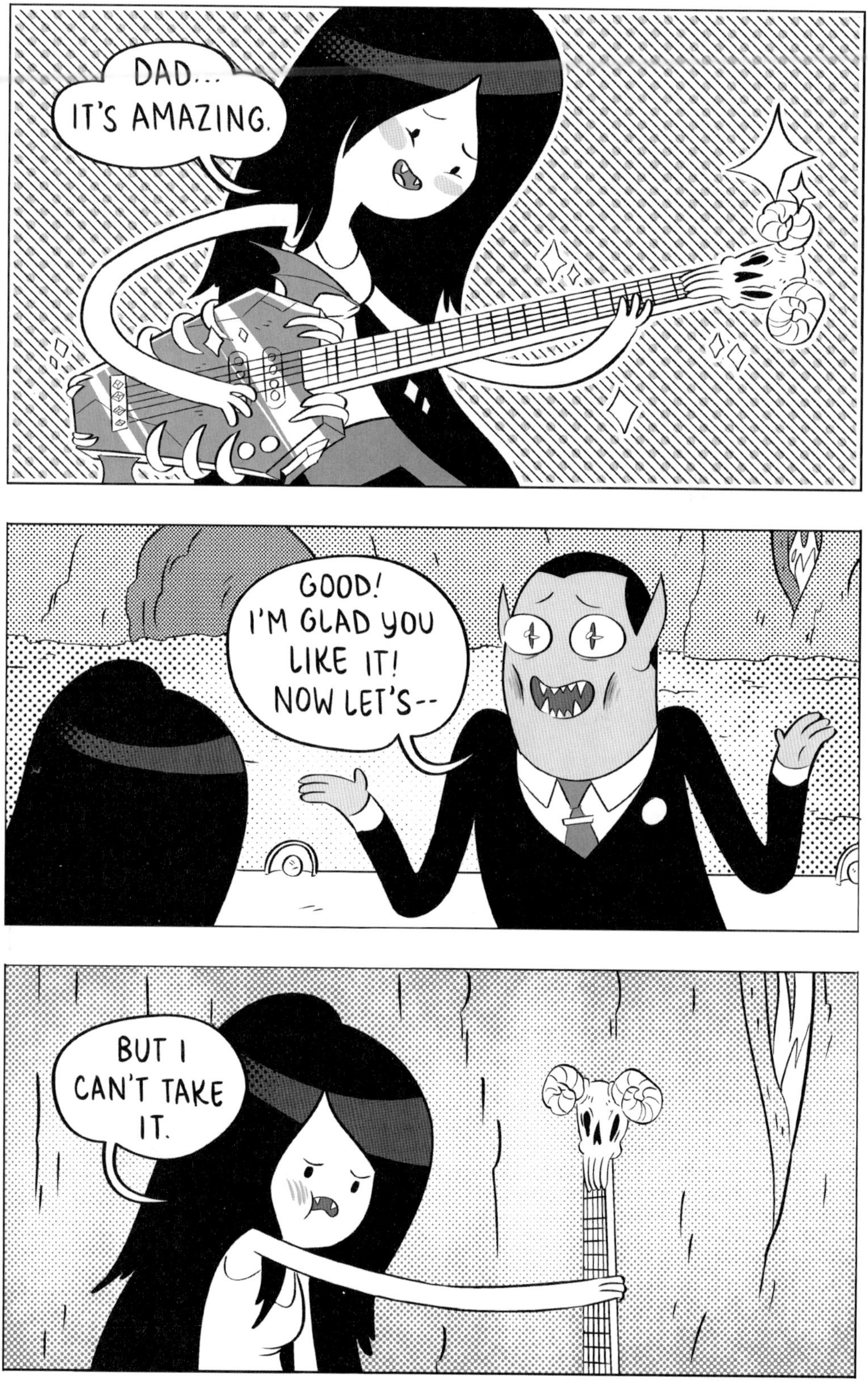
DAD... IT'S AMAZING.
GOOD! I'M GLAD YOU LIKE IT! NOW LET'S--
BUT I CAN'T TAKE IT.

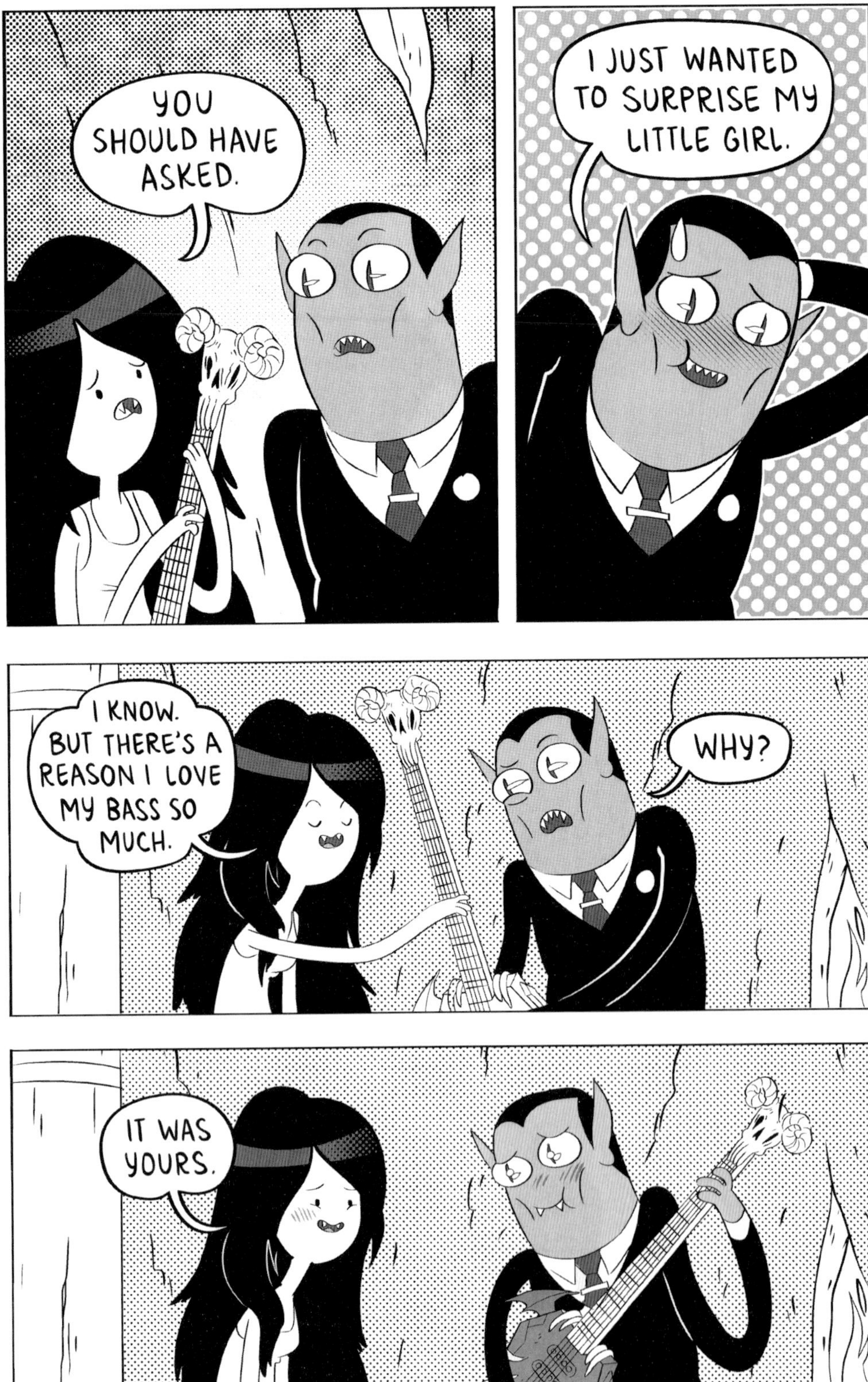
YOU SHOULD HAVE ASKED.
I JUST WANTED TO SURPRISE MY LITTLE GIRL.
I KNOW. BUT THERE'S A REASON I LOVE MY BASS SO MUCH.
WHY?
IT WAS YOURS.

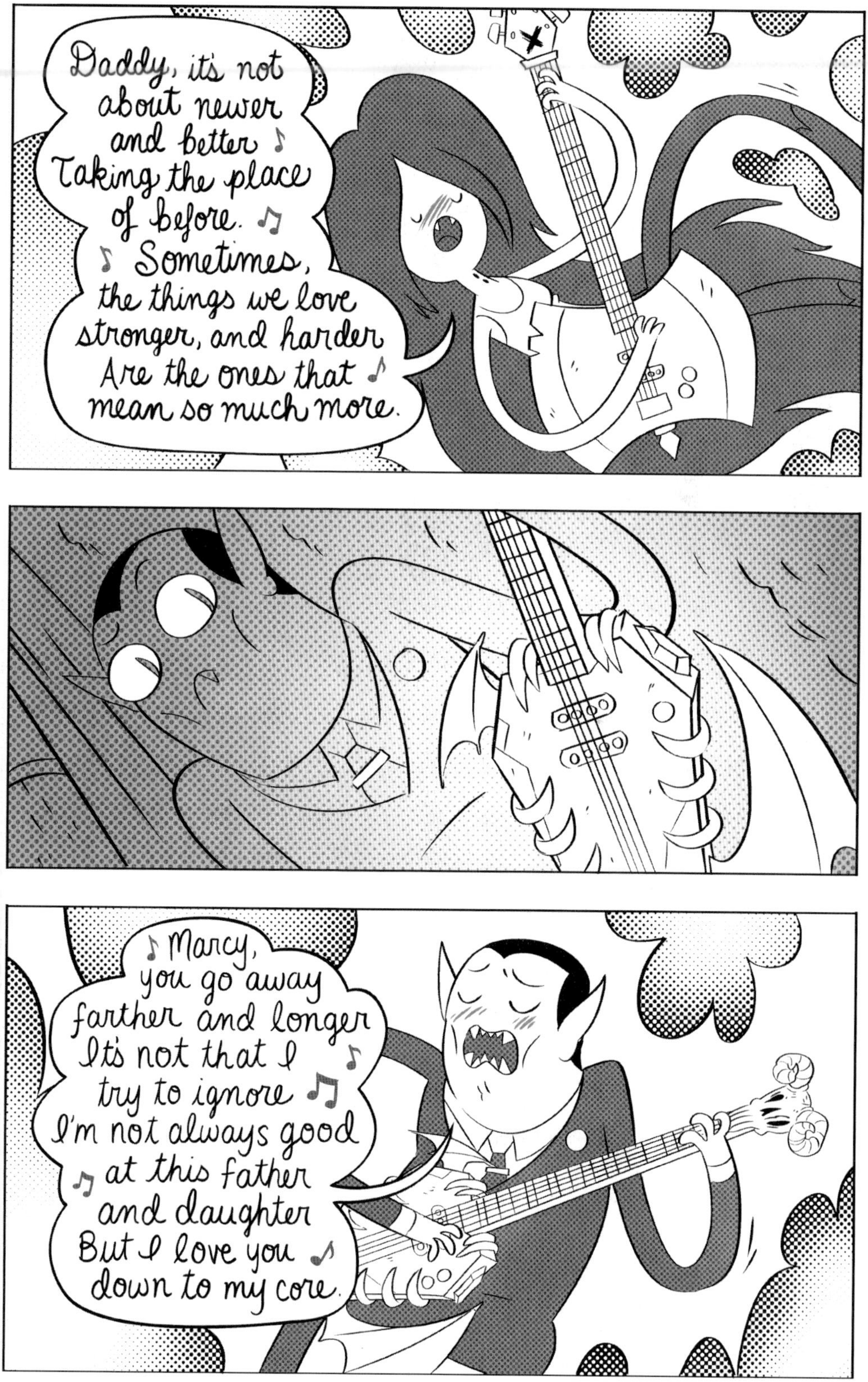
Daddy, it's not about newer and better ♪ Taking the place of before. ♫ ♪ Sometimes, the things we love stronger, and harder Are the ones that ♪ mean so much more.
♪ Marcy, you go away farther and longer It's not that I ♪ try to ignore ♫ I'm not always good ♫ at this father and daughter But I love you ♪ down to my core.

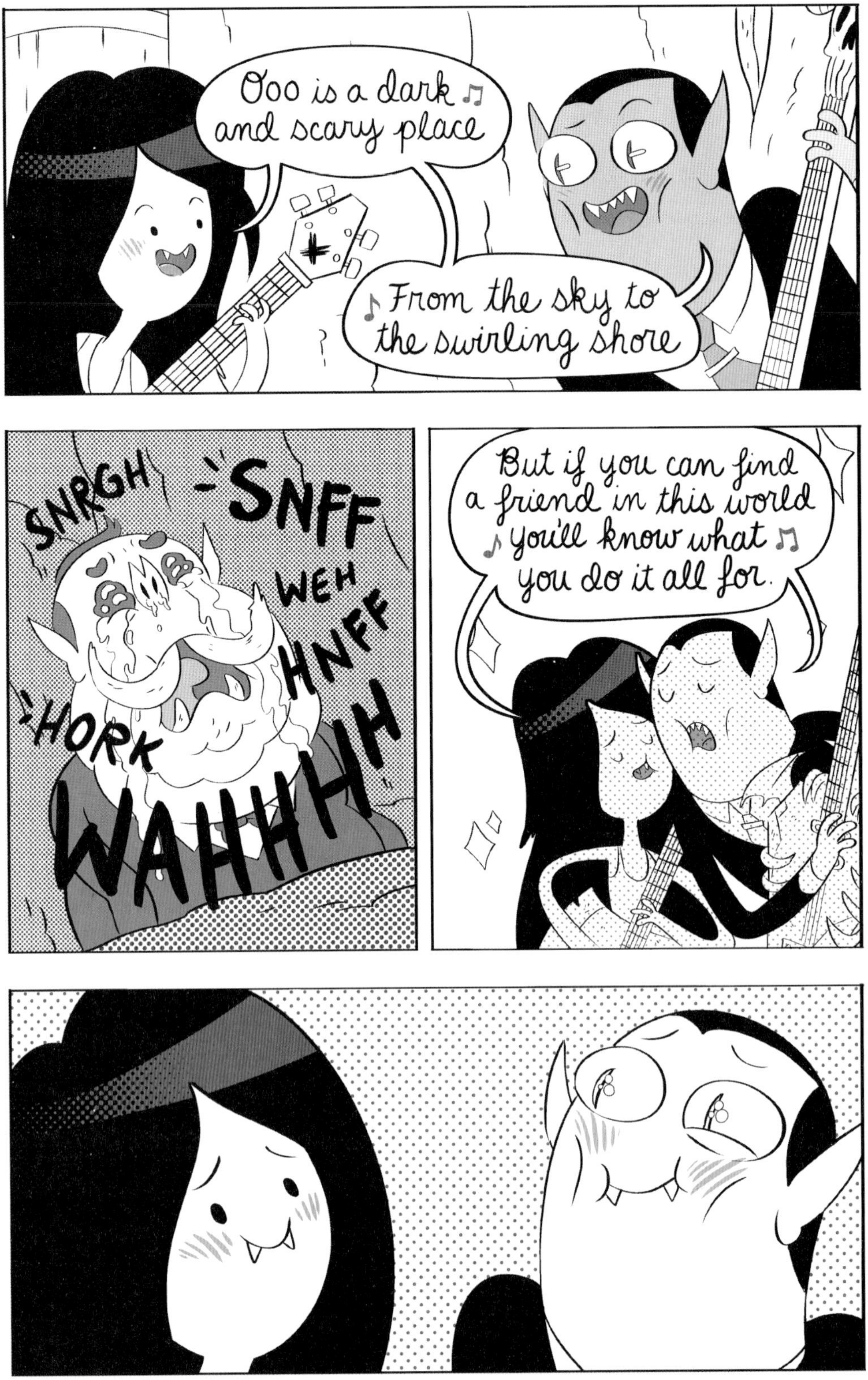
Ooo is a dark and scary place
From the sky to the swirling shore
SNRGH
SNFF
WEH
HNFF
HORK
WAHHHH
But if you can find a friend in this world you'll know what you do it all for.

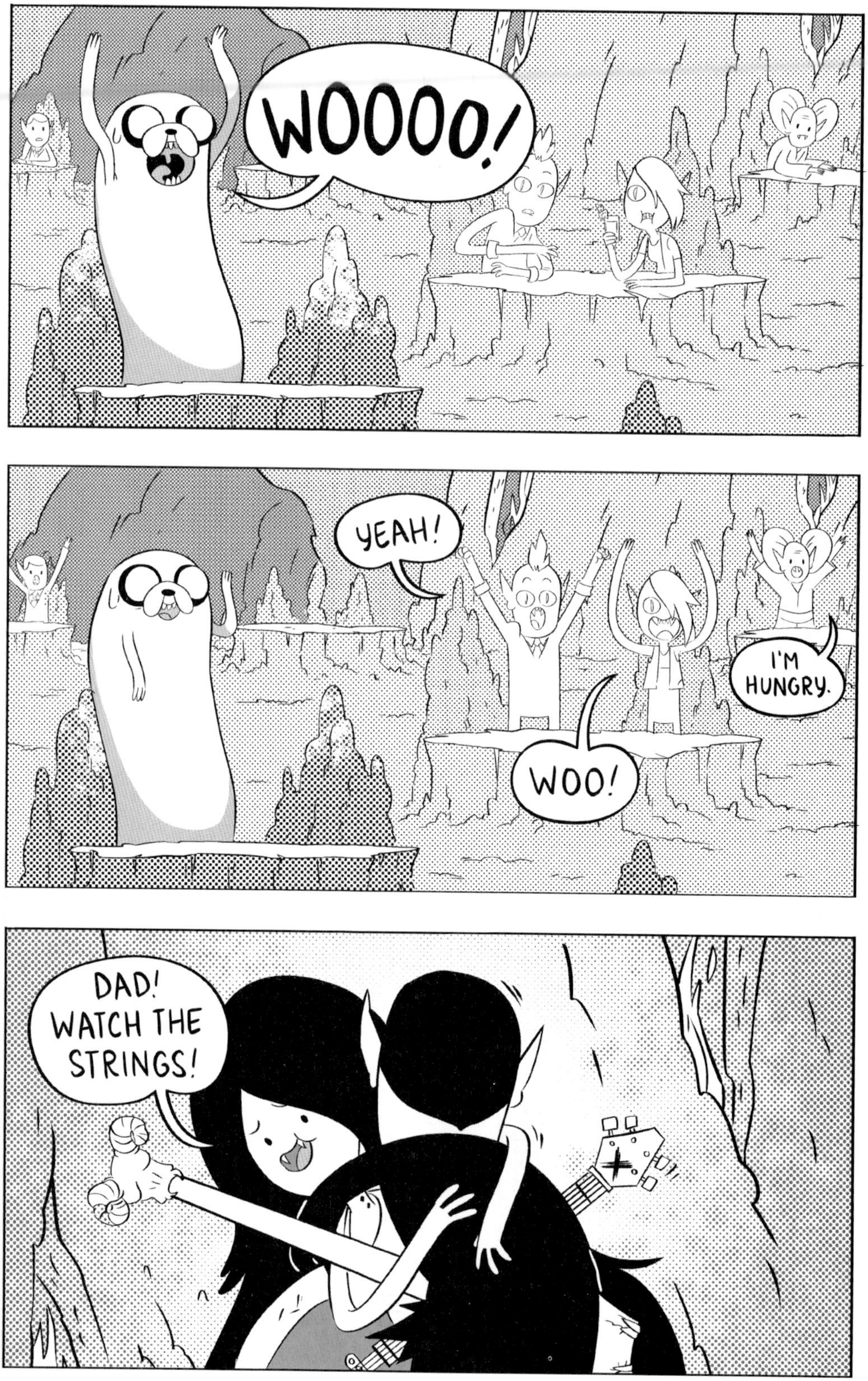
WOOOO!
YEAH!
I'M HUNGRY.
WOO!
DAD! WATCH THE STRINGS!

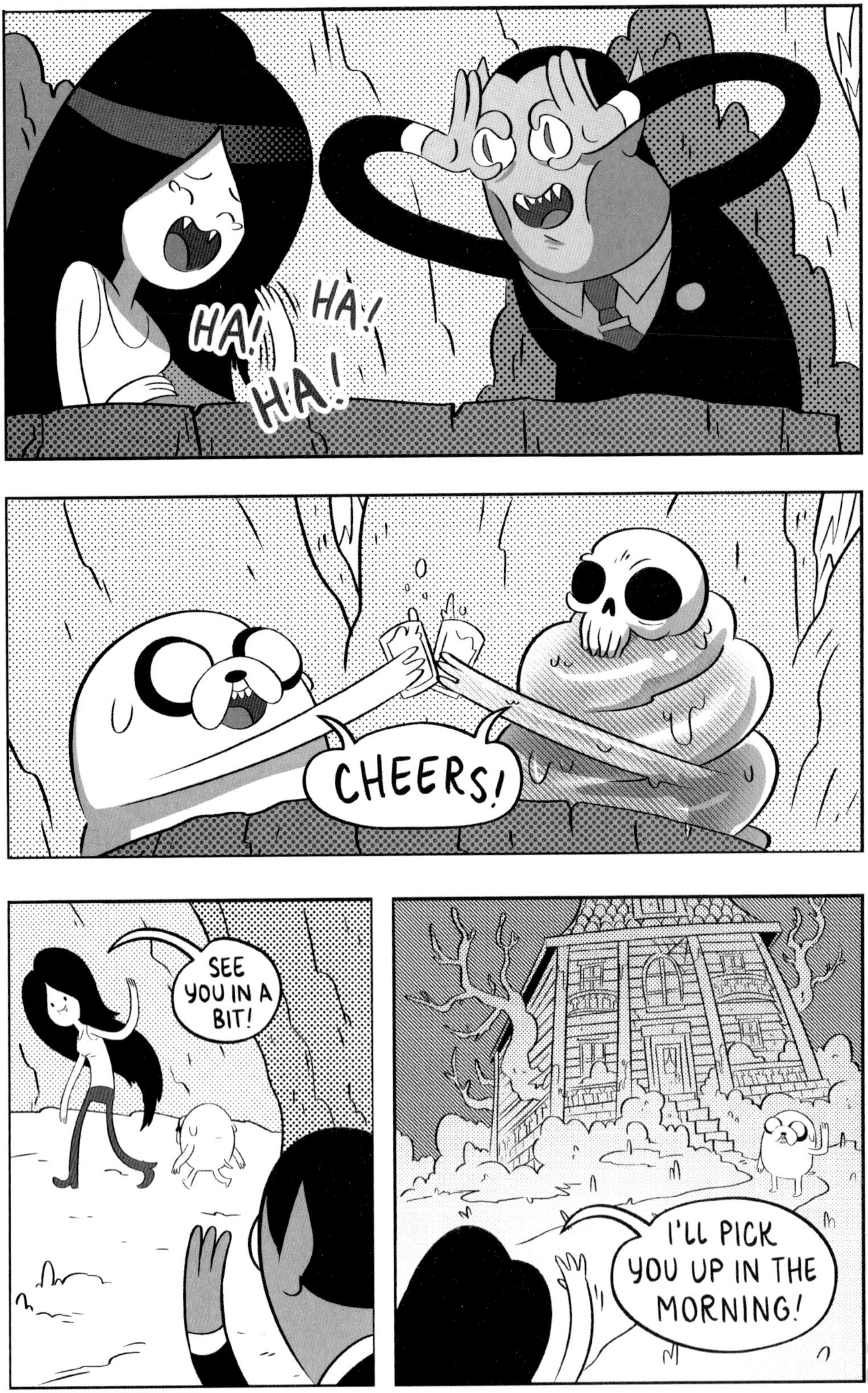
HA! HA! HA!
CHEERS!
SEE YOU IN A BIT!
I'LL PICK YOU UP IN THE MORNING!

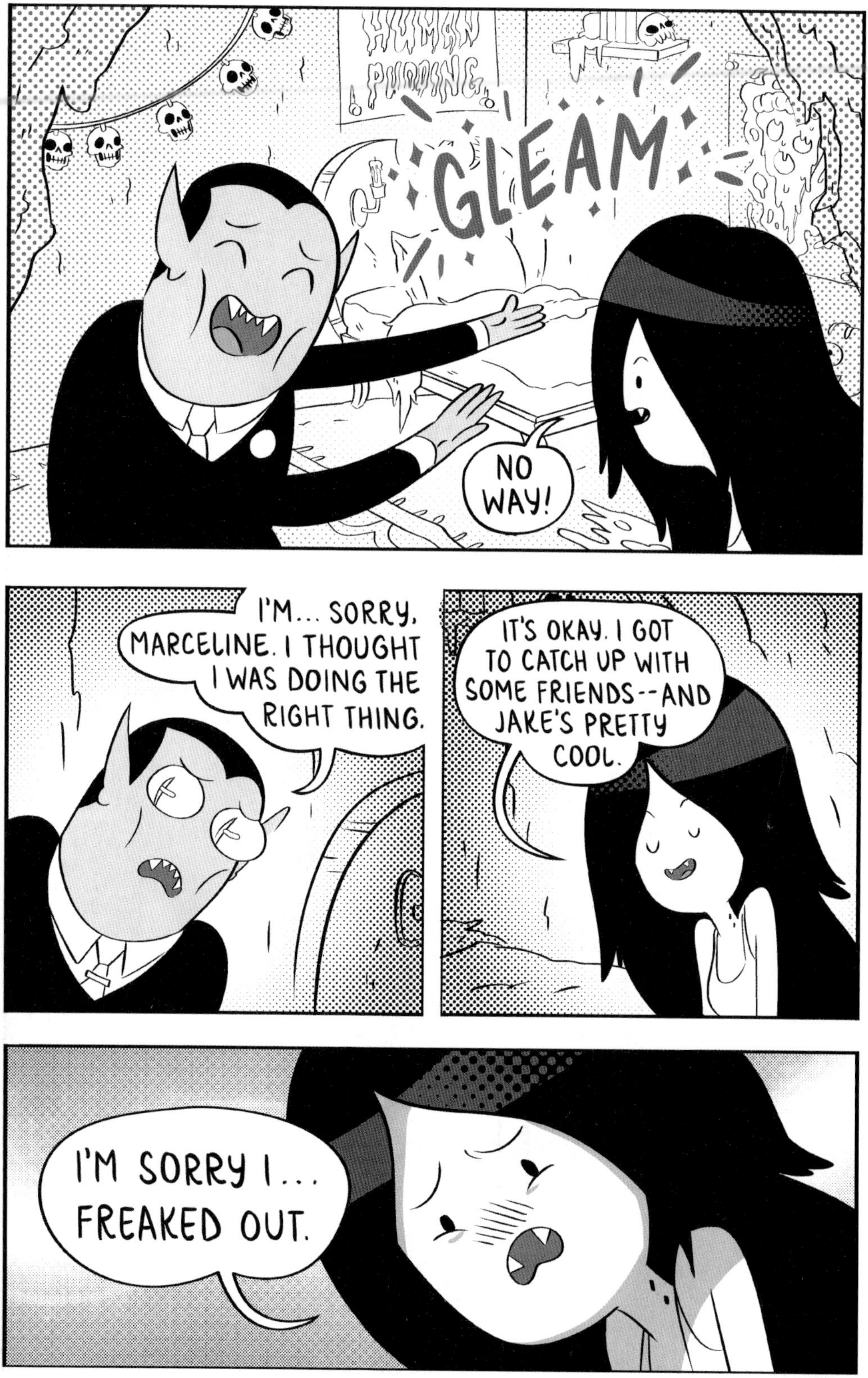
GLEAM
HUMAN PUDDING
NO WAY!
I'M... SORRY, MARCELINE. I THOUGHT I WAS DOING THE RIGHT THING.
IT'S OKAY. I GOT TO CATCH UP WITH SOME FRIENDS--AND JAKE'S PRETTY COOL.
I'M SORRY I... FREAKED OUT.

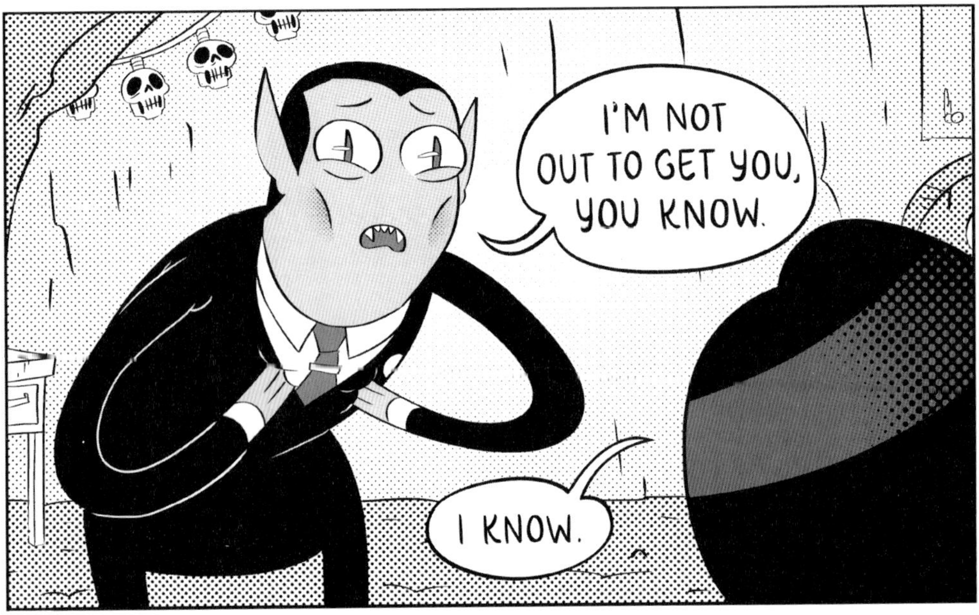
I'M NOT OUT TO GET YOU, YOU KNOW.
I KNOW.

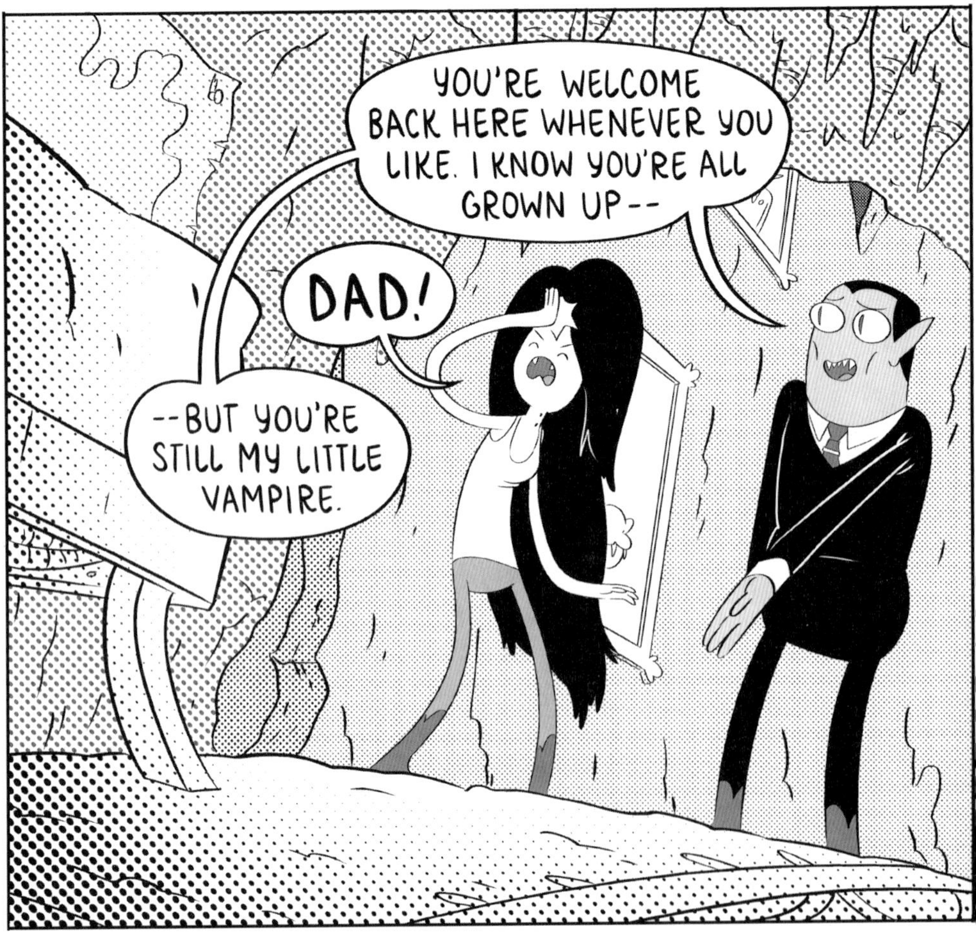
YOU'RE WELCOME BACK HERE WHENEVER YOU LIKE. I KNOW YOU'RE ALL GROWN UP--
DAD!
--BUT YOU'RE STILL MY LITTLE VAMPIRE.

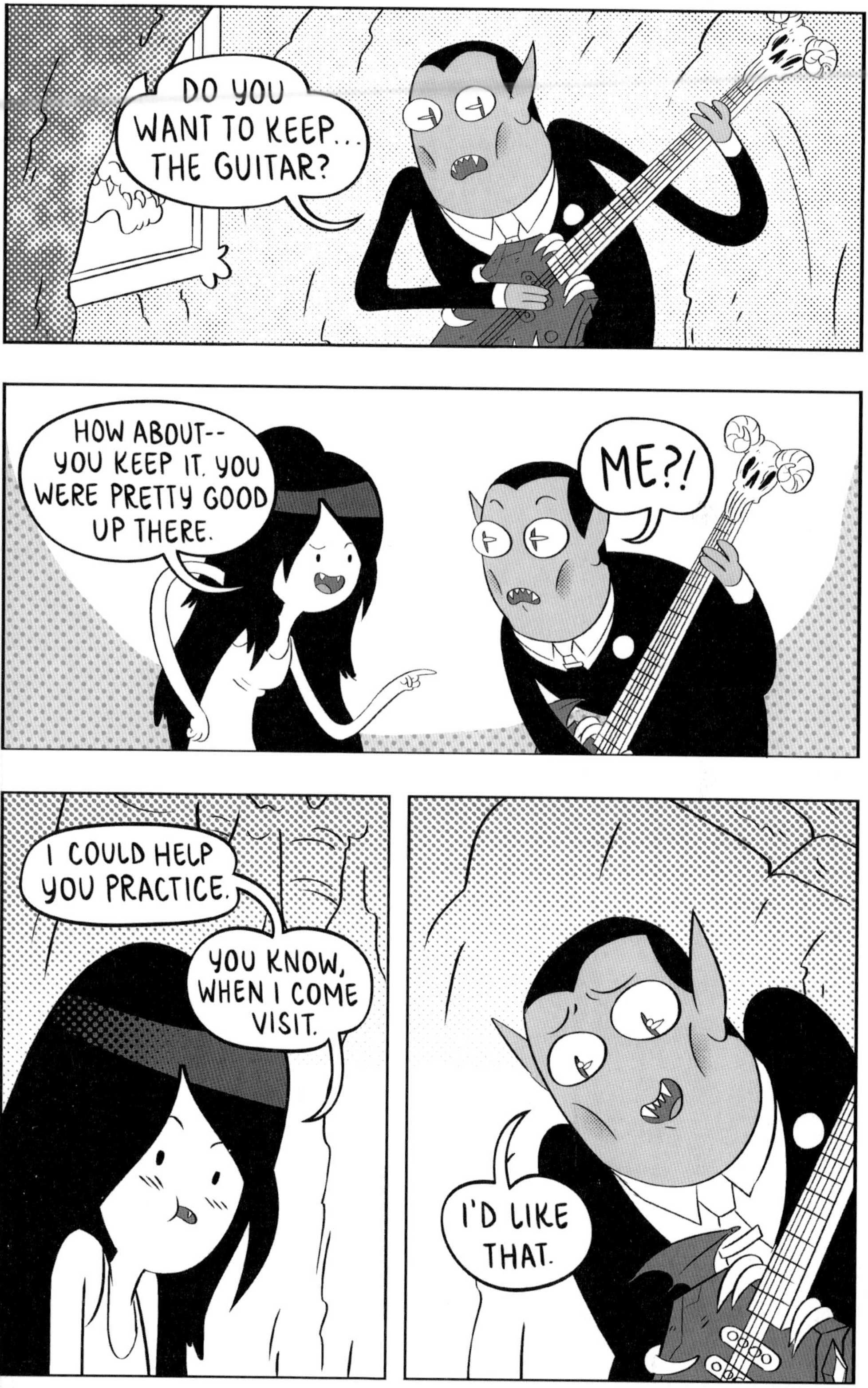
DO YOU WANT TO KEEP... THE GUITAR?
HOW ABOUT-- YOU KEEP IT. YOU WERE PRETTY GOOD UP THERE.
ME?!
I COULD HELP YOU PRACTICE.
YOU KNOW, WHEN I COME VISIT.
I'D LIKE THAT.

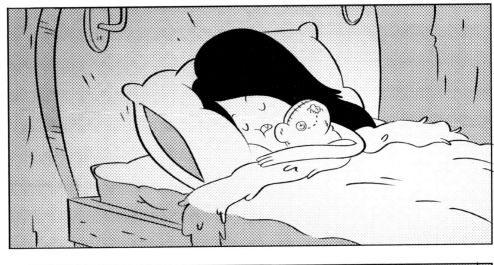

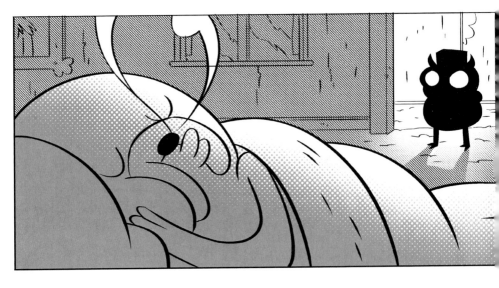

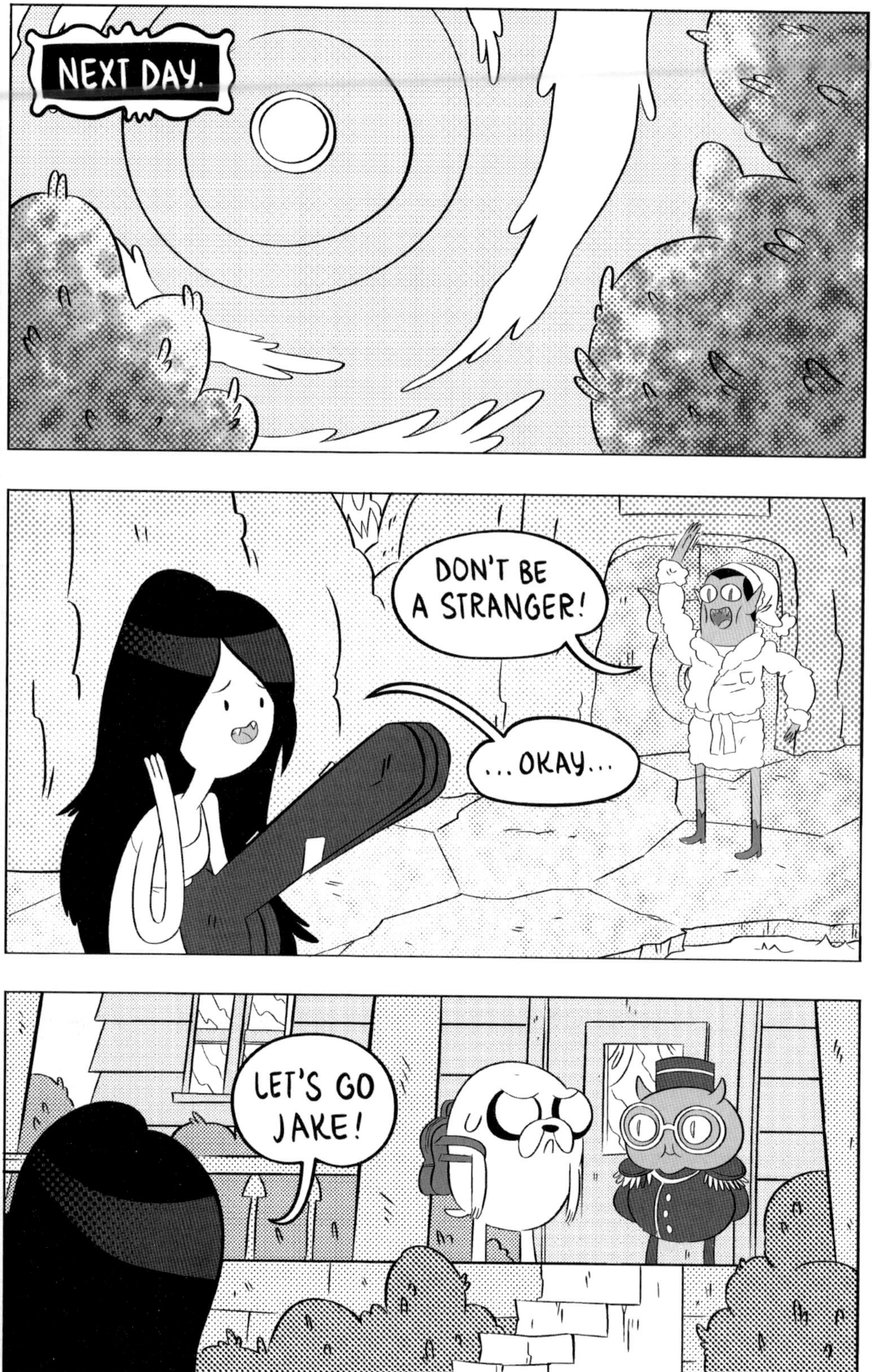
NEXT DAY.
DON'T BE A STRANGER!
...OKAY...
LET'S GO JAKE!

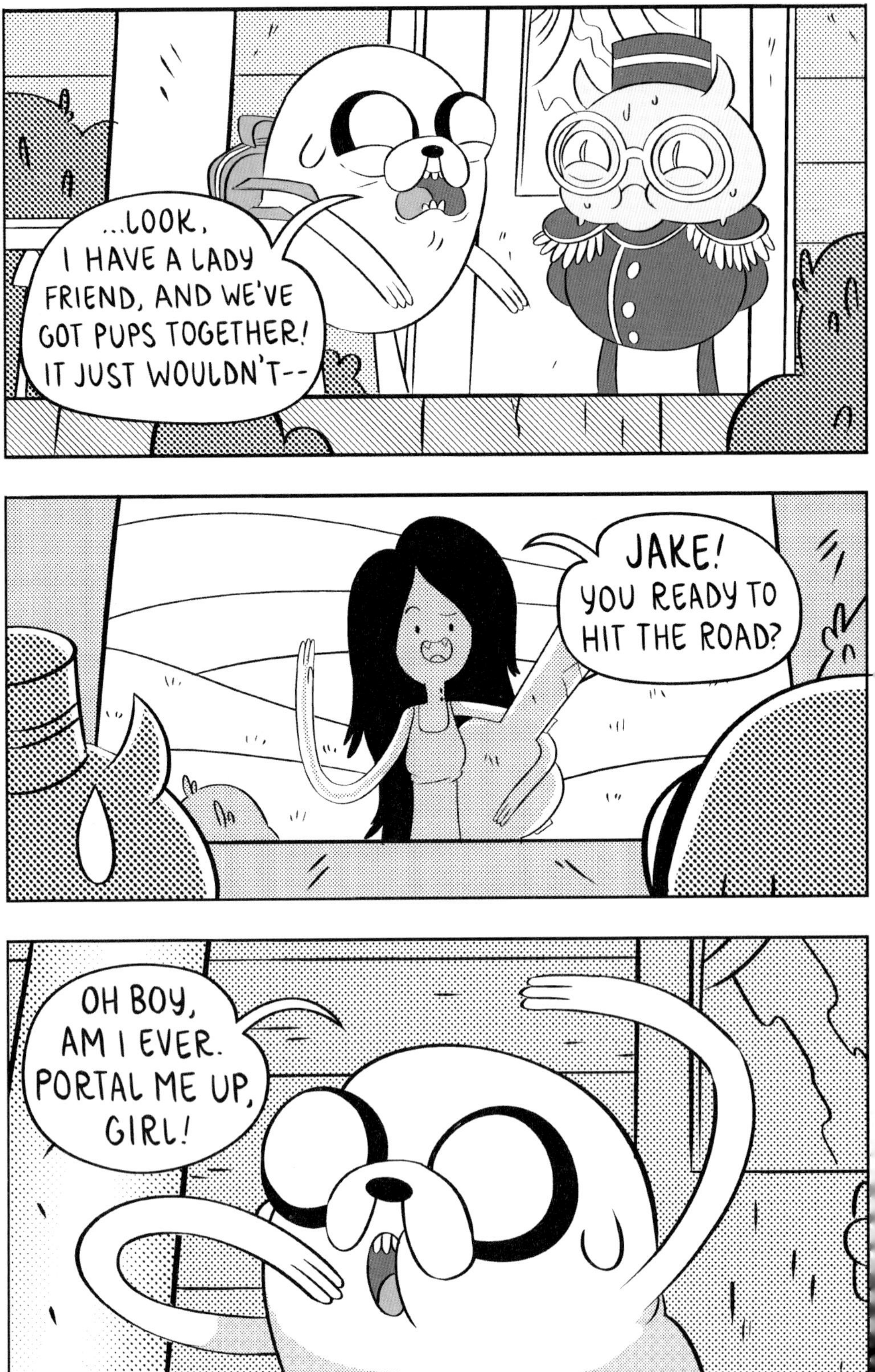
...LOOK, I HAVE A LADY FRIEND, AND WE'VE GOT PUPS TOGETHER! IT JUST WOULDN'T--
JAKE! YOU READY TO HIT THE ROAD?
OH BOY, AM I EVER. PORTAL ME UP, GIRL!

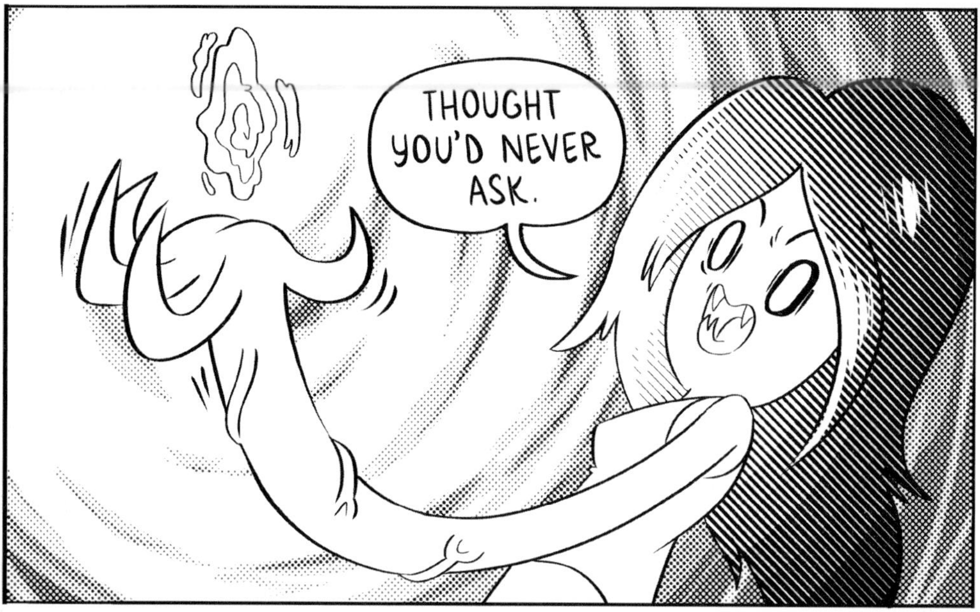
THOUGHT YOU'D NEVER ASK.

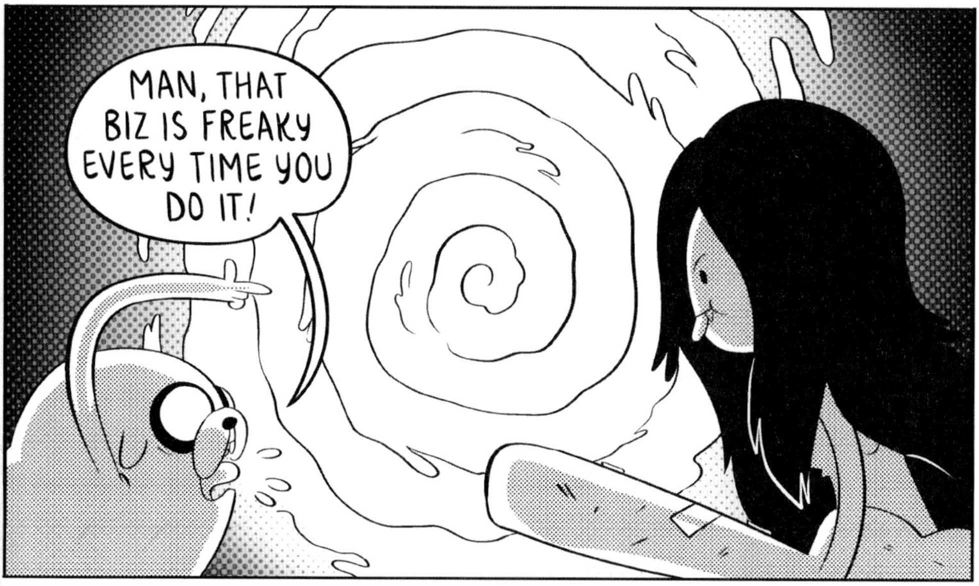
MAN, THAT BIZ IS FREAKY EVERY TIME YOU DO IT!

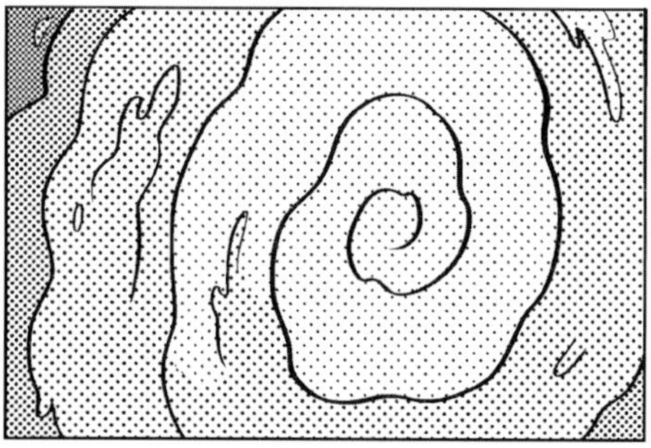

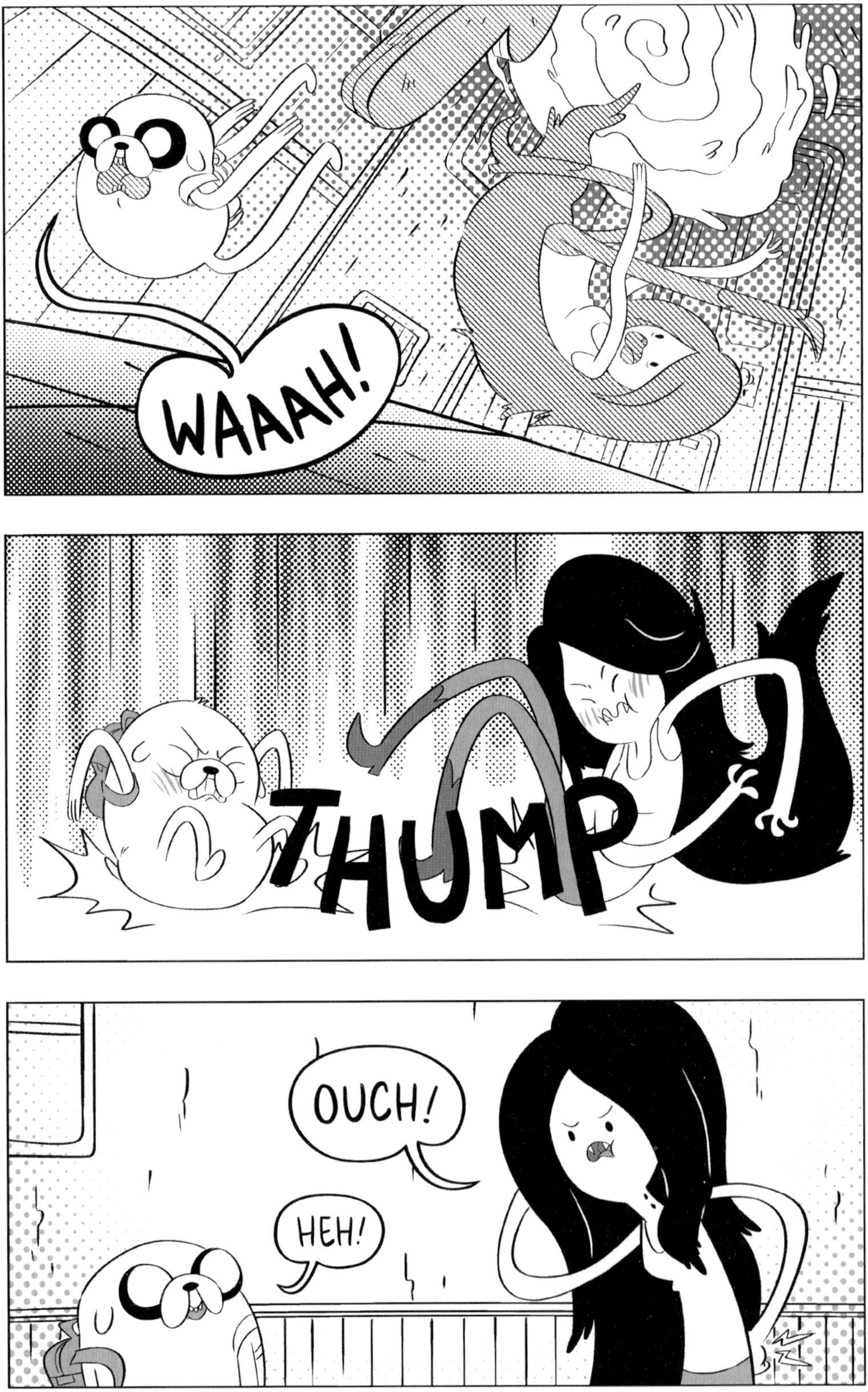
WAAAH!
THUMP
OUCH!
HEH!

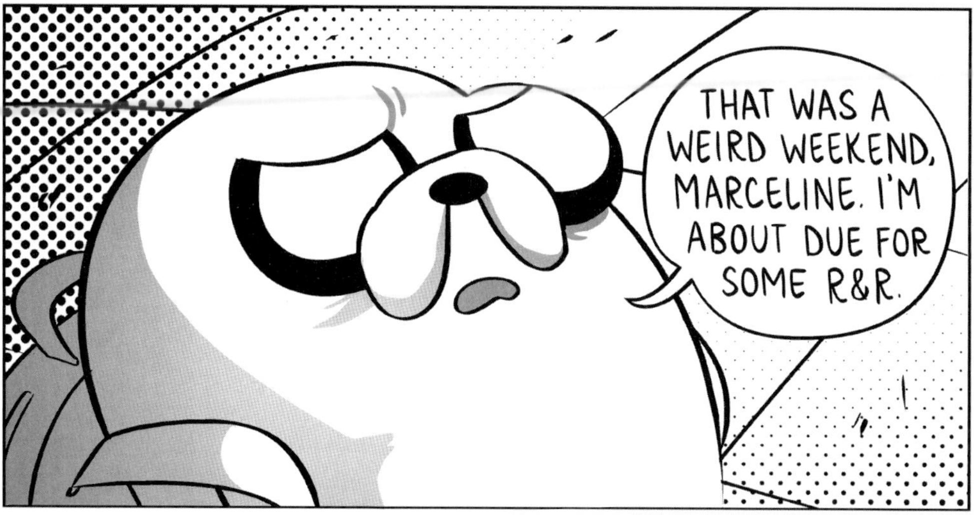
THAT WAS A WEIRD WEEKEND, MARCELINE. I'M ABOUT DUE FOR SOME R&R.

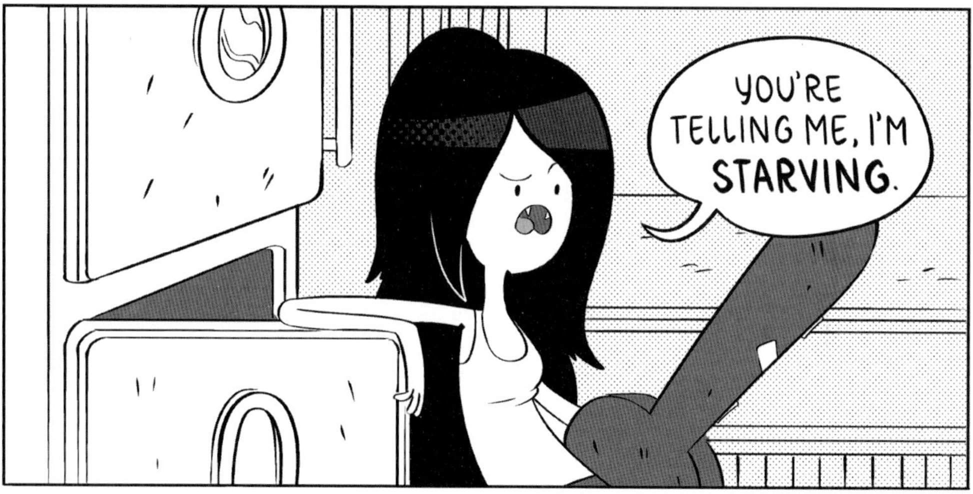
YOU'RE TELLING ME, I'M **STARVING**.

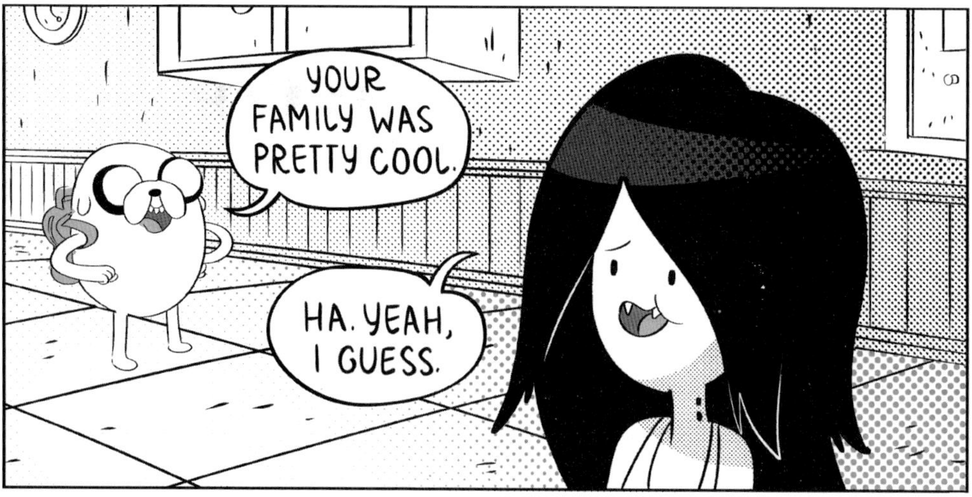
YOUR FAMILY WAS PRETTY COOL.
HA. YEAH, I GUESS.

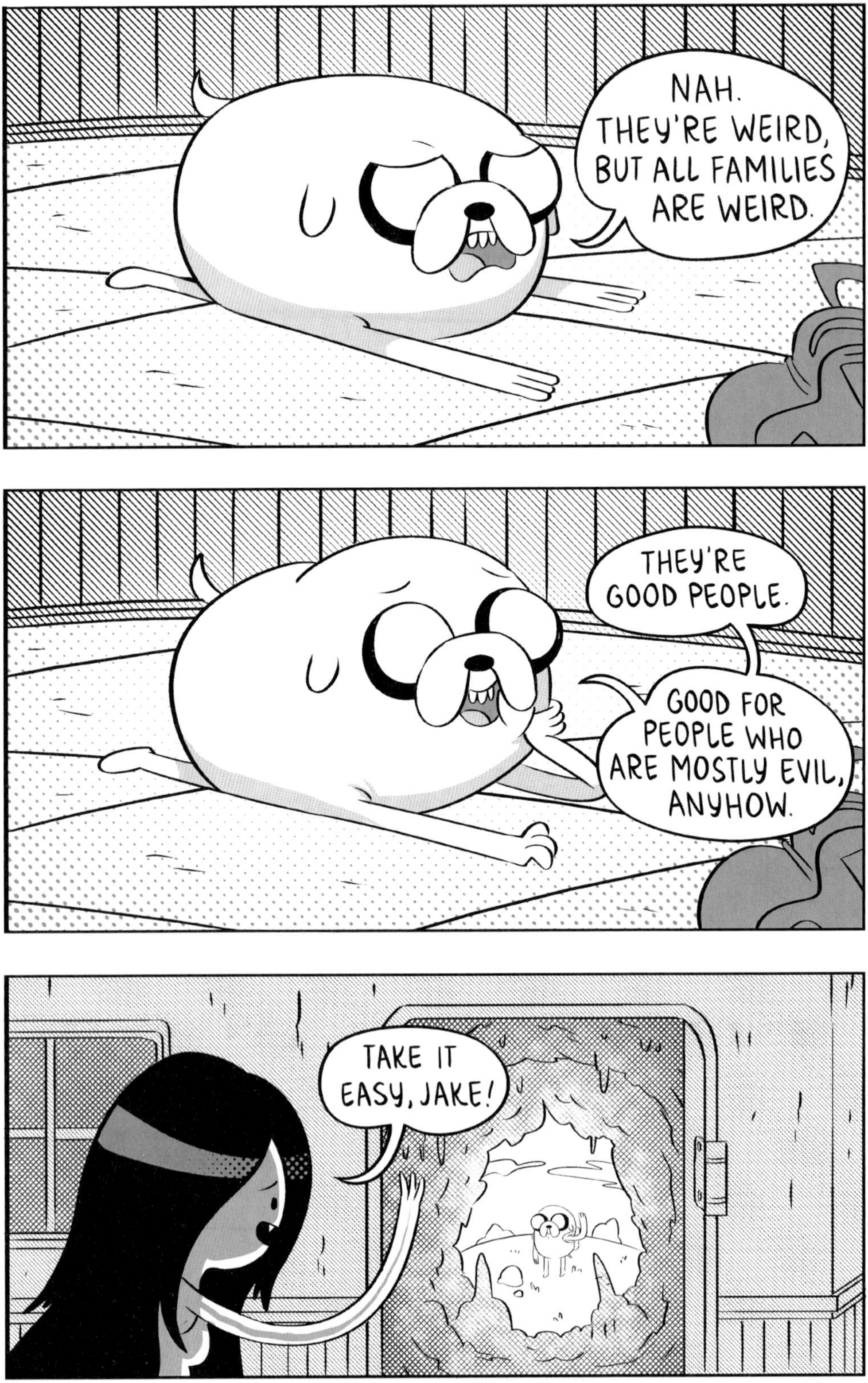
NAH. THEY'RE WEIRD, BUT ALL FAMILIES ARE WEIRD.
THEY'RE GOOD PEOPLE.
GOOD FOR PEOPLE WHO ARE MOSTLY EVIL, ANYHOW.
TAKE IT EASY, JAKE!

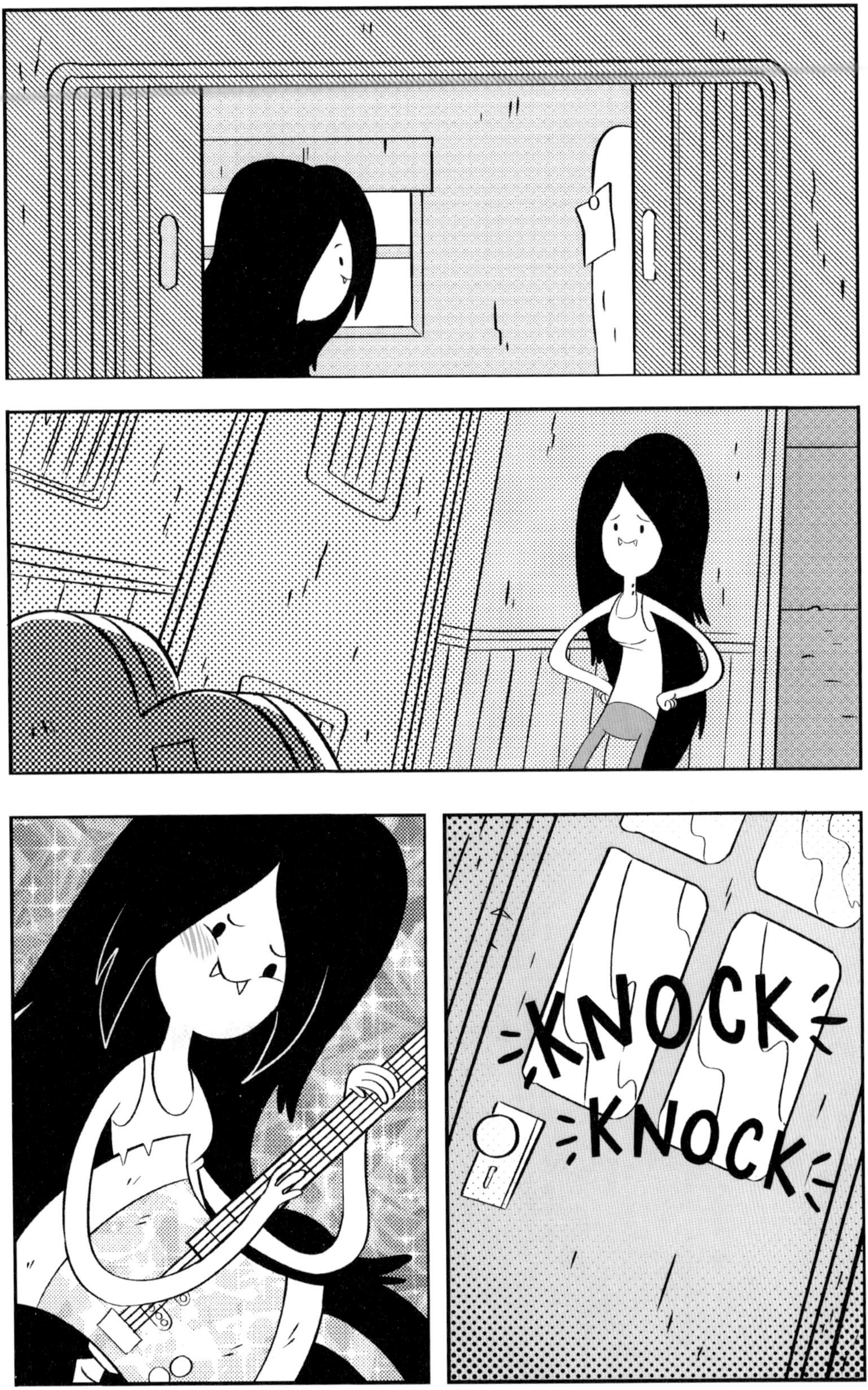
KNOCK
KNOCK

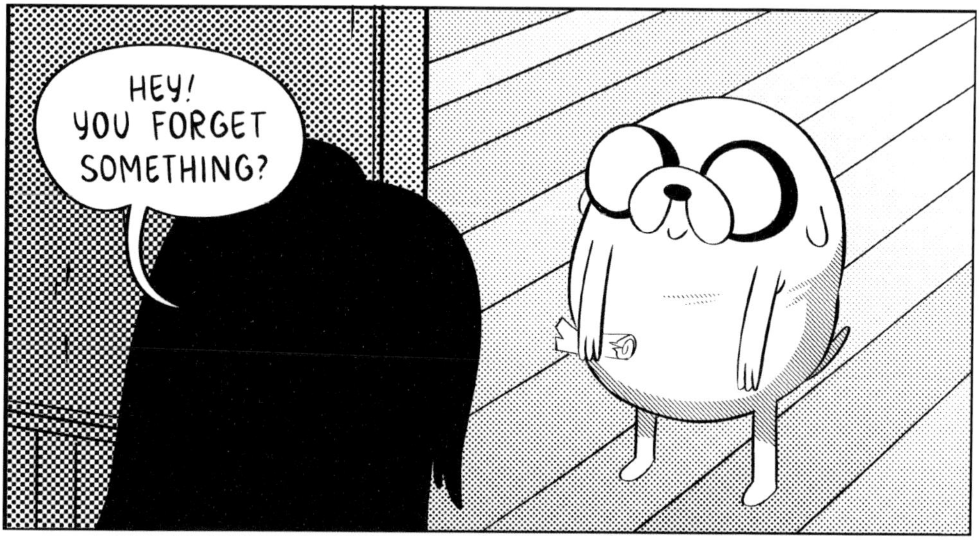
HEY! YOU FORGET SOMETHING?

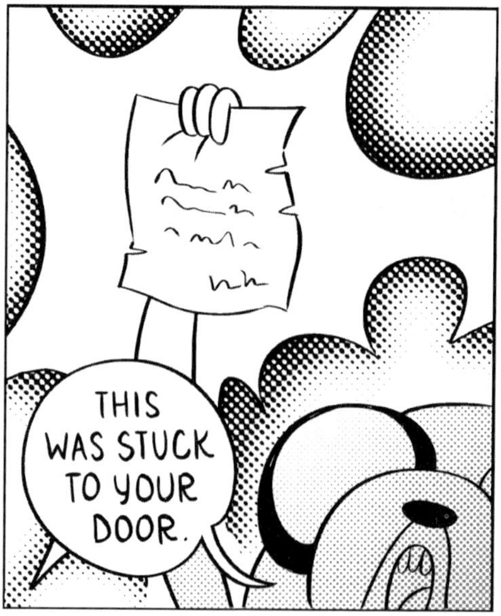
THIS WAS STUCK TO YOUR DOOR.

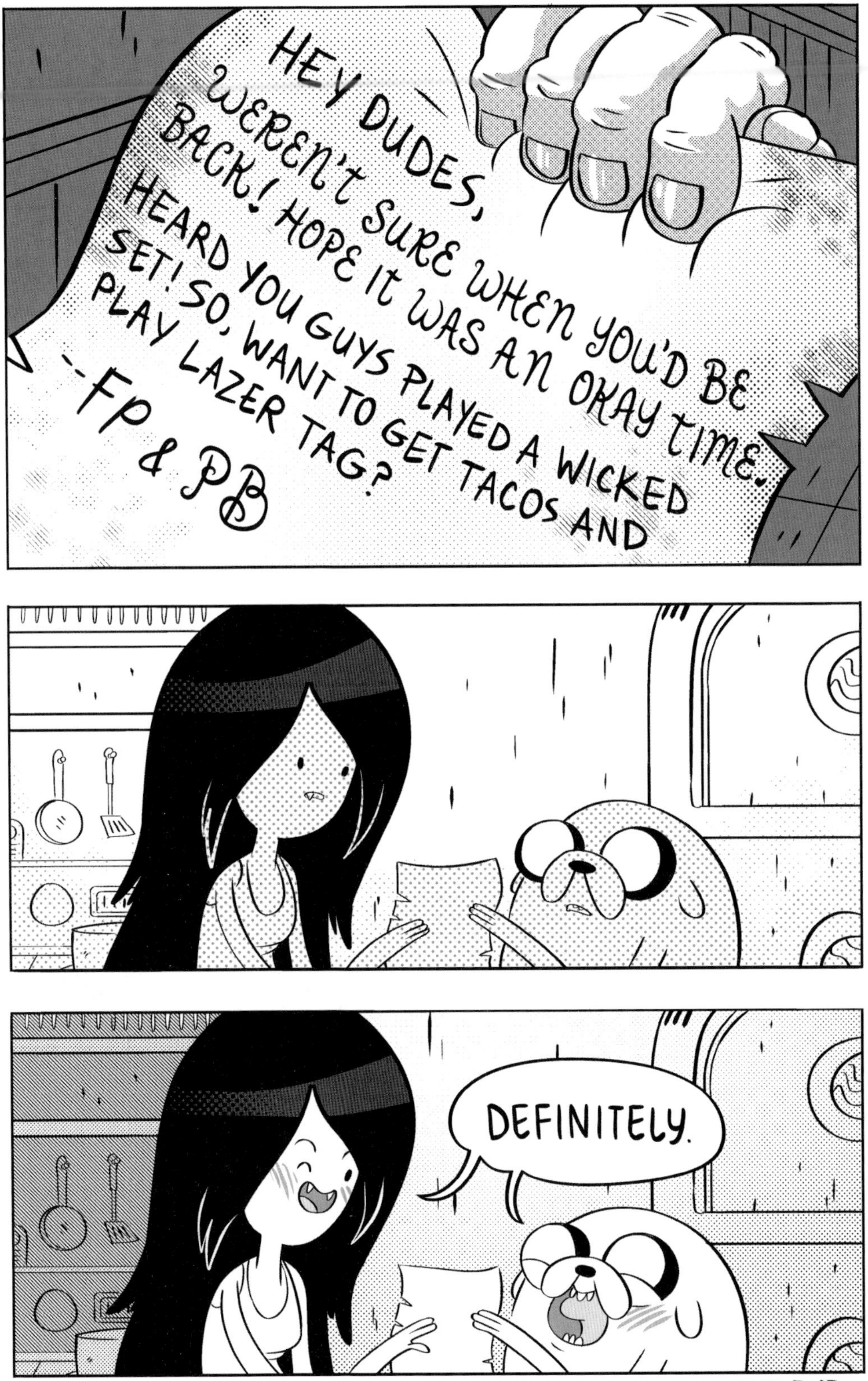
HEY DUDES,
WEREN'T SURE WHEN YOU'D BE
BACK! HOPE IT WAS AN OKAY TIME.
HEARD YOU GUYS PLAYED A WICKED
SET! SO, WANT TO GET TACOS AND
PLAY LAZER TAG?
--FP & PB
DEFINITELY.

THE END.

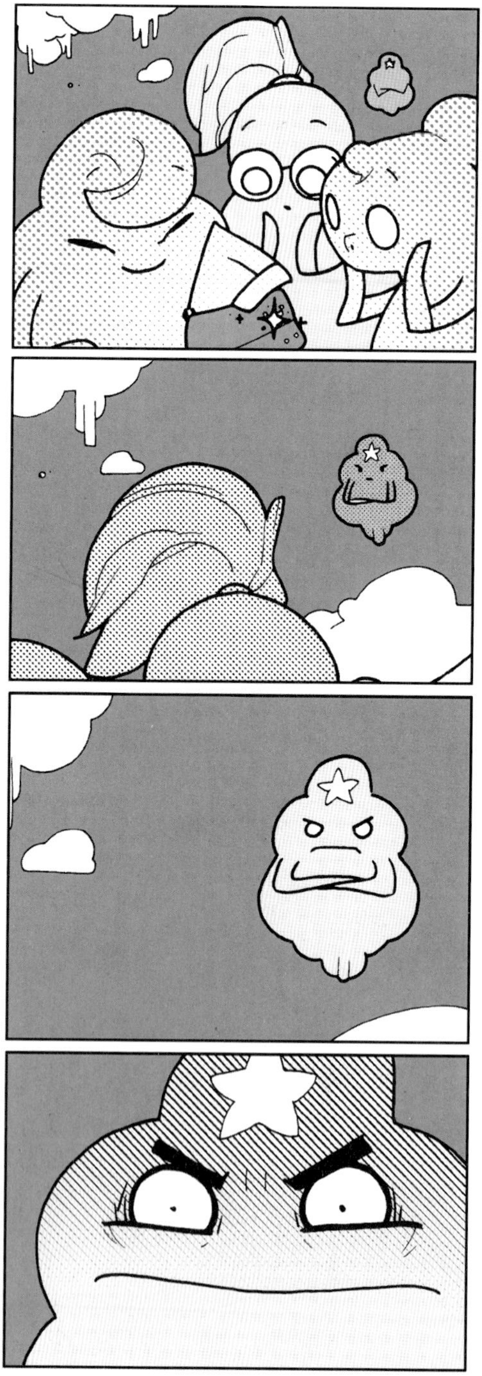

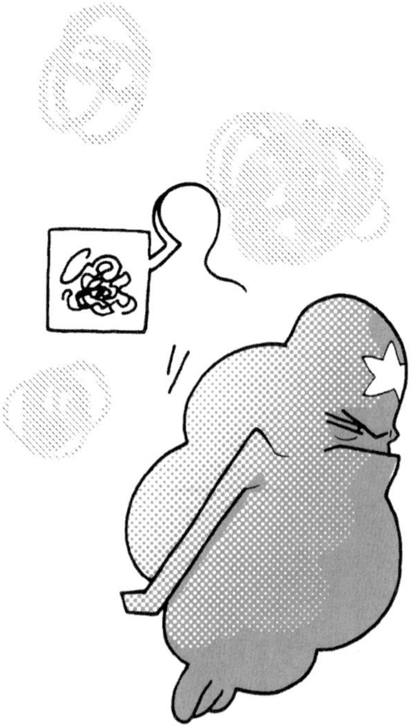

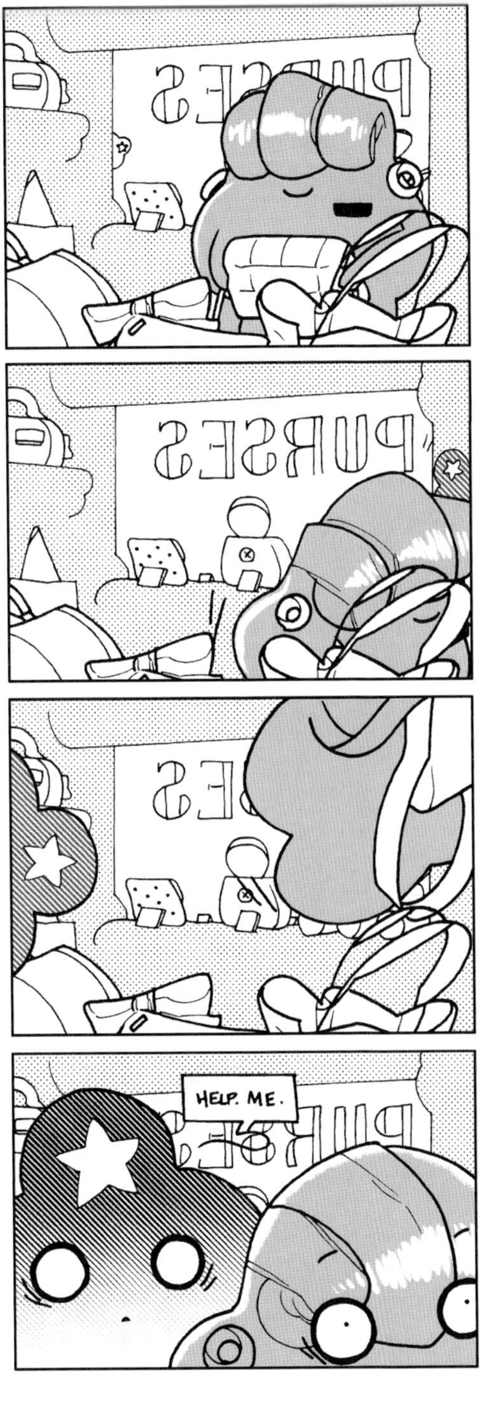
HELP. ME.

LSP
Gone Questin'

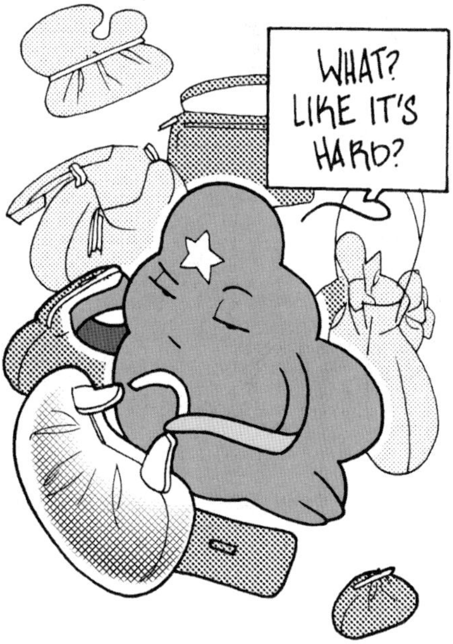
WHAT? LIKE IT'S HARD?

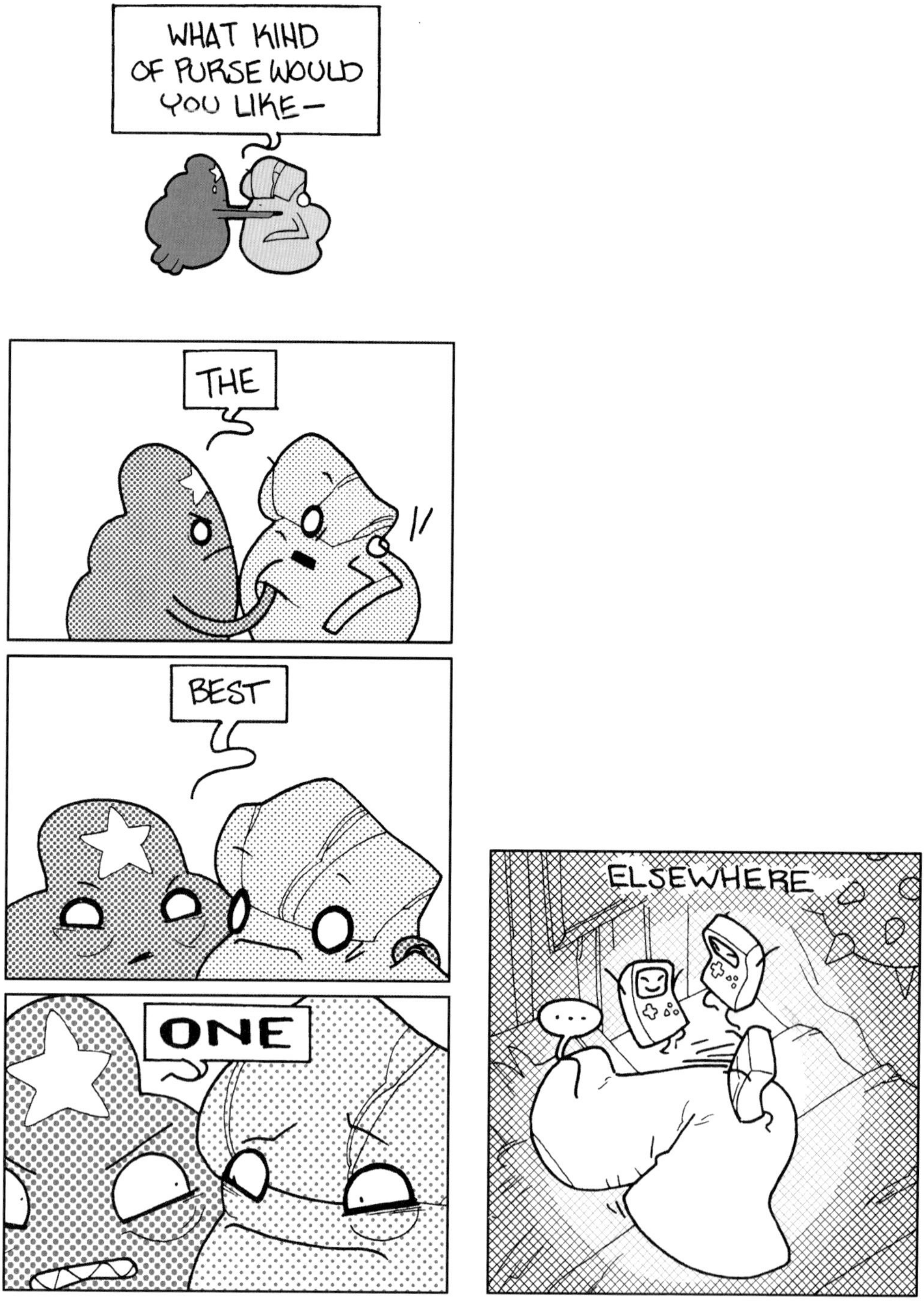
WHAT KIND OF PURSE WOULD YOU LIKE—
THE
BEST
ONE
ELSEWHERE
...

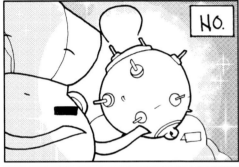

NONE OF THESE PURSES HAVE **WHAT I WANT**!!!

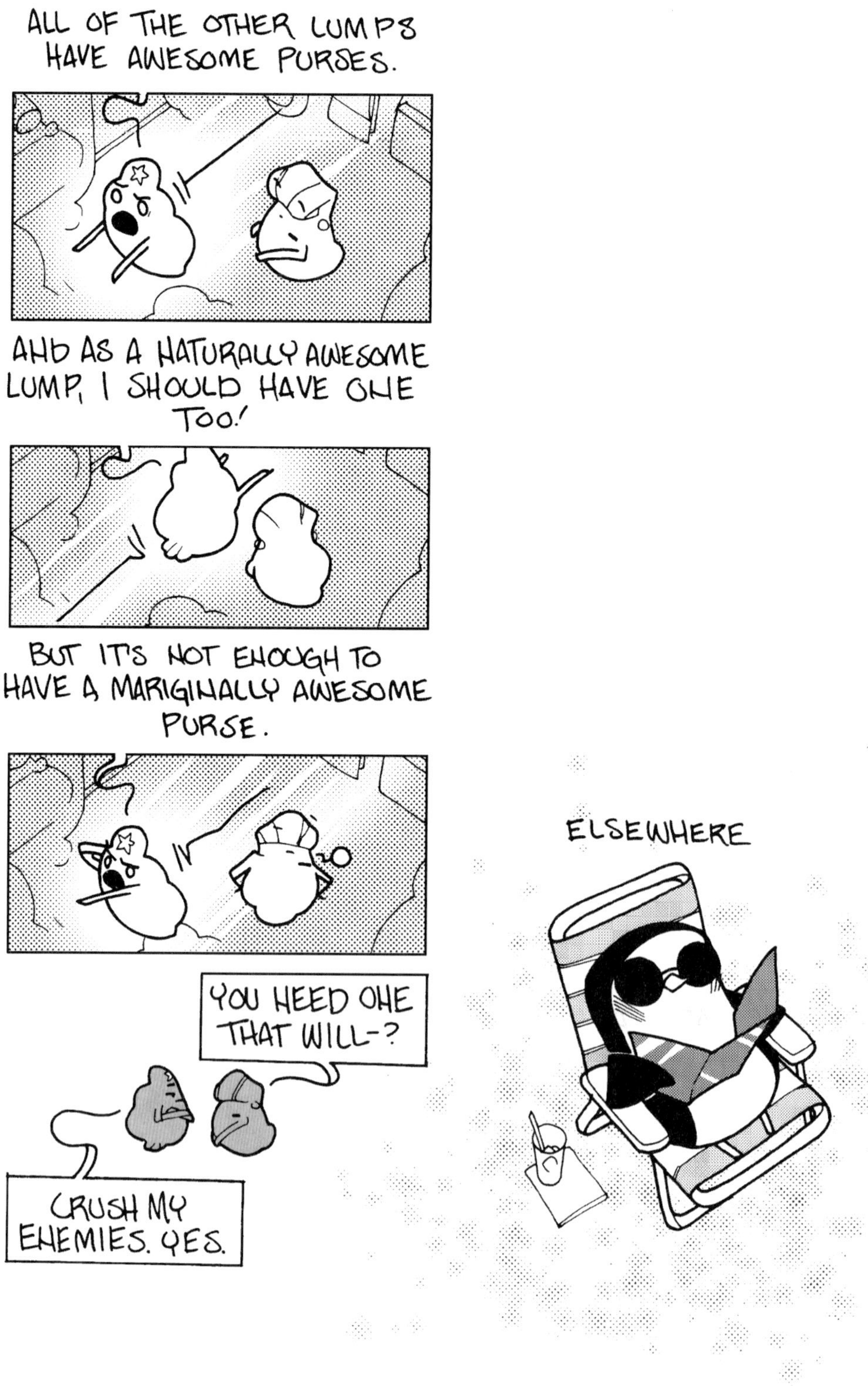
ALL OF THE OTHER LUMPS HAVE AWESOME PURSES.
AND AS A NATURALLY AWESOME LUMP, I SHOULD HAVE ONE TOO!
BUT IT'S NOT ENOUGH TO HAVE A MARIGINALLY AWESOME PURSE.
YOU NEED ONE THAT WILL-?
CRUSH MY ENEMIES. YES.
ELSEWHERE

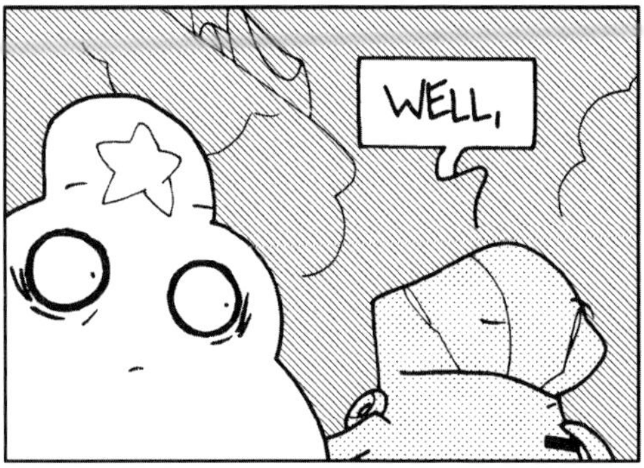
WELL,

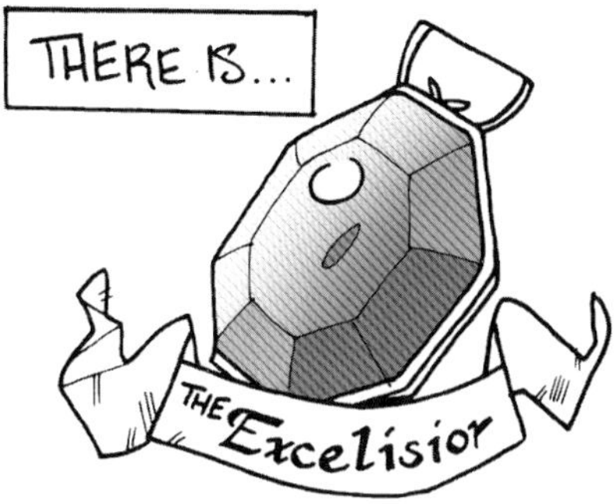
THERE IS...
THE Excelisior

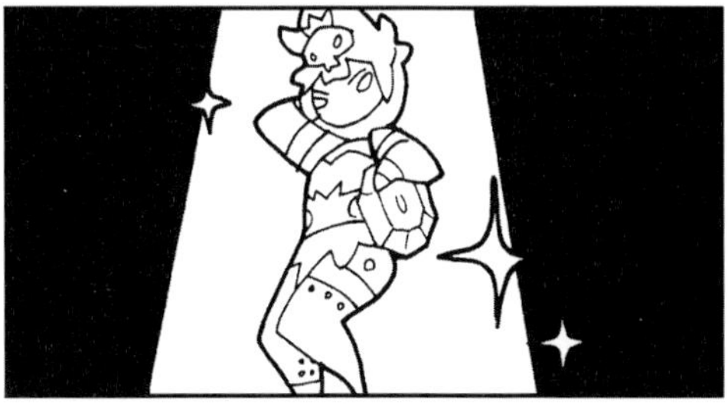

ITS NATURAL GLAMOUR WILL
FABULIZE ANY LOOK—
—AND IT'S INCINERATOR WILL
INCAPACITATE ANY CREEP.

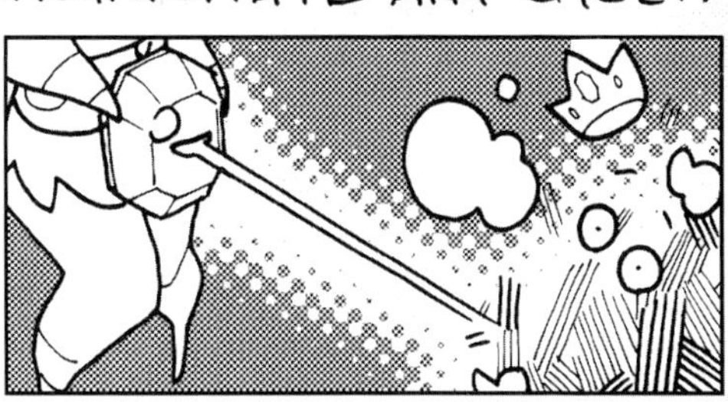

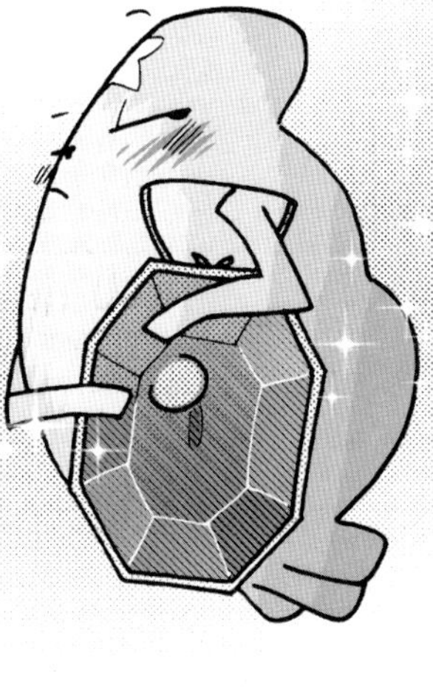

BUT FOR A NOMINAL FEE I
CAN SELL YOU THE MAP
FOR YOUR QUEST TO GET IT.

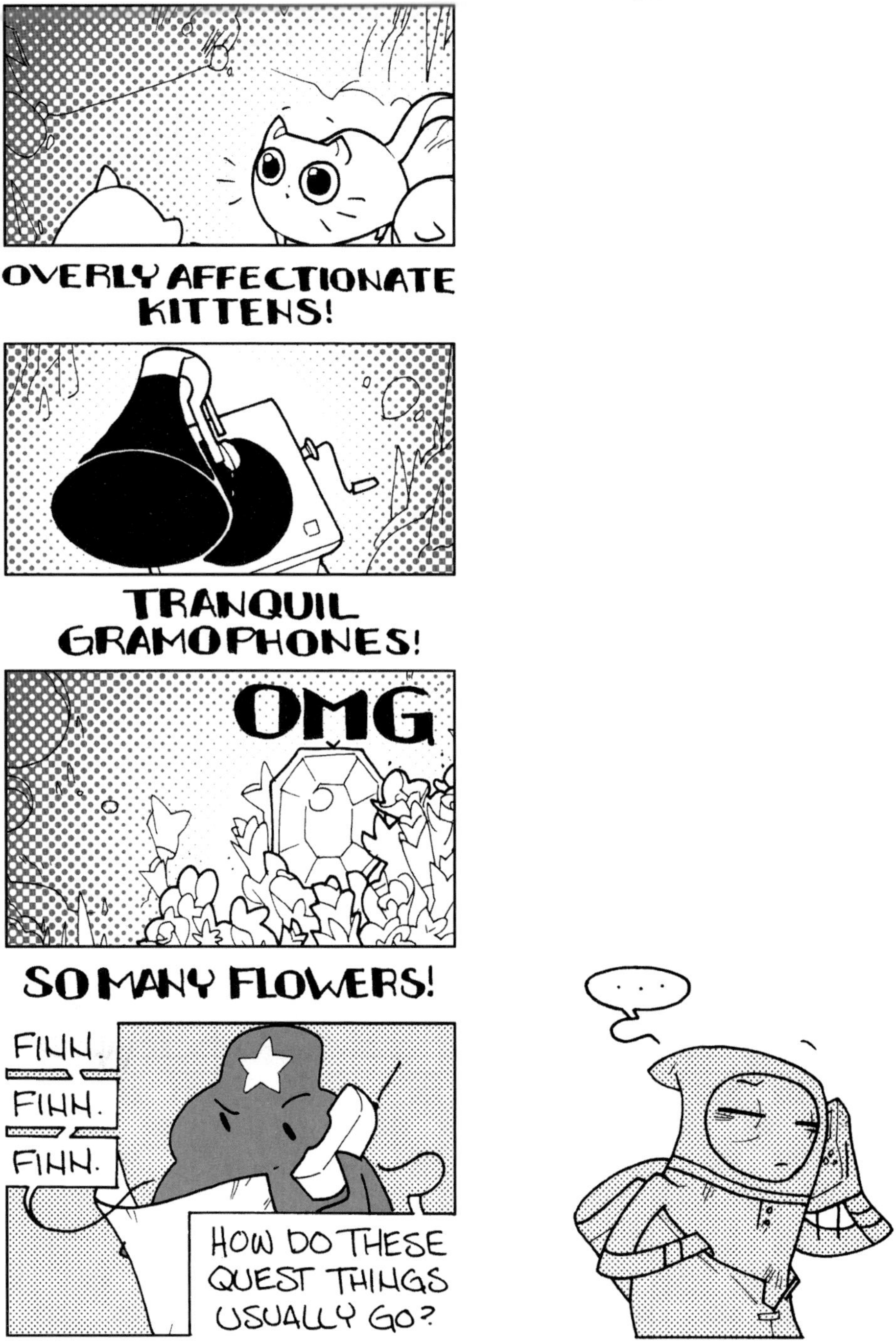
OVERLY AFFECTIONATE KITTENS!
TRANQUIL GRAMOPHONES!
OMG
SO MANY FLOWERS!
FINN.
FINN.
FINN.
HOW DO THESE QUEST THINGS USUALLY GO?
...

HUH. YOU GUYS **ARE** AFFECTIONATE...
UM.
OKAY.
WEIRD.
oh.
I THINK THIS QUEST HAS BEEN MISREPRESENTED.

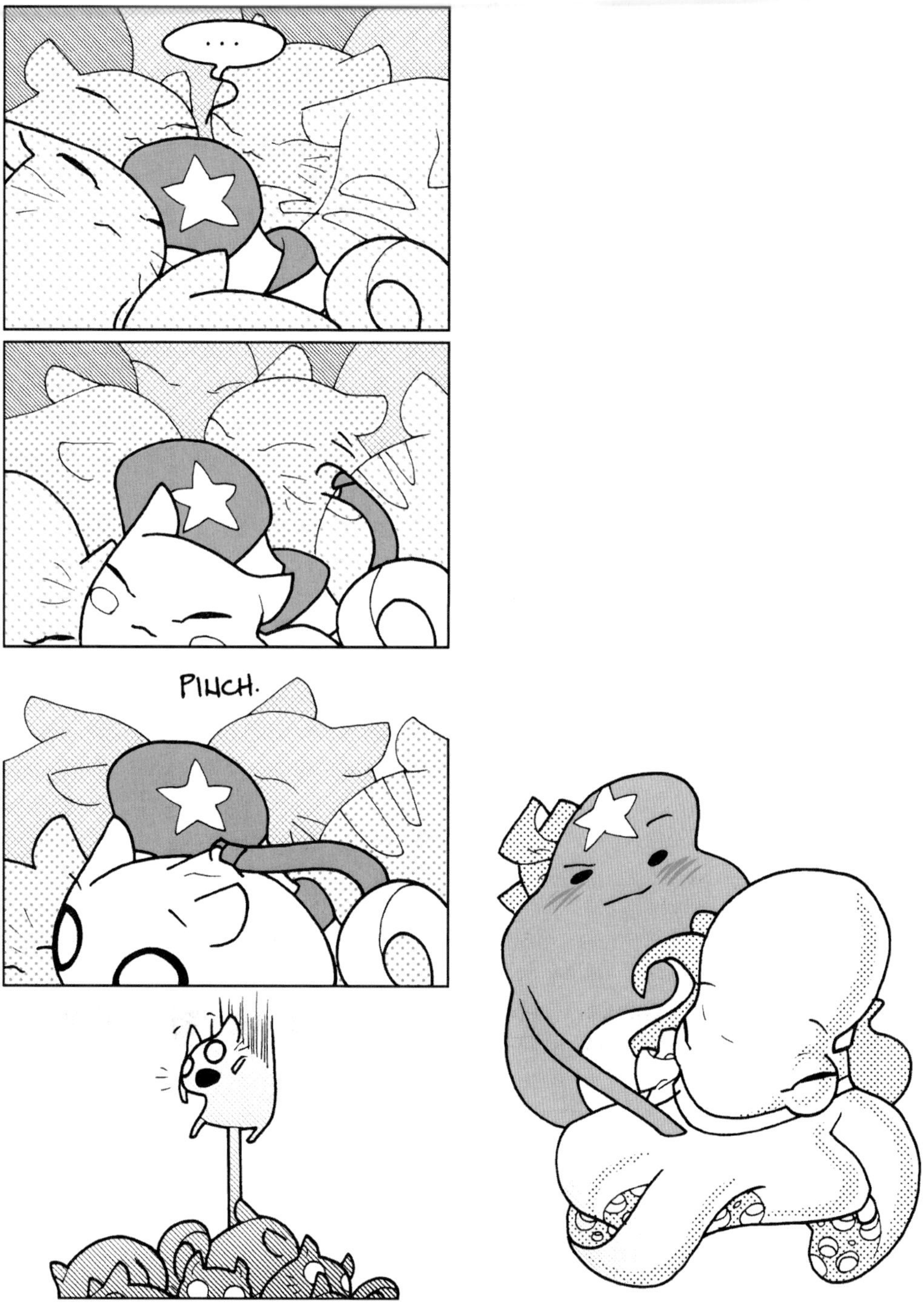
...
PINCH.

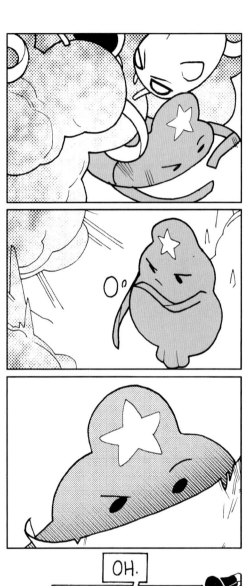

OH.

THIS IS GONNA
BE LAME.

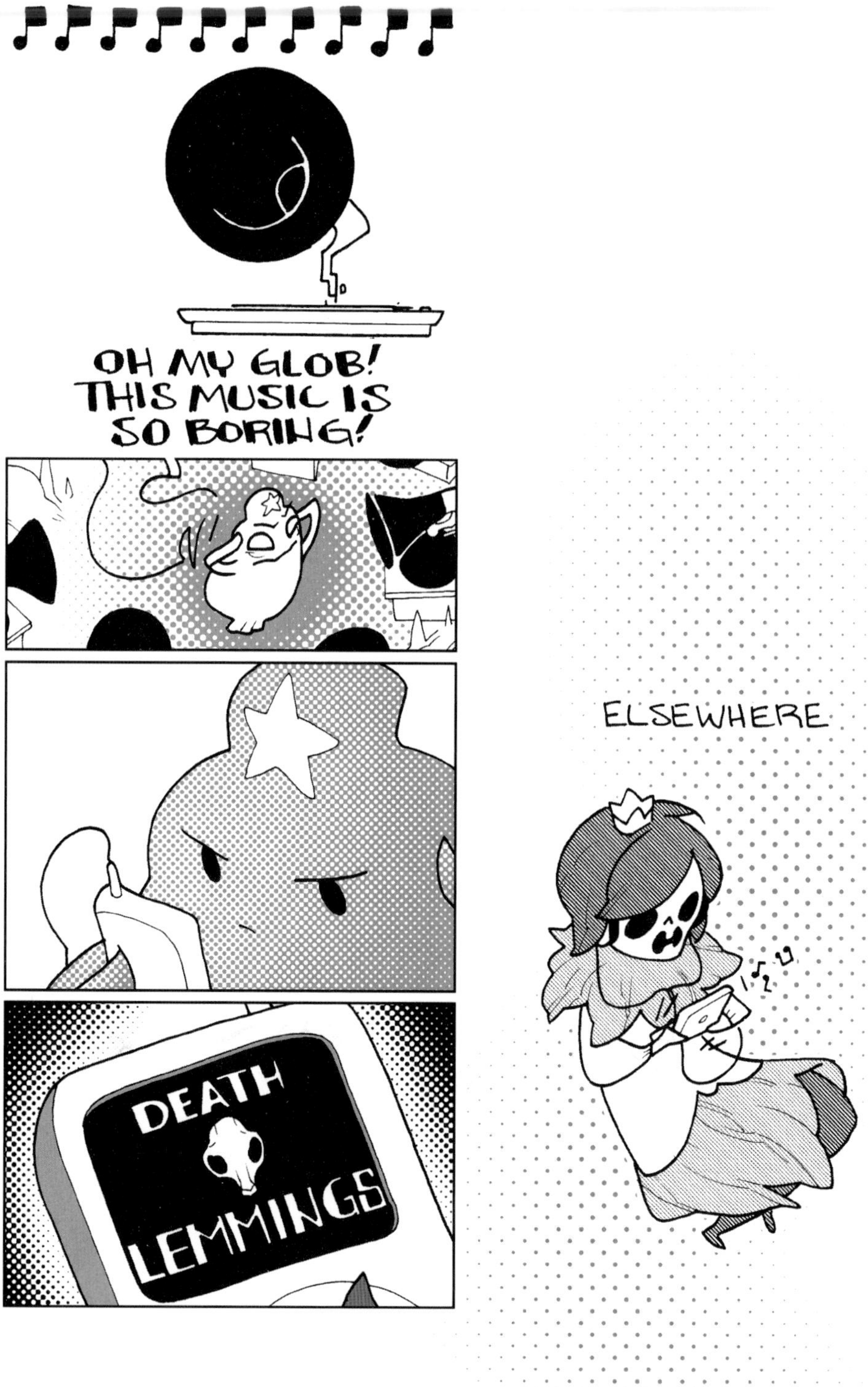
OH MY GLOB! THIS MUSIC IS SO BORING!
DEATH LEMMINGS
ELSEWHERE

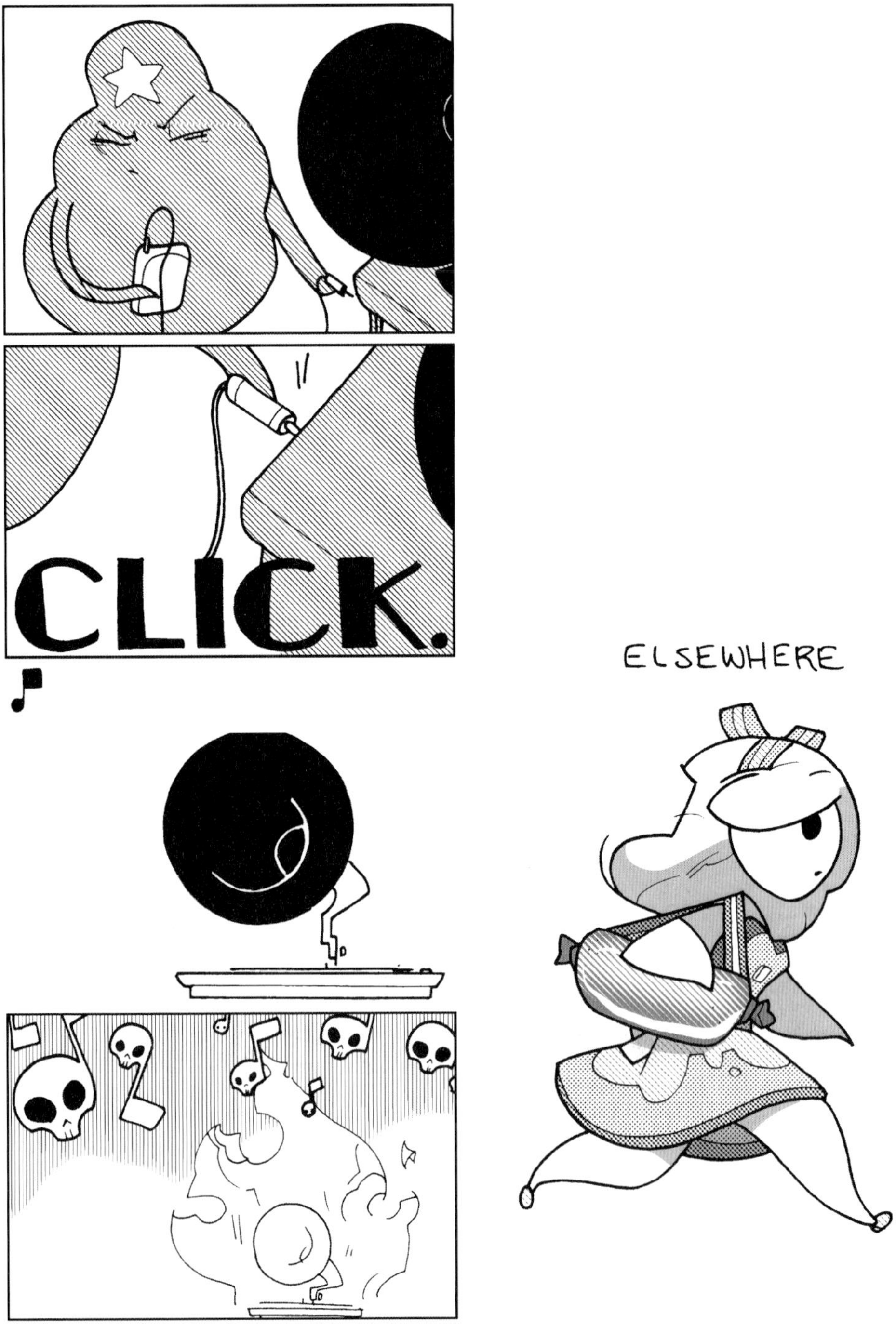
CLICK.
ELSEWHERE

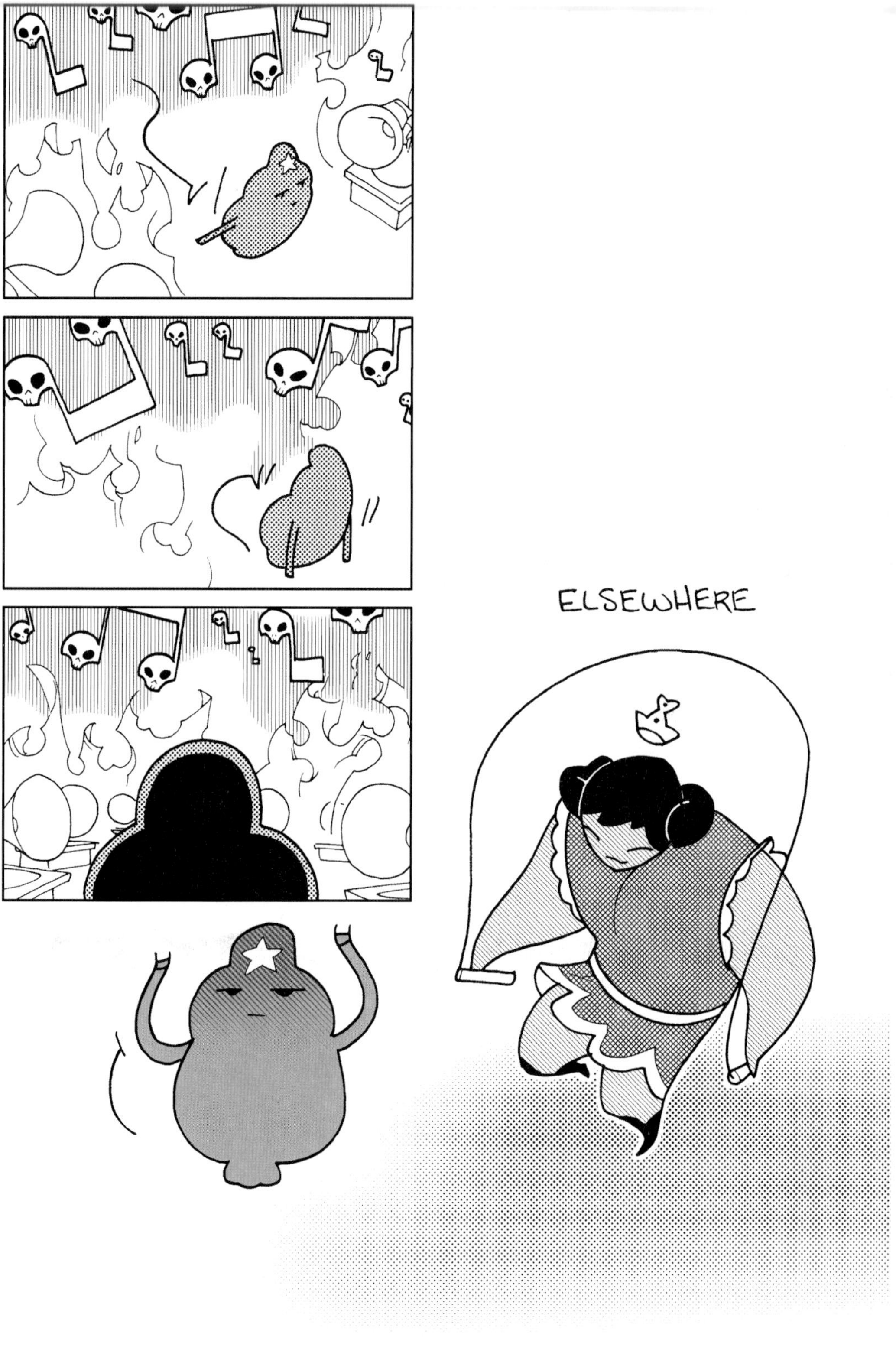
ELSEWHERE

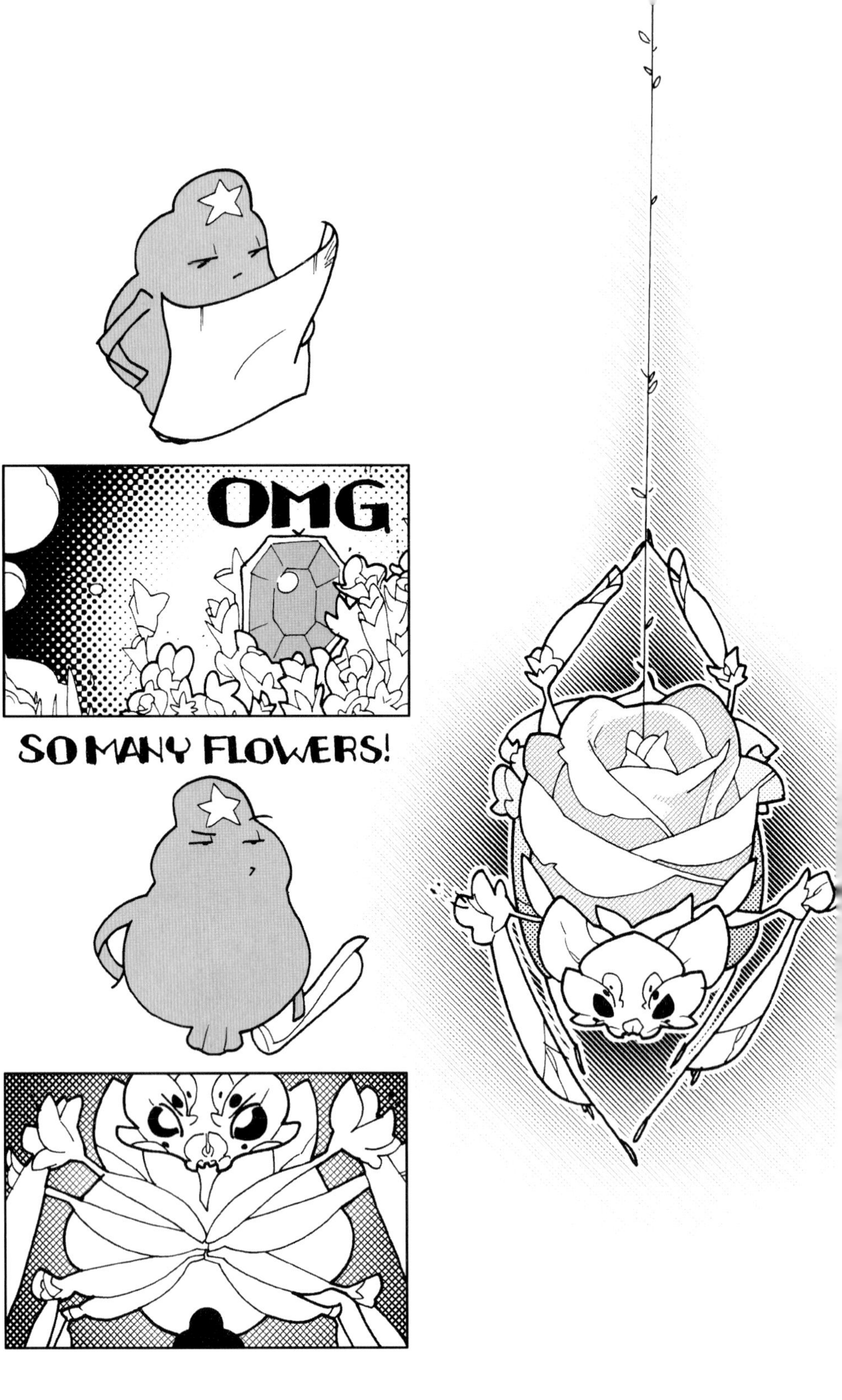
OMG
SO MANY FLOWERS!

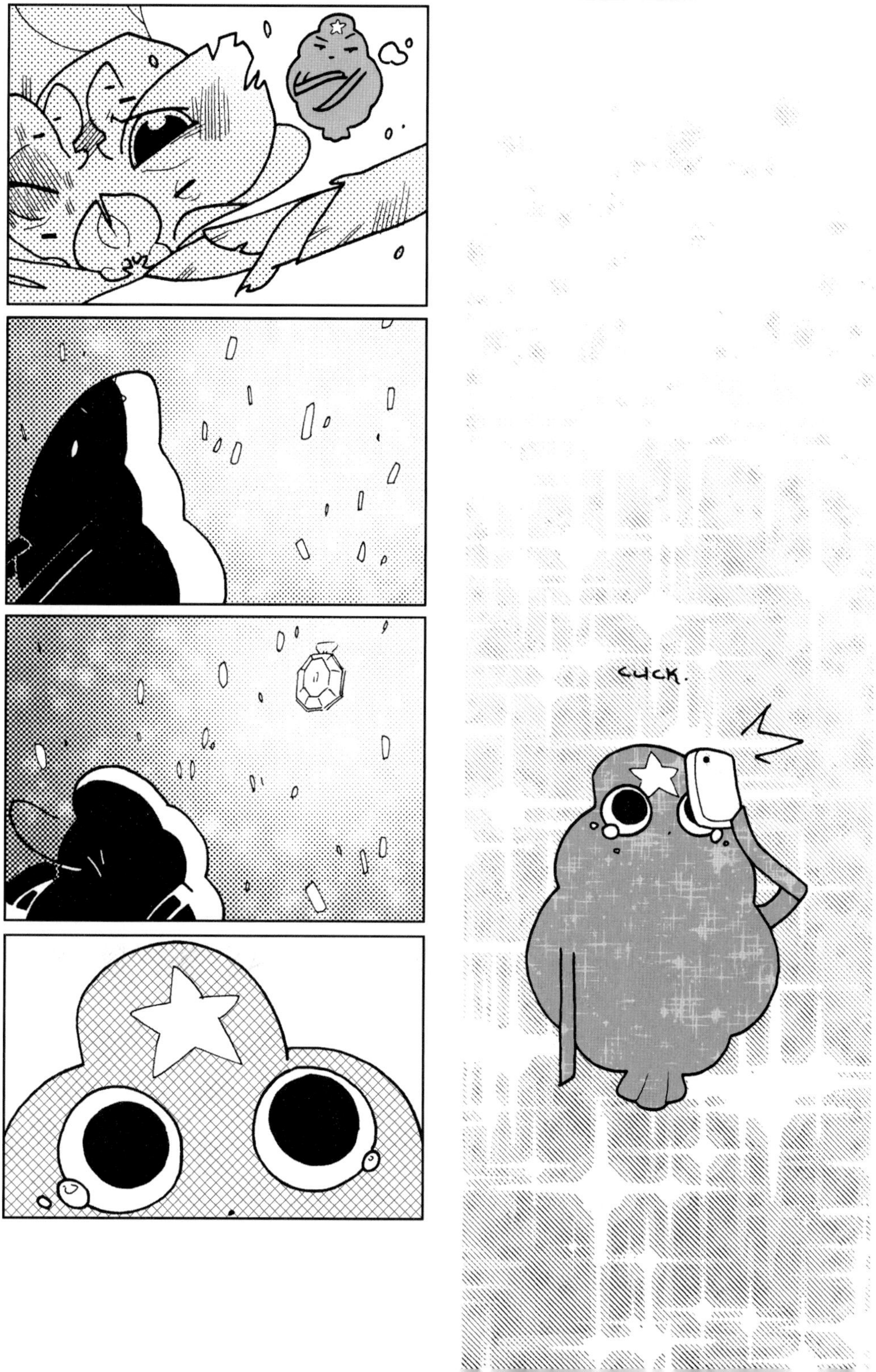
CLICK.

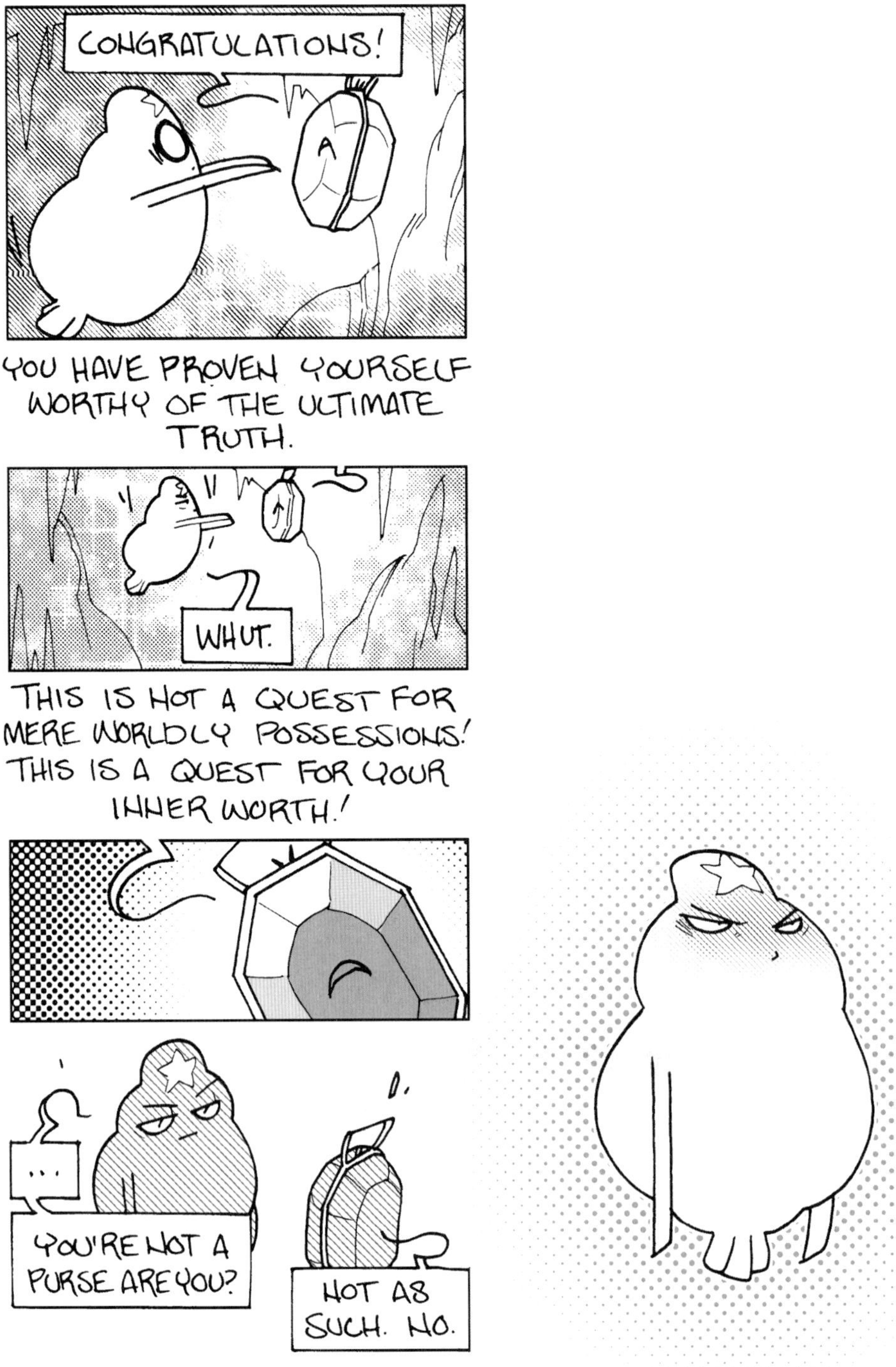
CONGRATULATIONS!
YOU HAVE PROVEN YOURSELF WORTHY OF THE ULTIMATE TRUTH.
WHUT.
THIS IS NOT A QUEST FOR MERE WORLDLY POSSESSIONS! THIS IS A QUEST FOR YOUR INNER WORTH!
...
YOU'RE NOT A PURSE ARE YOU?
NOT AS SUCH. NO.

LISTEN, SHINY, I DID NOT COME ALL THIS WAY JUST TO HEAR YOU TALK! I WANT MY PURSE. I EARNED MY PURSE. **GIVE ME THE GLOBBIN' PURSE!**

BUT.

BUT.

YOU DON'T NEED THE PURSE THE FABULOUSNESS WAS INSIDE YOU ALL ALONG!

ELSEWHERE

I ALREADY KNEW THAT.

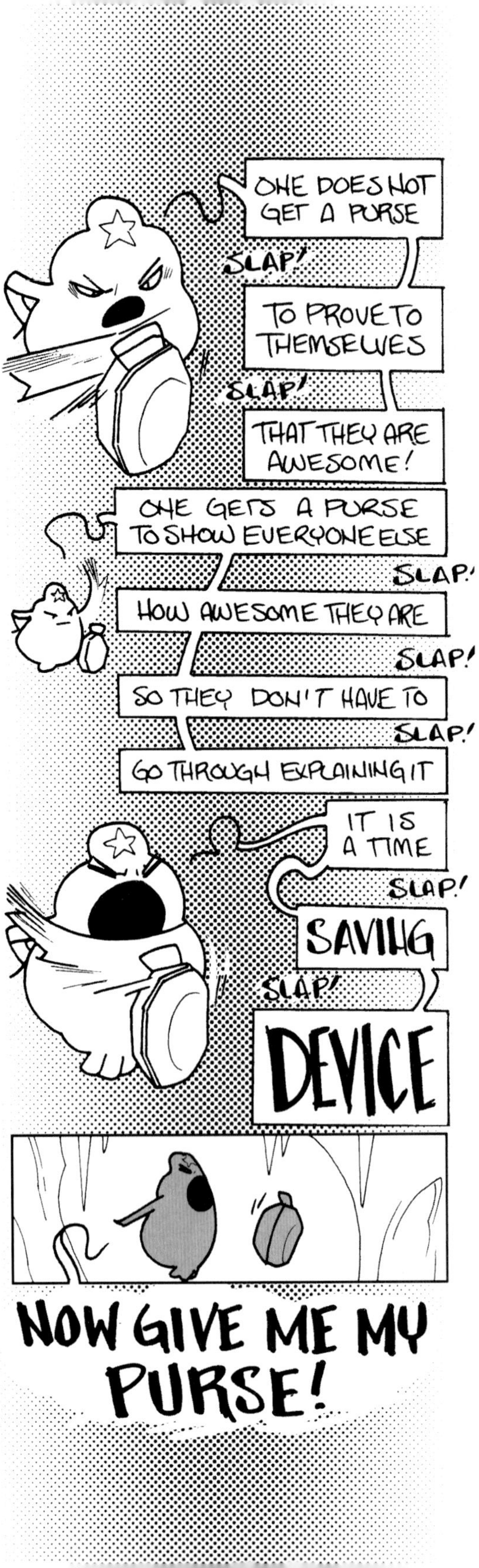
ONE DOES NOT GET A PURSE
SLAP!
TO PROVE TO THEMSELVES
SLAP!
THAT THEY ARE AWESOME!
ONE GETS A PURSE TO SHOW EVERYONE ELSE
SLAP!
HOW AWESOME THEY ARE
SLAP!
SO THEY DON'T HAVE TO
SLAP!
GO THROUGH EXPLAINING IT
IT IS A TIME
SLAP!
SAVING
SLAP!
DEVICE
NOW GIVE ME MY PURSE!

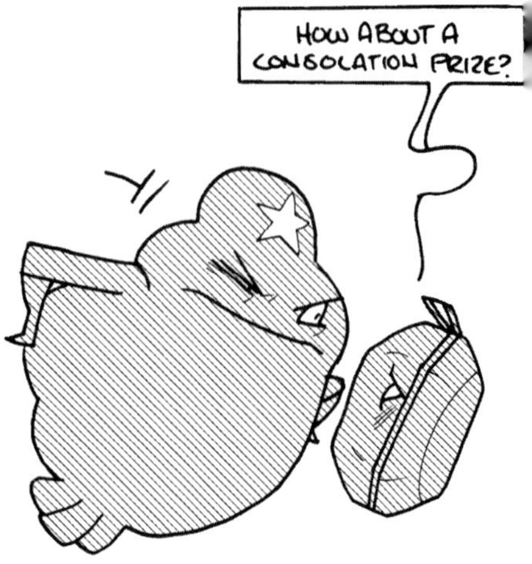
HOW ABOUT A CONSOLATION PRIZE?

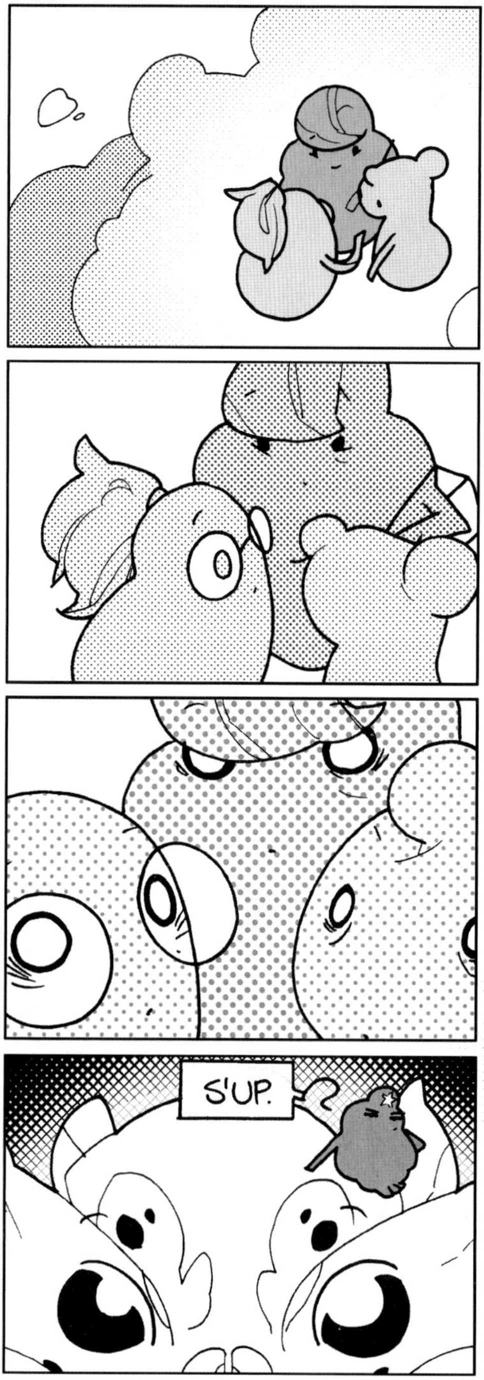
S'UP.

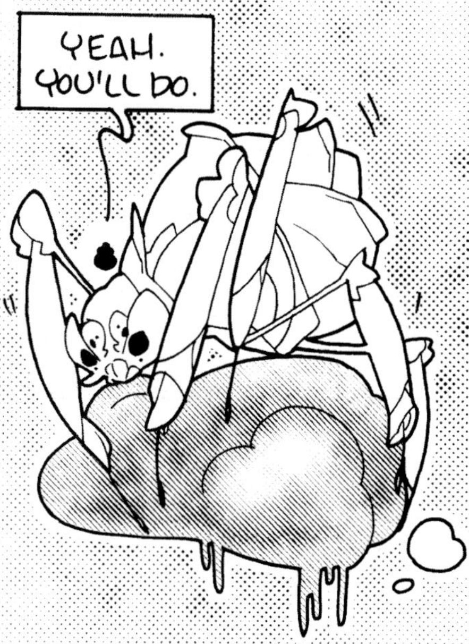
YEAH.
YOU'LL DO.

END.

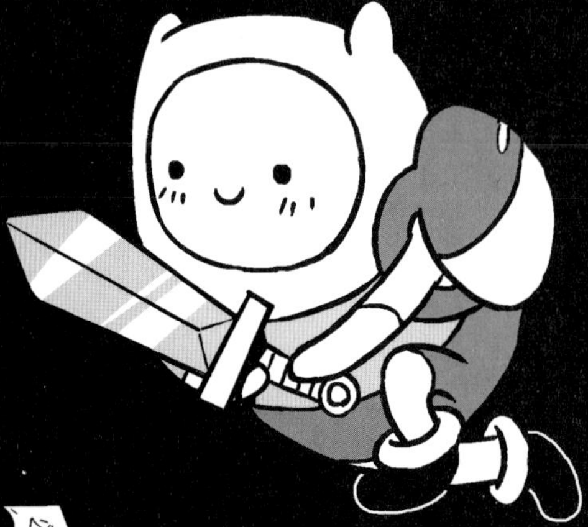

ADVENTURE TIME™

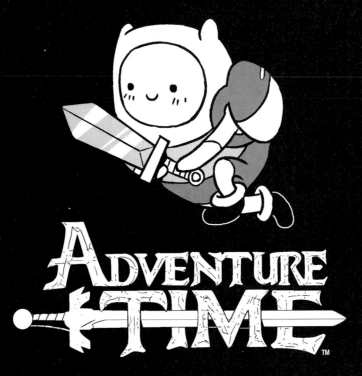

VOLUME 4

FALL 2014

Written by KATE LETH
Illustrated by ZACHARY STERLING